TARGETING THE TELOMERES

A THRILLER

R. N. SHAPIRO

REVIEWS

Five Stars

Targeting the Telomeres is the sequel to the author's debut novel in the same series, the acclaimed *Taming the Telomeres*. In the latest installment, Amanda Michaels is thrust into a dangerous web of intrigue, political artifice, and corporate expropriation when her family is unable to shake the pitfalls of her father's telomere discovery....The dialogue feels authentic and Amanda is a fabulous heroine, working with and against a whole cast of supporting characters that enhance and drive an already great plot.... I'd recommend this book to anyone who is looking for an awesome series that doesn't hold back as a thriller, fueled by an intelligent and articulate plot that feels like it could have been written to play out on the big screen.

—Reviewed By Jamie Michele for Readers' Favorite

Five Stars

Richard Shapiro provides a wonderful entertainment for fans of action-packed, cunningly plotted thrillers with great settings. Amanda Michaels didn't think her summer vacation would be eventful, but then with her family being targeted by powerful enemies bent on stealing her father's work, she is pulled into a whirlwind of action....I just became a fan of Richard Shapiro's writing, thanks to the masterful handling of plot and characters in this novel....The prose is crisp and it has descriptions of scenes, characters, and places that leave vivid images in the minds of readers and dialogues that help to build plot. The author is a master at creating surprising turns and exciting moments throughout the narrative. Targeting the Telomeres: A Thriller is engaging, a novel with a huge conflict and strong elements of sci-fi. One of those stories I read straight through the night.

—Reviewed By Romuald Dzemo for Readers' Favorite

Five Stars

The plot is fast moving and the conflict kept me totally engaged. There are no dull moments... the tension is superb, especially when Amanda and her ally enter China. I literally have no fingernails left. The ending was explosive and definitely not what I was expecting. The author is a true master of weaving elements of a suspense novel together and has provided a truly unforgettable story. I hope there is a sequel!

—Lesley Jones, Readers' Favorite Editorial Review

EPIGRAPH

Tel o mere: [Pronunciation: "tee-low-meer" or "tell-uh-meer"]
Noun; A compound structure at the end of a chromosome.
Controls cell life. And death.

- Three American scientists share the Nobel Prize for solving a puzzle involving cell biology, discovering the enzyme that influences cell telomeres, the protective tip of chromosomes that get shorter each time a cell divides, controlling cell life and death.
- Hackers aligned with China hack BBS servers, where secret US biological telomere researcher Ron Michaels has proved longer telomeres may extend human cell life.
- A Hemispheres Airways commuter jet mysteriously crashes, killing all aboard including researcher Ron Michaels & his wife, leaving one survivor: his 18 year old daughter Amanda Michaels.
- Major US news media leak claims the US gov't paid $200 Million to Hemispheres Airways to thwart investigation of the Hemispheres jet crash.

DEDICATION

For Terri, Rachel, and Dillon.

ACKNOWLEDGMENTS

The author thanks the NSA, CIA, and the FBI for background information, John and Chris for tactical information, Dillon Shapiro for neuroscience background, Mary for her editing, Claudia Sperl for cover art, Greg Johannesen for inside illustrations, and for those of you that offered suggestions.

PROLOGUE
SLEEPER

Lying on the cramped, lower bunk of the sleeper car, she feels with her fingertips along the thin foam-rubber pad masquerading as a mattress. *There it is.* She tugs on the lower portion of her backpack hiding the loaded pistol with the customized silencer, nestling what constitutes all her belongings in the crook of her right arm.

She thinks, all I wanted was to get some of my memory back from before the crash. Not this.

The bullet train hurtling northbound towards Beijing at 180 miles per hour suddenly lurches, causing a metallic screech that soon fades.

Amanda thinks for a moment about a family photo. Of her dad, her, and her mom, sitting on the front porch of the house they lived in before the crash. The one she hopes to recall, that her Uncle Andy showed her. She mentally photoshops her baby brother Justin in too. Nothing can stop fantasies no one else can see.

If my plan fails, I won't have to worry anymore, Amanda decides. Because I'll be dead.

CHAPTER 1

GAG REFLEX

Monday Morning
Washington, D.C.

THE TV in the background startles FBI counter-intelligence agent Steven Solarez during his early morning ritual of checking the weather on his tablet, sending a swig of burning hot French roast coffee everywhere.

Holy crap, he thinks, listening to the reporter on CNT.

"According to the *Washington Observer,* over 200 million dollars was transferred from the U.S. government to a Hemispheres Airlines bank account, effectively funding most of the death claims for the victims of Flight 310, which left D.C. for New York City and crashed in Quarryville, Pennsylvania about two years ago. Official sources with the Department of Justice are strenuously denying this claim."

Solarez feels his cell phone vibrating on his waist, slides it off its holster, and reads the incoming text message.

Emergency meeting @ 8:30 AM with Director. Confirm.

Once the proverbial cat is out of the bag, can you ever shove it back in? This is bad, for sure. But he didn't hear any details of why the money was paid to the airline, so maybe whoever leaked it doesn't have the whole story. Maybe.

He texts his confirmation to his assistant, Dean, then decides to add more.

Find Amanda Michaels now. Tell her not to talk to the reporters. Put an agent on her 24/7.

He smiles, knowing she stands far from helpless now. It was a prophetic move on his part to give her training at Quantico once school let out, virtually the same program a field agent undergoes. Weapons, hand-to-hand combat, and evasive driving techniques. He had to pull a lot of strings for approval, but given the secret research role her father, Ron Michaels, was undertaking, it made sense.

Next, he calls Andy Michaels and braces himself for an onslaught from the high-profile trial attorney.

"I just heard the report on the radio. Do you know what this'll do to my law practice? My reputation? Do you?" Andy says with a panicky voice as soon as he answers, mentally cataloging every material possession in his Georgetown home and imagining his lucrative Georgetown practice going right down the rat hole.

"Careful, this isn't a secure line. Yeah, I get how serious this is."

"How about my clients who settled their cases? What if someone decides I knew everything..."

Solarez interrupts him. "Stop! We need to talk in person. You did nothing wrong, so don't start panicking. We're putting protection on Amanda immediately. No one talks to any reporters until we have a solid response plan, hopefully around noon."

"What am I supposed to tell my partners and my staff?"

"Tell them you can't comment now, but you'll issue a statement soon."

"Are you kidding? I can't say that."

"You can't tell them anything until you look into the allegations. Better?"

Andy contemplates this a few seconds. "No. Completely unconvincing." He tries to come up with a logical explanation, but the more he thinks about it, the more furious and anxious he gets. He was never comfortable with the confidential information the DOJ lawyer had shared with him—that the U.S. did indeed pay the $200 million. His clients trusted him when he recommended they settle their wrongful death claims. Sure, they all were awarded major settlements, but that was before he learned of the secret government payout to the airline. He realized then if anything about sabotage leaked later on, there would be hell to pay.

"What about the press when they start calling?"

"Same thing."

"Can you call Stein at the Department of Justice to confirm everything is still okay? He assured me all my settlements were legal."

"I'll talk to him."

"My head is ready to explode."

"Tell you what, I have a meeting with the FBI director this morning, but when I'm done I'll call you."

Andy isn't listening. He's still thinking about the news story. Whoever leaked it must have an agenda. Why would the Chinese leak it and risk exposing their sabotage of the aircraft? Makes no sense. Maybe a disgruntled FBI or CIA employee? It's possible, but who, and what was their motive?

"We'll work this out," Solarez promises, but Andy has major doubts. What is it they say about hiding the truth? It usually floats back up to the surface, no matter how hard you try to weigh it down.

CHAPTER 2

SEPARATE TEAMS

Langley-CIA HQ
Monday afternoon

"CHUCK, GOOD TO SEE YOU."
Walter Zukoff firmly shakes CIA Director Charles Isaacson's hand. Built on a medium, stocky frame, Zukoff carries at least 15-20 extra pounds that he stopped worrying about long ago. Too much work and much less exercise means his belt buckle now angles downward under the extension of his belly.

"Always a pleasure, Z," Isaacson replies, using Zukoff's nickname reserved for friends. They both sit down at a small round table deep inside CIA headquarters in Langley, Virginia. Contrasted with Zukoff, Chuck Isaacson exercises religiously in his fully-equipped home gym to retain his trim frame.

"The president signed off on the directive." Isaacson continues, tapping a document on the table, then offering it to Zukoff to verify for himself. Sliding his glasses out of his sports jacket pocket, he reads it over and looks up.

"You weren't expecting otherwise, were you?"

"Not at all. In an off-the-books meeting I had with him and his national security team, he literally mentioned the 'Manhattan Project' in discussing our work. He said something like 'this does not have the urgency of that project, but in terms of long-term implications, this work could be more important because it would affect not tens of thousands, but potentially millions.' Not sure I agree with him, but it certainly added some gravity to the assignment."

Zukoff directs the biological research division of the CIA at a classified facility in a rural area of Maryland, affectionately called Sherwood Forest by those who know it exists. Locals realize it's some kind of government base, but they have no idea it's the headquarters for the development of biological weapons. Anthrax, chemical weapons, ricin, radioactive compounds for weaponry, basically anything outside of regular firearms or classic ammunitions.

In 1989, the U.S. Government enacted the Bioweapons Anti-Terrorism Act, which incorporated the earlier Bioweapons Convention Treaty, called the BWC for short. The act prohibited the research of "lethal" biological weapons. However, like much of the English language, the term "lethal" is open to differing interpretations. In this case, the CIA chooses to interpret the word "lethal" as killing someone immediately, making a biological weapon that slowly kills its target over a week or two "non-lethal," and therefore legal to develop under the BWC.

Isaacson begins again. "So, here are the details. I'm managing the commercialization aspect of the telomere project and covering any economic benefits to be derived from commercial licensing, like medications, rapid wound healing, and life-extending modalities. You'll be handling the non-lethal biological weaponry. But there's a bit of a twist." Isaacson pauses for dramatic impact, and Zukoff looks quizzically at him. "The commercial research part at Sherwood will be run by Ron Michaels."

Zukoff chuckles. "Ha! Putting a dead man in charge. That's quite a cover story. What brainiac thought that up?"

"Well, Michaels isn't dead."

"Yeah, right. He died in the Hemispheres crash and was buried with his wife. It was all over the news."

Isaacson decides not to fill him in on the entire story, even though they're friends. "Not exactly. Due to cooperation between the agency and FBI counter-intelligence, he wasn't on the jet. He assisted us in an operation before the plane crash, and we kept him in a safe house for months after we extracted him."

"I'll be damned. We *can* keep a secret. What was he assisting with, besides his own project? And where is he now?"

"I still can't share that information. But believe me, he's 100% alive and well and he's been continuing his research, at Sherwood."

"Do you mean to tell me he's been right under my nose and I didn't even know it?"

"That, my friend, is why I'm the director of the CIA and you head up biological research," Isaacson jokingly replies.

The truth is Isaacson knows how to work a room of spooks as easily as a room of politicians, and he keeps the intricate complexities of the CIA humming. Z is the consummate introvert, much more comfortable supervising lab results and orchestrating biological breakthroughs. His idea of professional satisfaction does not involve testimony on Capitol Hill before an intelligence subcommittee.

"All kidding aside, there was no good way to start without him, and we can't use a contractor like Biological Blood Services anymore, too many other nations want to get their hands on these breakthroughs. Each researcher working with Michaels at Sherwood was briefed on the classified status of this information, and for the foreseeable future we won't allow Michaels to leave. He is ensconced with his own team at Sherwood. He's been given a new identity on paper, and maybe we'll get him some plastic surgery down the road, or set him up on a remote farm in New Zealand. He can be put out to pasture later, but not until we use his telomere breakthroughs for medical and weaponry purposes. This isn't the first time secrets possessed by one division aren't being fully shared with another."

"True." Zukoff manages, doodling in the margin of his note pad. Nice five-point stars, which he shades in as he briefly wonders whether the Hemispheres crash was connected to Ron Michaels' research. But he doesn't ask Isaacson, who continues explaining the master plan.

"The bio-medical part of the research, which preliminarily demonstrated the extension of cell life, will continue under Michaels. Before the crash, he officially confirmed it on animals. Unofficially, on a few human test subjects as well, which we found out about later. So, no scientifically sound human trials exist, only animal trials. Still, the animal testing was nothing short of amazing. He extended the life span of fruit flies and mice over 50%, which could translate to a 15% to 25% extension of cell life in humans. Now, the issue of side effects? Well, that is still unknown.

"On the bio-medical commercialization side, the president's directive calls for licensing the technology within 18 months to American companies or majority-owned American companies. Because of other intelligence information, he also wants monthly progress reports on the telomere weaponization and a viable 'non-lethal' weapon within in the same timeframe. Desired features include easy delivery, non-detectability, and irreversible decline, causing death within less than seven days. He says it could be a game changer with some of our high-value terrorist targets."

"Wait a second, this is ludicrous. No clear path exists for this type of thing. Three years would be the soonest for any bioweapon according to my timeline. Please tell me you didn't say we could meet an 18-month window."

"I didn't say we couldn't."

"I don't want unnecessary pressure on myself or my team because of an unrealistic deadline."

"Look, the president and his advisors were adamant. Our current drone program saves troop lives, but it's a public relations disaster. Sure, we kill our targets, but there's collateral damage—family members, young kids, neighbors. Our field agents are saying with every drone strike that destroys a building, we create hundreds of new terrorists because the videos the extremists post all over the internet tie us to the damage. Some high-value targets call for drones, but we also need a weapon that can eliminate individual targets without creating new terrorist propaganda videos in the process. Understand?"

"Yes, I do. Out of curiosity, how do you envision this bioweapon working? By making cells die faster instead of making them last longer?"

"That's a possibility, but consider this: Michaels' original focus was on cancer, to slow the growth or spread of tumor cells. Then he showed rapamycin and mTOR hugely impact cell life. The telomerase enzyme signals the telomere somehow and increases the total number of divisions before it dies, extending cell life and, presumably, human life."

"Keep going."

"So, if telomerase can stimulate *healthy* cells to divide more than normal and live longer—"

Zukoff interrupts. "Then the same could possibly be done with *abnormal* cells, like cancerous cells, causing a victim to die far quicker than with natural forms of cancer." He stares at the crease where the conference room wall meets the ceiling, thinking. "Unfortunately, I don't see our enemies lining up for blood transfusions so we can infect them."

"Of course not. Michaels knows blood transfusions are far too invasive and not realistic for the commercial applications either, so he's already working on a different delivery system. You'll have immediate access to his findings, but your team should be brainstorming too."

Zukoff is now holding the pen vertically, resting just the tip on the note pad, eyeing Isaacson. "This reminds me of how they lambasted President Reagan when he said he wanted to develop a space laser to zap nuclear missiles, and the press called it 'Star Wars.' It sounds great, but can it be done? What about costs?"

"No budget constraints, just requisition in the usual fashion."

"I've already decided who my research director will be. He's been with us for less than a year."

"Who?"

"The name won't mean anything to you since you aren't acquainted with any of my key people. You do realize human testing will be required." Zukoff says.

"You do what you need to do, but it better be somewhere else in the world. And be damn sure no dots connect this work back to the agency."

"Got it." Zukoff's mind wanders to the infamous LSD studies the government secretly conducted stateside that were eventually declassified. There's no way any human trials he commissions will surface in declassified reports. Figuring out how to deliver a non-lethal bio-weapon comes before worrying about testing, he decides.

"Michaels' group can't know about your project," Isaacson insists. "Your group will be apprised of their progress, but not vice-versa."

"Impossible. They'll both be working at Sherwood." Zukoff says.

"I am damn serious. Besides, you didn't know Michaels was even there. During orientation, tell your team everything they learn and create is top secret, no exchange of information, even within the compound. Also, we know other nations will be working hard to get at our breakthroughs too."

"Okay, but why can't we trust our own people with classified information?"

"It's not that, it's Michaels. Every brilliant researcher is eccentric, and he is by no means an exception. I worry about his reaction if he found out his telomere breakthroughs might be used as a bio-weapon."

"Don't you trust him? You just disclosed he was assisting the agency before the Hemispheres crash."

"Let's say this. He's instrumental to these breakthroughs. I trust him implicitly as to the research. However, some circumstances, shall I say, raise some questions. One more thing. He fathered a son while in protective custody."

"Wait, what the hell?" Zukoff asks.

"Not with a mistress. His wife died when the plane went down, but they had frozen her eggs years ago. He used an agency-cleared surrogate to have another child. So Justin, his son, is with him, and someone who has worked at Sherwood for years is his live-in nanny. The kid's less than a year old, and Michaels can't really leave the compound since the outside world believes he's six feet under."

"We're talking about a top-secret situation with tremendous implications. Are you sure you trust someone who has a young toddler to think about?"

"I trust him." As he says this, Isaacson's mind wanders to Michaels' refusal to continue his research until the CIA and FBI agreed to let him see his daughter and brother. *Not the time for self-doubt*, he resolves.

Zukoff interrupts his thoughts. "I'm going to need all of Michaels' data as soon as possible. Then, as we move forward, how will I receive updates?"

"I'll give them to you directly as they supply them to me. We'll also have active surveillance all over the lab."

Zukoff nods.

"Let's get to work. Are you ready to change the world?" Isaacson asks as they walk towards the conference room door.

"Of course. That's why we came to work here, isn't it?"

Isaacson walks down the quiet hallway to his expansive corner office. There's an important telomere detail he did not share with Zukoff, but it resides in the foreground of his thoughts. Ron Michaels treated his own daughter with blood transfusions, making her the only human test subject, and this non-traditional "clinical trial" was successful. She beat the medical issues she suffered from, and hell, she was the only Hemispheres jet crash survivor. Solarez has reported no current problems, and she is under no ongoing medical care of any kind.

The questions he keeps returning to revolve around whether Amanda Michaels will live longer, and if she is also resistant to particular infections or traumas. Her situation may not necessarily create a completely new gateway to increased life spans for millions of other Americans, or for humankind for that matter. Nonetheless, Isaacson resolves to either discuss this issue directly with Ron Michaels or gain access to her blood or tissue to have it analyzed by government biologists and geneticists.

Before he reaches the doorway of his own office, he asks his assistant, Barbara, to come into his office. When they first started working together, she would appear with a notepad and pen, now she walks in with her tablet.

"I want you to call a couple of our research organizations and set up two different symposia. One needs to appeal to the top minds in the scientific community, so title it something like 'Ethical and Economic Implications of Extending Human Life 25 Percent.'"

"Isn't that a little vague? Shouldn't you say 'to 110 or 125 years of age?'"

"Whatever, you can create the exact title. It'll cover the potential healthcare system costs of such an extension—increased costs of Social Security, contributions to the workforce by senior workers, all of those issues."

"What's the second one?"

"How about 'Fast-Tracking Drug and Medication Approvals:

Current Cutting-Edge Methods to Expedite Human Trials and Obtain Approval.' Set them both up within 45 days if possible."

"Got it," she says, rising to walk out of his office. Isaacson can't help but appreciate the shape of her long legs as she leaves, but the dominant thought pervading his mind is the enormity of the challenge facing both Zukoff and himself.

CHAPTER 3
HOUSEGUEST

HER EYES open and she sees him still sleeping beside her. Smooth as silk, Angie Tipton, Andy Michaels' trusted paralegal, quietly lifts herself off the bed and grabs her nearly transparent, white knee-length robe from the carpeted floor next to her bed, tiptoeing toward her bathroom. She eases the door closed with a quiet click.

As she considers herself in the mirror above the sink, a touch of sadness and guilt builds. She realizes this situation is hopeless, but she forces a smile and throws some water on her face. After running a brush through her hair, she walks back into the bedroom. Paul Franklin turns to face her as she lifts the two empty wine glasses from the nightstand.

"Good morning. That was amazing. Come over here."

She puts the glasses down, slides on top of him and leans down to kiss him.

"God, I love what you do to me," she sighs.

"I have until about noon." He kisses her and holds her tightly against him. His other hand finds its way down to her thigh. He slides the bottom of her robe up and she immediately feels the cool air on her exposed skin.

"Where are you, supposedly?" Her voice is laced with sarcasm.

"I was at a hearing in Pennsylvania that required me to stay overnight and I'm driving home today by noon, which is mostly true."

"You realize this relationship is pretty toxic." Angie says half-heartedly, leaning away from him.

"What's that mean?"

She climbs off him and sits in the chaise, still facing him.

"Well, let's see. You're the defense lawyer who fought my boss in the high-profile Hemispheres crash case, which seems a bit unethical. Oh, and you're married."

"I disagree with you about the ethical part. You're a paralegal for the opposing firm, but we never talk about our work. Where's the violation? Plus, the cases are all over now."

Technically, it's true the cases are over, at least for now. But if all goes according to plan, Franklin will be unleashing a hailstorm on Andy Michaels like he's never experienced before. He sure as hell isn't going to share that with Angie though. He still needs her, and not just on a sexual level.

"Well, you are still married, which makes this is an affair, and your wife could file for divorce, or maybe kill you, or me, and there is this thing some folks call adultery, and also your kids would hate you...there's probably more." She reaches again for the two glasses, plus the empty wine bottle on the nightstand, and walks out of the room.

On her way out she uses her foot to gently push the very handy sex swing they used last night out of the doorway. She smiles, thinking of Paul's excitement as she hovered at the perfect height in the trapeze-like contraption. Tantalizing him, staying ahead of him sexually, is an art form she takes pride in.

Exactly why do they enjoy this? She loves the sexual energy and assumes he does too. He can't fake what they do for each other, she assures herself. She recognizes he derives some pleasure in bedding down his rival's paralegal too. Part of her believes Paul wouldn't slash Andy apart in one of their litigation battles, at least not without warning her somehow. She imagines Paul thinks he would get tipped off by her if the proverbial piano was falling toward him from the window as well.

While she is washing a few dishes in the kitchen sink, he walks up behind her wearing nothing but his boxer briefs and reaches inside her robe, caressing her intimately. He leaves his right hand on her breast, swirling two fingers around the nipple. "Do you think I'm evil for being a corporate defense attorney for companies like Hemispheres?" he says, withdrawing his hand slowly while asking.

"Well, I'd say you're on the wrong side of things, but I believe somewhere inside you is a good soul, or I wouldn't be with you. I thought you said we never talk about our work."

He walks away and sits at the breakfast bar, thinking a moment. "Contrary to what you might think, I do have a conscience."

"What about the way you fight every plaintiff's lawyer who seeks a dime in court? Believe me, I can think of a few notable war stories."

"I'm not a friend of greedy people who want millions for what I consider minor problems, and there is no shortage of fakers. I hate the money-grubbing malingerers."

"Are you suggesting people like the families of the 9/11 Pentagon victims you fought against in court are fakers? You sound like Ann Coulter. She went after 9/11 widows like they asked to become widowed. Jeez."

"There are exceptions. That might be one of them," Franklin says.

"What about those whose husbands and wives and children were killed in the plane crash that killed Andy's brother, Ron? Are you saying they were seeking jackpot justice?"

"You know the rules. Can't talk about any of that. Fortunately, we currently aren't on any opposing cases with you guys."

Paul nervously fidgets, moving the salt and pepper shakers in meaningless maneuvers on the table. "Would you be surprised to learn I've tanked cross-exam on some plaintiffs before?"

"How so?"

"Well, everyone feels for people who've lost a spouse or child, and you know your client is going to be paying, you're just fighting over how much. I've gone soft on my cross on a number of victims, but I'll never tell anyone who they were, including you."

He gets up and paces around the room, looking as if something is on his mind. Figuring the conversation is over, Angie starts to walk out.

"Would you consider coming to work for me? For a much higher salary?"

She stops in her tracks, turns, and stares. "I don't think that's a good idea on many levels. You're joking, right?"

"Not at all. I just want you to think about it. Maybe sometime down the road."

Angie doesn't answer. It's bad enough to be involved in this affair which would infuriate Andy, he would blow a brain synapse if he ever found out. Her leaving his practice to join Paul would cause a mental breakdown.

Paul decides to drop it. "I'm going to take a shower. Any ideas on breakfast?"

"We can't exactly saunter into any of the nearby cafes together, so I guess I'll fix something here. Scrambled eggs, wheat toast, jelly?"

Paul nods in agreement and heads to the bathroom.

As the hot water pelts him, he thinks about his plan, and his upcoming meeting with Ty Ryan, the private investigator. He couldn't hire Angie now even if she was willing to make the move. Her access inside Andy Michaels' firm may prove instrumental in the near future. He just has to make sure she doesn't figure out his true intentions.

CHAPTER 4
NEWSEUM

"THE PRESS IS on this like white on rice," Franklin whispers to Ty Ryan. They're both looking at interactive news stories about the Kennedy assassination on the third floor of the Newseum, one of the newer museums in D.C.

"Biggest story to hit this city in months."

"Any luck obtaining the info on the plaintiffs?"

Before contacting Ryan, the investigator who obtained some critical information for him during the plane crash cases, Franklin riffled through many of the litigation files himself. He was trying to find someone who would challenge the wrongful death settlements based on a new fraud or conspiracy claim. No rational family member would join a lawsuit that might force them to give their settlement money back, so his pitch would promise the safekeeping of their original proceeds. However, if the U.S. conspired with another person or company to secretly snuff out a search for the truth, that could violate the Racketeer Influenced and Corrupt Organizations (RICO) Act, which can carry both criminal and civil penalties.

Franklin's first target was Andy Michaels' law firm. Could he tie them to the government in a conspiracy of silence and deception? After his file review, Franklin hand-picked five of the settling plaintiffs by their white-collar occupations and his intuition as those who might be interested in suing. Then he hired Ryan to do deeper background work on each of them.

"Let's go to the men's room for the transfer." Ryan starts walking, trailed a short interval later by Franklin. They silently exchange envelopes in the restroom and file back out, heading in different directions before meeting again in another hall.

"You need to decide who you think would be the best to approach." Ryan says, walking slowly toward another alcove.

"I think for ethical purposes I should write a letter."

"Your call, but I wouldn't. What if they give it to Michaels?"

"True, but they can tell him if I show up in person too. I'll think it over. Any chance of you planting a bug in Michaels' office for me?"

"I told you I don't do B and E. There may be another way though."

"What's your idea?"

With a few steps between them, Ryan and Franklin wander through the museum. Both look at the next sequence of historical newspaper pages on the wall. "One Small Step for Mankind," the headlines declare.

"Another person with access to the office could do it. His paralegal might even do it," Ryan whispers.

Angie. Could I plant something on her without her knowing? Franklin quickly nixes that concept. Maybe Angie would do it for me?

"I'm already inside her," he replies, turning to Ryan with a smile.

"You're messing around with her?"

"I thought you knew everything."

"No, only what I need to, and that's something I never had a reason to know."

"Have your sources given you any further information on why the government paid the airline?" Franklin asks.

"Not yet, but I'm sure they will. I'm thinking to end any further investigation into sabotage, but I haven't figured out who or why."

"Did you figure out who detained you after the Hemispheres crash and returned you to the Department of Justice?"

"My money's on China."

"Unrelated question, but not entirely off topic. Why'd you leave the SEALs?" Franklin pries, now walking beside Ryan back down the JFK assassination hallway.

"What, are you my shrink now?"

"No, I just wondered. I read a lot about the SEAL team that got Bin Laden." This is a complete lie—Franklin is still determining Ryan's loyalties. After all, this plan of his must remain airtight.

Ryan doesn't say anything for several long seconds, trying the attorney's patience. "Too many funerals. So, I walked while still mostly intact. My emotional bandwidth is pretty narrow, not like yours or any other person in this museum."

"How about a pension?"

"I had to fight to get five years of veterans' benefits. I fell several years short of a full pension. Why do you think I do this investigative work for you?"

"Makes sense I guess," Franklins says, thinking that needing the cash is a solid reason, so long as cash won't make Ryan go astray if the chips are down.

"When I open my closet door," Ryan says, "there are clothes inside, but sometimes instead I see this teenage kid I trained my weapon on, decided to save him, and then...." Ryan flings his arms from his waist upward near both sides of Franklin's head. "Kapow! He detonated a suicide vest, blew me back against the opposite wall. Damn glad for my body armor, full helmet and all. We would kill high-value targets every night when we rampaged Iraq. Abbottabad, Al Asad, Ramadi, Baghdad, so many cities I can't remember 'em all. Killing only five or six meant a wasted night. The so-called 'surge' succeeded because of us, but when you look back, what did we accomplish? Neither side wants our asses in their business, we didn't consider we're just infidels. We had jobs to do, and we thought we were liberating Iraq."

"After your captives released you to the DOJ, did the U.S. compensate you?"

"Yeah. They gave me $50,000 and made me sign confidentiality papers. Whoever held me was certain I was FBI counter-intelligence, they wouldn't believe a word I said otherwise. Do you have any idea what it's like to be treated like a political prisoner, never being told what you did wrong or ever having a trial? The first day I figured they'd kill me, but when I found myself still breathing on day two I realized they were using me as some kind of bargaining chip. Now I want to know why."

"So that's why you're helping me?"

"Yep, I want to see where all this is going. And I can use the cash, of course."

"Get me a bug, and I'll work on Angie."

"Roger." The investigator walks away. His financial outlook is brighter for the next calendar year, and discovering why Hemispheres was paid $200 million by the U.S. will be an added bonus.

CHAPTER 5

VIDEOCONFERENCE

AFTER THE VIDEO conference is arranged, Solarez insists Amanda travel in an unmarked vehicle to FBI headquarters, given the recent leaks and subsequent media frenzy.

He meets her at the security desk and escorts her to the elevator after she is screened. As the door closes, she starts questioning him.

"How many months will this go on? Wait, it isn't going to be more than months, is it?"

"Can't say. It's out of my control."

"I thought everything about this was under your control."

"Hardly. I'm a supervisory agent, the director decides on things like this, not me."

They arrive on their desired floor, the door opens, and they proceed to the room where she's done prior video conferences with her dad, Ron Michaels.

"I don't want you in here," she tells him as she enters.

"I have to connect you, sorry." He follows her into the nondescript room with white walls, a table with a couple chairs, a flatscreen TV and a desktop computer. Tapping a few keys, he makes the connection and a room can be seen on the TV. As he leaves, he gives her the same instruction as before. "Tell the agent in the hall when you're done and she'll come get me."

The door closes behind Solarez and Ron walks onto the screen. Behind him she glimpses her little brother, Justin, and his nanny, Mrs. Kolfax. Amanda lets go of everything troubling her and feels truly happy.

"Hi Dad! So great to see you again!"

"You too! How's everything going? How's Crossroads?"

"Good. We've added a few new patients."

Her dad turns to the side and picks up Justin, who is holding a small panda toy. Looking curiously toward the monitor, he sees Amanda but doesn't recognize her.

"Hi Justin! Remember me? I'm your sister, Amanda. What do you have there?"

He moves the stuffed bear up and down.

"Can you say hello?" Ron asks, bouncing him gently on his knee.

"Ba-ba. Ba-da."

"What words has he been saying?"

"We think maybe dad or dada, hard telling."

Justin bangs the toy on the table, then sticks it in his mouth.

"Do you have any other animals, Justin?"

Ron answers for his son. "Oh he's got all kinds of little critters, and some Disney characters. He's creating a virtual animal playground."

"So how are you dealing with him walking now?"

"We've baby-proofed everything—drawers, cupboards, toilets, you name it. Can't open a thing without releasing some sort of lock. He keeps Mrs. Kolfax busy, especially since I'm spending a lot of time in the lab."

"How's that going? Are you making progress?"

"Oh, always."

Amanda doesn't pry.

"I want to get clearance to go off property to a parade in Annapolis. I hope it will be approved.

"Justin would get to see his first parade!"

"Yeah, we shall see." On the screen, Mrs. Kolfax walks over with a couple other small animals, a brown pony with a frizzy mane and a pink pig. Justin momentarily turns his attention to the pony, then goes back to the panda. *Must be his favorite,* Amanda thinks, *at least for today.*

"I wonder if they'll ever let me visit you guys in person."

"I wish I knew."

"I'm going to meet David after this. He's interning in this building."

"Really? I didn't know he was interested in FBI work."

"Me either. He hasn't finished school yet, so he's just here for the summer. I'm going to ask Solarez if I can tell him about you and Justin."

"Follow whatever instructions they give you. They may not seem fair to you, but they're for our safety."

"Did you hear the plane crash is back in the news?"

"No, what for? Wait a sec." Ron asks Mrs. Kolfax if she can take Justin to the next room, due to some personal things he needs to discuss with Amanda. Once she leaves the area, he turns back to the video cam.

"I kinda figured you hadn't heard," Amanda says. "Something about the government paying a lot of money to Hemispheres."

Her dad looks concerned. "Sounds like trouble."

"Solarez assigned agents to cover me 24/7. Not as bad as your situation, but he wants them on me wherever I go, which is pretty suffocating."

"Are you taking the pills every day?"

"Yep, unless I forget. Why can't I take them once a week or something?"

"Because, by lengthening your telomeres, you are more susceptible to other side effects, like reduced immunities, and I'm not sure what else. That's why. I check your cells every time I receive the vials of your blood here at the lab, and your telomeres are super long, like those of a five-year-old, but there are so many things we don't know yet."

"Fine. But will I age normally? I mean, I wonder about it when I look in the mirror most days, whether I'm aging like any other college kid is."

"Hopefully you'll live longer, so I guess that means you may age differently, maybe more gracefully. All the animal testing points to extended life, but I can't predict how that will play out for humans. There are lots of question marks, which we're working on now."

"That's not too reassuring since you didn't really answer me. It stresses me out."

"I'm sorry, but we have no scientific data to tell us what to expect. It never affected me so I don't know—"

"You transfused me for a lot longer though. I still feel, uh, I mean I know you transfused me to help me, but you didn't really know enough—"

"I knew it didn't have any adverse effects on me."

They visit for a few more minutes on confidential matters, trying to catch up on everything they can. Amanda then asks to say goodbye to Justin, who soon becomes agitated, and they end their teleconference on a downbeat. With some disappointment, Amanda exits the room and asks the woman posted outside to tell Solarez she's done.

"Agent Solarez, I want to tell David Owlsley my dad's alive. I don't know how it would be a problem, especially with the security clearance he needed to work here for the FBI this summer. You know that we've been through a lot of heavy duty stuff together, including going to Manhattan to try to figure out what was special about my dad's telomere research. He knows part of the story, but nothing about my dad surviving."

"I recently realized the same thing, so I had a brief meeting with him this morning and told him the truth."

"Wow, that was way easier than I thought it would be. I'm so used to you saying no."

"What I told David was very limited. He knows your father wasn't on the jet and about him being under witness protection, but not about the ongoing telomere research. And it needs to stay that way. Deal?"

"So I can say I've been in contact with my dad but nothing about what he's doing?"

"Right. Nothing about his research or his location."

"You've never told me his location."

"Well, consider it one less secret for you to keep. You're welcome."

CHAPTER 6

FBI VISIT

THE FBI CAFETERIA reminds David of a high school lunch room—the painted cinder-block walls, standard rectangular tables with fixed benches, and ubiquitous plastic trays. At least they aren't the same color. He spots Amanda, wearing a pair of faded jeans, a light tan button-down shirt and a black blazer with a visitor badge clipped on the lapel.

The moment they find an empty table, Amanda blurts out, "They told you my dad is alive. You understand I didn't know any of that when we went searching in New York."

"Yeah, I'm still processing it all..."

"Solarez told me it was top secret because the FBI was trying to uncover a mole, who they found after they killed off Pletcher, who was bait or something. Anyway, my dad was never aware of any of that, he helped them with something and they put him in a safe house to protect him. I wasn't allowed to tell you, I begged them to let me. I had a video conference with my dad and Justin today, which is why I'm here."

"With Justin? Wait, what are you talking about?"

"Justin, my baby brother. Oh wow, Solarez didn't tell you that part. He's nearly a year old now."

David jumps out of his chair and takes a few steps away from the table, a look of complete confusion crosses his face. Amanda realizes he's overwhelmed by the information and remembers how shaken and upset she was when she first found out.

"Come back and sit down, I need to explain." She gets up and touches his arm, trying not to make a scene among the tables of FBI administrative staff and agents. Several people stare questioningly their way.

"Solarez helped my dad retrieve frozen eggs and sperm from a fertility clinic my parents had used when they had trouble conceiving. Anyway, he also arranged for a surrogate. All this took place while my dad was protected at the safe house. He named the baby Justin, because that was the name I wanted. You know I always wanted a brother—"

"You didn't just want one, you kept saying you had a brother named Justin after the crash. You remembered things you did with him. But how could you keep all this from me since we went searching for answers in Manhattan?"

"Solarez told my Uncle Andy and me absolutely no one could know anything. It's been killing me. And yeah, the Justin thing is weird. Maybe my knowing about him and my amnesia are connected."

"No, that makes no sense. Memory stores what already happened, he hadn't even been born when you were telling everyone about him."

Amanda sees the distrust in David's eyes. "What else can I say? I'm telling the truth. You know how people say they have a sixth sense or a hunch? Maybe I do too. C'mon, let's get some lunch. What do you eat in this place?"

Being the kind of guy that normally analyzes and researches everything, including his meals, David barely looks at the food choices. Instead he thinks about the sixth sense theory but isn't buying it. No matter, it doesn't affect the way he views Amanda. After ordering and insisting on paying for both their meals, he sits back down at the table with her.

"I need to tell you something else," Amanda says. I remembered something about me and Jonathan. I think I dreamed it the other night, or maybe it was...I don't know when. The point is I remembered something. You know what that means?"

"No, what?"

"That they're all still there."

"Who's still there?"

"Not who, what. All my memories. I've read a lot about memory. They're forever stored in our brains, but head trauma like I had damages the neurons, blocking me from processing them right. If I can remember something about Jonathan from before, that confirms it--I still have them."

Sure, he initially urged Amanda to rekindle things with her old boyfriend because he thought it might help her gain back some of her prior self. But she had repeatedly refused, saying she had no memory of him or feelings for him. Now David wants a closer relationship with Amanda for himself. Selfish? No, he tells himself, yet again. They've gotten together a few times so far over their break from school, but more like old friends than what he wants. With or without the romance, he still cares deeply about her, but he's overwhelmed by what he's learned in the last few hours.

Her brings himself back to their lunch. "Um, yeah, that's great. Anything weird happening, like health-wise? What about the bleeding and stuff?"

"Nothing's changed there, I still barely bleed." Amanda doesn't mention her periods only last about a day. It seems unusual, but she can't compare them to before the crash since she doesn't remember them.

"I gotta get back to work. Can I come see you at the farm and hang out sometime?"

"Sure. An agent will be there since they're with me day and night, I mean right outside the house. Solarez is freaked out about the news leak."

"And for good reason. Somebody wanted that story out, hopefully we'll find out who and why soon." As David says this, he wonders if there are parts of the truth Amanda has not shared with him.

CHAPTER 7
EMBASSY

THE CHINESE EMBASSY intelligence analyst is focused on the four computer monitors in front of him when his supervisor, appears in the doorway.

"Fong wants to meet with us in five minutes."

"I'm sure he saw the news this morning. It wasn't us."

"We will explain everything then."

The two intelligence analysts are seated at a round conference table in the large open office of Ambassador Fong in the Chinese Embassy off Massachusetts Avenue in Washington, DC. Ambassador Fong's deputy chief sits on one side of him, and on the other side sits Jang-Chung. They all greet the familiar intelligence analysts as they enter the room.

Jang-Chung, the man accompanying the Ambassador, acts as the lead Chinese liaison with the Department of Justice and was the negotiator of the secret Hemispheres crash agreement between China and the U.S. Considered a rising star in the Chinese embassy, he was educated at Peking University, before honing his English while in the International Relations graduate school at Stanford in California.

"Gentlemen, you realize this news all over the American media is a problem. The U.S. could decide to release damaging information about the crash. Or the American press could discover the jet's electrical system was tampered with. Or that our nation was trying to steal their biological information. Where did this story come from?" The Ambassador demands.

"Not from anyone connected with the embassy. None of our people would do this," The intel supervisor replies.

"This is an effort to embarrass the People's Republic," the ambassador barks at them. "They're trying to make us look bad. How can you be certain we do not have a leak within our staff?"

"We received the last $25 million for following the agreement, and we do not want anyone claiming China had anything to do with it or the U.S. might ask us to pay it back." Jang-Chung explains. He personally negotiated with Stein from the Department of Justice to swap various people being held by each country. The deal gave the U.S. the option to trade in yuan at a higher valuation, which ultimately permitted the U.S. to recoup the millions they secretly funneled to the airline to keep the sensitive matter quiet.

"I don' t believe the U.S. would leak this. Some other nation planted the story to embarrass one of us, or some individual did it for financial gain." Jang-Chung continues, looking for input from the intel analysts.

No one mentions the issue was sensitive enough that a mercenary contractor had terminated Kent Perless over the issue—he was planning to go to the press with the theory the Chinese had sabotaged the jet.

The more junior analyst finally speaks up. "Even if no one in the PRC did it, the U.S. may still blame us, especially if the news keeps reporting on it. And we don't want them digging too much. We need to find the source so we can be sure nothing else will become public."

"Agreed. Your group needs to monitor the internet to determine any possible source of this disclosure. The premier asked that we use all available resources to secure timely updates about the American telomere research. What about your asset at the Sherwood lab?" Jang-Chung says.

"Yes, we think we can turn the researcher we have targeted, although we have not tried to get information yet. We need to have a special assignment, and the time is not yet right." The senior intelligence agent smiles. "The Americans think they fooled everyone, but they are wrong. We initiated a spear phish that embedded a remote access tool, which can quickly exit when any real-time security systems might detect it. This gives us access to the research lab server almost whenever we need it."

The junior analyst says: "Sir, I want authority to surveil Amanda and Andy Michaels. If you consider the sources of this leak, she clearly meets the parameters. Her uncle is more unlikely, but we cannot be sure. I want to monitor their mobile devices; we can hack their cell phones and wi-fi routers."

"We cannot use any of our assets for such a risky operation." Jang-Chung protests.

The ambassador raises his arm with his palm facing out. "No more details. So long as none of our agents are required to personally enter their residences, I will approve the surveillance you propose. I trust you will get results. That will be all for now."

CHAPTER 8
ANONYMOUS

STEVE SOLAREZ HATES MISSING his lunchtime workouts. He leaves no time for a regular lunch, often grabbing a sandwich on his way back to the office. His favorite haunts: the downtown YMCA and Manhattan Deli, just a block from FBI headquarters.

Standing beside the treadmill, he scrolls through his personal cell phone looking for a playlist. He hits shuffle and the first track begins: *Growin' Up* by Springsteen. *"I took month-long vacations in the stratosphere...."*

After working out and showering, he heads for the deli where the owner, cooks, and servers all recognize him. He orders his regular pastrami and Swiss on rye with spicy mustard and scrolls through his emails while he waits.

"You're all set."

Grabbing his sandwich with a quick wave of thanks and heading out the door, he's halfway down the block before he notices the folded piece of paper resting between a napkin and the edge of the bag. *What's this?* he thinks, pulling it out and unfolding it. The non-descript font reads:

Agent Solarez:

I work for the Chinese Government in the Embassy. I have valuable information regarding Ron Michaels and his son, which I'm willing to provide in exchange for fair compensation. I will email exact instructions to your personal account. Once I receive the first transfer of $50,000.00 USD, I will provide a portion of my *information. Each subsequent payment will result in additional intelligence.*

Sincerely,

X

Solarez does a slow 360, looking at the other people on the street who aren't paying any attention to him. He heads back to the deli, but no one has any idea how the note got in his bag.

There is an extremely small number of people in the world who know Ron Michaels didn't perish in the Hemispheres crash, and fewer still who are aware of Justin. Solarez concludes whoever wrote the note has knowledge of Michaels' telomere research, maybe even where he's hidden. Making his way out of the parking garage, he considers not only the source of information, but also whether an agent inside the Chinese Embassy would take this risk. If this is for real, this could be a counter-intelligence coup. But it might be a ruse, the Chinese fishing for intel.

This one goes straight to the director and Isaacson. It's way above my pay grade.

CHAPTER 9

BECCA'S

JUST BEFORE NOON, Andy texts Becca to say he's on his way and heads out of his office, up to M Street, and over to Wisconsin. The sun directly overhead radiates intense heat, so he loosens his tie as he jaywalks across the road. A long horn blast from a cab startles him, but he quickly realizes it's not directed at him. He looks up at the familiar "Becca's" sign before pulling the door open. A chime rings and he is enveloped by incense. Not seeing Rebecca right away, he walks past a customer and a pretty young clerk on his way to the cash register, then spots her.

"Are you ready?"

Things between them have been a little shaky as of late. For about 18 months they virtually lived together, but a couple months ago she started pressing him for a more substantial commitment. He loves her, no question in his mind, but he is still recovering after his divorce from Sarah and can't get married again. Not yet, at least. Upon learning of his reluctance to move ahead in their relationship, Becca started staying more often at her small flat on Olive Street, blocks away from him. A breakup was never declared, and they still see each other fairly regularly, but she has made it clear she considers them no longer exclusive. A longtime yoga enthusiast, she began teaching classes twice a week at a popular studio in Georgetown. Her friends multiplied from there, and he noticed a marked decline in their time together, including overnights.

"Sure, let me tell Andrea I'm heading out."

Moments later they walk north on Wisconsin toward Au Pied Du Cochon, a casual French restaurant.

"You didn't have to meet me today considering what's going on," Becca says.

"What am I going to do?"

Her hand reaches out instinctively for his to reassure him. "It was all over the news this morning. Is it true? Did the U.S. pay hush money? And why?"

He knows part of it is true, but he was never told the amount.

"I don't know what to believe, but I guarantee I settled every one of those claims legitimately."

"I'm sure you did. But if something went wrong with the jet, why would the U.S. give the airline money?"

Andy doesn't respond as his thoughts turn to his former clients and his meetings with Attorney Stein from the Department of Justice, who told him the government paid off Hemispheres to keep the national security part of the story confidential. It could become a huge scandal, like the Iran-Contra affair. No, he thinks, there's actually a big difference between the CIA using illegal drug profits to support rebels in Iran and them trying to stop China from stealing biomedical secrets.

"Andy, you didn't answer me." Becca pulls him from his thoughts.

"I'm not sure if the story is true, and I can't say anything until..."

"Until when? The media is blowing up over this. And I bet they're blowing up your phone too."

He needs to contact Stein to see what, if anything, he can do to keep him out of this ethical quagmire. Maybe national security trumps everything, even him having to talk to the press and being questioned about his ethics.

They haven't been seated five minutes when Andy feels his cell phone vibrating. A picture of Perry Carson appears. *No way I'm talking to a reporter now.* After the waiter takes their order and they hand over their menus, he texts him back.

Not now. Later.

He finally responds to Becca's question, "I'm going to talk to a few of my government contacts."

"Well, what if they did give them the money? Will all the

cases get reopened? Are you going to file a new lawsuit? You better be prepared to protect yourself and the firm."

Sue the U.S.? Stein and the DOJ would go absolutely bonkers. Not a chance. As far as my reputation goes, hmm.

"I don't know where this is going. Let's talk about something else, okay? How are things with the shop?"

"Fine, except I need to hire a new weekend part-timer. Ashley gave me notice, she's moving to San Francisco. Oh, I found a dress for the gala."

Andy barely hears her, but it reminds him they are going to the big DC Bar Association see-and-be-seen soiree. Not exactly good timing.

"Great, what color? I'm looking forward to seeing it."

Faking his way through the rest of lunch, Andy wonders whether or not his law practice will implode.

CHAPTER 10

MEETING STEIN

THE CAB PULLS UP in front of the Robert F. Kennedy Department of Justice building at 950 Pennsylvania Avenue. Andy Michaels shoves the earbuds into the inside pocket of his suit jacket. He had been listening to a peaceful acoustic piano playlist, trying to calm himself on the way to his meeting with Brett Stein, his DOJ attorney contact. Stepping away from the cab onto the sidewalk, he momentarily gazes up at the four huge pillars forming the facade of the building before entering. After clearing security, he makes his way to Stein's office where they shake hands and head to an expansive conference room with 16 chairs around an oversized table. The door sweeps closed, Andy sits down, and Stein takes his seat at the end closest to him.

"I specifically asked you before our deal was signed if you were going to protect me from any exposure if someone tried to say I conspired with the government on the Hemispheres crash. Now here I am, my integrity impugned and my law practice in ruins."

"We haven't breached anything, and I can't keep someone from illegally leaking information. All I can do is try to uncover the source of the leak. Unless you've got another idea," Stein challenges.

"Actually I do. If this is really a national-security-threatening classified secret, which you told me it was when we made this deal, the government can shut this thing down, and fast."

"We are already running down all leads--..." But Andy cuts him off.

"My reputation is being trashed. Are you following the news? 'Michaels conspired with the government.' 'Michaels withheld evidence from his clients.' How can I fight back when I'm under a confidentiality agreement and you're supposed to be protecting me?"

"I understand your pain, and we're going to do everything we can."

"Oh yeah, how are you going to compensate me for my reputation? If you were a potential client thinking of retaining an attorney, would you call me with this going on? Hell no!"

"I'm meeting with the U.S. attorneys who'll be handling our defense. I think we'll able to pay for your lawyer per the confidentiality agreement, but we have to keep that confidential also."

"That's the first almost positive thing I've heard in all this mess. Who'll defend me?"

"Probably a former assistant U.S. attorney we feel comfortable with who's now in private practice. We'll share the information under a joint defense arrangement so they understand the background and maintain its confidentiality as attorney-client privilege."

"Okay, please tell me who you propose as soon as possible. I need to go practice some law, what's left to practice anyway. What a goddam mess."

Minutes later Andy makes his way to the first floor and walks out to find a taxi. He scrolls through his text messages and notices one from his ex-wife.

Please give me a call as soon as you can. About calls for congressional investigation.

He looks around for a corner or a quiet spot so he can call Sarah, who is also the top administrative assistant to Senator Mike Pierce. *Congressional investigation?*

Sarah picks up after a couple rings.

"Thanks for calling me back. Let me go close the door." Andy hears her moving around. "I wanted to call you because the senator said the caucus has a lot of constituents demanding an investigation of the Hemisphere's crash. He asked me to call you, obviously because of our relationship, to find out whatever I could. Tell me this is wild overreaching by the press."

"I don't have a lot to tell. I'm going to defend this, get it dismissed, and there's nothing to it. I had no information about this alleged government payment when I was working on the wrongful death cases for my clients. Is there something specific you were hoping to find out?"

"Well, strictly between us, did the government pay $200 million to Hemispheres?"

Andy pauses briefly. "Sarah, I can't say anything right now. I would if I could."

She takes his hesitation as a sign there may be some truth to the stories.

"Could you recommend anyone at the Department of Justice to talk to?"

"Sure, Brett Stein. He knows what's going on. I'm just between a rock and a hard place."

Sarah can detect the intense anxiety in her ex's voice so she doesn't press further. Andy adds one more thing, unsolicited.

"I am completely innocent and will be exonerated from any wrongdoing, but you wouldn't believe what this is doing to my reputation and my practice."

"I can only imagine. But a number of senators are making noise about committee hearings on this, the same ones who always claim big government is spending taxpayer money for the wrong reasons, and they are like junkyard dogs on this $200 million payoff. I can try to persuade Senator Pierce none of it is true, but not the other senators, even if I think you're innocent."

"Thanks. If I can tell you more soon, I will."

He shoves the phone back into his pocket and heads to the street to hail a cab.

When did my life get so complicated, he wonders.

CHAPTER 11
THE NOTE

THE FBI DIRECTOR studies the now unfolded note, lays it on his desk, and looks at Solarez.

"We're treating this as legitimate until proven otherwise. Take it down to forensics. They won't find prints except yours, but they can check the source of the paper. Font style too, I guess, for whatever that might tell us, which will probably be nothing, but 20 different computer manufacturers, if not all of them. Get the customer and employee information from the deli for the day you found the note and the day before, and all surveillance footage for the same time. A pro would realize we're going to check all this, but it's the only approach I can think of. Maybe they slipped up somehow."

"Who's going to notify the CIA director, you or me?"

"You can. Are you sure you can't reach back out to the source somehow?"

"Except going back to the deli like usual and hoping I catch him leaving another note, no. I'll be hearing from him by email, just like he said."

"If or when he does contact you, make him believe you're interested. Ask him for information about how to wire the money and press him for why the info is so valuable. Then contact me for the authorization."

"The bureau will pay the 50 grand?"

"Depends. We're not paying 50 grand *only* for the Michaels information. If we pay, and I'm not saying we will, it would be for whatever *other* intel he might have. Never doubt the potential value of a double agent. Of course, the note could be a complete sham too." The FBI director mindlessly folds the 8½-by-11 sheet of paper back into eighths. He unfolds it again, thinking about the ramifications if the note is legit.

Reading his mind, Solarez says, "If this really is a Chinese operative inside the embassy and they're aware of Michaels, his research and his son, either our operation in Canada or at Sherwood has been compromised. We need to get to the bottom of this."

"Yep. They already seem to know way too much, like they have an asset at the lab, or they hacked our servers. We're counting on this research, and the whole thing may be in jeopardy. Keep me posted, and let me know if the CIA comes up with any ideas."

CHAPTER 12

FRANKLIN'S PITCH

WITH HIS WELL-REHEARSED pitch running through his mind, Franklin pushes the 31st floor button on the elevator. After announcing himself to the attractive receptionist seated behind the round, modern desk, he sits in one of the client chairs and looks at, but doesn't actually read, the headlines of the Wall Street Journal. Moments later, he is ushered back to a small conference room with an expansive view of the city's skyscrapers and the river. The CEO of Hemispheres Airline, David Merland, awaits him.

"David, so good to see you again. How's your wife?"

"Delores is doing well, thank you. And how about your wife, Melanie?" The businessman takes a seat at the table and Franklin follows suit.

"She's fine. With one in high school she stays quite busy, of course. Now, the reason I'm here—the plane crash and the $160 million Hemispheres fund used to settle the claims. I assume you've heard the news."

"As soon as the story hit the airwaves I must've had 20 emails and text messages. No one has confirmed anything. And if it was true, I should've been the first to know, right?" Merland rises and walks over to the window to gaze at the river, then whirls back around. "Surely our lead attorney realizes it's completely false."

In actuality, the leaked story is correct. But the how and why is quite complicated, and Merland was sworn to secrecy by the FBI and the counter-intelligence agents who met with him. The arrangement saved his company and its stockholders over $100 million—the massive self-insured portion of the airline's liability—and it made sense. If a foreign government sabotages a U.S. commercial airliner, why should the shareholders pay? Hemispheres' insurance carrier, ABG, didn't fair as well. The $50 million it paid wasn't reimbursed and never will be because of the national security issues and the secret payment involved.

"My sources are saying there was a monetary transfer—"

Merland cuts him off. "Is there any evidence? Again, do you understand how preposterous it would be for something like that to happen and me not to be aware?" *Pretty convincing performance if I do say so myself,* Merland thinks.

Franklin's turn at acting comes next, since he was the one who informed the media and doesn't exactly possess a cancelled check; he's trusting Ryan to find the documentation to back him up. "I don't...I haven't...seen any direct proof, but I'm sure the press has something or they wouldn't put it out there knowing the libel standards."

"Well, let's wait and see what they've got. What else is on your mind?" he asks, knowing the lawyer too well to think he came in person just to discuss a rumor.

"As I recall, your insurer paid $50 million, and between the airline and your suppliers, you came up with another $110 million. I want to try to get the money back. My office has already drafted a RICO Complaint for D.C Superior Court regarding fraud and concealment by both Andy Michaels' law firm and the U.S. Government. If they concealed the truth, like if the crash was caused by a terrorist or some type of sabotage, that would be a game changer for sure. The airline did nothing wrong—there was no faulty maintenance, no defective parts—so you shouldn't pay, and I could get it all back for you, and then some. I'll even work on a contingency fee—one-third of the settlement or recovery and reimbursement of our litigation expenses, if we don't recover them ourselves."

"Taking on the government?" Merland bellows in a gravel-filled baritone. "What if we lose? Does this RICO statute require us to pony up any attorneys' fees to Michaels—or the government for that matter? I imagine the United States can find more than a few government attorneys willing to fight a fraud charge." He pauses long enough to cool down. "Fine. I'll talk to the board. The thought of getting the money back is very enticing, but suing the U.S. and a well-known attorney who handled high-profile cases against us will make this airline part of a media circus yet again. Something we need to think about."

"I don't understand why you would hesitate, especially if the rumors are true and the government hoodwinked you."

Merland senses a serious knot forming in the upper part of his stomach. He wants to talk to his FBI contact, pronto. "Like I said, I'll discuss it with my officers and let you know."

"I've already talked to ABG."

"Are you kidding me? You should have consulted me first."

"Sorry, I didn't think the sequence mattered," Franklin lies again. He figured the insurer would want their $50 million back, and he was right. They were willing to cover the litigation costs if the attorneys' fees were contingent on a recovery, and also if Hemispheres agreed. Without the airline, they wouldn't commit to anything.

"They're willing if you are. Since they only paid a fraction of what you put together in the settlement funds, they won't file without you."

"They never called me."

"I asked them not to contact you until we talked. Bert Pritchard is who I spoke with, their general counsel. Here's his card. Give him a call and let me know what you two decide."

Franklin rises from his seat and Merland reaches across the table to shake hands. He walks Franklin to the conference room door, but no further. He sits back down at the table. *There's a fire burning, and I need to put it out and fast.*

By the time Franklin crosses the polished terrazzo flooring of the lobby, he has considered his options. What if he doesn't get cooperation from Hemispheres or ABG? He still could file the same action as long as he gets one or more family members who recovered funds from their death suits to participate. Yes, if

Hemispheres—for whatever maddening reason—won't act on it, he still can. He feels a renewed satisfaction thinking he may be able to compensate for the tens of thousands in hourly fees he was screwed out of when he was forced to settle every claim within only months of the crash. The silver lining may still come shining through after all.

CHAPTER 13

INTERNSHIP

DAVID FIDGETS in his chair in Solarez' office. When he first met the agent at an MIT job fair, he looked skeptically at his U.S. Department of Justice business card. It was a long shot, far from the career he envisioned on his first day of classes at the prestigious university. Yet here he is, a computer technology and surveillance intern for the FBI at the Washington, D.C. headquarters, working on matters affecting the nation's counterintelligence. He has wondered more than once if Solarez was aware of his relationship with Amanda, and if that was the reason they selected him for the summer internship. And with the information Solarez is telling him now, it seems even more likely.

"So you're telling me Ron Michaels didn't die? Wait, were you involved in his disappearance?"

The momentary pause before the agent's response tells David he's right. "Yes, I was on the team tasked with protecting him," he confirms, but offers no further details.

"Well, I have a lot of questions." David pauses, thinking about his train trip with Amanda to Manhattan, where they tried to uncover why a patent attorney named Pletcher had done business with her dad. "Did you follow us when we went to New York to find Pletcher? And the bombing of Pletcher's garage, was that you?"

"There are some things you don't need to know."

"Yes, I think I do."

Solarez hates having his hand forced by a 19-year-old intern, but the intel he might gain from using David's relationship with the girl should they ever need it makes him cave. "We were involved. But that information doesn't leave this room. Now the government is being accused of paying millions to Hemispheres, and we have no idea where the story came from."

"You don't think Amanda did it, do you? Or her Uncle Andy?"

"No, but we're concerned for their safety."

"Anything else?"

"That'll be all," Solarez responds.

As he walks to the cafeteria to meet Amanda for lunch, David wonders if this is the career path he ought to be following.

CHAPTER 14
LUCENT'S VIEW

CLAUSTROPHOBIC. The one word that Amanda keeps thinking while the MRI scanner does whatever it does to get views of her brain. An hour later she's at the reception window at Dr. Lucent's office adjacent to the hospital.

"How was your spring semester at UVA?" Lucent asks her as she enters his small office.

"Fine. Right now I'm enjoying working at the farm and helping out with some of the patients at Broken Halo."

"I saw the crash on the news again..."

"The press can't get enough of the rumors. I don't believe them, but it still opens old wounds for me." She sits in a patient chair across the desk from him.

"I understand. Any memories from before the crash you want to share with me?"

"Just one little thing about my high school boyfriend, Jonathan."

"Well that's encouraging. You remembered something about him from before?"

"Kind of. Jonathan and I were, uh, kissing and stuff when I woke up one morning, so I'm not sure if it was an actual memory or a dream. I've seen him a few times since everything happened, and I've been made well aware that we dated in high school, so I could have made it up. I'm so tired of being like this, leafing through scrapbooks and looking at photos on my phone to learn about my own life."

A silhouette stands outside the glass door of the doctor's office. "Let me go see who that is." Dr. Lucent opens the door and talks briefly with a man in the hall, then comes back in and closes the door.

"You didn't tell me you had bodyguards."

"Oh yeah, since the news broke about the government hush money they've been with me constantly. It's completely unnecessary, and annoying, but my uncle said the alternative, being put in protective custody, is worse."

"Your uncle is a smart man." Lucent turns to the flat-screen TV projecting several images of Amanda's brain. "The images on the left are from right after the plane crash, and the ones on the right are from the MRI you had today, but I don't have the radiology report for those yet."

Lucent starts to compare the images and immediately notices something unusual.

"Amanda, can you give me a few minutes? I want to talk to Dr. Wishart about these. He's one of the neuro-radiologists and I really trust his judgment. I'll be right back, feel free to peruse the magazines." He gestures to the rack on the wall on his way out. He calls Wishart from a phone in a hallway alcove and they agree to meet in the radiology room on a different floor of the building.

In the darkened radiology room, they examine the old and new images of Amanda's brain.

Dr. Wishart shifts a few around. "No evidence of bleeding or abnormalities on today's scan."

"Don't you have a tool to measure the size of the brain?"

He scrolls through several icons on the monitor and selects the one that places graphical anchors around the circumference of an image.

"Can you compare the measurements from both dates?"

Side-by-side images with various marks and numbers appear on the screen.

"Interesting. It's about five percent larger now."

"If we rule out swelling, that would be pretty unusual, right?"

"Absolutely. If there is any change in size after a TBI, the brain normally becomes smaller as the injured tissue is reabsorbed."

"Well I'm looking at the same films you're looking at. Do you see any telltale indications of swelling?"

Wishart reviews them again. "No."

"All right, thanks. I want to study these a bit more, particularly the new ones."

Lucent walks down the hall toward his office where he finds Amanda leafing through a dated *People* magazine.

Lucent brings up the same images and studies the orientation of Amanda's frontal lobe, central sulcus, and parietal lobe in relation to the inner aspect of her skull. Is the frontal lobe a little too close to the interior of the skull in some of those areas? A traumatic cerebral swelling would be the most logical explanation, but the lack of clinical signs of this condition increases the possibility of actual brain growth. Keeping in mind the hyper-rapid coagulation of blood she exhibited after the crash, he mulls over possible treatments. Whether or not medications or steroids will help her is unclear, and he decides to talk it over with Amanda.

"At your age, we wouldn't expect to see any meaningful expansion of your brain, but it appears to be larger in the recent scans."

"Why would it be bigger?"

"Honestly, I don't know. I'm going to prescribe an oral steroid for now. If the increase is being caused by swelling, we need to reduce it so your brain isn't pressing against your inner skull."

Amanda decides to tell the doctor something she has been holding back since he started treating her. "Dr. Lucent, remember when Uncle Andy and I came to your house and I cut myself with scissors to show you how I don't bleed normally? Well, my dad did blood transfusions on me when I was younger. I have no idea how they affect me, but I'm taking enzymes and nutrients now. I thought I should tell you, in case it's somehow connected to my surviving when no one else did, or now, connected to my enlarged brain."

The doctor is surprised by this information and Amanda's reluctance to tell him until now. "Why didn't you tell me before?"

Amanda feels like she betrayed him, one of the only medical doctors she likes and trusts. *Damn, secrets suck.* She wants to blurt it all out and tell him everything, but she knows it could harm her dad or her little brother. Maybe Uncle Andy too.

"Because I couldn't."

"I don't understand—"

"The government. I have to honor an agreement we made with them."

"Who's we? This doesn't make sense, Amanda."

Lucent thought the agent in the hall was some sort of over-protection resulting from the recent media frenzy. Now he's even more baffled.

"All I know is I was treated with blood transfusions to help with my medical problems and it affected my blood, and my heal-ing. That's all."

She abruptly gets up, looking down to avoid eye contact with Lucent, opens the door and walks out.

Dr. Lucent walks quickly toward the door.

"Amanda, wait a second."

She pauses long enough to look back and shake her head, then continues walking down the hall with the agent on duty trailing behind her, feeling like a big liar.

CHAPTER 15

FALLING MAN

HE STARES at the large photographic reproductions mounted along the wall of the exhibition hall from his vantage point on the bench. Several somber-looking people slowly shuffle through the alcove ensconced deep inside the 9/11 Memorial and Museum in lower Manhattan. They hardly notice Ty Ryan seated along the wall opposite the iconic photos. He sits like Buddha, hands resting along his thighs, motionless. His gaze is focused on the falling man, dwarfed against the enormous black-and-white grainy image of the World Trade Center.

What absolute hell impelled this seemingly voluntary decision? Ryan knows this man's decision wasn't really voluntary. He understands hell. Hell forced this man to free-fall from a high floor of the World Trade Center. Death by inferno or free-fall to death—not much of a choice. The image haunts him. Every time he returns to New York he finds his way here, like a magnetic pull. The free-fall guy didn't deserve to die, only the terrorists deserved to die, and wanted to. This conundrum bothers him.

He feels his phone vibrate in his pocket. He looks at the screen, a text from Liza.

I'll text you when I'm leaving the museum.

K, he replies.

CHAPTER 16

LIZA

THE PULSATING BASS line of the loud techno music pulsates inside Liza Chang's stomach. *Ba-ba boom. Ba-ba boom.* She sits two rows back from the catwalk at New York Fashion Week for her company's most important stateside presentation of the year. People are packed in like sardines on folding chairs lining either side of the runway under the mammoth white tent in Bryant Park, Manhattan. It has earned the nickname "7th on 6th" because most New York design houses are on Seventh Avenue, but Fashion Week events are held off Sixth Avenue at the park. The Michael Morse line is slated for 7:00 p.m., after Tom Lord.

Marco, one of the designers for Morse, leans over to Liza. "Oh my God, here we go! I can't stand it anymore!" Thundering synth music plays and a choreographed light display begins.

Camera flashes burst from all directions as the first model in the Morse line makes her way down the catwalk, looking frighteningly thin and somewhat androgynous. She has short dirty-blonde hair and exotic makeup in multiple shades, including pastels that would look ridiculous anywhere but here. Those lucky enough to be in the front row point and converse about every detail of the model's look, from her shoes and the dress to the jewelry and makeup. In quick succession, a series of additional models appear in Morse outfits until they fill the narrow stage in a single line. At the far end, the first model turns and walks back, giving the audience a second chance to see all the ensembles.

Leaning again toward Liza, Marco excitedly says, "Here's the dress that I managed! Don't you love it?"

"Absolutely, Marco. It's amazing."

The announcer comments on various facets of the clothing as the models stream by. Between the music, the clapping, and the chatter of the industry pros packing the venue, Liza can't hear herself think. Fortunately, the hour goes by quickly. Then Liza, Marco and five of the other designers and sales representatives rush behind the stage, hugging, giggling, and high-fiving each other.

"The reception was amazing!" Marco lifts his plastic champagne glass high in the air. "The Nordstrom and Dolce reps congratulated me on the way here. Can't wait to talk to the buyers at the after-party!"

Liza faintly hears the familiar tone of her phone emanating from her small purse. She glances at the message. Ty Ryan, her old friend and occasional fling is meeting her after the party at the Conrad. She texts back, confirming she'll find him in the lobby bar.

The MOMA after-party is an immense success for the Morse line. Liza and her colleagues foresee job security, at least for one more fashion cycle. Liza has a unique role as a regional sales and quality control representative with the company for their accessories. It's a well-kept secret that the accessories—and even some of the upscale clothing—is made in China. The mandatory "Made in China" labels are sewn into the clothing in the most discreet locations possible, away from the splashy hang tag stating "Designed by Michael Morse, Seventh Avenue."

An Asian-American woman, Liza is now 30 years old. Her mother and father emigrated to the United States from Beijing. She grew up in Brooklyn before her parents relocated to Arlington, Virginia, where her dad was a professor at nearby Mary Washington University and her mom ran a successful upscale nail salon. As a child she learned Mandarin, Beijing's main language, and Wu, commonly spoken in the Shanghai area, as well as Yue Cantonese. They traveled back to visit her extended family about once a year; her parents were hard-working and frugal, but reconnecting with family was a vital ritual for them.

Valedictorian of her high school class in Arlington, she was offered a scholarship at Yale, where she graduated summa cum laude and was recruited by the CIA. Speaking multiple Chinese languages at a time when keeping tabs on China was of increasing interest made her valuable to the agency. Her affinity for languages also allowed her to master Arabic while at Yale.

One of her first covert operations for the CIA was to Iraq, embedded with SEAL Team 8, when the U.S. thought it successfully marginalized the "insurgency." History proved it to be a hollow success—much like the entire Iraq war and ill-fated occupation thereafter. During her Iraq assignment, her world collided with Ty Ryan's. Every night the SEALs, along with Liza and their Iraqi interpreter, would engage in missions to take out terrorists and so-called insurgents. Liza didn't take out the bad guys, that was for the SEALs to do, including Ty, she handled mission organization and logistics. They also shared a bed on several random occasions, but those unscheduled trysts were mutually satisfying, perhaps due to the uncertainty of it all.

Ryan had observed her acumen with a pistol and semi-automatic at the firing ranges between their almost nightly SEAL missions, and between their secret liaisons and nightly work, he became smitten with the way Liza carried herself. There was something about her exotic beauty that hooked him. She was different from any woman he had been involved with in his life "BL," or "before Liza."

In their first months together, she often shared her innermost feelings with Ty and confided that she did not think their Iraqi missions would ever win over the hearts and minds of the Sunnis and Shiites, who had a centuries-old blood feud that would not be settled by a weak government propped up by Americans, who most Iraqis distrusted. During her time in Iraq, two SEALs died, and every few days an IED would kill or maim a U.S. soldier, sending a chill through every member of the unit.

To the chagrin of her supervisors at Langley, and Ryan, she tendered her resignation at her six-year anniversary and surprised everyone by taking a position with Michael Morse, filling their need for an East Coast representative willing to travel to China and handle interaction with their overseas factories. Getting as far away as possible from intense stress was her paramount thought.

She soon discovered she could earn significantly more taking private contracts than she did with the agency, though some of the shadowy figures were downright spooky. She often didn't know who hired her, but for the right money, usually paid in full up front, she didn't care.

Hong Kong has long had a cottage industry of managing agents tasked with retaining confidentiality for businessmen hiding their profits offshore. Liza established a managing agent and a bank account to receive her off-the-books funds. Her HK account was in the fictitious name on her fake U.S. passport.

Some other contract ops she accepted involved honeypotting a clueless businessman, which required the use of her femininity in seductive ways. With some assignments, she assumed the sex was filmed, but her marks never once suspected she targeted them. She was careful to wear disguises and not take any repeat jobs in the same cities.

Another lucrative side business for her was a bit of contraband smuggling from China to the U.S. Never expressly apprised of what was being smuggled, her involvement was oblique—she would simply advise her contact when various samples were being shipped from one of the Chinese factories back to the Morse warehouse in Brooklyn and her contact did the rest. She presumed they were paying intermediaries at the factory and the warehouse to handle the illicit contraband. She got paid for each shipment she initiated, and the money had encouraged her to collect as many potential accessories or clothing samples as reasonably plausible.

Approaching the hotel bar to meet Ty, she wears a sheer white button-down blouse and above-the-knee black suede skirt from the Morse line, black nylons with seams running up the back of each leg, and black stilettos. Ryan stands and gives her a big hug beside the barstools. His muscular, six-foot-tall frame easily envelopes her petite, trim body.

"Good to see you."

Liza looks him over carefully. His wavy brown hair does a few untidy flips and is slightly longer than a military cut. He has chiseled facial features, high cheekbones, and piercing blue eyes, and he wears a simple black t-shirt revealing his strong arms. She admires his faded jeans and black leather belt with silver diamond-shaped studs surrounding it.

"How was the big show?" Ryan smells the wine or champagne on her breath, recognizing she had a few drinks before catching a cab to meet him.

"Unbelievably stressful. With it being the biggest show of the year, the whole next buying season rides on it. As far as I can tell, it went very well, at least all the company reps think so. At the MOMA, everyone raved about our line, and you know Marco, my friend, he was really excited because a bunch of his designs were popular."

"Awesome. Can I buy you a drink?"

"Of course, let's celebrate. The show, all the glitz and glam. And why not celebrate us too?"

Deep down Liza hates the fact Ty shows up to fall into bed with her only once in a blue moon, such a completely undependable relationship, though she voices not a word of her frustration. She was trained to maintain a fierce front. She finally focuses on the small menu of specialty drinks, then sets it down on the bar, where it sticks to several drops of over-splash from the previous occupant's drink.

"How about a Stoli martini, dry, with two olives please."

Ryan gets the bartender's attention, and the bartender whips up the cocktail and slides it in front of her.

They exchange small talk before she asks if he wants to go to the Loopy Room rooftop bar. They down their cocktails and head to the elevators. As soon as the doors close they engage, bodies pressed tight, tongues diving and caressing. When they arrive on the roof, they release each other and find their way to the railing, passing a bunch of couples on couches near a glowing fire pit. They gaze out over the Hudson toward New Jersey, observing the myriad lights of office buildings and high-rises.

Ryan breaks the silence. "Your current job seems more copacetic for you than the agency."

"It is, but some of my private contracting work has been pretty damn stressful. The good part is I know I'm not locked into anything. I can just make good money, not ask a lot of questions, and move on."

"Be careful. You haven't been eliminating targets, have you?" He's actually curious because they've never discussed it.

"No." She turns and looks him in the eye. "I don't have to accept every proposed job, and I don't want that kind of guilt on my head. Who needs it? I'm not planning to die young. You?"

"Nah. I do some shady side stuff for the P.I. group, but its child's play compared to handling international assignments like you do."

"Not all of them have been in China."

"I thought—"

"Wrong. Sure, I won't work against the agency here at home. But if the job is just honeypotting..."

Ryan soaks this in, peering out across the Hudson, noticing the shimmers of various lights reflecting off the surface of the river. "I can't block out some of the things I did, particularly in Iraq. Like blowing away teenage insurgents. But I deal with it."

"One private job haunts me," she admits cryptically.

"Mind sharing?"

"Honeypot stuff on the surface, but I have a feeling it was a lot more."

"I'm sure that kind of work can take many different forms. I won't push it if you don't wanna tell."

Ty takes a swig of his drink and stares out over the city. The same bartender returns. Ty places another order but Liza declines, she started way before he did.

"I agreed to it because I could visit my parents in Arlington before the job," she explains. "It was in Northern Virginia. I was assigned to seduce a married guy. I honeypotted him at a bar he and his pals frequented. I needed to convince him to meet me at a hotel the next day, get him to call in sick, which I, um, accomplished."

"Yeah, I don't need the details about the seduction. But I gather that's not all."

"Right. The next day I boarded an Amtrak Acela train at Union Station and headed back to New York City. On the way, I saw the news on my laptop about the Hemispheres jet crash. Well, my target was the electrical inspection supervisor for the Hemispheres fleet at that airport." She looks out across the river as Ryan contemplates this bombshell for a moment.

"So, you're saying you were the reason he called in sick that day, and maybe someone sabotaged the jet?"

"Yep."

"That's pretty heavy." The wheels start turning fast in Ryan's mind. Unbelievable that Liza may have played a part in the crash without knowing it. "Who hired you?"

"I can't tell you that even if I wanted to, I don't know who it was. They use proxies."

"Can I ask how they paid you?"

"I have an agent who manages an account in Hong Kong. That's all I'll say."

Ryan mulls over mentioning he's working for a lawyer who is trying to unravel a $200 million mystery about why the government paid hush money to Hemispheres, but he decides not to go there, he can't even let her know about his confidential work. Not yet. Maybe after they head to her room he'll try to pry enough information from her to narrow the players involved.

CHAPTER 17

DIRTY DOZEN

FLETCHER, a scrawny 20-something with blond scraggly hair, now one of the teacher's pets, is already there.

Walston, wearing round John Lennon-style wire-rim glasses and his "Trust me, I'm a Jedi" t-shirt, sits next to him.

"Did you wonder what mysterious type of animal was terminated to become part of the meatloaf today?" Fletcher asks, taking another bite of pepperoni pizza.

"Not really, but I also did not partake." Walston looks up to see their chief coming toward them.

Ron Michaels stops at their table, a round one that seats four.

"Can I barge in on the esteemed members of my dream team?" he says, not waiting to be accepted or rejected.

"Sure. So how did you pick us? The team, I mean. Oh, and do you know what we call ourselves?" Fletcher asks.

"Researchers?" Ron answers, without missing a beat. He doesn't mind Fletcher's sarcastic and cynical attitude, and they have enjoyed many in-depth talks regarding worldly matters, often with a biological twist.

"No. The Dirty Dozen."

Walston laughs and Ron smirks. "I like that. And to answer your first question, I wanted to gather 12 thinkers from different disciplines to rival the innovations that happened in the late 1800s. Why were there so many amazing inventions then?"

"Cuz it was the Industrial Revolution. Duh." Walston blurts

out, but immediately knows he's wrong based on Ron's expression.

"Nope. Everyone was hanging out in the bars and taverns, and then the first coffee shops opened. People started drinking coffee and tea, both stimulants, and instead of being dulled down with alcohol, they were all hyper. It wasn't only the caffeine, it was the combination of people from all different backgrounds and walks of life gathering in the coffee shops. Alchemy."

"Sorry, that still doesn't explain why you put Kabo the chicken sexer on our team. He's got no grad school degree or biological training."

"That may be true, but what did he do day in and day out for a couple of years?"

"Lifted the rear ends of chickens on an assembly line to determine if they were male or female, which no normal person can do because a chicken's gender is virtually undetectable," Fletcher says.

"Precisely. Kabo's discerning eye is going to help us solve a problem. I'm not sure which one yet, but he will. We need to analyze DNA sequences, we are basically code breakers. I bet my bottom dollar Kabo will help us. It'll happen."

"Then I'm guessing you picked Forman for his memory since he's lacking any relevant schooling or experience," Walston ventures.

"Yep, he was the first American to win both the American and European Memory Championships. Has he shown you any of his tricks?"

Fletcher rolls his eyes. "He put two decks of cards on the table, looked at each card in both decks for less than two minutes, and then told us what every card in each deck was, in sequence, before we turned it over. There must be some kind of marks on the backs of the cards. We didn't fall for that B.S."

"It's no parlor trick, Fletcher. He's a memory athlete with intense training. You can google it. He creates vast memory palaces in his mind to accomplish these feats, and we need researchers like that."

"A memory palace, what the hell?"

"In his mind, he places items in various rooms in familiar buildings, like a home he grew up in. He links each number, like card 1, to a memorable palace room. When he needs to remember something, he walks through these rooms, mentally speaking, and "finds" each number in the sequence by assigning some sticky characteristic to each item. For example, for the 10 card in the sequence, lets say its the queen of hearts, he might imagine the queen melting on top of a piano that was in the living room with a picture of a huffing heart hanging on the wall. Then he'll place the other cards in each room, assigning an unusual action to each item to make it sticky, so its memorable. A simple mental stroll through this familiar territory allows him to correctly recall every card in numerical sequence. With lots of practice, of course.

"His ability to masterfully use the existing system of folders and subfolders inside his brain could prove very useful in our research. He may observe a sequence of biological compounds that you, Kabo, or Masterson would never notice. He has trained his brain to remember, instead of using the notes app on his phone to act as his external brain. Don't you see, the modern world is all about using external memory to offload our memory so we don't have to use our own. No one wants us to train their own brain anymore." Ron points to his skull. He eats a few bites of the green beans on his plate and swallows before getting back to the external hard drive discussion.

"The first serial strip movies—this is going way back, well before any of us were born—had lines of images, and the projector sequentially showed each image, one after the other. With slight changes as each strip moved, it seemed like continuous movement. Our DNA is like that, with our chromosomes lined up one after the next along the double helix. Our job is to figure out what sequence, what small changes to our chromosomal codes, will allow our telomeres to divide more times without suffering damage, making each cell last longer. Having all my researchers thinking in different ways, seeing things normal researchers don't, that's how we're going to make our breakthroughs. Don't worry about your team members' credentials, think about how we can work together to deliver the solution."

Later that afternoon in the lab, Ron walks by Fletcher, who is peering through a microscope with his ever-present earbuds in his ears.

"Hey Fletch, what's on your playlist?"

"A Mark Ronson mashup."

"Never heard of him."

"He's a brilliant rock producer, worked with Bruno Mars, Amy Winehouse. Got his start working as a DJ in New York, even though he was born in Great Britain where I think he lives. Anyway, he says nothing new exists, everything is remixed. I listened to a TED talk he gave, where he talked about putting together some of his best music."

"So, kind of like what we do as scientists. We build with a little from this and a little from that, drawing on natural combinations and sequences," Ron muses, then pats him on the shoulder and walks away, thinking about the mashup he's trying to create.

Ron doesn't spend all his days in the lab, he also devotes a number of hours to searching the internet, reading every article he can about topics remotely tangential to those involved in his current telomere research. Maybe by lifting something from here, merging it with something from there...one never knows.

He looks at his watch and decides to head to the nursery for a quick visit with Justin.

CHAPTER 18

INBOX

THE EMAIL ARRIVES THROUGH SOLAREZ' personal Gmail account.

> *From: Birdie234@gmail.com*
>
> *Re: Embassy*
>
> *You must first establish an encrypted account through software available online. Download Zapped. Once you do so, you will be able to open and view my next email.*

Solarez downloads the software, establishes the necessary account, and clicks on the next email from the same fictitious name.

> *I suppose you've had time to think about how valuable my information may be. I have access to information you can only dream about. As I said, we begin with Ron Michaels and his son. The world believes he's dead, and there are few people outside of American intelligence who know this.*
>
> *Wire instructions: $100,000 USD*
>
> *Bank Account: BTR8-67312 A, Commerce Bank of Eritrea*
>
> *Account Name: Steve Solars*
>
> *SWIFT CODE 56134.*
>
> *Once the deposit is confirmed I will provide the first install-ment of information about Michaels' son, Justin. Next will be about our asset at Sherwood, with more to follow.*
>
> *—Birdie*

"What could they possibly know about Justin?" Director Isaacson asks Solarez after he fills him in on the email. "Even if they know he exists, he's protected at our Sherwood facility."

"No idea. But if they planted an asset inside Sherwood or hacked into our servers, this intel could be very valuable. Whoever *they* might be."

"I'm trying to think of something we could ask this contact to verify they work inside the Chinese embassy and have appropriate clearance. But if we drag our feet, it might be too late for the information to be relevant. Or he or she may change their mind or demand even more cash."

"Anyone who's willing to take these kinds of risks has an agenda that goes beyond making money. Their value to us is their alleged access to the Chinese embassy. I am assuming Chinese embassy, not Russian or some other embassy."

The director swivels slightly in his chair, thinking things through for a few seconds. "Let's do it. We have too much riding on this operation for the research to land in the hands of the Chinese. We'll know if this is worth pursuing further once we receive the initial information. Send Birdie a one-line email confirming the wire transfer when it's complete. And advise me as soon as you get the info on the kid."

CHAPTER 19

JONATHAN

AMANDA HAD TROLLED Jonathan's Facebook page and learned he would be playing lacrosse for Johns Hopkins against College Park in their annual rivalry. College Park's stadium in Maryland is one of the finest lacrosse venues in the nation according to their website, and it should be packed. She bought her ticket in advance on the Johns Hopkins side and is taking her seat when Jonathan enters the field as the starting attacker for his team. The score seesaws back and forth, and is tied after two periods, but Maryland ekes out a 3-2 victory. One of the Hopkins' scores is Jonathan's, fired from outside the goal crease.

Immediately after the game, Amanda presses through departing fans to a metal fence dividing the stands from the visitors' bench. The dejected Hopkins players begin to walk from the sidelines to the locker room at the far end of the field. About that time, she notices Amber Fields and another girl standing in the aisle about 30 feet to her right. From various social media posts, Amanda knows Amber and Jonathan are in a relationship and she turns and quickly walks away, not wanting to cause trouble. Jonathan spots her and takes off after her just as Amber recognizes her as well.

He catches up to her and calls out. "Amanda! Amanda, hey, stop!"

She keeps moving, but he continues following her on the other side of the fence, one level down from the walkway. She finally stops and turns to face him. He puts both arms upward against the chain link and laces his fingers through the holes.

"Why didn't you say hello? You didn't tell me you were going to be here."

"I wanted to see you play, and I was going to talk to you, but I chickened out. You didn't have to come after me."

"I'm glad to see you. Was there something in particular you wanted to say?"

A bunch of people curiously pause, then walk around her as she looks down at him, deciding whether or not to tell him.

"I remembered something."

"What's that supposed to mean?"

"Something about you and me. I still can't remember anything else, you know, from before."

"I didn't realize that, we haven't talked in a long time. Not really since graduation."

"I saw Amber, and you're seeing each other, so I ran. I'm not trying to get in between you two."

"Well, I tried to forget what we had. You pretty much crushed me after the crash when you blew me off like I was nobody."

"I'm sorry. I couldn't reinvent what I couldn't remember."

"Did you expect me to wait? Or to keep believing in something you told me didn't exist anymore? Put yourself in my shoes."

Amanda doesn't say anything. The memory of him holding her tightly had touched her so deeply. She clings tightly to any shred of her pre-crash memory.

Jonathan says, "I still have some of the letters you sent me when I was at lacrosse camp the summer after junior year. I was reading them not long ago."

"I would like to read them. Could you scan them and send them to me?"

"Sure."

"I'm staying at Crossroads until I go back to school."

"Will do." He stares an extra second, both oblivious to the many noises surrounding them.

"Anyhow, great seeing you Jonathan. You played great, really." She locks eyes with him again, searching for meaning.

"Thanks for coming. Let's stay in touch."

With that, he turns and trots toward the visitors' locker room.

Seconds later, tears well up and fall down her face. She wipes them with the sleeves of her hoodie. As she finds her way to her car, not twenty feet behind is the FBI agent trying not to interfere or look too obvious. Amanda stops abruptly and the agent almost bumps into her from behind. *I'm emotional enough to cry*, she suddenly realizes, brushing tears from her cheeks, *over a memory that likely was before the crash.*

I may not be a lost cause after all.

CHAPTER 20

PRESENTATIONS

RON MICHAELS PULLS the key card out of his lab coat pocket and swipes it over the reader, and a large glass door slides horizontally. He feels the rush of the airlock as the first door closes and the second door opens into the research area housing the rodents used in many of the projects. Their small cages line one entire wall. Wearing his less-than-designer hair cap and nylon gloves, he strides several steps past the guinea pigs to the mice. Grasping one small container with five mice, he walks out of the room.

He makes it a practice to be involved in certain aspects of the experimental trials rather than relying exclusively on his research teams. On the second floor, he exits the elevator, holds his card up to the security reader, clears the airlock doors, and passes several large freezers and refrigerators. Upon entering the room where a dozen researchers have their workstations with microscopes and other various lab equipment, he takes a seat at his workstation, which is no more different than any of the others on the floor—at his insistence. He looks at his watch—1:00 p.m. The weekly progress meeting isn't until 2:00 p.m., giving him a little more time for research.

Right before the meeting, he grabs a seat in the center of the room. A massive flat-screen TV hangs on one wall and his team is crowded inside.

"All right, let's start with the heterochronic parabiosis group. Bob, you're up."

Though it sounds like a Frankenstein-type experiment, fusing the circulatory systems of live young and old mice allows some of the older animals' organs to be rejuvenated, most likely due to some type of molecular factor present across the blood types. The simple transfusion of blood from younger ones to older ones has shown health benefits in past studies. Much of the current research in this field isolates and identifies what factors cause this phenomenon in the hopes of reversing age-associated organ function declines.

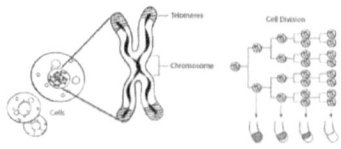

Bob heads to the front of the room and slides his small flash drive into a laptop. His PowerPoint presentation addressing the specific procedures and methods of the experiment appears on the screen. The team discusses their means of isolating potential anti-aging factors present in younger blood. Most of the questions arise from researchers not privy to the project, curious about different specifics or conceptual implications. Then they discuss the results. Some molecular factors in the blood of the young mice didn't seem to cause a significant change in health when provided to some of the older mice, but in others, the trends were more promising. Ron poses several questions about the concentrations his researchers used, why they decided on certain methods, and, in the more positive trials, suggests a higher concentration of the factors or a larger sample of mice might bump the findings into the statistically significant range.

"So, on the suggestion of Dr. Michaels, we are trying to move away from having to stitch together the skins of the young and the old mice to join their circulatory systems, because he says it's unrealistic as a commercially viable delivery system in humans. I guess I have to agree." The junior researcher smirks toward Ron.

"Yes, you do. Clearly we're not going to sew people to each other to commercialize this breakthrough. The method needs to be simple."

"Exactly, so what we've been doing is injecting the plasma with our cocktail of enzymes into the young mouse, then withdrawing it and re-injecting it in the older one, eliminating the need for the circulatory connection or contemporaneous transfusion."

"Thanks Bob." Ron turns to James, the leader of the free radical group. James replaces Bob and starts his slide show.

Prior research has established that free radicals produced by routine mitochondrial cell function inexorably leads to genetic degradation—the symptoms of the aging process. Though far from proven, the same could be said for many theories of aging. The free radical group aspires to reduce free radical proliferation in cells by supplementing them with antioxidants, or working with mutant mouse strains that produce less free radicals. Then, the researchers carefully study their tissue and age-associated changes. The slide show shows some promising prospects, but as with most lab experiments, there is both supporting and contrary evidence. Several antioxidant interventions reduced aspects tied to the aging process, while others did nothing at all, even though in the conceptual framework of the free radical theory, they should have.

Par for the course, Ron thinks to himself. The free radical project is still getting off the ground, so he doesn't grill them too hard. Instead, he obtains clarification on a few of the results and offers suggestions on the future direction of the research. He then reminds the team to scour the current telomere research online and to include it in their report for the next meeting.

Next up is the genetic engineering group. Samuel, the leader, begins his presentation. Ron is particularly interested in this project, though he gives no indication. With the advent of supercomputers and more efficient genome analysis, it is becoming increasingly simple to identify genes that accomplish different tasks, even if researchers didn't grasp how or the why at first.

By taking genetic samples from a bunch of people who lived past 100 and comparing them to the public at large, researchers can identify the genes that are more pronounced in a centenarian and examine the molecular factors associated with them. The synthesis of computer science and biology will likely pave the way for many biomedical advancements like this in the future. With that in mind, Ron pays close attention to what genes seem to be implicated in permitting longevity and their known functions, and correlates this with whether the centenarians have longer or shorter telomeres.

He notes the genes associated with those over 100 years old often seem random, nonsensical, or previously associated with processes wholly removed from aging. However, if the data suggests a random protein linked with some obscure biochemical pathway slowed the aging process, then it is certainly worth investigating this and any connection with short or longer telomeres. The most difficult question for the researchers to explain is how and why these obscure genes profoundly impact the aging process. When Ron poses this question, he gets a chance to see who's been doing their homework.

Finally, the last group addresses gene editing using CRISPR/Cas9, the type of gene editing methodology that allows biologists to hone in on and modify one or two of 22,000 genes or more. Bart, the team leader, explains how the team is working to delete certain gene expressions to prove whether gene editing could control muscular dystrophy or cystic fibrosis, diseases with no known cures. Another goal of this gene-editing research is to determine whether it can be useful in teasing out longer telomeres in human stem cells and if they can be reproduced throughout the body.

All in all, the presentations show forward progress, although meeting the 18-month mandate remains highly uncertain. Ron's own research on devising a unique delivery system has not even arrived at a launch pad. His dream of targeting the telomeres requires a convenient, patient-friendly method of ingesting the telomere therapy to be successful. Transfusions or shots won't suffice.

CHAPTER 21

DISTORTION

"BOSS, we tracked the email IP address to the internet café you asked us to and we confirmed "Birdie" used one of the desktop computers. There's a row of five of them and we know which one he used. Unfortunately there's no surveillance footage."

"You told me they had a surveillance camera trained on the front exterior of the café and one directed inside the store," Solarez says.

"Yeah, I did tell you that. So what happened was once we went to the store owner and sat in the back of the store with him reviewing footage on the date that we're looking for, all of a sudden the camera image blurs, My guess is our target sprayed some kind of solution on the video camera. They had no clear footage for days before one of the store clerks realized there was something on the lens and they cleaned it off."

"So you're saying you've got nothing."

"Unfortunately. We also checked all the outside camera surveillance for hours before the time of the email and hours after and there's nothing we can find that gives us a clue.

"This guy is good. And he probably won't go back to that café again."

CHAPTER 22
CROSSROADS TROT

AMANDA STUDIES *the miniscule lines meandering horizontally from the outer corner of each eye. Have they changed? No, they seem the same. Will I age normally? How will I tell? Maybe I am now a freak of nature. A freak of my dad's telomere transfusions. I don't know, it makes me cray crazy sometimes.*

She opens the medicine cabinet looking for nothing in particular and briefly ponders the words on the small water-stained paper inside the door:

Nothing's beautiful from every point of view. - Horace
Money often costs too much. - Ralph Waldo Emerson

Next, her eyes drift to the rectangular piece taped right below the other scrap removed from Kent's bedroom wall:

Strength is born in the deep silence of long-suffering souls, not amid joy. -Felicia Hemans

Strength. Yeah. A near smile forms as she considers the words, and how they bring back a rush of thoughts. After softly touching the scrap of paper with her fingers, like a caress, she eases the cabinet door shut, ready to see David for his first visit to the farm in quite a while.

Amanda greets David on the front porch of the farmhouse, ignoring the FBI agent standing beside his unmarked SUV. She gives him a big hug.

"You ready to do some riding today?"

"I'm not exactly an equestrian."

"We'll keep it at a walk. I'll ride Voodoo and you're on Francine. I think you'll like her."

David takes in the pungency of the stable. Strong odors. He mentally contrasts them with the absence of noticeable scents in the FBI HQ. Manuel helps him with the necessary tack, and within a few minutes he and Amanda are side by side on horseback, on a slow trot down a well-worn path under a canopy of trees.

"How's the interning?"

"Fine. I've seen Solarez a few times, but not every day."

"I guess it would be a nice change for you from all that science at MIT."

"Yeah. So how's Cognitive, uh, what's your UVA academic program again?"

"You got it, Cog Science, and I'm taking some cognitive psychology courses too. I took a class last semester called Memory Distortion. For obvious reasons."

"Gotcha. How's your house, are you right on Rugby Road?

Naw, but not far, we're a couple blocks off Rugby, just off Grady. It's an old restored house, I have 3 roommates. But, none went to Middleburg Academy, oh, but Sarah was dating Archer

Thompson a while. Sarah told me he graduated a year before us."
Amanda looks over at him while they both bounce up and down
on the horses.

"Didn't he throw that huge party our senior year, where some
kid backed into his front driveway, uh, thingy?"

"You know I don't remember, that was before..." She says,
referring to life before the crash.

"Duh. But, I meant a brick light pillar, a kid knocked it down,
it was brick too, but Archer never knew who did it."

Amanda has no recollection of the notorious event. "Okay," is
all she musters.

The awkward lost memory moment passes, David knows he
botched it big time. They continue riding in silence. David still
feels a little awkward around Amanda since their lunch at the
FBI, and he's not sure what else to talk about, he wants to
rekindle a real relationship with her, but won't push it, he knows
better. He decides to ask a few questions about some of their
mutual acquaintances and the car Kent Perless was killed in,
which he noticed was no longer on the property.

"Have you seen Charlyne much since you moved to the
house? I haven't seen her since we graduated."

Amanda thinks back to her binge-drinking days and Charlyne
having to call her uncle to intervene.

"Not as much. She's probably happy to not have me screwing
up her world."

"Whaddya mean by that?"

"You know I was a basket case freshman year. Hell, I guess
I'm still a basket case. I ran into her on Rugby Road one night a
few months ago, but she was with a guy so we only talked a
minute."

"What happened to the Alfa Romeo, did you sell it?"

"I paid a foreign car mechanic to fix it up. It's in a storage
place in Middleburg. I didn't like looking at it every day, but I did
learn how to drive a stick shift, in case I ever decide to drive it one
day."

"That's cool. My dad taught me when I was 17, but I don't
remember how. What about Britt Hayes, the pretend drug-addict,
undercover agent?"

"Of course not. For all I know she's assassinating some third
world leader for the CIA, assuming she's still alive."

"I figured you two didn't keep in touch. Have you been following your doppelgänger in New York?"

"Huh? What doppelgänger?"

"I read a couple different internet stories about her, she was written up in *People* magazine too. Here, have a look at your pictures side by side. I saved it on my phone cuz I was blown away by the similarities. Maybe she's your long-lost sister."

They stop the horses so David can scroll through his phone and find the picture. Amanda leans toward him to check it out while he holds it over towards her.

"Wow, she's like my body double!"

"She's been ushered through lines outside a couple of the hottest clubs in New York because everyone assumes she's you."

"Good for her. It would be fun to meet her, you know, maybe get her to come to D.C. We could dress exactly the same and put it on Instagram. I haven't put anything up on the charity Facebook page in a while either. It could be fun, and maybe we'd raise some money for Healing Heroes too."

"People are still so curious about you, you'd crash the internet. But you're under FBI protection, did you forget about that?"

"Don't be such a killjoy. We can figure something out."

"So, how much are your working in the facility here at Crossroads over the summer?"

"Like a half day, all weekdays. I'm just a volunteer, but I like it."

"Are you going to take nursing classes and stuff?"

"They're in the nursing school, not part of my college program. Who knows. I'm really don't know what I wanna do. I need to decide pretty soon though."

My doppelgänger, she thinks. How crazy it would be to meet her.

CHAPTER 23

A WEAKNESS

AGENT FORSYTH DROPS a file folder on Solarez' desk. "Your guy Franklin's got some interesting, uh, hobbies going on for a supposedly reputable married attorney with kids."

"What are you talking about?"

"Well let's see. First, he's having an affair with a paralegal. Guess where she works."

"The FBI?"

"No, Andy Michaels' law firm."

"Are you kidding?"

"I wouldn't do that, sir. The pictures are in the file. He's sleeping with a young attorney at his own firm too. One other thing: He's been meeting with a guy who's some kind of undercover investigator with a legit agency. I did a background check and his name is Ty Ryan. Former SEAL, worked on a number of special ops with the FBI and CIA."

"So, Franklin's covering as many angles as possible. Banging Michaels' paralegal, and he's got a SEAL who was held hostage and released after the Hemisphere's plane crash digging up dirt for him. Now I can guess who leaked the story. But he hasn't filed any kinda lawsuit yet...not enough solid evidence maybe." Solarez theorizes.

"Could be, but he met with Barbara Grofelt, the attorney who works with every wronged celebrity or A-lister. She represented several of the women who alleged Phil Lusby drugged and raped them, and Kelly Moore, who sued Wright News Group for sexual harassment. She knows how to work the publicity. Seems like every time I turn on *Entertainment Universe* she's talking about some celebrity she's representing."

"If Franklin convinces Grofelt to join him in this RICO action, we'll be on the front page of the tabloids for the foreseeable future." We've gotta torch this guy, I mean make him feel excruciating pain. Legally of course, and nothing requiring a search warrant. We need to share these photos with his wife. And the mistresses. Get 'em into their hands pronto. It might not stop him from filing this lawsuit, but having his personal life blown up might slow him down. What else? Is there something unethical he's done that his law partners should know about? I need you to keep digging, and stay on him."

Solarez glances at the glossy photos arrayed on his blotter.

"You can hang onto those, sir, I have another set. Shouldn't take long to find more on this dirtbag."

CHAPTER 24

THE SPOKES

THE THREE OF them are focused on the whiteboard on the wall inside a secured portion of the D.C. Chinese embassy. Red and black names and places. In the center there's a blue circle and inside is the English word "Franklin" in black. Then there are several black spokes heading outwards at different angles. One of the black spokes points to Ryan, and 180 degrees in the other direction a black spoke points to Angie Tipton. Two more spokes point to Merland and Bogofski/V.E.B.

The senior Chinese intelligence analyst stands at the whiteboard with a dry-erase marker in his hand, gesturing. His junior wingman is a few feet back observing, and beside him stands Jang-Chung, the top Chinese-U.S. liaison involved in the Hemispheres affair.

He begins: "According to all of our surveillance, Franklin is at the center of the leaks. First of all, there is someone working with him. His name is Ty Ryan. We really don't know if he's been planted there by the FBI. He was a U.S. SEAL, and we detained him to keep him from causing disturbances. He certainly doesn't think highly of us, but we treated him with respect and then released him."

He then taps his magic marker on Angie's name. "Franklin appears to have a secret relationship with the paralegal at Andy Michaels' law firm. We are not sure if she purposely got involved with Franklin or if he enlisted her to try to get insider information on Michaels' law firm."

"Things get even more complicated. The law firm Franklin works for does extensive work for V.E.B., which is a Russian bank controlled by an oligarch; the principal is Bogofski. It seems to be a funnel for the Soviet Premier's skimmed-off funds. But we don't know if this has anything to do with the leaks. Although the Russians might be trying to embarrass us, we have found no direct connection between that bank and Franklin except the law firm does work for the bank."

"Here's where the trouble begins. Franklin has gone to Hemispheres Airways and is trying to convince them to join him in a lawsuit against the government and against Michael's law firm. He wants to sue over secret payments the United States made to Hemispheres Airways, which may expose the secret deal we made with the U.S.," The senior analyst nods, indicating his intelligence briefing is complete.

"It looks to me like Franklin is being financed or pushed by one of these other players. I have trouble believing he would be able to mobilize all this by himself," Jang-Chung says.

"Don't be so sure," The senior analyst replies. "Franklin hates Michaels, and he was forced to settle all of the crash lawsuits, which obviously cost his law firm substantial sums of money. And basically reduced his fee income tremendously too. But he may believe this matter is so high profile it will create new business for him and his law firm."

"Would his efforts to bring a lawsuit go forward even if he was unable to lead the effort?" The junior analyst asks.

"That's a good question, the U.S. system is so unpredictable. I'm not sure if anyone would be as capable as Franklin. But I see your point. If he was not around to spearhead this..." The senior analyst ponders.

"Get 24/7 surveillance on this Ryan guy. And on Franklin. Keep watching the situation carefully, then we can make a decision." Jang-Chung says, and given his rank in the embassy hierarchy, Jang-Chung's decision is the final say.

"Yes sir."

CHAPTER 25

A REQUEST

RON MICHAELS HAD PUT in the request to leave Sherwood a month before the Disney Costume Parade, the biggest parade held in Annapolis, Maryland. It would be the first Disney event experienced by his young son Justin.

Dear Agent Solarez:

I am requesting leave, with FBI bodyguards, to attend the Annapolis Disney Day Costume Parade with my son. As you know, this is my first time asking for leave and I think it would be enriching for him to see it. We would attend the parade and return the same afternoon. I'm sure you can put together some kind of simple disguise for me, and we would have no intentional or meaningful contact with anyone. Please contact me with your decision as soon as possible.

Sincerely yours,

Ron Michaels

Solarez thinks it's a reasonable request made far enough in advance, so he grants permission and arranges for plainclothes FBI agents to serve as escorts. Sure, this outing will involve some risk, but why would anyone attending a Disney parade suspect some guy watching the characters with his son is anything but a random dad?

CHAPTER 26

RICO

"MERLAND, the CEO of Hemispheres, called me. The attorney who represented them against the crash victims' families, this guy Franklin, comes to his office and says he's got a plan. He wants to sue the government and Andy Michaels' firm for fraud and concealment under the RICO statute. He tells Merland he'll take the case on a contingency and only asked them to kick in part of the expenses. On top of that, he's gone to their insurance carrier, the one that paid out millions in the settlement, and they're interested as long as Hemispheres is in. I already filled in my director and he asked me to brief you ASAP."

CIA Director Isaacson shifts in his chair and fiddles with the frame of his glasses as he contemplates Solarez' news.

"We've got a problem, I agree, but I'm out of immediate answers. You?"

"If Hemispheres won't get involved—and we'll strongly encourage them not to—maybe the insurer won't either."

"Yeah, but here's another issue. We provided the money so their stockholders weren't paying for it, but we never told the insurance company, which at the time made sense."

"We can't exactly pull out our checkbook and write them a check now. It would confirm what most people currently think is simply a rumor."

"Doesn't look like we're going to contain this easily. I don't know where Franklin got his inside information, but winning his case requires him to prove it. Are you with me so far? The court will want evidence of the payment to Hemispheres, creating a national security issue we can use to end this whole thing. Yeah, we'll take the heat for it, but what other choice is there?"

"Assuming a judge agrees with us, we win. But what about the guaranteed PR disaster while this thing works its way through court? And while it may be the least of our concerns, we made a binding agreement with the Chinese government too. We can't stop Franklin from filing it, however we do have some personal dirt that might slow him down a bit." Solarez smirks.

"What's that?"

"Photos showing he's having an affair with Andy Michaels' paralegal and a female attorney at his firm. His wife will not be happy when they anonymously find their way to her."

"Nice. Wouldn't want to be him when she receives them. Wait, do you thinkAndy Michaels' paralegal is feeding inside information to him?"

"I would certainly hope not. Screwing your boss's enemy is one thing, but pilfering classified information? That's a whole different level. We can keep an eye on her if you want."

"Alright. It would be a stretch to go to the FISA courts seeking a warrantless search because we think he might possess national security information obtained illegally. We need to have a serious talk with Andy Michaels, though. Since he and his law firm will also be named, they'll surely try to make him talk. We can't stop them from taking his deposition, can we?" Isaacson asks.

"I'm not sure. I'll contact the DOJ. Stein can advise whether we can assert national security privilege on behalf of Andy Michaels also. I suppose he'll need to retain a separate attorney?"

"Ask Stein about that too. What about the daughter? Is Franklin roping her into this?"

"No, he told Merland just Andy Michaels law firm and the government. But she's in protective custody in case this suit is about more than a pissed-off lawyer who thinks we screwed him out of defending dozens of death cases. What a crock, right? Here we are protecting everybody from terrorism, and they're trying to imply we sabotaged the jet."

"Such is the world we live in," Isaacson muses. "Find out

whatever you can on Franklin without a warrant, preferably something we can use to convince him this suit is a very bad idea. Given that his possible reward is millions, it'll be a tough sell. And do more homework on the paralegal and the former SEAL. Maybe we can make one of them see things our way."

CHAPTER 27

BANDAGED

THE LAB MANAGER walks toward Ron Michaels, who is removing several glass slides from an electron microscope, and hands him a note. He reads it, gets up, and rushes through the lab and out the sliding glass doors. Once across the courtyard, he flashes his I.D. and places his fingers over the detector to enter the nursery building. The young lady at the front desk recognizes him.

"I believe Justin's in the infirmary. Down the hall, next-to-the-last door on the right. Mrs. Kolfax is with him."

Ron trots down the hall and turns into the infirmary.

"One of the other kids unscrewed a loose screw holding up a wall on the pretend kitchen, and it fell down and hit Justin right below his left eye, on the cheekbone. Made a jagged cut."

Ron inspects Justin, who still has moisture around his eyes from crying and a long bandage on his cheek, which stopped the minor bleeding.

"Are you okay little buddy?"

Justin nods his head up and down.

"I think he's going to be fine." Ron lifts the toddler up off the small chair and clutches him to his chest. Justin rests his head, bandage and all, in the nape of Ron's neck and holds onto him with his little arms.

"You're alright, it's okay." Ron lightly pats him on the back.

"Do you think he can go back to the nursery, or should I take him home?" Mrs. Kolfax asks.

"You can keep him here, he'll be fine."

They all stand and turn to walk out of the infirmary. Ron notices a small wipe with Justin's blood on it, which he discreetly sweeps off the table into his right lab coat pocket.

CHAPTER 28

VWD

RON STANDS at a counter with microscopes, various glass beakers, and test tubes aligned in their appropriate plastic racks. Using shiny stainless steel tweezers, he removes a very small piece of the bloody wipe and places it on a clear glass slide. He puts another slide on top and carries it down to one of the researchers in the lab.

"Run this for the composition of the blood plasma."

"Roger that, Dr. Michaels."

The next day the results are printed out and emailed over the encrypted intranet to Ron, whose eyes dart through every parameter of the various compositional elements of the blood.

As soon as he finishes reviewing the data, he leans his chair back and rubs his temples with two fingers on each hand. The results show Justin does not carry any characteristics for Von Willebrand disease, or VWD, a genetic blood disorder involving varying levels of hemophilia, excess bleeding. *That explains why Justin's blood had coagulated normally and there were no used bandages, even though the cut was deep. But how could this be?*

Upon Justin's birth, his blood characteristics were provided to Ron by the hospital. They clearly showed Justin was a carrier for VWD, which made sense medically and scientifically since he and his wife Rochelle both passed the trait down, first to Amanda and now to Justin. Amanda's VWD had always been controllable, and with her telomere treatment, the attributes of the disease had been completely erased.

Ron contemplates how this current test could be incorrect.

Could it be the wipe was from a different child and it wasn't Justin's blood? Or his researcher returned a false negative?

Or, could it be that Justin is...not really Justin?

CHAPTER 29

LAPTOP

RON MICHAELS ARRIVES at his apartment within the Sherwood housing complex and changes out of his lab clothes into a pair of sweatpants and a T-shirt. He flips open his laptop on the small desk adjacent the kitchen to catch up on the news.

As the computer screen brightens, the password and login request does not appear. Instead, the image pixelates into an opened email.

Important message about Justin

He quickly reads further:

Dr. Michaels: We have Justin. He is safe and doing fine. So long as you continue your research, your son will be unharmed. However, if we detect any change in your practices or data entry, you will never see your son again. We will know if you are complying. Do not report this email to anyone.

This message will be deleted in 30 seconds.

Ron leaps from his chair and stares at the laptop, his heart pounding and his mind whirling. He immediately scans the room looking for a surveillance camera. One could be hidden inside a book on the shelf or in some other unnoticeable place. A bug perhaps, or more than one? Is that possible in a secure government apartment? He glances back at the computer screen and sure enough, the email disappears, replaced by his homepage.

I was there when Justin was born, he thinks, and we've both been in protective custody ever since. How could this happen? Think, think. As a surrogate, Odette did require her privacy, and she asked that only the delivery staff and doctor remain in the room during the actual birth. Ron's mind pulses as he tries to remember the first moment he saw his son. They cleaned up the baby and he was holding him within minutes. Within minutes? Did something happen in those first minutes?

No! This can't be!

CHAPTER 30
RANDI'S HELP

RANDI MIDDLETON vigorously chews her gum while typing the report on her desktop, depressed knowing she has, what, three or four more after this one. As the only administrative assistant whose job it is to type and organize all the reporting for the dirty dozen team members, she keeps the balls in the air. The days approaching lab presentation day always suck. Trying to ignore the papers arrayed on both sides of her desk, she sighs and taps repetitively on her keyboard. Ron enjoys her irreverence and caustic sense of humor.

"Don't you have a Microsoft laptop, Randi?"

She barely glances at Ron, continuing her typing. "Yeah, why?"

"Do you have Excel? I don't on my Mac."

"You know we can't carry any of this top-secret work outta here, right?" She winks at him, the words heavy with sarcasm.

"Do you think I could borrow it just for tonight, to work on some spreadsheets?"

Randi looks at him quizzically. "I guess so. Lemme write down the password you'll need." She grabs a Post-it, picks up the computer from the right side of her desk, flips it open briefly, and scribbles the password on the little square of paper, which she sticks near the touchpad before closing the lid.

"I underlined the first letter because it's capitalized."

"I'll bring it back to you first thing tomorrow morning, I promise. Thanks."

Ron notices the half-eaten blueberry muffin and crumb trail on the napkin under the left corner of her monitor as he tucks the laptop under his arm and walks away.

At the desk in his apartment, Ron types out the instructions to his brother Andy. He explains who he is to contact, in person. Next, he composes a letter to Amanda. He protects each file with a password and saves them on separate flash drives, then deletes both documents from Randi's laptop.

Ron closes his eyes and tilts back in his desk chair, thinking.

There had to be a swap at delivery, inside players at the hospital...orchestrated right under the nose of Solarez and the CIA. What about Odette, the surrogate? No, she couldn't be involved...it must've taken a lot of cash to pull this off. Where is Justin, how can I possibly get him back? Can I somehow talk to Solarez...or will they know?

CHAPTER 31

PRESSER

BEFORE ANDY COULD EVEN LEAVE his Georgetown home, every media outlet was reporting on the lawsuit filed by Franklin and Grofelt. The ultimate publicity hound, Grofelt had arranged a news conference to notify the entire country about their allegations that the United States secretly paid as much as $200 million to Hemispheres just to cover up the truth about what happened to the jet before the crash. When Grofelt states document subpoenas have been issued to the government, and that the suit alleges Andy Michaels was a co-conspirator who agreed to keep quiet and cooperate with the government, Andy angrily stabs the power button on his remote, unable to tolerate another second.

Myra, his receptionist, has a changed look on her face when he walks into the office. Her eyes dart downward immediately as she barely whispers, "Good morning, Andy." He strides by her to his office, drops his briefcase, tosses his jacket on a chair, and heads directly to see Hunter Ross, his senior partner. Peering around the doorframe, he sees the silver-haired man writing something on a yellow pad.

"Can we talk?" Andy asks.

"Sure, why don't you close the door."

He complies and sits in a client chair. They regard each other for a second or two before Ross breaks the silence. "I guess my first question is, did the U.S. really pay the money?"

"I know this sounds bad since we're partners, but the government swore me to secrecy."

His partner's face reddens. "Andy, we work for the same firm, and you're saying you can't tell me? Who gives a goddamn what the government said you can or can't talk about!"

"With the assumption this information will stay between us, and theoretically you're my attorney, which makes this conversation privileged, yes, they paid the money."

"Holy hell. When did you find out? Please tell me it was after you settled all those cases for the families and your niece."

"Of course it was. I didn't know anything until after we settled them. But then Stein, your man at the DOJ, told me. I freaked out when he first told me, and I'm still freaking out. I keep thinking what if the clients find out? They'll think I did something illegal, but I didn't. He assured me I would be protected under the cloak of national security, but it hasn't helped my conscience."

"I don't get it. Why would the U.S. pay Hemispheres?"

"I'm not supposed to say."

"I don't give a damn! I'm acting as your attorney, and representing our firm too. I have no idea if this is covered by our malpractice insurance, maybe it is."

"You know we shouldn't represent ourselves."

"Yeah, we'll need outside counsel." Ross concedes. "Let's go back to where you were going to tell me everything."

"Okay, they paid the money to suppress the fact China had sabotaged the Hemispheres flight. Chinese intelligence officials were desperately trying to prevent a scientist from sharing information about a biological breakthrough. They thought the technology might be sold to the Russians." At the last second, something tells Andy not to divulge what the research was about or that the target was his brother.

"That's it? $200 million for that? Why didn't they just tell the press the truth?"

"I wonder that myself, but you'd have to ask the CIA or FBI. Stein told me there were various high-level negotiations between us and China. We got some concessions, but he never told me what they were, other than China repaid all the losses."

Ross moves some papers around on his desk for no reason, and without realizing it taps a pen in his hand against them.

"Okay, I feel a little better, but this firm is taking a big hit.

Sounds to me like you did nothing wrong, but getting you dismissed entirely from this thing, who knows how long that'll take."

"What about my reputation, and our firm's reputation? How do we fight back against all the negative press?" Andy wonders aloud.

Ross looks at Andy, but no reassuring words come out. He stands up and walks to the window.

"We'll figure out a way, I've survived big storms before and this will be no exception."

"I'll set a meeting with Stein, pronto." Andy says, thinking back to the bad feeling he had when Stein first unloaded the truth on him, *after* he had settled all the cases.

CHAPTER 32
SHOCK VALUE

A FEW MINUTES after her husband, Paul, leaves for work, her 17-year-old senior pulls out of the driveway in the Jeep heading for school. Melanie Franklin changes into her exercise clothes and drives to the Emperor's Fitness Center. She works through her personalized training regimen, feeling like she's sweating off five pounds. In reality it would be hard to shed even two pounds off her enviable hourglass figure. At 5' 6" and 115 pounds, even 20-somethings drool over her rock-solid body. Choosing to bypass the gym's locker room after her workout, she decides to follow her almost daily routine of getting back into her Lexus, stopping at a drive-thru to pick up a Café Americano, and heading back home to get ready for the rest of her day.

However, a ticking time-bomb awaits her. As she passes the front desk on the way to the parking lot, Francine, the receptionist, calls out to her.

"Melanie, someone dropped this off for you, said he was your travel agent and you would know what it is." She sets a large sealed envelope on the counter.

"Travel agent?"

Always efficient, Francine moves on to the next customer without answering, handing him a rolled towel, swiping his membership card, and giving it back to him.

Melanie doesn't recall talking to anyone about traveling, but she sees her handwritten name on the label and picks up the envelope. Once inside her car, she tears open the flap.

A series of black-and-white 8x10 glossy photographs pour into her lap. The first few are of her husband and a woman she doesn't recognize intimately kissing in front of an apartment. The next several have been taken through a window and show the same woman in lingerie with him.

With trembling fingers, she then flips through pictures of her husband with a different woman, whom she recognizes immediately as a petite, young attorney at his law firm. Both of them are entering an apartment in one picture, and in another one they are kissing by his car. She rifles frantically through the photos looking for a note, but there is none. Heat and rage erupt in her body. She can feel the blood coursing through her head, her temples throbbing. The tightness in her chest is not a heart attack, but an attack on her heart by uncontrollable external forces.

Driving home is a blur. She realizes she forgot to get her coffee as she pulls into the driveway. Once home, she strips off her exercise clothes and gets into a steaming hot shower, her mind racing, wondering how she'll confront Paul. *When, how?* All of her hard work to keep their world running. The surgery she got to enhance her breasts, the facelift that was so painful but worth it. *Bastard. How could he?* Later, she marches back out to the kitchen counter and grabs the envelope again, barely able to breathe. She studies the photos more closely and turns a couple of them over. Someone has written "Angie Tipton, paralegal at Wilson, Hopper & Michaels" on one of the pictures of the woman she doesn't know. *How convenient, they captioned it. But who did this? Hmmm, who would bust Paul? If it was one of the bitches in the photos, why would she include pictures of herself? Too stupid.* She double-checks, but none of the others have anything on the reverse side. *Whoever did this knew I would recognize the woman from Paul's firm in the pictures, so this person knows us,* she concludes. *Maybe a friend who wants me to know...*

She jumps on the laptop at her small desk and within minutes locates the Wilson, Hopper & Michaels website and confirms Angie Tipton works as a paralegal there. One of Paul's top rivals, the lawyer who sued Hemispheres for the largest group of passengers and represented Amanda Michaels and her family also.

How will I make Paul pay for this? In the most brutal way imaginable.

Hell hath no fury like...

CHAPTER 33

GOING VIRAL

PERUSING the latest biology and genetics journal articles is an evening ritual for Ron at Sherwood. Every night or two, to vary his routine, he goes to the Nobel Prize homepage, where speeches of the winners are recorded in each discipline. If the speaker had slides, they can be viewed too, and he has reviewed every speech on antibiotic breakthroughs. Tonight he finds the last award in the field of physiology or medicine relating to the study of viruses, which was given to three scientists: one who discovered the human papillary virus that causes cervical cancer and two others for their human immunodeficiency virus (HIV) research.

While watching the HIV presentation, Ron finds one particular aspect interesting: "Retroviruses are relatively uncommon among the viruses affecting humans, and rely on the host's cellular machinery to make their viral DNA."

Rely on the host's cellular machinery to make their viral DNA...That's it!

He instinctively leaves his chair and strides to the bathroom to pee, goes through the motions—flushing, stepping over to the sink, washing his hands—not seeing himself in the mirror, but rather the possibilities.

Viruses. Delivery system. Retroviruses. They don't hold energy, they don't metabolize, they don't evolve, they are beholden to the cells they infect to replicate. Without a host cell, viruses are an inert packet of materials. The hosts do the work for them. What if these packets can also carry telomerase and lengthen the telomeres of each hijacked cell? A delivery system requiring no transfusions, no injections, just a capsule containing the viral concoction along with the telomerase enzyme.

Forgoing the hand towel, he dries his hands on his pants and returns to his laptop where he rapidly taps in the methods, the tests he plans to do, which viruses to test, how he can piggyback the telomerase enzymes on various strains. He can hardly wait to get to the lab in the morning and begin experimenting. *I'm not going to tell any of the others about this without some evidence it can work. No need to crow about any breakthrough without support.*

As with many brilliant people, Ron gets caught up in his thoughts and his mind loses any situational awareness whatsoever. He forgets momentarily that his apartment might be bugged and any number of hackers could be recording every keystroke.

The next morning, Ron's workspace holds at least a dozen petri dishes and a similar amount of small test tubes with different-colored caps on a Lucite rack.

"You seem very focused on your work, but that's nothing new," Walston says as he walks by Ron hunched over the counter.

"No different than you. Definitely staying busy. Are you getting ready for this Friday?"

"Yes sir, and I'm looking forward to going to Bethesda to see my folks this weekend too."

"Good for you. I don't have that luxury, I mean, of leaving the compound."

Bethesda, Maryland is right outside D.C., Ron thinks. Maybe Walston will be my courier.

CHAPTER 34

JOGGER DOWN

NOT EVEN 15 seconds into his morning run through Rock Creek Park, Andy notices her when she passes unusually close to him. He picks up the scent of her perfume while scanning her pink running shorts, dry-fit pink-and-white T-shirt, and matching earbuds. He loses her, becoming immersed in the music pumping through his earbuds as people run by on the popular trail. A few minutes later he spies her again not far ahead, and admires her trim body and natural gait. Suddenly she glances off another runner, a relatively large gentleman jogging in the opposite direction. She spins and lands with one leg under her to the right of the paved path a few paces ahead of him. Instinctively, he rips one of the earbuds out of his ear when he reaches her and leans down as she grasps her right ankle.

"Wow, are you okay? What'd you hurt?"

"My ankle. That guy bumped into me and I fell."

She continues to gently hold and rub her ankle in apparent pain.

"I think I need to sit on one of those benches for a minute."

She starts to try to stand without putting pressure on her right leg. Andy reaches out to her.

"Let me help you."

She puts one of her arms over his shoulder and their sweaty bodies work as one, with him supporting her as they slowly make their way the few feet over to a bench. Andy hovers as she sits down and lightly touches her tender ankle.

"I can't believe he did that!" She's irritated and shaken.

Andy takes a seat a reasonable distance away from her, figuring he will confirm she's OK, then be on his way. The smell of her perfume wafts toward him again, noticeable but not overwhelming.

"Yeah, a lot of people use this trail, and you have to look out. Obviously he didn't." Andy's thinking it's time to continue on his way southbound. "Are you going to be okay?"

"Let me check..." She gets up and gingerly tries taking a few steps. "I'll walk for a few minutes and see how it goes."

Andy walks beside her.

"You look familiar. Do I know you?"

"I don't think so, but I'm Andy Michaels, and I'm an attorney. I handled a bunch of the Hemispheres crash cases."

"That's it! I saw you on the news. I'm a court reporter, my name's Cathi."

"Nice to meet you." They exchange a cordial handshake.

"Do you live or work near here?" She asks.

"Yeah, my office is right down the street in Georgetown, and I live in Dumbarton Oaks."

"I'm going to be at Gold Coast Tavern in the New Horizons Hotel having drinks with some friends tonight during the football game, assuming this isn't anything more than a sprain of course. You should stop by, and have a drink with us."

"Could be fun. Put me down as a maybe. Hope your ankle's not broken." Andy turns and jogs away.

One of the great things about living near Georgetown that Andy doesn't take for granted is the ability to walk to the hotels, bars, and shops. Becca's shop stays open until 9:00 p.m. and it's only 7:30, so he decides to head by the Gold Coast to see if Cathi's actually there. The scent of her perfume mixed with a touch of sweat lingers in his mind.

He surveys the long copper-covered bar and several of the

tables but doesn't spot her. Maneuvering past a crowd of people filling the narrow area between a divider and the barstools, he finally thinks he sees her seated further down, facing away from him.

"Cathi?"

Her head turns. "Oh, glad you could make it. How are you?"

He tries to concentrate, but he's mesmerized by her black, sheer long-sleeve blouse and burgundy-and-black brocade skirt.

"I should be asking how you're doing. Your ankle, I mean."

"We're both fine. I walked about 100 yards, and I was able to run slowly, although I did head back to my car. Took a couple ibuprofen right away. Glad you stopped by, it should be a good game tonight."

"Where are your friends?"

"Oh, Tina wandered off a minute ago and a couple others still may show up by kickoff."

"So, you're a court reporter, huh? With the number of lawyers in Washington, I guess I shouldn't be surprised we've never met. Do you do criminal or civil?"

"I used to do both. I don't work full-time anymore, just free-lance a little. I was with Forrester-Horn Group. Have you heard of them?"

"We don't use them but yeah, I know the name." Andy studies her eyeliner. It has a hint of green that matches her beautiful eyes. He admires her high cheekbones and sees the small heart on her necklace on his way to a fairly wide-open view of her cleavage with the extra button on her blouse unbuttoned. And again, her same perfume. She gets the bartender's attention and he orders vodka with a splash of soda. After they both finish a round of drinks, she becomes increasingly touchy, running her fingers softly along his forearm a number of times to emphasize points during their animated conversation.

"So, what was it like to fight that lawyer for the airline, what's his name again?"

"You mean Paul Franklin?"

"Yeah, that sounds right. One night he's on the news saying there's no evidence Hemispheres did anything wrong, and a few weeks later they settled with like every family. A snake in the grass if you ask me. What do you think?"

"He's a worthy adversary. Somebody has to do their bidding,

if not him, it would be another suit like him," Andy says before sipping his vodka. *Always be careful when asked to comment on opponents,* he thinks. *You never know who it will get back to.*

Leaning toward him, she whispers, "You said your office was nearby, didn't you?"

He simultaneously catches a whiff of her perfume and glimpses the upper portion of her breasts. An inquisitive look crosses his face. "Yeah, only a block and a half away. Why do you ask?"

"I thought you might want to show it to me." Her leg brushes against his.

Andy's mind whirls. "Uh, possibilities. I'll be right back."

He quickly decides to head to the restroom and texts Becca to see what her plans are. Just as he gets up from the barstool, he feels his phone vibrate in his pocket. He pulls it out and looks down at a message from Becca—she trumped him.

In car accident. They're taking me to Georgetown U Med Ctr. Can you come?

Andy stares at the message, both concerned and disappointed. He reaches down and taps in the response.

On my way.

Andy uses the restroom and heads back to tell Cathi the breaking news.

"Hey, you won't believe this, but I just got a text. A friend of mine was in a car accident, I'm going to meet her at the ER."

"Was it something I said? Are you joking?"

"No, I wish I was. It was nice seeing you again. Will you take a rain check on the office tour?"

She fumbles through her small clutch, finds a pen, and scrawls her name and phone number on the napkin from under her drink.

"Sure, of course. Here's my number. Let's do lunch or something."

She hands it to him with two hands, touching him for an extra moment before she moves her hands away.

"Yeah, okay."

Fairly certain he will never make that call, Andy turns and pushes through the Monday night football revelers.

The emergency room receptionist repeats herself.

"I'm telling you we have no Rebecca Patricks brought in by any rescue squad. No Patricks on my intake sheets at all, and I've been here all evening. Are you spelling her last name correctly?"

"Of course I'm spelling her last name right. She's my girlfriend, I can spell it. Any chance she got taken somewhere else connected with Georgetown?"

"Can't think of anywhere else they'd go. This is the only emergency room around here. You can call around to some of the other area hospitals, like GW."

Andy stalks away from her and immediately texts Becca.

Are you here at the ER? At Georgetown?

He waits for what seems an eternity, even though it's only 60 seconds.

What are you talking about? I'm closing down at the shop.

Andy stares incredulously at the text from Becca. Then he scrolls above to the one he received at the bar to make sure he didn't read it incorrectly and decides to call her.

"You didn't text me about being in a car accident and meeting you at the ER?"

"No, why?"

"Guess I got a misdirected text message, but I'm looking at it on my phone. Crazy."

Andy heads out of the emergency room.

"You shouldn't have done that, even if you thought it was the right thing to do," Solarez tells the young analyst.

"Sir, your instructions were to keep eyes and ears on this target 24/7, and I had no clue who this woman was or what her sudden interest meant. *If in doubt, get him out.* That's what my training taught me. I didn't have time to call for permission. Would you like to know who she is?"

"Let me guess. Chinese operative?"

"No, Melanie Franklin, Paul Franklin's wife. Andy Michaels had no idea who she really was."

"She's trying to seduce him. I didn't expect that." Solarez says.

Some kind of sicko payback, yes sir."

"So, your text created an impromptu exit plan? Extricating him before he explored further. Pretty slick. Sorry I doubted you, but he'll be wondering where it came from." Solarez pats the analyst apologetically on the shoulder before walking away.

CHAPTER 35
JUNIOR CRUSH

ALMOST NO MAIL ever comes for her. In fact, more still arrives addressed to Kyle Perless, the former farm owner, than to her. Amanda takes them over to the Crossroads Broken Halo rehab facility and asks Helen, the coordinator, to forward them to him at his condo. Once in a while there's a stray letter to Kent. Every time one arrives it still hits her right in the gut, robbing her of her breath. She thinks of the first time she walked in his room in the farmhouse, the feeling of it all. But this one is addressed to her, so she flips the envelope over and checks the return address as she tears open a corner. If the contents are what she thinks they are, they might help her remember something, anything.

Looking for somewhere comfortable, she walks down the hallway to her room and plops down on the bed, the perfect spot to read her old high school letters she wrote to Jonathan. Before she starts reading, she lays the folded papers down and gets up to light some incense. She blows air over it, ensuring the stick is lit, and takes in the pine-needle scent. Back on the bed, she unfolds several pages and her eyes focus in on the one on top:

Jonathan:

It's so boring here this summer without you. My mom's always trying to do stuff with me. Not what I want to be doing though. I'm doing the club soccer team with Reston and practicing twice a week. Charlyne and Iris and I went to a movie last night at the Starr Center. Brad Pitt and Angelina Jolie were spies or something. I didn't think it was any good.

Bobby Firstine totaled his dad's Suburban after Michael Beasley's party last Saturday night. Holy shit. The cops arrested him, he flunked the DUI test. Big trouble! His parents were out of town and he's up shit creek. Wonder where that creek is, anyway. Ha ha.

Jonathan – I miss you sooo much. Can't wait until you're back!! Can you come home now?

xxooxx Amanda

The second page is a photocopy of a handwritten letter, just like the first:

July 16

Jonathan:

I saw your mom at the Giant supermarket with your sister. Your mom's always so nice to me. She wants me to come on another trip with your family. She says the ski trip we went on was one of her favorite family trips ever. Do you remember how cold the weather was at Seven Springs? And the night we had that snowball fight outside the cottage after dinner? Your sister was so mad at you when you stuffed that snow down the back of her coat, I thought she was going to kill you. We have a game tomorrow at the Loudoun Striker Field. You know I hate the Strikers team. They beat us on penalty kicks the last time we played. Anyway, I miss you and wish you were here right now.

xxooxx Amanda

P.S.: What day are you getting home again? I always forget, is it the 15th or the 16th of August? Write me back!!

Instinctively she closes her eyes: Jonathan, in a dark blue puffy ski jacket; chasing his sister, he pounces on her in the snow and stuffs the mushy snowball right between the nape of her neck and the top of her pink coat.

Why didn't I help her? Why did I laugh at her?

She's crying. Her brother climbs off. Seeking revenge, she

jumps up and grabs any snow she can, throwing it at him, tears running down her cheeks. I'm still laughing. So mean...

"Help me Amanda, help me!"

Oh my God, I remember? Why didn't I help her? What a bitch I am. I was.

She opens her laptop, finds Jonathan's profile on Popchat, and sends him a private message:

I got the old letters. Thank you for sending them. Remember when you shoved the snowball down your sister's ski coat at Seven Springs? I remembered it! Maybe things will keep coming back to me. I saw David the other day, we rode horses here at the farm.

Amanda waits, hoping for a quick response, and just before bedtime she notices his reply:

I thought they might help. Hope to see you later this summer? I'm coming home at some point.

Amanda starts imagining herself getting back together with Jonathan, imagining what that will be like.

CHAPTER 36

WALSTON

"WALSTON, YOU HAVE ANY PLANS TONIGHT?"

"No, Dr. Michaels, why?"

"Wanna have dinner with me? 7:00?"

"Uh, sure, I can hang around."

The semi-private dining area holds only eight tables and is open to supervisory scientists and directors and their guests only. Featuring a special menu not unlike an elite resort, this is where Ron eats seven days a week, unless he skips dinner, which he frequently does. It offers white tablecloths, shiny silver utensils, and a second-floor view looking out over the river birch, oak trees, and trimmed hedges dotting the grounds beside the research building. Sometimes he spies a deer wandering warily through the tree line.

After they are seated and order, Ron gets down to business.

"You're quite a thinker, Walston. You seem to enjoy thinking things through, like the big picture, not the small minutiae."

"Uh, sure Dr. Michaels."

"Call me Ron. No more doctor."

"All right, sir."

The young research scientist is being ultra-careful. He wears a rumpled Tattersall checkered button-down shirt, having ditched his white lab coat earlier. Being in his late 20s, he's still amazed by how he got here. A recruiter contacted him by email at Stanford and wanted to arrange an interview with an unnamed but prestigious bio-genetics lab. He only learned toward the end of the vetting that the position would be at a facility operating under the general direction of the CIA somewhere on the East Coast and his actual employer would remain confidential. He'd receive a significant raise to work on research having a major impact on all Americans. As soon as the recruiter spoke those words, he knew he would accept the position.

"Walston, do you think about the effects of the typical American living to be 100 or longer?"

"Well sir, sure, we're all aware our research targets life expectancy."

Ron stares at one of the empty wine glasses and taps it with his fingernail, creating a high-pitched clinking sound. He watches the waitress enter the kitchen, one of the two swinging doors swooshes toward the dining room and back. The other table across the room is occupied by a couple researchers who aren't on their project.

"Stem cells are always discussed when we consider how to deliver a telomere solution. But if we have to modify the stem-cell level at birth and let it run its course, do you realize our research would not affect the majority of the population clamoring for solutions to aging?"

"So—you're suggesting we find a different time to transmit the telomere change?"

"Yep. Dozens of genetics labs not only in the United States but in Europe are trying to develop a proprietary medicine that will become the leading anti-aging miracle drug. If our solution only works with newborns, it'll be of no use to millions of seniors. And we could fall behind the competition if theirs can be applied to the elderly in the next few years."

"Huh, I hadn't really thought about it, Dr. Michaels. We've been focused on devising a delivery method."

"I told you, just Ron, not Dr. Michaels. Anyway, our solution must be deliverable at any stage in life, not just birth. Hell, those wanting a magic pill or whatever we come up with aren't going to be babies or 18-year-olds. They're going to be 65, 70, 85-year-olds who want to lead meaningful lives for another decade or more. What would you pay if you were, say 70, and you can get a drug that buys you, 10 or 20 more years to live? Even two more decades of decent health. How much would that be worth?"

"A lot. A whole lot."

"Precisely. It's not a matter of whether we'll come up with the solution, we will. But it must be deliverable at any point in life."

The waiter presents a bottle of wine to Ron.

"Walston, do you drink red?"

"Sure."

A glass is poured for each of them.

"Resveratrol. Caloric restriction. Do you think they might have some meaningful effect on aging?" Ron asks him.

"Sure, but aren't we shooting light years beyond a phenol like resveratrol? Or a temporary change like caloric restriction? Antioxidants, caloric restriction, all those things are efforts to cause an external compound to possibly impact the cell. Altering the internal structure of the cell by modifying and lengthening all the telomeres is a better biological solution to extending its life than using some agents with unclear impacts. If we propagate longer telomeres, that means more series of DNA code to divide, and so on."

Walston takes a sip of his wine, feeling like he made some darn solid arguments, but another analogy pops into his mind. "It's the difference between adding a new synthetic oil to an existing car engine that might make it run smoother by lubricating the parts, versus replacing the entire thing with a new one proven to last longer."

"I considered all the blood treatment methods that could deliver enzymes to coax cells into creating longer telomeres. Some of the presentations were excellent, but I don't think any of them will be viable." Ron says.

"Why not? A bunch of the things the teams are working on show promise. You lost me."

"None of them will spread fast enough, I mean, to every cell in a human body. Blood transfusions, daily medications, every one of those methods are non-starters. They will either take too long or be too invasive."

"So, what would be better?"

Ron looks around, then whispers, "Viruses. Because the virus hijacks a cell and directs it to spread the viral code to other cells. And a small number of them can quickly spread throughout the body. They're micro-robots with one specific task. We've got to create a virus with chromosomal directions to lengthen each telomere. It might carry telomerase, directing cells to lengthen the telomeres, or maybe it carries telomerase and rapamycin. The consumer just swallows a capsule with the viral concoction or something. We gotta figure out that part."

"Sure, better than transfusions or repeated oral medications, but we can't control a cold virus much less a telomere-targeting one."

Michaels taps his fingernail lightly on his glass again, now partially full. "I devour every journal article about viruses as soon as it appears. They're already experimenting with cancer treatments using a virus and have made headway with herpes simplex viruses. Don't you see? A virus is the logical way to spread something rapidly that can *structurally change each cell* without us doing anything except dropping the virus into the body. It works its way through the bloodstream on its own, targeting the telomeres."

Silence pervades the table for about 30 seconds while they both think this over.

"I read your thesis, Walston. It's the reason you're here."

"You did? How'd you get it?"

"I was searching for viral research and found it. I was intrigued by your thoughts on the herpes simplex virus and your proposition on how to suppress its expression."

"Wow, I thought I was recruited based on my academic rank."

"No, I sent our recruiter because of your paper. Now I have a bigger question for you. Let's say we can increase the age of every human being to 100 on average. What becomes of all the pesky diseases and cancers? Alzheimers, ALS, heart disease? Won't extending lifespan automatically decrease the incidences of these killers known for randomly picking off people before their life expectancies?

"If lengthening the telomeres means longer cell lives, it's gotta reduce them, because they contribute to thinning out the longest-living humans. I hate to be overdramatic, but you realize we'd effectively be destroying the entire underpinning of natural selection and survival of the fittest, right?" Ron says.

"I agree. But all kinds of modern drugs contribute to that also. Look at GMOs and the chemical-resistant insects now evolving to counteract the new crop chemicals we've developed. We're turning natural selection on its head, creating a world of artificial, unnatural selection, or even worse. We're selecting what we want to do within our own species and without affecting others. No, actually, we're affecting them too, come to think of it. Longer lives may adversely affect other species by consuming more meat and plant life, by creating massive increases in carbon dioxide, every human expanding their carbon footprint with every additional year they live." Walston says.

After another slow sip, Walston places his glass back down on the white tablecloth. "I haven't had a discussion like this since grad school biology and genetics."

"It's important for us to consider." Ron continues. "If we succeed, and the average human lives to be 100 or older, it completely blows up natural selection, which says our species needs to procreate, but once we deliver our kids and prepare them for this world, we're no longer materially contributing to humankind procreation. What is there, evolution-wise, that makes humankind more successful by having a lot of 100-year-old people hanging around who aren't contributing more offspring for our species?" Ron says.

"Older persons may contribute other advantages to mankind beyond procreating."

"Give me one."

"I don't know if I can, Ron," he congratulates himself for remembering to use his first name, "Unless a 100-year-old figures out how to make humans live to be 125, how to utilize renewable resources, or how to ensure it doesn't adversely affect all the other species on Earth."

Ron's young guest looks at his glass, which is about empty. Ron reads the nonverbal cue and fills it before continuing. He takes a sip from his own glass, then continues.

"Switch back to our research projects. Let's say I put you and your team on viruses. We know Rapamycin inhibits TOR, which extends the lifespan in mice even if they're fairly old when treatment begins. And Rapamycin is being used to prevent the immune system from rejecting transplanted organs. It could help for cancer treatment, sure, but may make the body not quite as capable of fighting other infections. What if the treated cells show increased chromosomal mutations? What if what we're doing could be the ultimate genetic modification, the stuff you read about in sci-fi books decades ago?"

"Maybe if we could lengthen telomeres without genetically modifying the cell, just kind of coaxing the longer telomere in a stem cell and then using—"

Ron cuts off Walston's brainstorm. "I'm sure you studied something called antagonistic pleiotropy theory in one of your post-graduate classes."

Walston rolls his eyes a moment and peers back at his boss. "The theory of aging that says our cells have better cancer-fighting attributes when we're younger, then they lose that ability as we get older?"

"Yep. Let me give you a refresher course. In William's model, aging evolves due to the pleiotropic effect of some genes that are beneficial to you earlier in your life, then they become harmful at later ages. There's a different theory about mutation accumulation, and some scientists think each of those theories of aging have merit, but no single right answer has emerged. I'm a believer in the antagonistic pleiotropy theory of aging. That's why I invited you to have dinner tonight."

Walston takes several small bites of his salmon and swallows while thinking. "Well, you got me. I don't see how antagonistic pleiotropy relates to elongating telomeres and making cells live longer. We would actually be partly defeating the theory, wouldn't we? Wait, is that what you're driving at?"

"Do you believe in God? No specific religion, I don't care which one. But do you think there's a god at all?"

Taken aback, Walston glances at Ron with a very odd and slightly cold expression. He knows his boss was raised Jewish but has never heard him talk about religion before.

"I was raised a Catholic, and obviously, there are some pretty rigid beliefs within the church. I believe in God. I wouldn't say I'm devout, I think some things are explained by science and medicine and genetics, and I think some of the religious teachings can provide us guidance."

"Do you think God created us and put us on this planet, or was it evolution?"

"I don't know, never reconciled it in my mind. It forces me to choose between believing in God and wondering if we all started from a single-cell amoeba. Are you linking this to the pleiotropy theory?"

"Let me ask another question instead of answering you. Let's say we succeed, no, we will succeed. And when we do, and the average lifespan increases to 100 or longer, what about antagonistic pleiotropy? Are we tampering with that?"

Silence.

Finally, Walston answers. "I think the ramifications are too intellectually deep to predict yet. If we are lengthening the telomeres and extending human life, there will still be diseases, there will still be cancers, but will the cell's ability to fight any of those be modified? We don't really know, do we?"

"Well, with the 18-month window the president gave us, I doubt we're going to be able to find out unless answers miraculously turn up during our research. But this stuff worries me." Ron lifts his glass. "A toast, Walston. God forbid we mess this up."

"Here, here."

They clink their glasses together.

"So, you're visiting your folks this coming weekend?"

"Yeah. Heading to Bethesda to see them."

"Would you mind stopping in Georgetown and delivering a folder to my brother? His law firm is right off Wisconsin. They have a mail slot in the entrance door for weekend drop-offs."

"No problem."

"Great, and keep it under your hat if you would please. I mean, that I'm having you drop something to my brother."

"Okay." Walston finds the request odd, but realizes Ron is compound-bound. *Probably just a personal note to his brother,* he thinks.

CHAPTER 37

DIVERSITY

FRANKLIN'S LAW partners were pleasantly surprised when he announced he joined the D.C. Bar Diversity Committee as a pro bono activity. Bob Greznick, chair of the firm's pro bono committee, stopped by his office as soon as he found out. The diversity committee, as one would expect, is dominated by minorities: African-Americans, Hispanics, Asians and those with mixed ethnicities. Franklin was one of the few Caucasians in the group.

"Great news, Paul. Any pro bono work by our lawyers, especially this type, is excellent. What made you decide to get involved with diversity?"

He launches into his scripted back story. "Carol Smith-Vincent is one of the assistant U.S. attorneys who does federal tort claims defense. Do you know her? Anyway, she said something to me about the committee and a light bulb went on. Why don't I get involved too? I called her, and she talked to someone else, and now I'm involved. The next meeting is tomorrow at the Georgian."

"Very nice, indeed. Good stuff Paul." Greznick taps the door frame of Franklin's office and ducks back out.

Angie is one of the few non-lawyer professionals in the organization, which allows a small number of paralegals to take part. After all, the idea of the diversity group is to help minorities receive a fair shake when interviewing with D.C.-area law firms, in-house corporate legal departments, or the courts, regardless of whether they are young lawyers or para-professionals. She had

texted Paul confirming his attendance at the bimonthly conference. The hotel is ideally located next door to the tall office
building housing the D.C. Bar Library, available to all members
and the bar's administrative staff. Naturally, the rest of the floors
are dominated by law firms.

While everyone is exchanging pleasantries before the coordinator announces the agenda, Paul gets a text from Angie and
strides toward the door. Spring hinges pull the door closed quietly
behind him as he steps into the outer hallway. She's wearing a
black-and-white plaid pleated skirt, a sheer black blouse unbuttoned a couple buttons down, black nylons and heels. As they
approach each other, Paul detects her familiar scent.

"Our first guest is Valrey Cooper, the assistant dean of admis-
sions from George Washington University, discussing the GWU
law school diversity program. Please give her a warm round of
applause." Paul's mind is far from Cooper's talk. His focus is on
Angie.

Paul virtually jumps when his cellphone suddenly vibrates
on the left side of his body. He pulls the phone from its holster,
unlocks it, and reads the message:

Bar Library, lawyer carrel 1-A. See ya there.

Within minutes, Angie enters the office building immediately
beside the hotel, now out of remote range. She presses the "up"
button at the bank of four elevators and finds her way to the
ninth floor, entering with her keycard provided to member firms
and their designated staff. At 6:30 p.m. on a Wednesday, there
are few people in the library. Law clerks, maybe an attorney, all
the unfortunate folks who have a deadline or are working as
associates.

She finds her way to one of the two large tables littered with
books and a couple magazines. She opens a book and pretends to
read it, awaiting Paul's entrance.

When he finally enters, he finds her seated at the table and
walks over. "Now what?"

"Follow me," she whispers.

In the back hallway are three workroom carrels. They have
room for a built-in desk, a shelf, and a chair, and they typically
contain a dozen or more law volumes for those working on major
briefs or appeals.

She quickly enters 1A and closes the door. Moments later,

Paul taps lightly on the door. The doorknob turns and he pushes it open. Her plaid pleated skirt and hot-pink thong is the first thing he notices on the floor below the desk. Next are her thigh-high nylons. She puts one leg on each side of his body and pushes the carrel door shut with her foot.

In just under 15 minutes they are both presentable and satisfied, at least for the evening. After walking through the library at decent intervals to the restroom, she decides to hold the elevator for him.

"I need to ask you a big favor, a very confidential favor," he says, facing her.

"What kind of favor?"

"I have a listening device, smaller than my thumb," he holds his right thumb up as a visual. "Can you attach it under Michaels' desk sometime when he's not in the office?"

"Are you kidding? That's stepping over—"

The elevator stops on the fifth floor and a woman enters and stands between them, facing the doors. Angie stays silent until the elevator reaches the first floor and the woman walks briskly ahead of them through the lobby.

"Absolutely not. What you're asking is way past what I'm willing—"

"Way past what? 'Us' is already 'way past' whatever."

"Paul, we couldn't be seen together before, but now that you sued Andy, we shouldn't even be seen in the same state. You're asking me to wiretap my boss. Absolutely not. Doesn't matter what or why."

"There's no way he would ever know you did it."

"So what? I don't agree with any part of your conspiracy lawsuit or what you're doing to Andy, so we better not talk about it again, like ever."

From inside the taxi she hailed, Angie stares out the window at the buildings, pedestrians, row houses. Paul has miscalculated her, she tells herself. Good sex does not mean she will be a traitor to Andy. She has always had misgivings about the affair, but at this point she wonders if Paul has lost his entire moral compass. Maybe she has too, for that matter.

CHAPTER 38
LOCO LIAISON

AS SOON AS the door to the house closes behind Amanda, the agent calls Solarez.

"She came out of the house and told me she understands my job, but that she was going to meet a high school friend, a Jonathan Parkinson, at Café Loco in Middleburg. She said she'd be back before 6:00 p.m. and that you'd approve it. Should I just tail her anyway?"

"Yes, but not too closely. Assuming she drives her own car, we can locate her. I'll patch you in to the GPS on your tablet. Let her believe she's alone, but stay near the Café once she arrives."

While driving his road-worn Land Cruiser through the streets of Middleburg, Jonathan still hears Amber's words from their recent phone call.

"I swear if you get back together with that bitch, I'll kill you."

Why is it that when your significant other makes a crazy-ass statement like that you want to go do it even more? He knows Amber has been incredibly jealous of Amanda since high school.

She wasted no time snagging him after the Hemispheres crash left Amanda with no memory of him, even though she was well aware they were pretty much inseparable for two years before the tragedy.

As Jonathan enters Café Loco, Amanda stands near the register in a pair of jean shorts and a billowy peasant-style shirt. Amanda turns to face him and there is an awkward split second before they lean in and hug.

"Great to see you," Jonathan tells her.

"Yeah, I'm glad we could get together. Let's get some coffee."

Her memory of everything after the crash is extremely vivid, including every visit to Café Loco. After they get their coffees, Amanda sees Kyle Perless' dobro, mandolin, and various guitars on a vertical rack on the way to a small round-top table situated between two older women at one table and a tall 20-something with earbuds working on his laptop at another. The barista tells Amanda Kyle Perless isn't in, and she realizes he might be teaching a music class to the brain injured at Crossroads.

Amanda takes one sip of her latte, then begins. "It was so weird reading my letters to you from before the crash and not remembering any of it."

"Yeah, I guess it would be."

"How's your summer been going? Are you home working, or are you just here visiting your parents?"

"I'm not working, just came home for a few days. You said you wanted to meet so I kind of had that in the back of my mind too."

"And how's Amber?" Amanda can't resist asking just to confirm they're still an item.

"She's doing well, going to UNC at Chapel Hill. She's got some kind of internship thing with a digital marketing company there."

It's a beautiful summer day, and within a few minutes of visiting, Amanda gets antsy. She asks Jonathan if he would like to drive down some of the country back roads since it's so nice out. He agrees, and soon they're in his Land Cruiser, their two unfinished coffees in the center console. He's at the wheel, and music from his phone is playing through the car speakers. He glances at Amanda.

"Where do you want to go?"

"Let's take Route 50 toward Paris and just look at the farms and enjoy going nowhere."

The song playing is one Amanda happens to know, "Animal" by Miike Snow. It's about him trying to make up his mind and whether he's free or tied up. *Wow,* Amanda thinks, *free or tied up. Prophetic.*

Neither of them say anything until they get onto 50 westbound and start passing the large farms of Middleburg, some with seemingly picture-book white picket fences, others with vertical metal fencing, quite different from the typical country style. Amanda decides to try to clear up some things that have been bothering her.

"Was I the first girl you ever...um...ever made love to?" Amanda asks over the music, starting with almost the most direct question conceivable. Before he can answer, she places her left hand lightly on his right thigh.

Jonathan keeps both hands on the wheel. "Yeah," he answers, adding nothing more, but turning to face her for a second before looking back to the road ahead.

"Do you know if you were my first?" She moves her fingertips just slightly toward his knee with a light caress.

"I only know what you told me, and you said I was."

Amanda contemplates asking for a few details, then decides against it. She really doesn't want Jonathan thinking she's insecure about it. After a while she has no idea where they are, but she notices a huge grassy field on the right side of the road with no fence around it.

"Hey, why don't you pull over here?"

Jonathan slowly eases the Land Cruiser off the road. He cuts the engine and pulls the key from the ignition. "Now what?"

"Let's walk out into the field."

Jonathan has a look she can't quite translate, like a moment of silent mental protest, but it passes, and he exits the car as Amanda closes her door. The two of them walk toward the rear of the Land Cruiser, where he grabs a folded blanket from inside, and Amanda begins to walk out into the high grass of the pasture with him a few steps behind. The grass, about a month overdue for cutting, has patches of colorful wildflowers growing in it. Jonathan figures some big tractor comes through and mows it down, but only when necessary.

Amanda, deep down, feels no sense of guilt about Jonathan's relationship with Amber, and the reason is simple. Jonathan was hers before the crash, and it wasn't her fault she lost all memory of any relationship with him. Once they walk about 40 yards out, Amanda turns and Jonathan steps closer. A soft breeze blows, creating softly undulating waves through the high grass, and blowing some of Amanda's hair over her eyes. She ignores it, reaches toward Jonathan and takes his hand, and they continue walking a little further away from the highway.

"Jonathan, I owe you an apology."

"What do you mean?"

"When I was in the hospital and at Café Loco for my 18th birthday party, I treated you like crap. See, I remember that, my memory is great after the jet crash. But I didn't feel anything, I didn't remember anything, and I still only have one or two tiny glimpses of what we had before. I had this dream, not long ago, where I remember you kissing me and laying on top of me, and I think it's based on a real memory. This may sound stupid, but I want to see if we can get back what we had."

He stops walking and presses against her, kissing her deeply. She can feel him against her thigh and knows he is excited to be intimate with her after so long. Amanda presses her left hand against his butt, pulling him towards her. His hands begin to explore her breasts.

Amanda takes a step back from him and takes off her blouse. He lifts his shirt over his head and drops it on the blanket partially spread in the long grass. She begins unbuckling his belt and helps tugs his jeans down. They drop slowly to the blanket, facing each other, legs partly touching, her breasts pressing against his chest, hands and fingers caressing each other.

Once they are back in the SUV, Jonathan continues driving random back roads, confident that with the GPS on his phone, finding the way back will be easy.

"You can't mention a word about this to anyone. At least for the time being," Jonathan says.

"What do you think I'm gonna do, go on the internet and announce it?"

What does this mean about us anyway?"

"I don't know, what do you want it to mean?"

"I don't know. I mean, Amber and I have a good relationship."

Why do you like that backstabbing bitch? Amanda thinks, but decides to play nice. "How many days are you home for?"

Just a couple, I'll probably head back to school Sunday morning.

"Are you going to see David while you're here?"

"Yeah, we're supposed to get together Saturday."

"Are you going to tell him you saw me? I mean, you can tell him we had coffee. We're pretty tight now, so I don't want to hide anything except, you know."

"Yeah, okay."

"You've been dating Amber a long time. Do you think it's gonna last?"

"Who knows? Am I supposed to factor you into that equation now?"

"Good question. Let's just see."

Jonathan parks next to her car in the Café Loco lot. She leans from the passenger seat and kisses him deeply, pressing her tongue up and around his. He likes the way she smells, different from the scent Amber exudes.

As they separate he stares in her eyes.

"Hey, are you wearing tinted contact lenses now? Your eyes look more green." He says.

"No. More green?"

"Well, they were always blue flecked with some green. But I would swear they are greener now."

"I have no idea—...." Amanda says while getting out, when Jonathan asks, "Do you want to get together again before I go back?"

She pokes her head back in. "Maybe, text me. I enjoyed it."

She looks him in the eye for a moment before closing the door. A smile crosses his face as he shifts the SUV into drive.

Amanda walks away wondering about her and Jonathan. And about whether her eyes could really change colors.

CHAPTER 39

ZUKOFF PLANS

DR. PETER LARSEN was personally selected by Zukoff to lead the development of the telomere bio-weapon based on Ron Michaels' research. Boston born and bred, Harvard biology degree and medical school. Zukoff was impressed with Larsen's take-charge approach from the first month he arrived at Sherwood.

Now, in turn, Larsen selects Dr. Kobi Albena, a brilliant magna cum laude med school graduate. A resident at Georgetown University Medical Center in Washington, Albena has assisted the U.S. government before, but is clueless about this current project.

Larsen ushers Albena into the spacious conference room at the CIA's headquarters in Northern Virginia. Zukoff stands for the introduction. They all take their seats, and Larsen begins the meeting.

"Dr. Albena, have you ever read about renditions carried out by the CIA?"

"I've heard of rendition, the use of third parties or untrackable operatives to sweep up terrorists and take them to prisons operated outside the U.S. by our allies. That's about the extent of my knowledge."

Larsen nods at Zukoff to fill in the details. "We operate a classified facility in Mogadishu. The compound itself is maintained by Somalia's National Security Agency. They run and protect the building. We paid to build an entire underground prison and we control one runway tucked in a little corner at the Aden Adde Airport. Your mission involves being transferred there and overseeing medical trials we plan to begin. We need you to leave in three days."

"What about my fellowship?"

"It will be marked as complete, even though you're a couple months short. Our relationship with Harvard is solid."

"We're going to give you a new name and back story, but you'll still be a doctor," Larsen explains. "As you know, Somalia is a complete mess, no centralized government, terrorist cells all over the country, hostile groups control about half of the country. But we maintain a safe toehold in Mogadishu and we house some of the most high-value terrorists from Somalia, Yemen, and Syria there. Rather than extraditing them to be executed in their home countries, we keep them, or I should say the Somalis do, we have no verifiable presence. As for these terrorists, in their minds they're getting a reprieve by not being shot on day one, but these cretins are the ones who'll be undergoing the medical testing."

Zukoff speaks up. "Dr. Albena, the most important thing I must impress upon you is anything you do has no connection to this agency. You will work for a proxy company, Somalian Essence Oils, Limited, to order any chemicals or supplies you need for the clinic. We're going to set up a special room in one area of the prison, right beside the existing clinic. The prisoners won't know you're conducting tests, only that you're the prison doctor."

"What kind of medical tests will I be performing?"

"No official records will be maintained. You'll use a secure laptop to upload the results and they'll be transmitted to us via satellite. You are not to identify any test subjects by name or communicate with me or with Director Zukoff while in Mogadishu. Do you understand?"

"Yeah, total secrecy, I get it. But you still didn't tell me what I'll be testing."

"You'll be testing how viruses affect some of the prisoners so we can develop vaccinations to counteract the viruses. The Russians and Chinese are developing viral bio-weapons and our intel indicates we are their intended target. We need to stay ahead of the curve by getting these tests rolling soon and making them completely untraceable. We'll give you a series of instructions on how start the clinic, and an agent with the Somalian company I mentioned will communicate with you about transferring materials to be used for the tests. Your staff will include a nursing assistant who's also an agency operative. She's already in place."

Zukoff is anxious to wrap up the meeting before the doctor can ask any more questions. "Take a few days to get your affairs in order. We're counting on you Dr. Albena, this is an important mission. Thanks."

After the doctor exits the conference room and is led down the hall by Zukoff's administrative assistant, the director looks at Larsen as they sit back down.

"Are you sure the virus delivery system is ready for us to begin actual human testing?"

"Absolutely, it's brilliant. We just studied Michaels' research, and we know he's serious about it. Every other plan they've been working on requires stem cell therapy starting at birth or some other elaborate scheme. This is the only one that uses a small number of pills ingested within a short time, say a week. The viruses in the capsules clamp onto the human cells and generate more cells with the same DNA to replicate and lengthen each cell's telomeres. For us to utilize this same research in the opposite way—to make the cells go crazy and start a cancer-like process—is what we need to test."

"What's your plan for infecting the prisoners without them knowing what's going on? And to prevent contaminating someone else by accident? I'm assuming you won't be using pills."

"We're still working out those details. We'll probably deliver the virus on rice in sealed food containers given to the prisoners on a very controlled basis. You're not going soft on me, are you? Remember, these are terrorists who have taken many innocent lives already."

"I get that, I just want to be sure our testing is secure, that the strictest controls are in place so no one is inadvertently infected."

"I'll travel down there myself and go over everything with Dr. Albena before they start the experiment. It will be a secret side trip so I don't draw attention to the project."

Zukoff stares at Larsen, wondering if they'll make the 18-month deadline the president demanded. Equally as important, he's going to make damn sure no one connects the dots back to his agency.

CHAPTER 40

FOR CHARITY

"BECCA, you look smashing, but we're late, and getting later by the minute. Are you almost done?"

Becca finishes applying her lipstick and sprays a touch of perfume along the nape of her neck. She walks out of the bathroom and Andy admires her powder-blue satin dress with its plunging neckline and spaghetti straps. The annual D.C. Bar American Cancer Society black tie fundraiser has long been the biggest charitable event for lawyers. This year, the bar selected the All Seasons Hotel as the venue with a casino night theme, featuring professional gaming tables and dealers.

"Do you have the tickets?" Becca asks Andy as they get in his car.

"Right here." He indicates his inside tuxedo pocket.

The ballroom teems with hundreds of attorneys, spouses, and significant others. Andy takes the ticket from the coat check attendant and puts a couple dollar bills in her tip jar. He and Becca walk past a huge swan ice sculpture and stop at the first bar where Andy works his way to the front of the line while he and Becca exchange hellos with a number of lawyers and their wives. He notices a group nearby talking with Judge Easton, who handled the Hemispheres crash cases, but quickly decides not to try patronizing her tonight.

While a friend's spouse engages Becca in a conversation about her store, gushing about how she just loves it, Andy slowly scans the large room of who's who in the D.C. legal world. On the other side of the room he spots his ex-wife, Sarah, with Mark Roth, the lawyer she's been dating for a year. She told him all about Mark when he finally gave in to her numerous text messages and they met for coffee the week before. It was quite pleasant chatting with her, although he would never breathe a word of it to Becca. In the back of his mind, he's aware Sarah is toxic for him, but another part of him simply will not allow that door to completely close.

Later, he and Becca situate themselves at one of the blackjack tables and they gamble for various donated gifts. Andy gets up from the table to find another drink, and as he walks toward the bar, Cathi appears. His heart skips a few beats. *How strange. No, she's a court reporter*, he reminds himself, *so it makes sense for her to be here.* She hasn't spotted him so he continues on his way, watching her out of the corner of his eye. She approaches a table and hovers behind someone. Andy pauses to take a closer look and sees that it's Paul Franklin. His hatred for Franklin is boundless since the RICO suit was filed, and his teeth begin to clench. He takes a diagonal route for a better perspective. She leans in behind Franklin in a way only a girlfriend or a spouse does. Andy realizes he has never seen Franklin's wife. His heart pounds. He is taking the new drink back to his own table when Cathi leaves and heads somewhere. Reversing direction, he sets the cocktail down on a table and takes up pursuit, assuming she is heading to the bar or the restroom. He's just a few steps behind her and closing. She heads down the hall leading to the ladies' room as he closes the gap and taps a little more than lightly on her left shoulder.

"Why? That's what I want to know!"

She turns toward Andy with a look of surprise on her face. "Why? Let me explain."

Abruptly veering away from the restroom alcove, she grabs his hand on the way, and before he can resist she pushes open a gray metal door and tugs him several feet into the stairwell. Thankfully, Andy hears no alarm.

"Are you crazy?" he protests as the door latches behind them.

"Sometimes."

She shoves him against the concrete wall. Her lips immediately find his as she leans into him. Her breasts momentarily press against his chest before he escapes her hungry kiss and forcibly pushes her away.

"You're not a court reporter. Your name probably isn't even Cathi. You're Franklin's wife!"

"You've restored my faith in your investigative skills, Attorney Michaels."

She advances again, passionately kissing him. Her mouth presses against his, and for some reason he responds, allowing her tongue to dart inside. There is that perfume again. He pulls away from her a second time.

"What're you doing? I'm here with someone. And you're married! Why?"

It takes every ounce of his willpower to pull away from her and open the door. She follows him through the door and back toward the party.

"I know who Rebecca is. But you must be the last to know about Paul and your paralegal, Angie."

Andy stops in his tracks, whirls around and glares at her.

"Angie? And Paul? What?"

"You can ask her yourself. That bastard will rot in hell, mark my words."

With that, she sashays past him with some extra sway in her hips and disappears into the ladies' room.

Andy's mind is racing, and he takes three deep breaths to try to calm himself. *Could Angie be sleeping with Franklin? Preposterous! No, could she be? No!*

He feels drunk, but not from the alcohol. Instead it's mental intoxication making him unsteady. He walks back across the room somehow and sits in his chair beside Becca.

"Where've you been? I had to fight off several lawyers." She keeps her eyes on the table and her cards. "I'll take a hit," she tells the tuxedoed charity dealer.

"Just talking to a court reporter," Andy replies, staring at nothing in particular, nearly in a state of apoplexy due to the throbbing in his brain.

"Here, you can have some of my chips, I can spare them." She pushes a couple stacks toward him.

Well after midnight, after he and Becca make it into the bedroom back at his place, she turns and asks, "Can you unzip me please?"

Andy slides the tiny zipper down to the small of her back, and Becca seductively allows the dress to drop right to the carpeted floor, revealing her black lace bra and matching thong. She takes a step away from the gown, turns toward him and lays a long, romantic kiss on his lips. She begins to unbuckle his belt, but Andy suddenly backs away from her a couple steps.

"I've got to tell you. I can't think about anything else." He plops down on the corner of the bed. "I found out tonight Angie may be having an affair with Franklin. My brain is ready to explode."

"What? You don't believe it, do you? Who says?"

"Franklin's wife. She stopped me in the hall near the restrooms. She said she found out and I should confront Angie."

"Wait a second, his wife told you this? That doesn't make sense. Do you know her?"

"No. Not really. I mean, I've seen them together," he answers, tactfully leaving out a few things.

"What makes you think she's telling the truth? What if she's got some twisted reason to try to get back at her husband?"

"She didn't give me any details. What am I supposed to do, find her and say, 'Hey, show me the videotape?'"

They both stare at each other, thinking. Becca picks up the gown, and carries it towards his walk-in closet.

When Becca re-enters the room, Andy hasn't moved, a dazed look is on his face, his mind somewhere else.

"So what are you going to do?"

"I don't know yet. But I'm going to proceed with caution, that's for sure."

"You don't think it could've—"

"Made a difference on all the settlements?" He finishes her

sentence. "I refuse to believe that for a second. For all I know she's lying. I'm also wondering about her motives, I mean Franklin's wife's motives."

CHAPTER 41

BLAME GAME

AS THE BLACK SUV drives under the covered portico at the Chinese Embassy, two guards stand at attention at both sides of the entrance, below the waving Chinese flags. Several small glass globes unobtrusively record every movement from the portico ceiling. Stein's driver stays seated in the SUV when he exits from the passenger side.

On the steps stands Jang-Chung, the lead Chinese negotiator who worked to settle matters between the two countries relating to the Hemisphere's jet crash and the messy aftermath. The complicated deal involved body bags, an exchange of hostages and secret currency manipulations. After the perfunctory greetings are complete, the two make their way to a conference room on the first floor. A round table is set for four with a teapot and small cups. The Chinese ambassador, Fong, enters the room and the parties exchange pleasantries. A young woman pours the tea and the three wait until she finishes and exits the room.

"Thank you for coming today, Mr. Stein. I thought it would be best to discuss this lawsuit in person. We are concerned sensitive information, protected under our agreement, will be disclosed in the American press. Can you provide me assurances that this will not occur?"

"Well, you realize in the United States any attorney with a law license can file a civil lawsuit. But our courts recognize certain privileges, one of which prevents the disclosure of information pertaining to national security."

The ambassador stares coldly. "Why did you let this attorney file this court paper?"

Stein decides asking if he understands the freedoms on which the U.S. was founded would be a bit too condescending, so he recalibrates his answer. "Like I said, we can't stop the filing of the action, but we can file a motion in response to assert national security as a defense and prevent any of the witnesses from disclosing classified information. We believe everything relating to these allegations should not be made public."

"You did not file the papers yet?" Jang-Chung asks.

"Our attorneys are researching the case law and writing the appropriate motion as we speak. I'm told they'll be filing it in the next seven days."

"It was stated at a news conference that they issued a subpoena to the United States for information about the alleged payment. Will your government be providing them any of that information?"

"No." Stein folds both of his hands in front of him and decides to fan the flames already burning between himself and the other two men. "How do we know China didn't leak this information?"

The ambassador's face turns noticeably red. "Outrageous! This embassy would never leak sensitive information. We are confident it came from your side."

"You have no basis to pin it on the U.S. We're going to find out who leaked it. Let's hope your country is doing nothing to undermine our agreement." Stein stands. "Are we done here?"

"Yes, thank you for coming to meet with us," the ambassador replies.

As Stein walks through the main hall of the embassy, he realizes another shoe will be dropping, it's just a matter of when.

CHAPTER 42
DEX

AMANDA KICKS some small pebbles with her sneakers, walking from the farmhouse to the Broken Halo facility. The smell of Roosevelt pines in the nearby woods carries on the wind. She enters the expansive room with a number of couches and recliners facing televisions mounted on the walls. Loud random noises fill the room as patients play computer games.

"Hi Julia. Do you think I can borrow Dexter for a little while and take him out to the stables?"

As Julia, his aide, starts to answer, Dexter turns and sees her. Leaping to his feet, he drops the controller in his hand and it clatters to the floor.

"Jenna! I been waiting for you!"

Before Amanda can make a move, Dex wraps his arms around in a bear hug, forcing most of the air out of her. Several of the other patients crane their necks to see what the commotion is about.

Releasing her, Dex begins clapping his hands and launches into a rap.

"Booty, booty, that's what I need.
Jenna, Jenna, the booty queen ..."

"Gimme some of those ..." He reaches his powerful hands out for her boobs, but she easily deflects them. *Some of that Quantico training paying off.*

"No, no, Dex..."

"Booty, booty, some of that booty..."

Dex continues his rap, now spinning around while clapping. "Sorry Amanda, you know Dexter." Julia apologizes.

But the apology is unnecessary. Amanda knows the story all too well. Dex, then a freshman at William & Mary, was helping out with a wedding reception at a privately owned lighthouse on Chesapeake Bay. Someone—never identified—left a gangway up, and in the darkness of that moonless July night, Dex fell through the opening almost 20 feet to the hard surface of the supply boat deck docked below. He lay unconscious for an unknown length of time before being discovered. By the time he was rushed ashore and transported to the trauma center, the damage was done. At 19 years old, a permanent brain injury wiped out his promising future.

A dashing six-foot-two high school lacrosse star, no one would never know it from afar, it only becomes apparent when conversing with or standing close to him. His parents, proud working-class Virginians, heard about the Crossroads program and enrolled him for a full year. He became fast friends with Amanda.

"Dex, will you help me feed some of the horses?"

"Yeah, yeah."

Amanda holds Dex's hand as they walk through the center of the stable, and she carries a bag of long carrots in her other hand. The FBI agent on duty stands outside the entrance.

"Give some of the carrots to Voodoo, my favorite horse, okay?"

He doesn't respond and Amanda feels his hand grabbing her butt.

"Dex, keep your hand off my booty." Amanda swats his hand away. She accepts his behavior as uncontrolled and harmless. They hear Voodoo neighing. "Here's a big carrot. I want you to hold this up and feed it to Voodoo. Can you do that for me?"

"Yes Jenna, let me feed him." No one knows why Dex calls Amanda "Jenna," just one of his many Dex-isms. He grabs the carrot out of Amanda's hand and holds it in front of Voodoo while he nibbles on it. He laughs like a three-year-old when the horse's tongue slurps over his fingers.

"That tickles. Haaa...! Look at his big teeth! It stinks. Poop, poop, poop."

"They eat food so they poop, Dexter. We poop too." Amanda picks up a bucket and walks to the nearest faucet with Dexter right beside her.

"Water, water. I love water Jenna. You know I operated cruise ships. Bigger than this stable."

"Really? Were you the captain?"

"The biggest ship you ever seen. I'm licensed. I'm a captain of Queen Elizabeth. I take ships through dark tunnels. I have ships that fly too, ships with wings that fly."

"Cool Dex, how high do they go?"

She holds his hand as they walk toward the door. Outside, he points up at the sky. "Do you see those clouds right there?"

The blue sky is dotted by a few cottony cirrus clouds forming a delicate, meandering string.

"As high as those clouds. Higher than those clouds, and I can go right through them. Oh, oh, a caterpillar."

Dex kneels down and releases Amanda's hand to scoop up the caterpillar, which he cups gently in both hands.

"Can I keep her, Jenna? I will be good to her."

"It needs food to become a butterfly, Dex, and they don't allow insects or animals inside."

The teen mopes, staring at the fuzzy insect in his hand. Amanda asks him to let it find its way home to its family and he finally relents. He kneels near some shrubs and places the caterpillar softly on the ground, staring at it slowly moving along the ground.

Amanda tries to distract him from having to leave his new friend as they walk back to the rehab center. "What does it look like when you're up in the sky, when you look down from the clouds while you're steering your ship?"

"Green and blue, blue rivers. But it rained yesterday. It rained really hard. You could hear the rain so loud I covered my ears. It hurt my ears."

"You didn't get wet, did you?"

"Yes, I got so wet, it was a flood right through the room. I was,

I was swimming, trying to swim away, the water was taking everything away, the horses were in the water, the trees were in the water, but I stopped the water. I stopped it."

"Amazing! You saved the day."

"Saved the day. I have to pee-pee. I gotta pee."

Dexter starts holding his crotch with both hands. Julia has been monitoring them unobtrusively, but now she notices Dex holding himself. She walks over and tells Amanda she'll escort him to the restroom.

"I'll see you soon, Dexie."

"Booty, booty, gimme that booty ..."

She hears Dex singing as he and Julia walk back into the facility, and it brings a smile to Amanda's face. Turning toward the farmhouse, she kicks a few of the small rocks on the road with the toe of her shoe again.

CHAPTER 43

LULIXI

SOLAREZ SCANS through the emails on his phone, refreshing incessantly, and sees the new one from Birdie he had been waiting for since he confirmed the transfer of the $100,000 almost four entire minutes ago. He clicks open the email:

LuLiXi Pharm Co., largest Chinese research and development company in pharmaceuticals. Heavily subsidized by Chinese government. Contractors working for LuLiXi kidnapped Justin Michaels just after birth, with help from the government. Don't know where Justin is being held. If discovered, will provide later.

-- Birdie

This must be fabricated, Solarez decides. No way my operation was compromised. I vetted Odette, the surrogate, myself. No chance this info is accurate.

He can't begin to wrap his head around the implications. Should I call Ron Michaels? No, I should drive to Sherwood and talk to him face-to-face.

He looks at his watch and decides he can't go today, then he remembers he has to talk to Isaacson and relay the information first anyway. He buzzes Director Isaacson's administrative assistant and makes arrangements to be at his office as soon as he can get to Langley.

Solarez resolves to throw every available analyst on LuLiXi and dig in to every possible place the company has labs and offices. And he provides direction to surreptitiously obtain DNA samples from Ron Michaels son, Justin. Or whoever the boy is.

CHAPTER 44
CONFLICT CHECK

TY RYAN HATES GOING to the office because no meaningful work happens within its walls. But sadly, the owner of the private investigation agency requires him to stop in regularly. He's scanning his inbox when a conflict of interest check email catches his eye. Investigative firms have to be careful about such conflicts, particularly with work relating to divorces. Ethics are sketchy at best in this field, but any half-decent agency avoids working for both spouses in a failing marriage.

The email is from Stephanie DeFalzo. The subject line reads "Conflict Check," normal for an email like this at their agency. However, the content is anything but routine:

Potential Client: Melanie Franklin
Opposing Potential Party: Paul Franklin, Attorney.
Any conflict with this one?
--Steph

Ty freezes a moment. No one at the agency is aware Franklin is the principal for the front company, Litigation Support Associates, that he does Franklin's investigative work, or that he played a role in the current RICO suit. And now one of his co-workers is going to be investigating Paul on behalf of his rightfully pissed-off wife.

Should I tell Steph? He knows he can't. So what the hell am I going to do? Tell Paul? He'll have to think about that.

CHAPTER 45

BIRDIE

SOLAREZ DEBRIEFED ISAACSON, who encouraged Solarez to travel to Sherwood to meet with Michaels.

They also discuss the topic of security at Sherwood in light of the confirmation that the largest pharma company in China was responsible for kidnapping Ron Michaels' baby.

"Steve, you realize this could be coming from the top of Chinese intelligence, they may be using LuLiXi as a surrogate to carry out their bidding. We've known for years that this company is responsible for black market fentanyl dumping. Some of the fentanyl comes straight from China, while other shipments funnel through Mexico or Canada. Raw fentanyl, precursors, analogues, fentanyl-laced counterfeit prescription drugs, you name it. Reports I have seen suggest LuLiXi may be the biggest illicit Chinese exporter, who knows how much money they are raking in. But, getting back to the issue at hand, China, and LuLiXI as its largest pharma company, both stand to gain from the commercialization of the telomere biology."

Isaacson sprawls on the small couch that sits opposite four client chairs in front of his massive cherry desk. Solarez sits in one of the client chairs, tapping softly on the right chair arm with his middle finger.

"I need to engage Birdie in more emails. We need to isolate any likely city or region where Justin could be held. Something tells me Birdie knows, or can find out."

"You're convinced he's inside the embassy here in D.C.?"

"That's the most likely scenario, because he reached out to me. It makes sense that Birdie knows exactly who I am, but I don't have enough intel to figure out who he is yet. I have a list of all known personnel, which I've narrowed to perhaps 10 suspects. Also, the reply times make it likely Birdie is on Eastern Daylight Time or in a nearby time zone."

"What if he has pondered defecting?" Isaacson asks.

"I doubt that's his or her plan. No one working in the Chinese embassy is allowed to bring their families with them to the U.S., that's one of their government's strongest leverage devices. If Birdie defects we both know they'll round up his family and send them away to a work camp, never to be seen again. No, I think it's about money, plain and simple."

Solarez sends an encrypted email from his office desktop computer.

Subject: Justin

Birdie: We need to know an exact GPS on Justin. If you don't have that, we need a probable city or region based on your knowledge. Secondly, we need the names of any assets you have inside Sherwood and what electronic surveillance you are running.

After lunch, a reply arrives.

Steven:

I don't have details on the location of Justin Michaels. LuLiXi has a principal business office in a suburb of Beijing, and its largest pharmaceutical factory is further west of Beijing in Fang-shan district. The Beijing area is most logical. I am familiar with our assets at Sherwood, but that is far more confidential intelligence, and far more valuable, surely you agree?

Solarez digests the Justin Michaels info and resolves to meet with Isaacson on mobilizing CIA assets in Beijing to ramp up their efforts as to Justin. But he immediately emails Birdie back on the Sherwood issue.

Subject: Sherwood

What's your $$$ request to give us the asset at Sherwood and explain how electronic surveillance is getting past our cybersecurity efforts there?

Solarez gets no response that day or night. Maybe Birdie is not ready to commit that kind of treason, the kind that might get him or his family killed.

CHAPTER 46
ANGIE DECIDES

ANGIE'S HANDS shake as she reviews each of the photos from the unmarked envelope. Impulsively she grabs her cell phone to call Paul, but changes her mind before she hits "send." She drops the phone on the coffee table and falls onto the couch, letting her thoughts run wild.

Once she returns to some semblance of rationality, she exchanges several text messages with Paul and agrees to meet him for lunch the next day at an out-of-the-way Chinese restaurant they have frequented before.

Grinding through her work the next morning, Angie's mind refuses to focus on the tasks at hand. Over and over she rehashes exactly how she's going to handle the situation. Based on his behavior she's convinced his wife hasn't confronted him yet.

As she walks toward him at the restaurant he rises from his chair, but she avoids his embrace, instead maintaining a businesslike demeanor.

"It's great seeing you. You look fantastic."

Ignoring his compliment, she dives right in. "I guess I'm not surprised I wasn't your only one. I mean, besides Melanie obviously. But—"

"Angie, what are you talking about?"

"I'm talking about you having an affair with me and someone else at the same time. Who the hell is she?"

"Someone's lying to you."

With that, Angie withdraws the folded envelope from her purse and sets it in the middle of the table. "These pictures aren't lying, you are."

Franklin glances at several of the photos. "Angie, look, she's an associate at the firm. She literally seduced me, and it only happened once—"

"You can forget about me coming to work for you or helping you bug Andy's office. He is ethical and honest, traits you are sorely lacking. As a matter of fact, maybe I should tell Andy about your plans to bug his office."

"Angie, you can't do that, I mean don't do that, I'm begging you."

"We're through. You can sweat it out. Don't call or text me ever again."

Angie stands, slightly pulling on the tablecloth and knocking over the salt shaker. She grabs her purse and storms out of the restaurant.

Paul Franklin knows he has a big, big problem on his hands. And at precisely the wrong moment.

CHAPTER 47

PARADE ROUTE

IN ANTICIPATION OF THE PARADE, Ron ordered a Mickey Mouse costume for Justin to wear. Ron is also dressed up, but in a disguise involving spray-painted dirty-blond hair, a handlebar mustache and a pair of nerdy tortoise-frame glasses. He's completely unrecognizable. The entourage leaving Sherwood includes four FBI agents, Ron, Justin, and the nanny, divided between two black SUVs with tinted windows.

"Justin will be so excited to see his first parade," Mrs. Kolfax says.

"No doubt. This will be great," Ron agrees, staring out the window at the passing countryside.

The Disney Costume Parade route occupies no more than three blocks near the waterfront in Annapolis. Speakers are mounted along the parade route, and families from far beyond the city limits line the streets. Kids squirm anxiously on the curb in front of multiple rows of adults, many well-prepared with folding chairs. Familiar Disney songs blare from the speakers, heightening the anticipation.

The Sherwood group arrives 30 minutes early and locates a spot in the middle of the route, near an Applebee's and opposite Walgreen's. Justin sits on the ground between Ron's legs and Mrs. Kolfax stands beside him with a lightweight folding stroller and diaper bag.

Hearing the word "Da-da," from Justin breaks Ron's heart, now that he's convinced *this* Justin is not *his* Justin. Ron's eyes dart around to the faces of the dozens of kids around him, looking into the eyes of the boys similar in age to Justin. *How will I ever find him?* He's brought back to reality by the increased noise as the first of the characters and parade floats appear.

Music continues to vibrate from the speakers and a line of fancifully-dressed men appear, banging on snare drums mounted at waist level. They move in choreographed sequences, circling each other and twirling their drumsticks in the air between beats. Next is a pastel-painted float featuring at least a dozen Disney characters, including Minnie Mouse, Mickey Mouse, Donald Duck, and Goofy. They wave to the crowds on both sides.

"Justin, that's Minnie Mouse, and right next to Minnie is Mickey Mouse." Ron points out the characters and Justin's eyes widen in amazement. Stilt-walkers in brightly-colored costumes dance into view with long walking sticks and pumpkins on top of their heads. Just beyond them, the next float carries Peter Pan, Captain Hook, and Tinkerbell.

Ron leans over to Mrs. Kolfax and excuses himself to go to the restroom. She sits beside Justin on the curb and continues to point out characters to the delighted toddler.

"How the hell did this happen?" Solarez demands of the agent assigned to Ron.

"Sir, I was right with him," Simpson nervously reports. "He

went in, and then he vanished. I searched both inside and behind the building in the alley. He just up and vanished, left the other two right on the sidewalk. We questioned her and she had no clue. He must've been abducted, surely he wouldn't leave them, especially the kid. The only lead we got is that he borrowed her phone earlier."

He gives Solarez the number.

"Where are the nanny and the boy now?"

"They're with Agent Dashiell, still watching the parade. Do you think we should extricate them?"

"Tell Dashiell and one other agent to take them back to Sherwood. You stay and supervise the ground search. Surveil for any suspicious activity within a quarter mile immediately. We'll ask the county police to set up a perimeter no more than a mile outside Annapolis, and we'll start reviewing surveillance footage of the highways. I'll get back to you on the perimeter and the roadblock details. That'll be all," Solarez practically shrieks, his voice an octave above his usual tone.

He thinks a moment, lowers the phone from his ear, then addresses the analyst seated in front of him in the FBI situation room. "Andrews, put agents on this immediately and coordinate with local law enforcement. We need the surveillance cams, license plate checks and a satellite feed. Send me some coordinates on that cell phone ASAP. We have a fluid situation here!"

Solarez pans his gaze along the various monitors arrayed before the other analysts. Who grabbed Michaels? Who could be audacious enough? And does it relate to the contacts he got from the Chinese double agent?

The man places the phone in the holster, holding the groggy animal still. He then steps cautiously away from it, and it trots away. He runs to the rental car parked along the park roadway.

Within minutes, the analysts are picking up pings from Kolfax's cell phone.

"Agent Solarez, we're getting pings from Fort Belvedere Park."

"Mobilize the SWAT team pronto and open a channel so we can communicate as soon as they're in position. Confirm when our perimeter is in place."

Within minutes, two FBI SWAT teams roar into the parking areas closest to the cellphone pings.

"Patch me into them," Solarez tells the analyst in front of him.

"You're live, sir."

"Team, this is Agent Solarez. Let's stage from both the east and west side. No telling what we're going to find. We have a very valuable government researcher who we believe was kidnapped by foreign agents. Do not shoot to kill, we need this guy alive. We'll send you a headshot of him. No one else from our side should be there. Again, do not shoot to kill."

The east and west teams, all in camo and equipped with GPS locators, coordinate their communications and begin entering the forested area. On the monitor, Solarez watches their progress as the cellphone pings move in an evasive zig-zag up a steep hill.

After both teams advance several hundred yards into the forest brush and patchwork of mature oaks and pines, the east team leader consults the feed being sent from FBI headquarters showing the location of the pings in relation to their approach.

"A hundred yards from target, sir," he whispers.

"Seventy-five yards from target," the west team leader adds.

"Any visual yet?" Solarez responds.

"Negative sir, east team."

"Negative, west team."

"Report when you get a visual on hostiles or the missing researcher."

Suddenly the ping reverses direction and starts descending the hill.

"Target changing direction."

"Any visual?"

"Yes sir. It's...an animal sir. I see the antlers, a deer," the west team leader reports hesitantly.

"Could be a decoy, disable it!" Solarez shouts.

The agent shoots a tranquilizer dart from a pistol and the large deer falls with a thump into a bed of leaves. With guns drawn, both teams warily approach the downed deer, fearing some kind of ambush. But nothing happens. They find a makeshift holster holding a cellphone strapped to the buck's shoulder.

"Agent Solarez, we've got the phone, but still no sign of your researcher. No sign of any humans at all, actually. Looks to be a ruse, sir."

"We've been taken for fools! They strapped the phone to a freaking deer. We've been wasting precious time!"

"We're still holding the perimeter, and we've been checking every suspicious vehicle," an analyst in the situation room tells the agitated Solarez.

"Fine. Any ideas on where we should be looking now?"

"Planes, trains, automobiles, the usual. Guess we can add boats too. With the hundreds of waterways in the area, they could slip him out virtually anywhere."

"Besides our perimeter, we've got nothing. I want surveillance footage of the roads leading out of downtown from one hour before he went missing. Get the manifests for all ferries and public boats in Annapolis and have an agent check them for suspicious activity."

Solarez tries unsuccessfully to untie the knot in his stomach. It wouldn't make sense for a foreign government to kill Ron Michaels, which is good news because that means he's probably still alive, and bad news because they will torture him for his telomere research.

CHAPTER 48

THE AXING

FRANKLIN LOOKS AT HIS LUNCH, then his watch—1:05 p.m. *Where is Ryan?* A tap from behind startles him. He turns and sees Ryan standing behind the park bench facing the Washington Monument.

"Daddy, can we go all the way to the top?" a little girl asks a man pushing a toddler in the umbrella stroller past them, momentarily distracting Franklin.

The former SEAL walks around the bench and sits beside him.

"What's so urgent? And why are we meeting here? Have you seen one too many spy movies?" Ryan asks, looking at the monument behind a pair of blue-tinted aviator sunglasses.

"It's Angie. She's going to tell him."

"Michaels?"

Franklin nods.

Ryan scans the horizon and the people nearby—a couple laying on the grass 20 feet away, a guy flying a box kite. Ryan has a plastic cup for his chew, and Franklin notices the subtle bulge along Ryan's right cheek.

"I hate to say it, but something has to be done, we have to protect ourselves. I slipped once and told her some details about how the government paid off Hemispheres. And I asked her to bug Michaels' office and she turned me down."

"You just said 'we.' She doesn't have any idea who I am, right?" Ryan asks, eyeing Franklin.

"I'm not sure."

"Not sure? How the hell could she know who I am? Did you ever use my name?"

"No, not that I recall. But somehow she found out I was also, uh, involved, with a young female lawyer at my law firm. She said to never contact her again, but--...."

"Now I get it." Ryan says, before spitting some chew into the cup. "What do you propose?"

"Is there a way to, uh, do this so it can never be traced to us?"

Ryan knew this was what Franklin would propose, but wanted to make him say it. After she risked her job and reputation for him, this spineless excuse for a man wants to knock her off. Better yet, he wants me to knock her off.

"It could be an unfortunate accident," Franklin adds.

"Or the suicide of a distraught lover?"

"Well my wife is bound to find out, if she doesn't know already, and truthfully, I don't want to leave her. Suicide could make it look like I broke it off with her, which might help save my marriage."

"What if it looks like she did it in your office while you're out?"

"In my office? No way."

They spend a few moments watching the tourists walking by, taking pictures of the pool and monuments.

"How about in the tub at her apartment? Too many pills or something?" Ryan suggests.

"That sounds better."

"Be sure you have an airtight alibi. Sending emails from your office would be good. That way there's a paper trail showing where you were."

"Yeah, that's good. But how will you get into her place? She never gave me a key."

"The less you know, the better. Don't text or call my cell on Thursday. I'll give you a landline you can call from a payphone if necessary. Stay at your office at least until 8:00, and send an email every 15 minutes or so. Do you understand?"

"Yes. We can discuss your payment afterward."

"That's fine, I know you're good for it."

CHAPTER 49
TERRIBLE THUD

.

ANGIE TIPTON DIPS her spoon into the pint-size Cherry Garcia frozen yogurt while watching the 11:00 p.m. news.

"We have breaking news from the district. Paul Franklin, a local attorney, died tonight around 8:00 p.m. after what police are investigating as a possible suicide."

"Oh my God," Angie says out loud to the emptiness of her kitchen as she hears a spoon clatter to the tile floor, unaware she overturned the container. She leans on the kitchen counter, closer to the TV.

"It appears Franklin, a partner with Leftwish & Franklin, jumped from the 12th floor of his office building at 1873 K Street, N.W. His body landed on the corner, near 19th, in front of several shocked eyewitnesses. Our reporter, Paul Slocumb, is at the scene with some of them now. Paul?"

"Yes, this is eyewitness reporter Walt Slocumb, reporting from 19th and K Streets. You can see the police tape behind us where investigators are still examining the scene. With me is Mona Washington, who's employed at the G&C Electronics store right across the street from where the victim fell. Ms. Washington, can you tell our viewers what you witnessed?"

The camera shot widens from Slocumb to include the eyewitness.

"I was out on the sidewalk, pulling in a cart with some of our display items, and I heard a terrible thud in the street. I looked over and I saw the guy right after he fell. A couple of cars stopped right away and I ran out there to see what was going on. Jesus, it was the worst thing I've ever seen. There was blood all around his head. I think he was still alive when I first saw him cuz his eyes were open for a few seconds. I leaned down close, but he didn't say anything. Then an ambulance pulled up and I just backed away to let them do their job. It was horrible. Oh, and then someone pointed up at the building and there was a hole in the window on the 12th floor."

"Thanks Ms. Washington. I'll provide updates as we receive them."

The anchor at the studio continues the story.

"Forty-eight-year-old Paul Franklin gained some notoriety in defending Hemispheres Airways when one of its jets crashed in Quarryville, Pennsylvania, and had recently filed a lawsuit against the U.S. and D.C. attorney Andy Michaels, alleging a secret payoff to Hemispheres airline by the government. Franklin leaves behind his wife and two teenage children. We will keep you posted as we learn more about the victim and any possible motives."

Angie grabs a tissue from the box in the guest bathroom and sobs, wondering who she can call. Ultimately, she decides it would be best not to call anyone. She curls up on the couch where she finally falls asleep until about 3:00 a.m., when she awakens and groggily changes into her nightshirt before heading to bed.

CHAPTER 50

MOBILIZATION

SOLAREZ CALLS TOGETHER his lead analyst and 10 other FBI counterintelligence agents. They gather in a lopsided semi-circle around him in a large situation room full of half-wall dividers and non-descript desks scattered with monitors, printers, keyboards, and scanners. Large flat-screens hang on several walls, as well as a whiteboard where Solarez stands, dry-erase marker in hand.

"Listen up. Whatever you're currently working on has to wait. This investigation is now your highest priority. A government biologist was working under an assumed identity at the Sherwood lab when he vanished at a parade in Annapolis this afternoon. His name is Ron Michaels, the public believes he was killed in the Hemispheres plane crash, but he wasn't on the doomed jet. He's the father of Amanda Michaels, the sole survivor of the crash. Also, an attorney named Paul Franklin committed suicide by jumping from a window at his law office today. We're thinking the two are connected because Franklin was the guy filing the lawsuit on behalf of Hemispheres against the government and Andy Michaels."

"Yesterday we received credible intelligence that the one-year-old boy Michaels has been raising at Sherwood is not his biological son. We aren't sure how his real son was kidnapped, or where he is, but we think it happened in the first minutes after he was born in Canada and that the boy is being used as some sort of bargaining chip."

One of the analysts raises his hand and Solarez acknowledges him.

"Why was he born in Canada?"

"That's not important. Let's focus on what is. The surrogate was a French-Canadian named Odette something—her last name's in the file. We've got to find her, and if we can't, we need to review her parents' email and phone records and interview them. Next, we'll investigate everyone involved in the delivery—doctors, nurses, aides—to see if any of them were paid by a foreign intelligence agency to help in the kidnapping. Michaels may have figured out the boy wasn't his son and decided he would try to find him, without our help. Or, it could be the kidnappers are extorting him and he went to pay them off. Or maybe they took him too and are promising they'll reunite him with his real son if he researches for them. All theories are plausible until proven otherwise.

"As far as the suspects in Canada, I discussed the operation with the Canadian Security Intelligence Service in Québec, where the baby was born. They are giving us access to the computer and phone data for Odette, her parents, and everyone involved in the hospital delivery.

"I'm pretty sure this baby and Michaels are alive because frankly, if they've been kidnapped, they're worth more alive than dead. Oh, and since this work is in Canada, we will team with CIA operatives because it's out of our jurisdiction."

A question from another analyst, this time a young female. "What type of research was he working on?"

"All I can say is it was being done under a highly classified White House directive. This case is your number-one priority. Jones, Epstein, divide the available agents. Jones team focuses on Ron Michaels; Epstein's team on the boy, Justin. That'll be all."

CHAPTER 51

DONE?

THURSDAY, 7:50 p.m. Paul Franklin hits the send button on another alibi email.

A man makes his way down a back hall and looks at his watch: 7:52 p.m. He notices the light under the closed door to Franklin's office. When he turns the doorknob with his gloved hand and enters the office, he startles the already on-edge attorney. Ignoring the two client chairs and Franklin, he strides past the mahogany desk to the floor-to-ceiling glass windows allowing the city lights to twinkle into the room.

"Is it done?" Franklin asks, standing slightly behind him.

No answer. Instead the other man simply stares out the windows toward the White House, visible between two highrises. Beyond is the dome of the U.S. Capitol to the left and the Washington Monument to the right.

"Why won't you answer me?" The redness of Franklin's face now extends down his neck. He takes a few steps toward the windows to see what his visitor seems fixated upon.

"It'll be done soon," Ryan finally whispers.

Franklin turns toward him angrily.

"It's still not done? How could you delay this? I've hardly been able to function for the last couple days, let alone work!"

With lightning speed, Ryan sweeps a small hammer-like tool from his rear pants pocket and strikes the window. The tempered glass shatters into thousands of tiny pieces. Franklin throws his hands up instinctively to protect himself from the shards, simultaneously Ryan donkey kicks Franklin in his midsection. Franklin's body bends into an unnatural u-shape as the inertia propels him through the remaining stalagmites and stalactites of glass. His shocked face, still facing toward the inside of the building, emits a blood-curdling scream that fades as he falls from the upper floor of the office building. Then it abruptly ends.

Ryan picks up the tool and shoves it back in his pocket. He surveys the room, confident he hasn't touched anything, before placing the suicide note—typed on Franklin's computer the day before through remote access—on the blotter. He fishes out the hammer Franklin kept in his desk drawer and puts it on the floor by the gaping hole in the glass, which allows the soft night wind to blow into the room. He drops one of the earrings he stole from Melanie Franklin's jewelry box earlier in the day near the opening surrounded by jagged glass shards, then walks out.

Retracing his steps through the interior hall to the stairwell and back up to the fitness center, he avoids all surveillance cameras. In a bathroom stall of the locker room he changes into a disguise drastically different from the grungy dreadlocks he wore when entering the building earlier. He stuffs the other clothing along with the adhesive plastic pieces he placed on his shoe soles to disguise his footprints back into his gym bag. His new lawyerly disguise consists of a black trench coat, tortoise-rim glasses and wing-tipped shoes. Last, he stuffs the gym bag into a black rolling briefcase before exiting the building.

Joining the growing crowd of rubberneckers, he silently exhibits his horror while thinking to himself that the street is only a temporary barrier to Franklin's further descent to hell. *Another falling man, remindful of the photo in the 9/11 museum.*

Convinced the surveillance cameras have documented his *concerned bystander* reactions, he briskly walks away.

CHAPTER 52

FLASH DRIVES

AFTER THE MONDAY morning mail-sorting ritual, Myra drops Andy's mail on his desk, including a non-descript mailer with no postage marked "Personal and Confidential." Andy opens it first, figuring one of his clients dropped it through the slot on the office door over the weekend. Inside are two identical flash drives attached with scotch tape to a piece of paper. One line of typed text runs below the drives:

The password is in your email.

He quickly reviews his office emails back to the previous Friday. No password. Then he opens his personal account and scrolls through the past 24 hours.

Flash drive password

Andy clicks into it and the message reads:

Ironman 3-1

Andy thinks for a moment. He decides "Ironman" could refer to the triathlons he did with Ron and one of their closest friends. The three probably refers to Ron, Alex Erickson and himself, and the minus one is Alex, who ended up being a mole for the Chinese government at the company where Ron worked before the plane crash. Alex was quickly terminated by Chinese intelligence when no longer needed, and his death was made to look like an accidental drowning.

Andy looks down again at the two flash drives and notices his name is written on one with a thin black marker and Amanda's name is on the other.

He places the flash drive with his name on it into the USB port on his computer and brings up a folder containing two files: "Andy" and "The List." Andy clicks on the one with his name and types in the password.

Dear Andy:

This is going to sound crazy, and I don't know how it happened, but Justin was swapped for another baby. I've been raising a child who's not mine! About the time I suspected this, I was contacted by someone trying to extort me. If I don't continue my research and allow them to access it through my computer, I'd never see Justin again. So I either keep doing my research, knowing it will be stolen, or try to figure out what happened to Justin. I can't tell you any more about what I'm doing, but please deliver the attached list to Dr. Vance and ask him to help me. Don't tell the FBI or anyone else with the government about this and don't save this file anywhere on your computer. I'm sorry I can't tell you more.

Love, Ron

Andy closes the file. Before opening the other one, Andy calls Amanda.

"I need you to come to my office. Can you get here right away?"

"I'm kinda busy here, but you sound pretty serious."

"I am. It involves, well, I don't want to say anything on this phone. Can you leave now?"

"I guess so. You realize my FBI escort will be with me."

"He can wait out in the reception area. Please hurry, but drive safely."

He glances down at his watch, figuring it will take her about 45 minutes. Before he can open the second file, his cell phone rings and displays a familiar number he is not at all surprised to see.

"Andy, Steve Solarez here. We have a crisis. Over the weekend, Ron vanished while he and Mrs. Kolfax and Justin were at a parade in Annapolis. He was in disguise and was escorted by four FBI agents. We have no idea what happened. I have some other disturbing information too, about Justin, but I want to talk to you in person."

This is too much for Andy to take in all at once. Solarez knows about Justin? How long has he known? And now Ron is missing?

"I assume you're doing everything in your power to find him. How could he disappear?"

"We have agents in Annapolis and D.C. assigned exclusively to this case. All of them are searching the entire region."

"Amanda should be here within an hour. Can you meet us at 11:30?"

"Yes, and that's great Amanda will be there too. I'll see you then."

Right after the call with Solarez it dawns on him that Amanda needs to bring her password. He texts her to confirm she got an email with a password and tells her he will explain more when she arrives. Only after sending the text does it dawn on Andy someone may be tapping into his text messages.

CHAPTER 53
TELOGURL 13

AMANDA MIRACULOUSLY FINDS a parking space a couple blocks off M Street, a reasonable walking distance from her uncle's Georgetown office. The FBI agent following her parks in a space not available to the general public. She walks down the cobblestone sidewalk and he picks up next to her as they walk the remaining block.

"I wouldn't mind working on this block, it's a cool neighborhood," Amanda says, trying to make small talk. The agent smiles slightly and nods.

Once they arrive at the office, the agent takes a seat on the couch in the reception area. Myra announces Amanda to Andy. They exchange hugs and Amanda follows Andy to a conference room where his laptop is set up. As soon as he closes the door, Amanda asks him about the urgency.

"This is only about the third time you've asked me to come here. Something bad must've happened."

"It's your dad. He vanished."

"From a government-run facility? How is that even possible? Have they checked their surveillance cameras?"

Andy motions to a chair. "Take a seat. He didn't vanish from inside the compound, he was in Annapolis with Justin and the nanny. Someone delivered an envelope here over the weekend with flash drives for you and me from your dad. Do you have the email I texted you about?"

"Yeah."

Amanda scrolls through the emails on her phone and finds the one called "Flash drive password." She opens it and finds one phrase: *Telogurl 13*. Andy pushes his laptop with the flash drive inserted across the table to her and she types in the password.

Amanda:

Believe it or not, Justin is not our Justin. Someone kidnapped him somehow after Odette gave birth. I don't know who has him, but they've been sending me messages. They said I need to keep researching. They hacked into my laptop and the servers at the lab, and if I don't cooperate or if they find out I told the government anything, I'll never seen Justin again.

I struggled with this for several days and finally decided I couldn't keep going. I couldn't continue to give them my research, and I couldn't live knowing they might kill Justin if I didn't cooperate, so I made a decision. I'm going to do everything I can to find Justin without handing my research over to whoever took him. I'm not sure when you'll hear from me again, but remember I love you more than the moon, the sun and the stars.

Love, Dad

Amanda can barely breathe. She gets up from the conference room table and starts pacing. "Our family seems cursed. Why?"

"I don't know, I really don't. First the plane crash and you being kidnapped, then the newspapers suggesting I'm part of some government cover up, and now this—"

"It's got to be the Chinese again, right?"

"Makes sense to me, but who knows. I got a call from Solarez literally a minute after I hung up with you. He'll be here at 11:30. You and I need to figure out what the hell we're going to ask him. He told me Ron disappeared from a parade he took Justin to. Oh, and get this, Solarez wants to tell us something about Justin. I'll bet he knows about the swap, so why didn't he tell us before? How long has he been keeping that from us? One thing is clear though, we're not telling him anything about these flash drives. Agreed?"

"Yep. We gotta figure this out. Hopefully Dad will contact us soon."

CHAPTER 54

THE HUNT

SOLAREZ GREETS his agent on Amanda's detail when he gets off the elevator at Andy's office. Rather than joining Amanda and Andy in the conference room, he asks them to take a walk with him, not trusting the law firm isn't bugged. He tells the agent they will be back soon and to remain in the reception area.

The three of them walk north down the cobblestone sidewalk toward M Street, Solarez between the other two.

"Remember when I told you both if I brought Ron back into the United States to do research it would have to be a well-guarded secret? Well, obviously someone found out, and one of the foreign intelligence agencies is using Justin as leverage. Ron never gave you any idea he was under pressure from anyone, did he?"

"Absolutely not," Andy says.

"When did you find out Justin isn't my real brother?" Amanda demands, "because if my dad found out and disappeared...well?"

"I found out a few days ago, and wasn't sure the information was credible. I was planning to drive to Sherwood to discuss it with your dad in person, but he vanished first."

"Who told you?"

"I'm not at liberty to tell you that, but it's a credible source. We reviewed the medical records from the infirmary at Sherwood and we had a simple pinprick test done on Justin, or whoever he is. We confirmed he doesn't have the right blood type or carry the vWD gene that is hereditary in your family.

"I have a team of 10 agents working on finding Justin and your dad. We're tracking down Odette and her parents, I've got agents investigating every person at the hospital who had anything to do with Justin's delivery, agents and officers are scouring the area between here and Annapolis, and we're analyzing all possible motives so we can find both of them."

"Have you got any ideas or leads? Is it the Chinese?"

"We're operating under the assumption the Chinese are involved, given the close connection to the research your dad was doing."

Andy chimes in, "Have you questioned their liaison to the United States government? And all those contacts from before?"

A temporary logjam of people appears on M Street. They pass them single file before returning to each other's sides.

"Yes, Andy. I talked to Stein and we're pinging our Chinese contacts. The first responses were total denials, as you would expect. I don't know enough yet to give you my opinion on whether or not they were being truthful."

They turn around and start re-tracing their route back to Andy's office.

"By us taking this walk, are you suggesting my office is compromised?"

"It's a possibility. We shouldn't discuss any issues relating to Ron or Justin in your office."

"Great, just great. And my cell phone?"

"Ditto."

Amanda looks at her phone, "I guess that goes for mine too. I wonder who's been listening or tracking me."

At the entry door to the office, Solarez stops. "Amanda, it's incredibly important that you keep our agents with you 24/7. No more side missions, your safety is even more jeopardized now."

Andy gives Amanda a questioning look as Solarez opens the door for the three of them.

"I wanted to meet Jonathan without any agents hanging around, sorry. You have been stripping me of any privacy I once had."

Amanda knows Solarez worries about her, but she's not at all convinced the FBI will find Justin or her dad. "Why don't you hire me to help find them?"

"What? Not a chance," Solarez says.

"I'm more motivated than 10 of your analysts."

Andy looks at her with a frown. "I agree with Solarez, let their agents keep working on it."

Amanda narrows her eyes and exhales with disgust through her nearly closed lips. *If they don't find them, I will,* she thinks.

They say goodbye to Solarez and she walks up the stairs to Andy's office with him.

"I don't think your dad's been kidnapped or taken hostage," he whispers to her.

"Why? What did the file on your flash drive say?"

"You just have to trust me on this one, but let's be extra careful from here on out. Are you doing okay at Crossroads, I mean besides this mess?"

"Yeah, except it's lonely there. I talk to David some. And I saw Jonathan, we met up at Cafe Loco."

"Jonathan Parkinson? That's surprising."

"Whatever. I'm not a child, you know."

"Yes, I know, just be careful. There's too much happening right now. Let the FBI protect you and don't get involved in any hijinks, please."

"Hijinks?" Amanda rolls her eyes.

CHAPTER 55

LAB LIST

THE REASON ANDY was so confident his brother was alive and not being held hostage was the second password-protected file on his flash drive, the one he didn't share with Amanda.

Andy:

Please provide this list and instructions to Dr. Sid Vance, my former professor. He should be able to obtain all these materials without difficulty from the labs at Georgetown. Please stress to him how important it is to keep this confidential.

Materials:

Adenoviral vector constructs (engineered to target P_{21} locus)

qPCR equipment, specific to aforementioned gene targets (minimum four complete sets)

CRE enzymes (at least 50 mL)

DNA polymerase and electrophoresis machinery (and associated ultraviolet imager)

Centrifuge, automatic pipets (50)

Confocal microscopes with lasers corresponding to aforementioned stains (2)

Consumer nail polish (Minimum 10 bottles)

Vectashield fluid (10 bottles, as least 4 oz each)

Mitochondria-targeting antibodies for microscope imaging

Mounting slides and cover slides (50 each)

Place all materials, surrounded by bubble wrap, in sealed boxes no larger than 32 x 32 x 32 labeled "fragile" and have them inside your office within 7 days if possible. Type XX in the top third of your faculty webpage and someone will pick up the boxes when you aren't present.

Andy decides to deliver the materials list to Dr. Vance right away. He struggles with keeping his brother's wishes from the FBI. Solarez is hustling and doing all he can. *What if I'm failing to provide information that could lead his team to either or both of them?*

He suddenly remembers the big deposition of one of his expert witnesses scheduled for tomorrow and realizes he has to spend at least an hour or two preparing.

CHAPTER 56

ACCOSTED

THE SUBJECT of Andy's case, a 26-year-old graduate student, was driving his two-month-old SUV on a rainy night when it lost traction and rolled over twice. The second roll crushed the roof inward, and he died before the rescue squad arrived. The wrongful death lawsuit filed on behalf of his family claims the manufacturer knowingly installed a roof that would not support the weight of the vehicle in a rollover.

The deposition of the engineering expert took six hours, thanks to the relentless manufacturer's attorney's endless droning. However, it felt twice as long with the awkwardness between him and Angie. He has a feeling she is aware he knows because she had avoided him as much as possible for the last few days, ducking into the restroom if he headed her way down the hall, or stepping back into her office as he passed by her doorway.

Ever since he found out about her and Franklin, Andy has been torn between having an open conversation with her to hear her side of the story and just firing her outright. She has worked for him for years and has always been nothing but an asset to his practice, but the thought of her being intimate with his opponent and what confidential information she might have shared with him in the heat of the moment makes Andy wonder if he can ever fully trust her again. This indecisiveness is what stuck the two of them in a room together for the last several hours, avoiding eye contact and only speaking to each other when absolutely necessary.

Bleary eyed and exhausted, his cognitive abilities reduced to only automatic functions, Andy feels fortunate to locate his car in the K Street underground parking garage. He drives the few short miles in the early evening darkness to his Georgetown home. After pulling his Mini Cooper into his driveway and getting out, he presses the lock button on his key fob and turns toward his front door.

A man in a black hoodie and ski mask materializes out of nowhere and points the muzzle of a Glock in Andy's face. "Unlock the car, get back in, and look straight ahead." The attacker's voice is electronically distorted to avoid recognition.

Andy complies, slowly pushing the unlock button and sliding back into the front seat. The man continues to aim the pistol at him while making his way into the back seat.

Andy barely turns his head—

"Face forward!"

The Glock presses into the back of Andy's head as he turns back to face the windshield.

"Don't do anything stupid. I want some answers. Why did Hemispheres settle all the lawsuits without a fight?"

"Good question. It was totally out of character for Franklin and the airline. I don't know why."

"I don't believe you. Did the government pay Hemispheres the $200 million? Don't feed me any bullshit."

Even with the assailant tapping the Glock against the back of his head to convey his seriousness, Andy decides to honor his promise to Stein.

"I don't... know," he stammers.

"You're lying!" The gun knocks harder against the back of his head. "I'm gonna to give you three seconds to come clean, then I'm blowing your lawyer brains all over this windshield. Amanda will be next."

"Okay, okay! They paid the money, but I didn't know until after I settled all those cases, I had nothing to do with any of it."

"Why did they pay?"

"The government didn't want the media to find out they were running a counterintelligence operation involving my brother and his research. China had a mole inside his research lab and the government wanted to expose the mole. Then China sabotaged the jet because they thought my brother was going to sell his research to Russia. That's the truth, I swear."

"China sabotaged the jet?"

"Yeah. You have my brother, right?"

"How many brothers do you have?"

"Only Ron. What do I have to do to get him back?"

"Your brother died in the crash."

"So you're not here about Ron? Then what do you want from me?"

"I ask the questions. What's your supposedly dead brother doing if he's still alive?"

"Research for the government."

"What kind of research?"

"Uh, I just know it has to do with telomeres."

"What about them?"

"I don't understand it since I'm not a biologist, something about extending cell life, longer lifespans."

"China wanted this research bad enough to sabotage a jet?"

"They thought Ron was gonna sell the technology to the Russians, at least that's what I was told. But it was all a setup by the U.S."

"You better not be lying to me."

"Why would I tell you Ron's alive if he was dead? That would be stupid. He vanished yesterday from the research lab, so I assumed you were here to demand ransom money or something."

Andy refuses to believe there's no connection between the gunman and Ron's disappearance, and is now wondering if Ron is still alive or not.

"You have the jet maintenance files from the crash lawsuits, right?" the masked man asks. "The files showing all the electrical work for the week before the crash?"

"Yeah, I've got a box or so."

"What did the evidence show?"

"That the electrical system likely failed. But personal injury lawyers typically are looking for preventable defects, we don't try to prove criminal sabotage."

"Put those files by the side door of your house when you come home tomorrow. Don't say a word about this visit, especially to your FBI friends. Believe me, I'll found out if you do. Sit here and look straight ahead for five minutes before you get out. You'll be hearing from me again."

Andy hears the rear door open and softly close. He notices both of his hands shaking uncontrollably, and tries to steady them on the steering wheel.

Nothing makes sense anymore. *What do they want, and why?*

Dashing through the unfenced yard behind Andy's home, into the front yard of the home on the adjacent street, then turning and racing along the sidewalk past several homes, Ryan locates the bike he stashed in the hedge where Rock Creek Park borders the Georgetown neighborhood. He stashes the ski mask in the black cinch sack before cycling away.

CHAPTER 57

BAD BLOOD

ANGIE CAN'T TAKE it anymore. This polite awkwardness between her and Andy is worse than being outed as a mistress. Worse than being fired. He knows about her and Franklin, but she's not sure how he found out. She confirms with Myra that he's alone in his office and walks in unannounced.

"Andy."

He slowly turns away from the monitor on his credenza to face her. He has played this moment in his head a dozen times and prepared as many different dialogues, but is caught off-guard by her initiating the inevitable confrontation.

"Andy," she says again.

He meets her gaze, but nothing comes out.

Guess it's up to me, she decides. "I can't imagine...no, I don't want to imagine what you must think of me."

"I don't understand. Why him?"

"This is going to sound stupid, but I always do what's right—putting myself through school, working for the good guys, eating healthy, paying my bills on time. I needed to do something wrong. Having an affair with a married man who was also my boss's enemy, it doesn't get much worse than that."

"And?"

"Something made it exciting. I liked having control over Paul, even if it was only in bed. And for a while I believed I could wring some good out of him, but that ended when he asked me to plant a bug in your office and I found out I wasn't the only one he was cheating with."

"Um, back up. He asked you to bug my office?"

"I didn't do it."

"But you never told me either. I feel like I don't know anything about you anymore. Did you give him information to use against me in the RICO suit?"

"Of course not! I never did or said anything that would put you or the firm in jeopardy. Our relationship and my work were completely separate. That was my main rule."

"I'm not sure I believe you. Why didn't you tell me about you guys?"

Angie finds herself going on the defensive. "Because I knew you'd lose it, like you are right now!"

"You don't think I have a right to be pissed about this? I trusted you, took a chance on you, even hired your friend Myra, against my better judgment. I expect this kind of behavior from her, not from you. God knows I'm not perfect in the relationship department, and who you shack up with after-hours would normally be none of my business. But I worked hard to build a solid reputation in this town and your choice of sex paramour could have destroyed everything."

Andy catches his breath, then continues, "I've been tiptoeing around my own office for days, trying to figure out how to make this situation work, how to trust you again, but now, I'm not sure—"

"Tell you what, I'll save you the trouble. I quit."

"Wait a second!" he calls out, but she is already gone.

Angie storms back to her office, grabs a couple personal items and her purse, and walks out.

A few moments pass before Myra appears in his doorway. "Uh, Angie just left and said she's done here. What's that mean?"

"It means...she may not be working here anymore. Tell anyone asking for her she's out of the office for now."

CHAPTER 58

CHINESE WORM

AS AN ANALYST FOR RON MICHAELS, Fletcher processes blood samples and reports his findings to other members of the Dirty Dozen team at Sherwood. He also recently picked up a lucrative side job with definite fringe benefits.

He met Monica at a bar not far from the research lab a few months ago. Walston, his wing man, had gone home early, leaving Fletcher with no one to consult when the gorgeous woman made her subtle approach, and he asked if he could buy her a drink. He was so taken with her he never questioned why a woman like her would cozy up to a relatively nerdy lab rat like him.

The amazing sex that ensued in her room at the Constable Inn that night convinced him he did the right thing by not looking a gift horse in the mouth. They exchanged numbers before he reluctantly left in the early morning hours and they continued to meet at the motel once a week.

About four weeks into their arrangement, Monica asks him if he'd like to make some extra money. Intrigued by the thought of getting cash in addition to sex, he asks for more details.

"You know those vials of blood you process for your boss?"

Fletcher knows exactly which ones she's talking about. Although there is no name or patient ID on the vials, he determined a while back the blood belongs to Ron's daughter, Amanda. The fact Monica knows anything about what he does puzzles him, but not enough to nix further discussions.

"What about them?"

"The company I work for is really intrigued by Amanda Michaels and how she survived the plane crash, and I know the blood in those vials is hers. They'll give me a promotion for a tiny sample of her blood, and they'll pay whoever gave it to me. If you get me a sample, you'll be $10,000 richer and I'll be a very happy woman. You know what that means..."

As her words trail off, Monica runs her hand down Fletcher's chest toward the zipper of his jeans, and any chance of him saying no disappears. *By just supplying the blood and not the test results, I'm not selling any state secrets,* Fletcher rationalizes. And after not having sex for over a year, he doesn't want to lose her.

"Okay, I'll see what I can do."

"Oh, thank you, Fletch! You won't regret it."

Now every week, when the unmarked tubes of blood arrive, Fletcher skims the tiniest bit of blood off the top and puts it in a separate vial for Monica. After he delivers it to her, she pays him $10,000, and they spend the rest of the night in bed. When his body isn't entwined with hers, he occasionally wonders about this arrangement and toys with the idea of telling Walston. But when he's with her, he can't bring himself to end it.

Monica supplies the blood as directed to her contact and has no idea what a *LuLiXi looks like or what a Chinese worm is.* But the worm pays her well.

CHAPTER 59

HOMICIDE

LESS THAN 24 hours after Franklin's death, a homicide detective calls Stephanie DeFalzo and asks if he could interview her about one of her clients, Melanie Franklin. That morning, Ryan is making one of his appearances at the shop—getting a mediocre cup of coffee from the ancient pot in the neglected break room and talking to Mike Robinson, another PI with a pocket protector full of pens and a comb-over meant to disguise his still-obvious hair loss—when Stephanie casually asks for their advice.

"Guys, a detective wants to talk to me about Paul Franklin. Do you think I need a lawyer? Who was the one the agency recommended for Miller when he needed one?"

The men regard each other for a second before Robinson answers. "You only need one if you've got a problem. There's no problem, is there?"

"No, all my contact with Mrs. Franklin was confidential, and there's no court order."

"Then you can talk to him, but remind him your conversations with the wife are off limits. Do you think she was involved?" Ryan asks.

"No. Considering what the bastard was doing, I wouldn't blame her for wanting him dead, but I don't think she had anything to do with it."

"Sounds like you have nothing to worry about then. Give him a bunch of general stuff and he'll move on."

The detective arrives at the Franklin home. With its stamped-concrete semi-circle drive and tiered fountain in the immaculately manicured front yard, the mid-century modern reeks of new money and a desperate desire to keep up with the Joneses. He walks up to the furniture-less porch and pushes the doorbell, setting off a series of canned chimes, and a teenage boy who appears to be about 17 comes to the door.

"Hi, is Melanie Franklin home?"

He's holding his badge despite no request to present it, and his car in the driveway isn't marked, but anyone who has watched a cop show on TV would realize it's a government-issued sedan. A few moments later Melanie Franklin appears at the door and tells her son to go do his homework. Her freshly manicured nails and well-pressed linen suit hardly fit the image of a grieving spouse.

"Mrs. Franklin, I'm Detective Upshaw from the D.C. homicide branch. Could I ask you a few questions relating to your husband's death?"

Melanie nods and steps aside. Once inside, Upshaw admires the expansive marble foyer and fine paintings and fanciful glass pieces on display. Before she can lead him to the white leather couch in the formal living room, he asks a seemingly harmless question: "Can I take a look in your bedroom as part of my investigation?"

"Detective, my husband may have been the attorney, but I still know you can't search our home or belongings without a warrant."

Upshaw pulls a single sheet of paper folded in thirds from his pocket and hands it over. Melanie steps aside to let him pass.

Twenty minutes later, the detective returns to the first floor and Melanie gestures to the kitchen table where two glasses of water are waiting. They each take a seat on opposite sides of the table.

"How would you describe your relationship with your husband in the last few months before he died?"

Melanie meets his gaze without blinking. "We had a solid marriage for many years, but it became a little strained recently." She doesn't volunteer any information about Paul's affairs.

"Tell me about Angie Tipton."

"You obviously did your homework." She takes a few sips of water from a glass before setting it back down on the round, sand-colored porcelain coaster in front of her.

"How long had you known about her and your husband, Mrs. Franklin?"

He notices her eyes following a lone fly buzzing around to his left. He can tell she wants to kill it because it is so out of place in her immaculate home, but she reluctantly returns her focus to him, the much larger pest sitting at her kitchen table.

"Not that long, less than two weeks. I was given an anonymous envelope of photos at the gym."

Upshaw weighs her demeanor and concludes she must be seething, must want to tell him more. But she's still not talking.

"So you went to a private investigator?"

"Of course. Why else do spouses hire them? I wanted to know what he was doing, and who he was doing it with."

"What did you find out?"

"That he was involved with more than one. Surprise, surprise."

"So your husband was cheating on you with multiple women? Some people would say that might make you a very angry spouse."

"Look, if you're implying I could have killed him, well, you're wrong. So if you're looking for someone with a real motive, it's Angie. Plus, I agreed to talk to you without an attorney. Would a lawyer's wife agree to do that if she had anything to hide?"

The Detective doesn't answer. "Do you mind if I look around your home one more time?" he asks, seeing if she's going to cut him short.

"Help yourself."

His instincts tell him she's not the killer, but he's not sure Angie Tipton is either. And why would Melanie's earring be in Franklin's office on the night he died if she wasn't involved?

CHAPTER 60

FARMER VANCE

THE FOUR BLACK cars speed down the one-lane dirt road leading off State Route 18, kicking up swirls of dust along the eighth-mile stretch. They drive under the branches of blooming crepe myrtles lining the road and pass several head of cattle before reaching the farmhouse. It sits on 130 acres, not a huge farm in rural Loudoun County, but certainly a respectable size for a family-run operation. Three of the plain-clothes agents trot into position, two on either side of the door, one in front. The door opens and a woman with close-cropped hair and an apron printed with red and green apples appears. She looks at the men, bewildered.

One of the agents flashes his badge at her.

"Mrs. Vance, I'm with the FBI. We're here to talk to your husband. Is he inside?"

"Why? What's this about?"

"Mrs. Vance, please tell us if your husband inside. We don't want anyone to panic or get hurt."

"He's here, but he's out at the pond, picking raspberries. Larry and John are out that way too. We pay them to come help us with our cattle. He's supposed to be bringing the berries back so I can make a pie."

"Where is the pond, Mrs. Vance?"

"That way," she says, waving her hand in a general direction. "Follow the road 'round that way and you'll find it."

"Men, back in the vehicles."

Four FBI agents form a ring around Dr. Vance under a live oak tree draped with Spanish moss. The men instinctively position themselves under the shade of the tree's canopy to avoid the sun beaming down from overhead.

"Dr. Vance, we understand you were close with Ron Michaels."

"Ron was a good student, but that's not why you gentlemen came all the way out here I suspect. Ron is dead. It was a goddam tragedy what happened to him and his family."

"Let's cut to the chase. You provided a laundry list of equipment to someone, and we think it was for Mr. Michaels."

"Are you saying Ron rose from the dead?"

The agent kicks around a few pebbles on the gravel drive. "I'm saying I want to know who requested the equipment and who received it."

"Me too, but I don't. I was asked to obtain legal, off-the-shelf laboratory equipment, put it in a box, and leave it in my office."

"Who picked it up Dr. Vance?" the agent demands again, scowling.

"I just told you, I have no idea."

The agent takes out his card and hands it to the professor.

"Dr. Vance, you want to help your government any way you can, particularly against the threat of some kind of biological terrorism, don't you?"

Vance looks down at the card. "Of course. If I find out anything I'll give you a call."

As the black sedans stream down the road, Vance kneels down, picks up the bucket filled with raspberries, and begins walking back toward the house.

Those guys are the last people who would get any information about Ron Michaels out of me.

CHAPTER 61
PALE MOON

THE MAN SITS in a rickety rocking chair in front of the Pale Moon tattoo shop, enjoying a smoke. He hears the unmistakable rumble of a Harley slowly making its way down the Middleburg back street and swears he can feel the vibration inside his body even though the bike is still several hundred feet away.

The man on the Harley steers into an open parking space in front of the store down the block. After strapping his helmet to the bike, the rider strides into the smoke shop next door and emerges a few minutes later.

In a hoarse southern drawl the smoker says, "That's a fine hog you got there. Like them stars and stripes on the gas tank, solid custom work. What year is it?"

"It's a rebuilt '03 Road King," the biker replies in an accent the smoker can't exactly pinpoint.

"Never seen you round here before, what brings you to Middleburg?"

The biker ponders whether to give out any information about his visit to Crossroads Farm, then decides a lot of people must go there to visit relatives who are being rehabilitated. Answering won't blow his cover.

"Going over to the rehab place at Crossroads Farm to see my nephew. He's got a brain injury and he's being treated there."

"You mean cold bitch farm, don't ya?" the smoker sarcastically responds.

This catches the biker's attention.

"Why do you call it that?"

"Because I knew Kent Perless and Kyle, his daddy. Kent was a fine young man, was friends with Erika, my youngest. All the bad stuff started happening once that girl done came into his life. Next thing I know, Kyle doesn't own the farm anymore, she does, and his boy is dead. That's why I call it that. I know she was the only survivor of that famous crash, but that don't mean nuthin' to me.

"Don't see Kyle much anymore, but he goes over there and teaches music. I'd like to know how the hell she ends up with the farm and he ends up teaching messed-up kids there. That's him gettin' the shaft and her gettin' the whole mine."

"Reminds me of my girl Erika and her dolls. She loved Barbies when she was, what, seven, maybe eight. One of her Barbies was talking back to the rest of them one day, so she took it and put it in the freezer for a few days to teach her a lesson. I think someone oughta put that Michaels girl's ass in a deep freeze like Erika's damn doll."

"You got some mighty strong views about her. She did start that place for people like my nephew," the biker says, mildly defending Amanda even though he's never met her.

"What good does that do for anybody in Middleburg, having them treated over there instead of at the hospital? No offense man. I can tell you I ain't winnin' no popularity contests around here anyway. They all fought me like hell when I tried to open my tattoo joint here in their highfalutin' horse country."

"Yeah, I bet."

"Not breaking any records on sales, but tats are pickin' up in popularity, even with them e-ques-tree-an types. I notice you got a couple on your biceps," gesturing toward the biker's arms just below his shirt sleeves.

He decides not to explain his tattoos, though he knows that's what the old guy wants.

"You ever talk to the girl yourself?"

"I got nuthin' to say to her. She ain't never been in my shop. Probably thinks she's above me."

The biker spits some brown liquid into a small plastic cup he picked up somewhere, presumably at the smoke shop. "How far is it from here?"

"About a mile. Make a right up there at the end of the street, then make the second left and follow it down and you'll see it on the left side. Guess I shouldn't a said all that stuff since you got a relative in there, but everyone here knows I don't filter nuthin'."

"No offense taken. Take it easy."

He tosses the plastic cup into a trashcan, straps on his helmet, starts up his bike, and heads down the road, wondering if he'll feel the same way about Amanda Michaels.

CHAPTER 62

UNCLE PHIL

HE RIDES the Harley up the two-lane road to Crossroads Farm, noticing the occupied but unmarked SUV parked at the end of the driveway. A couple miles past the entrance, he locates a spot to park on the side of the road. After studying the map on his phone, he takes a few items out of his saddlebags and enters the dense forest surrounding the property on foot. A sturdy old oak with a wide trunk catches his eye. Within minutes, he is perched high in the tree with a direct line of sight to the farmhouse and rehab facility. Through his binoculars he sees another male, who he quickly concludes is FBI, standing in the driveway not far from the house. *One by the entrance, one close to her at all times.* About 30 minutes later he observes his mark, Amanda Michaels, walking with a woman who appears to be some kind of nurse, along with the same young man she had been escorting around during his prior surveillance visit. One day spent surveilling the facility as a fake sprinkler and irrigation system worker had paid immense dividends. Feigning work on sprinkler heads while Amanda had escorted Dexter around outside and to the horse stables provided the intel Ty Ryan needed to acquire the patient's name.

When he returns the next day, he parks his motorcycle by the rehab facility and checks in at the front desk before approaching the male patient he surveilled before.

"Hey Dex, it's been a while. I'm Uncle Phil, remember?"

The man goes in for a hug, and Dex wraps his arms around him, seeming to confirm their closeness.

"How've you been? Is everything good here?"

"I'm a captain, did you know that? My ship's out there. I'll take you on it."

"I'd love to go on your ship sometime. Maybe I could give you a ride on my bike too. Is Amanda coming by today?"

"Amanda's my best friend. She takes me out and shows me things. She takes me to the horses, she walks me down through the woods. She's my booty booty," Dex gushes proudly.

Dex yells across the room to the aide at the reception desk. "Where's Amanda? She comin' today?"

The woman looks up, then gets out of her chair and walks toward them. "I don't know, Dex."

"Can't you ask her to come over, please?"

"I guess I can ask, but only for you, Dex."

The nurse walks back to her station and texts Amanda.

Dex plays checkers well. Sometimes. Other times he executes completely inappropriate moves, like trying to move sideways instead of diagonally, for no good reason. Uncle Phil looks up from their game to see Amanda enter the room with one of the men he saw during his recon the day before. The agent eyes the new visitor with Dex, but stays near the door as Amanda begins to walk toward them.

"Hi there, I'm Amanda Michaels."

"Yes, I'm Phil, Uncle Phil."

"Well, it's a pleasure to meet you. Dex is one of my favorite patients. We've gotten acquainted over the last few weeks."

Amanda takes a seat at the table where the men had been playing. Dex loses interest in their conversation and wanders off to find a game console and play Super Smash Brothers.

"Look, I'm not Dex's uncle," Uncle Phil whispers.

Amanda starts to panic and looks anxiously toward the agent.

"Don't get up, please, everything's okay. And it took a lot to get in here. My name is Ty Ryan, I'm a former Navy SEAL. I know your dad's still alive and doing research for the government. After the plane crash, I was kidnapped by the Chinese and released later under whatever deal the U.S. cut. The government didn't tell me anything, I gathered all my information from other sources. What I don't know is why you're being protected by the FBI or why our government paid over $200 million to Hemispheres, do you?"

"How'd you get in here? I mean if you're not Dex's uncle—"

"Don't worry about it. What's this I hear about your dad disappearing?"

"What? How did you hear about my dad?"

"I told you, I have my sources. I know about Justin too."

Amanda eyes Ryan warily. There's no question the man in front of her is rock solid, despite his unkempt appearance. She looks at his arms and notices the ripple of muscles along his biceps. *Maybe he was special forces, maybe a SEAL.*

"If you won't answer how you got in, how about telling me why you came here."

"Let's just say I was curious about you. And for some crazy-ass reason I was thinking about offering you my services. For a fee, of course."

"I don't believe you. And even if I did, it wouldn't be logical for you to show up here. Who are you working for?"

"You can call the Navy Special Warfare Command in California and ask them about Ty Ryan. They'll confirm I'm who I say I am. As for logic...it's never really been my strong suit. Soldier of fortune is closer to the proper description."

"Look, all kinds of people have approached me because they heard about me surviving the crash. You could be an ax murderer for all I know." She stands up. "There's an FBI agent standing right over there, and I think I need to go talk to him."

"Whoah! Please sit back down, Amanda. Sure, everyone knows your story, but how many people know your dad's alive and he recently disappeared?"

Amanda sits back down, slowly. "Who sent you? Are you holding my dad? Or my brother?"

"I'm not working for anyone now, I guess you could say I'm a free agent. I came here because I want to help you find them."

"And you're not with the government?"

"Far from it. Never worked for the FBI or the CIA, and I left the SEALs years ago. Look, I'm damn good at what I do, and I know the Chinese government sabotaged the jet. I have a feeling they're behind your dad disappearing too."

Now that part may be true. Amanda finds herself believing him, although she can't quite decide why. "Convince me you're not FBI or working for someone involved with nabbing my brother."

"Look, I do private investigation work. On one of my jobs I came across some evidence suggesting the U.S. paid Hemispheres a hefty amount of cash, and it's been bothering the hell out of me ever since." Ryan decides not to say anything about working for Franklin. "That's what motivated me to come meet you."

Amanda hesitantly opens up. "I got a message from Dad. I think he's alive, and I have to believe my real brother is too, somewhere..."

Amanda starts to tear up, but wrestles her emotions back under control. She turns to check on Dex, who remains engrossed in his game.

"Your real brother?" Ryan is taken aback by this new information.

"Yeah. My dad's note said he ran a blood test on the boy he's been raising for the last year, and he's definitely not Justin. And my dad knows a thing or two about genetic research."

"But you think your actual brother's still alive?"

"Definitely. Whoever kidnapped him is probably using him to get at my dad."

"What's so important about your dad's research that opera-tives would kill for it?"

Amanda won't give this information up, for all she knows Ryan is working for a foreign agency. "I don't know all the reasons, and the ones I do know I'm not sharing with you."

Ryan thinks for a moment. Between his own curiosity and the prospect of getting paid, he decides he doesn't want to lose this opportunity. Besides, he can always raise this issue again later. "I'll do some homework and see what I can find out about 'em."

"That would be great, thanks. How do I get in touch with you?"

Ryan takes out a pen and scratches down a phone number.

"Don't call me on your cell in case it's being monitored. Use one of the landlines in here."

"Not to be rude or anything, but why do you think you can do a better job of finding them than the CIA or FBI?"

"Let's just say I've developed some skills since I left the SEALs, but I'm not promising anything. Don't tell anyone, not even your uncle, or the feds will do everything they can to shut me down. I'm not exactly high on their list of favorite people. Remember, I'm not doing this out of the kindness of my heart, I expect to be paid. My services are unique, and damn valuable."

Amanda starts to tell Ryan not to boss her around, she can and will talk to whoever she wants, but she stops because she knows he's right. Instead, she gets up and walks across the room toward Dex.

Ryan has followed her over to Dex and starts chatting with him. Amanda wonders about Uncle Phil, whether his aim is true or not, and walks out of the center, lost in thought. Ryan watches her leave, thinking how rude it was of her to simply walk out. He quickly says his goodbyes to Dex and heads out the entrance to find her but she's gone.

CHAPTER 63

CONVINCING

THE NEXT MORNING, Amanda visits with Dex, and after a decent interval of time she calls Ryan from a landline. He agrees to come visit that afternoon, about 3:00 p.m. Her curiosity about Ryan and what he could accomplish was like a powerful magnet attracting her attention.

Amanda returns to the rec room a little after 3:00 p.m. and sits beside "Uncle Phil" after greeting Dex, who momentarily drops his controller and hollers "Jenna! Jenna!" He gets his hug from her and immediately re-immerses himself in the game. Phil continues to play with Dex while he and Amanda talk.

"I don't believe the FBI or the CIA are making any progress. According to Solarez they're all over it, checking every Chinese diplomatic post. They are looking for any child matching Justin's description. You'd think a Caucasian kid would stick out like a sore thumb among of bunch of Asian diplomats. But he says they're focused on China, mainly Beijing."

Ryan whispers to Amanda, who somehow manages to keep

playing the video game and never comments. When she is finished, he finally speaks.

"So, lets assume he's in China, could you get us in, find my brother, and then get us all back out? Everything will be in lock-down with the North Korean leader's upcoming visit with the Chinese premier. We have to escape alive, with a child."

"Nice move Dex, you're the man!" Ryan says.

"You're the man, yes Dex, you're the man," Dex repeats loudly. "Jenna, we play next, right?"

"Maybe Dex, we'll see."

She turns back to eye Ryan.

"I thought you'd be willing to do anything to get your brother back? And its only money. I thought you had plenty now...." Ryan doesn't turn, doesn't even look her in the eye.

Amanda shoots a searing glare at Ryan, who won't meet her glare.

"How much money?" She asks him.

"A million." He says matter of factly. "It's just money. I wouldn't hesitate to pay it get my baby brother back. I mean if I had one. Three-quarters up front, the rest when Justin is safely out of China."

Ryan goes back to playing the video game, he can tell Amanda's mental wheels are turning.

Finally some real cash. But it won't do me much good if I'm dead, he reasons. Liza would be the perfect connection once I'm in China. And with logistical plans. What would her logistical services cost, $100,000? Probably more since I'll need weapons, safe houses, and untraceable transportation of some sort. More like $150,000 or 200,000.

"Is the fee the same if I go with you?" Amanda asks.

"It should be higher."

"Assume I'm comin' with you."

"We'll see. Same fee, but I wanna check out your skills, and maybe teach you a few. Not a word about this to anyone. No internet searching either, I assume it's being monitored. You read me? I'll be in touch very soon. I have solid connections inside China, but we need to develop a plan that could succeed."

"Dex, Jenna will play you now, but she's definitely no match for *the man*. Come give Uncle Phil a hug please, I have to go."

CHAPTER 64
OCEAN CITY

IN OCEAN CITY, Maryland, southeast of Annapolis, four men book a room at a no-name three-star hotel a couple blocks from the harbor. Two of them venture out well after dark and find the scuba boat. The engine department is cramped, smelly and hot, so they move on to Plan B. The flat cushions forming the aft and starboard bunk bow each hide storage compartments large enough to hold a person laying down. They drill several one-inch holes in the wood covers before replacing the cushions and returning to their room.

Per their arrangement with the Ocean City Dive Club, the men are waiting on the dock at 7:00 a.m. They will be exploring the Kathleen Riggin shipwreck site 12 miles off shore. A small clammer, the Kathleen Riggin sank after a huge swell capsized it in November, 1991. The three men presented the advanced certifications required for a cold-water, open-ocean dive to the dive master a couple days before.

A brilliant sun has risen in the deep blue sky over the harbor. The dozens of boats in the marina create a cacophony of metallic chiming as lines tap against the masts and booms, and flags wave back and forth in the blustery, shifting winds.

"Can we help you with anything?" Riess, one of the three men, calls out as he and the others watch the captain and the first mate busily organizing the wet suits, fins and masks.

"Nope, we've got everything lined up. It should be a great day," the captain replies. "So, you guys in school at the Naval Academy?"

"Myself and Barber here are visiting instructors. Paul's my friend and one excellent diving partner. We've dived wrecks in the Caribbean and were looking for something interesting to do here. I heard you sometimes see sharks?"

"Occasional black tips, duskies, sharpnose and sandbar sharks," the first mate says. "All kinds of fish hang out in the wreck, so lets hope for some good visibility."

When the boat finally arrives at the dive site, a series of buoys are placed as the ship trolls through the moderately choppy water. There's almost no other nautical activity, with the exception of one fishing boat nearby. The men can make out one or two fishermen in their seats near the stern of the boat. Once everything is organized, the captain asks the men to give their attention to Bobby, the first mate, while he goes over the safety instructions.

After the protocols are reviewed, Jones suddenly announces, "Guys, I feel like death warmed over."

Riess is irked. "We paid all this money to come out here and you don't feel well? You're still diving with us, aren't you?"

"This is the first time I've ever been seasick. I hate to do it, but I'm gonna pass." Jones dejectedly holds on to the starboard side of the boat with both hands and watches the water, giving the impression he might vomit at any moment.

"Are you sure?" Barber asks him. "What if we cut our dive short and come back to check on you? Maybe you'll feel better after a while?"

"If you want to come back and check on me that's fine, but I doubt I'll be joining you. I'll stay here with the captain."

When it appears there's nothing more they can do for Jones, the first mate, Riess and Barber finish gearing up, drop to the swim platform and make their way into the ocean.

"How about a ginger ale?" the captain suggests, "might help you feel better."

"Sure, thanks."

The captain heads to the rear of the open deck, flips open a large white cooler and pulls a ginger ale out of the ice before closing the lid and walking back over to Jones. After he hands the can to his queasy passenger, he saunters over to his chair and assumes his normal position, splaying one of his legs on top of the instrument dash and opening a newspaper. Jones tells him he's going below to use the head. Once out of sight, he lifts one of the berth cushions.

"It's time."

He removes the plywood he drilled holes in the night before and helps the man out of the storage compartment. Then he grabs a small duffel bag containing extra scuba gear.

"I'll create a diversion. When you hear his footsteps moving toward the bow, go."

The stowaway hurriedly puts on his wetsuit and positions his 15-minute oxygen tank on his back with the rest of his gear.

The captain hears a commotion and looks over to see Jones fall to the floor of the bow, yelling and writhing in pain. He drops his newspaper and hurries over to assist him. While he's attending to the distressed passenger, the stowaway slips unseen to the swim platform off the stern before silently sliding into the water. He gets a visual of his destination, then disappears under the surface.

The captain leads Jones to the cushioned seating area in the stern.

"I was headed below to puke, but then I tripped over something. God, that was painful."

"Just lay down a while, hopefully your foot will feel better, and maybe the queasiness will pass. If it doesn't, hit the head and let 'er rip."

Within 30 minutes the other divers return, having cut their dive short to check on Jones, who indicates he won't be able to dive with the group. They decide to end the excursion and ask the captain to head back into the harbor early. Once they're out of their wetsuits and gear, Riess heads dockside. He notices a small, triangular red, white and blue flag has been raised on the fishing boat bobbing in the distance. He gives a thumbs up to Barber and Jones.

Two fishermen assist the stowaway in the wetsuit onto the boat from the fold-down ladder off the stern, and one assists him with removing the small oxygen tank. They raise a small, triangular flag before pulling in the lines and cruising south.

Within several days, the exfiltration team and their stowaway on board enter the harbor in Freeport, Bahamas. One of the crew members and Ron Michaels board a Panama-bound Air Panama jet later in the day at Grand Bahama International Airport. The last leg of their journey is on a charter jet, which makes a refueling stop in Hawaii and continues westerly along the equator to their ultimate destination.

CHAPTER 65

FRENCH SIDE

ELIZABETH GARDNER CHECKS in to her hotel room on the Dutch side of Saint Martin, props open her laptop, and surfs the websites of companies offering sailing charters. The captain she chooses has a one-day sail that day, but she books a three-day trip leaving the next day, which will stop first on the French side of the island. She explains that TripAdvisor highly recommends several restaurants there and she hopes they can travel during the day and take the dinghy to the island for dinner.

The next morning, she carries one dark blue duffel bag onto the vessel. Her captain, Douglas Caperton, introduces her to his first mate, Hector. Normally the yacht sleeps two couples in addition to the crew, but Elizabeth rented the entire boat, so the three of them sail out of Simpson Bay toward Grand Case, a harbor on the French side. The seas are calm, almost glassy, and only a few occasional slivers of cloud dot the sky, not enough to block the sun even fleetingly. A small flock of brown pelicans fly overhead, gracefully flapping their wings, gliding, then flapping again.

Elizabeth enjoys much of the sail stretched out topside near the bow, her back supported by the small windows of the master berth, large-rimmed sunglasses hiding her eyes, her nose stuck in a paperback. She remains aloof to the crew, rerunning her back story through her mind: assistant at a Wall Street bond-trading firm, vacationing alone for few days before her broker boyfriend joins her after tying up some last-minute loose ends at work.

One of the analysts on the Solarez' situation team had noticed several international phone calls from Canada to Megan's Mango on the island of Saint Martin in the Caribbean. Further searching revealed Megan's was a beachfront restaurant and bar purchased about a year before. Because a significant French-Canadian community populates the French side of the island, it was deduced that Odette bought the business under an alias after Justin's delivery.

Solarez instructed a female agent familiar with the case to pose as a tourist sailing in and out of the island's harbors and extract the truth from the surrogate. After all, if Brittney Hayes could pretend to be a mental patient and meth addict to gain access to Amanda, she could play any role, including Elizabeth Gardner.

The sailboat reaches Grand Case by late afternoon and Elizabeth requests they go ashore in a dinghy for a cocktail before dinner. While traveling the short distance to shore, Hector offers to accompany her, but she politely declines. Wearing a cropped top over her bikini and a colorful wraparound on her waist, Elizabeth drops her flip-flops in the sand out of reach of the gently lapping waves of the harbor. Sounds of reggae music carry on the wind from one of the restaurants or bars, she can't tell which one. Looking around, she sees the sign for Megan's Mango a few doors down, so she walks along the beach past a few young tourists seated at a wooden picnic table. She navigates the well-worn salt-treated steps to the open-air café.

Another couple speaking in a strong accent, which she surmises is South African, enjoys two colorful frozen cocktails she doesn't recognize, each with pineapple and mango on spears beside their straws, and they laugh at something the man said. Elizabeth bides her time at a high-top table, staring out into the harbor, patiently waiting to meet Odette. The end of "Scarlet Begonias" by the Grateful Dead plays through some unseen speakers, followed by "St. Patrick's Day" by John Mayer. *What a strange musical segue,* she thinks. Although Solarez still refuses to believe Odette, the surrogate momma was in any way involved with a baby swap, primarily since he personally vetted her, buying this café and leaving Canada rather abruptly leads Elizabeth to suspect money had the desired effect for whoever needed her cooperation.

Unfortunately, she doesn't see Odette at the bar, waitressing tables, or anywhere else. After ordering a stoli and soda on the rocks, which she nurses for several minutes, she heads to the restroom to survey the rest of the establishment. On the way, she notices a small area where local artists' creations are for sale. Behind the small glass counter, Odette sits on a stool. Elizabeth recognizes her from the photos she was provided, but doesn't stop, deciding instead to continue to the restroom. By the time she comes out, Odette has left her post and stands beside the bar talking to a waitress. Elizabeth walks over to the women.

"I like the necklaces and bracelets in your case. Can I get a closer look at some of them?"

"Of course, follow me," Odette says. "Are you visiting?"

"Yes, on a charter. We're anchored out in the harbor."

They return to the retail corner and Elizabeth feigns interest in several of the colorful pieces. "The local jewelry is very cool."

"A little extra something for folks like you, people touring the islands, wanting to take a piece of the Caribbean home with them."

Elizabeth detects a slight French-Canadian accent in Odette's near-perfect English. "I'm Elizabeth. And you are?"

"I'm Natalie," she answers, confirming she does not want to be traced.

"Is your family from France? I hear a hint of a French accent."

"No, Canada. I bought this place about a year ago."

"Must've cost a small fortune, but what a fantastic location, right on the water."

The woman pauses before responding. "I was very fortunate. I inherited some money when my dad passed away, and I always wanted to run a café on a beach. My family came to Saint Martin once when I was younger and I dreamed of coming back. Now it's a dream come true. I have the pleasure of meeting people like you from all over the world during the day, then retire to my boat. I love being rocked to sleep by the waves."

Elizabeth knows Odette's father is alive and well, but says nothing. She buys one of the bracelets with cash and heads back to her seat. She orders another drink, barely touches it, then meets Hector at the dinghy to head back to the sailboat. Once on board, she sends an encrypted message to Solarez who suggests she first determine if Odette stays alone on her boat, and if she does, to visit her the next evening and confront her on the swap of Justin.

Elizabeth watches the sunset from the yacht most of the evening after enjoying her dinner with the captain and Hector at one of the fine French restaurants along the beach. When she and the men part company, she uses her small binoculars to watch for a dinghy leaving somewhere near the café to try to determine which boat Odette lives on. But she fails to locate her that night. She wonders if she stayed with a boyfriend on shore or if she somehow missed her. So many dinghies had gone back and forth in the course of the evening, figuring out which one ferried her target was a daunting mission, especially from the moored sailboat.

CHAPTER 66
HOPELESS PLACE

WHILE ODETTE PERUSES a magazine in the sleeping berth of her sloop, she listens to an acoustic piano playlist through Spotify. She never hears the rowboat or the intruder who slips aboard, silent as a tiger targeting an unsuspecting gazelle. When she senses someone in the room with her, she glances up from her reading and sees a black face mask and a pistol with a silencer pointed at her head.

"If you want to live, don't scream."

The intruder drops a backpack on the bed near where she lays.

"Who are you?" she asks, sitting up on the bed. "If you want money, I'll give it to you." She tries to remain calm.

Using a few front teeth, he rips a 6-inch piece of duct tape off the roll he withdrew from his pack, keeping the pistol trained on her.

"This is temporary, until I know you're not gonna scream. I'll take it off soon because I want you to answer some questions. Cooperate and this bullet won't go through your skull."

He slaps the duct tape over her mouth with latex-gloved hands.

"Turn over and lay down on your stomach."

With her heart pounding and tears streaming down her cheeks, Odette slowly rolls over.

"Put your hands behind your back."

She doesn't move them at first.

"Now!"

She hesitantly complies.

The man tries to tighten a zip tie around her wrists but realizes he can't without putting his gun down. The moment he lays it on the bed, Odette kicks her legs out against his body, causing him to fall backward. He manages to grasp the pistol on the foot of the bed as he falls to the floor. In a second, he's on his feet and trains the muzzle at her again as she tries to scramble out of the cabin.

"Stop right there!"

Odette freezes only steps away from him, her eyes wide with terror. He backhands her across the face. "You dumb bitch. Try that again and it'll be the last thing you do. Lay back down."

Out of options, she gets back on the bed, wondering if falling prey to the almighty dollar is coming back to haunt her. She should have known it was too good to be true when the Asian man told her he had a simple way she could earn a lot of money—$100,000 down and another $200,000 after the delivery of her surrogate baby. All she had to do was not react to the slight change in the baby's appearance when the nurses cleaned up the newborn and handed him to her.

He zip-ties her ankles, and she doesn't try to escape this time.

"You know what, I changed my mind, I'm keeping that damn duct tape over your big mouth. I'm allowed to do that, right? Ever hear of BTK?" he asks her, fully aware she can't answer him. "It stands for bind, torture, kill."

He reaches into the backpack and pulls out a long hypodermic syringe, which he sets on the counter beside the bed along with the small vial of liquid. Odette sees the needle and the meds and her fear amps up to sheer terror. She shimmies her body toward the foot of the bed and flops to the floor.

"Binding done, time for the torture part," he says, turning around and realizing she's not on the bed anymore.

"Stop movin' around!"

He pulls her up with two hands and flops her back on the bed. He fills the syringe three-quarters full and jabs it into her right buttock. Odette tries to scream but only manages a muffled groan through the tape, then nothing at all as the paralytic agent squelches any further movement. The intruder takes several other vials out of his pack and fills a second hypodermic needle with a cocktail of their contents.

He plunges that one into her left buttock, supplying an overdose of Lorazepam and two other medications that together cause her breathing to become shallow. He waits about 20 minutes, periodically checking her pulse until it is barely perceptible. He gathers up the extra zip ties, syringes, and small vials from the counter with his gloved hands and replaces them with loose pills and a few unmarked prescription bottles. He begins whistling the melody to "We Found Love in a Hopeless Place" by Rihanna and Calvin Harris.

"I wonder if Calvin Harris wrote all those lyrics?" he asks his semi-conscious victim while opening up a small, clear plastic bag and locating his roll of duct tape. "Ya know he's a musical genius. Ya think Rihanna wrote any of them? Damn, all she has to do is sing and move her body. Who cares if she can write lyrics, you agree?"

He slides the bag over her head and tapes it shut around her neck with a double layer of tape. Her faint exhalations partially fill the bag like a half-deflated helium balloon for a few seconds before she suffocates.

Charon holds no personal grudge against this woman, just wants to do the job right. After he checks for a pulse and fails to find one, he surveys the cabin area carefully, assuring himself nothing but the random prescription meds are being left behind. Using a pair of scissors, he cuts the zip ties from her wrists and ankles takes the bag off of her head, and removes the duct tape from her neck and mouth, being extra careful not to cut her skin.

Why does he think of this kind of upbeat music while killing? He hadn't been born a killer, he was desperate for money and couldn't be picky about the type of work he got. The jobs had haunted him at first. That's why he'd try to lighten the mood by listening to some catchy songs before or during the act. What once distracted him from the depravity of what he did was now part of his routine.

He shoves the used tape and ties into the plastic bag, then slips off the sloop stern with his supplies into the rowboat and silently rows back to shore.

Word of Odette's untimely demise travels like lightning through the shops and restaurants of St. Martin the next morning and is soon confirmed by local websites. Minutes after messaging the bad news back to the U.S., Elizabeth receives a response: There's a new mission at hand and she will receive her instructions within 24 hours. She closes the laptop, prepared to move on to the next job but feeling like she missed a golden opportunity to discover the truth about Justin.

Charon hits the end key on his burner phone, confirming the successful operation, then turns away from the view of the bobbing boats in the harbor. *As usual, he doesn't know his true employer, but he assumes a Chinese source. He traced his last incoming wire transfer to a Hong Kong bank.*

Pushing the balcony door closed behind him, he walks back into his hotel room to the king-size bed where his luggage sits. He sets his wheeled bag on the floor and extends the pull handle, then slings his black backpack over his right shoulder. After taking two steps toward the door, he stops. He slides the pack off his back and on to the bed, slides out his laptop, and flips it open near the white pillows he barely touched during his stay. Flopping down in front of the screen, he taps in his password, establishes his secure connection, and types into the search bar: "who wrote the song we found love in a hopeless place?"

"I thought so," he says out loud, while sliding the laptop back into his backpack. He grabs the handle of his other bag and hurries out of the room so he doesn't miss his flight.

CHAPTER 67
SURVEY

"SIR, we may have a lead on a mother who gave up a baby for adoption near Tillsonburg a week before the Michaels' delivery occurred," the FBI analyst tells Solarez. "She's in Simcoe, the next town over."

"Let me guess, 50 people live there and any sniffing around we do will raise all kinds of red flags."

"No red flags will be raised. When a child is adopted in Ontario, it's done through the Ministry of Children and Youth Services. About a year after the adoption occurs, the Child's Aid Society of Hamilton, or CAS, reaches out to the mother who gave up the newborn to check on her well-being and assess how she felt the adoption was handled."

"So, we're going to get that information from CAS on this mother?"

"Actually, almost everything I told you is fake, I wanted to see if it sounded believable. We're going to send one of our agents to talk to her under the guise of working for CAS."

"Well, you had me fooled. Good work."

A Canada Air jet touches down in Hamilton, Ontario, and after clearing customs, the operative finds her French-Canadian contact, the one holding up a small sign with the words "Elizabeth Gardner" written on it in black permanent marker. They get in the car and he drives the 50 kilometers to the Lazy River Inn, one of the few places to stay in Simcoe. Elizabeth knows, because she checked out the hotel situation herself. She also researched the origin of the name Simcoe, since it sounded to her like some kind of manufactured product. But the city was named after a British Army general who had helped pioneer the area. She imagines General Simcoe riding on horseback down Main Street to the Canadian trading posts as they make their way to the inn.

Elizabeth first reaches out to Natalie Michele through a voicemail, which goes unreturned. She calls a second time and leaves another polite message about the need for the one-year adoption follow-up survey, stating she would like to meet Natalie at the Ontario Community and Social Services building and can "be available at Ms. Michele's convenience." She finally receives a text:

Do I have to do this? I really don't want to.

Elizabeth responds during normal business hours the next morning to avoid arousing suspicion.

I can understand your hesitancy, and I realize this is a difficult subject for you. However, the Child and Family Services Act requires that I conduct this survey with you. Are you available later this morning?

Okay, 11:30, where in the building are we meeting?

On the first floor there are some square tables in the lobby inside the front door. I'll meet you there. I'm about 5-7, shoulder-length brown hair. I'll be wearing reading glasses and a nametag.

Elizabeth adjusts the prop glasses on her nose and clips her fictitious ID badge to her tan blazer as she settles in at a table to wait for Natalie.

This takes me back to my high school drama club days, she thinks. I always enjoyed pretending to be someone else. Hopefully no real Ministry employees will notice me before I get the information I need from her.

Around 11:25 Elizabeth looks out the window of the government building and sees a thin young woman in a loose-fitting tweed coat using her shoe to put out a cigarette perhaps 20 feet from the entrance. Elizabeth knows it's Natalie based on several photos she was given, and carefully notes the spot where the butt is situated. The girl enters through the double doors and begins scanning the tables. Elizabeth stands up and waves to get her attention. As Natalie cautiously approaches, Elizabeth gives her a warm smile.

"Ms. Gardner?"

"Yes, but please, call me Elizabeth. I appreciate you coming in for our survey. Take a seat."

Natalie can't be more than 110 pounds, perhaps five-foot three, including her shoes with a bit of a heel. She avoids eye contact and fidgets, visibly uncomfortable with the situation.

Elizabeth goes through a list of general questions before she asks the ones that will help her determine whether or not Natalie Michele was in on some kind of scam, giving up her son for a considerable sum of money paid by the people the FBI and CIA want to find.

"What was the primary reason you decided to give up your son for adoption?"

Natalie squirms, and her eyes dart around while several

seconds tick by. "Look, I was working in the Odyssey Club. Do you know about it?"

"I've heard of it."

"It's one of the best nightclubs around here. The same locals come in night after night, and I was, uh, doing some things I shouldn't a' been. Please, I don't wanna get in trouble."

Elizabeth looks at her compassionately. "Drugs?"

"I...I felt like my life was spiraling out of control. I was in the middle of the pregnancy when I realized I was such a train wreck I couldn't give him the home he deserved. One of the cocktail waitresses at Odyssey had a friend who gave up a baby for adoption and she's the one who suggested it. I contacted CAS, and they did the rest."

"Was it CAS that recommended the hospital in Tillsonburg?"

"Yeah, I think it was them."

"How long were you there?"

"Well, it was my first child. I went in the night my water broke, and I was there a little over a day, I believe."

"The records reflect it was a natural childbirth?"

"Correct."

"Were you satisfied with the labor and delivery process?"

"What's that got to do with anything?"

"Service satisfaction is part of our survey. We ask all adoptive mothers about it."

"They were fine I guess, but I was very conflicted about giving up the baby. So that kind of clouded up everything for me."

"Who came to the hospital to support you during your labor and delivery?"

"My parents came, but not the father, I didn't want him there. We only went out a few weeks, and he ended up being a drug dealer, which is where I got my...Anyway once I decided to give up the baby, there was no reason to involve him." Natalie's voice catches on the last few words.

"I see. All right —"

"Look, this is why I didn't want to do this. It just opens wounds for me. There isn't a day that goes by that I don't think about what would have happened if I had kept him."

"Well, I can assure you your son is in good hands, and his parents are taking great care of him." Elizabeth delivers this line smoothly, while recognizing that there is a decent chance that Ron Michaels has been unwittingly raising her son.

"Can you tell me who they are?"

"Not in this type of adoption, I'm afraid. But we screen all adopters thoroughly and our file indicates no adverse information on them whatsoever."

"Oh, okay. So are we done?"

Elizabeth pretends to be reviewing her notes and deciding if she has other questions. After a minute or two, she looks up sympathetically at Natalie. "Yes, I think we're done for today. If we need anything else, we'll contact you. Best of luck to you, Natalie."

"Thanks."

With that, the young woman rises, heads toward the doors and exits without looking back.

Elizabeth waits a few minutes before also exiting the building. Using a latex glove, she stoops to pick up the cigarette butt, placing it in the small ziplock bag, then continuing back to the inn. Once she's in her room, she sends an encrypted message to Solarez, advising that she probably has a good DNA sample.

I would not consider Natalie Michele a suspect. Based on her appearance, I don't believe she was paid, and she has no idea where her baby ended up.

Solarez responds, That's consistent with our financial analysis of her. There's no money in any of her accounts and she's been overdrawn twice in the last six months.

Within two days, Solarez has one burning question answered: Natalie Michele's DNA is a familial match for the DNA obtained from Ron Michaels son at Sherwood.

CHAPTER 68
CROSS-TRAIN

AMANDA LOCATES the slip of paper with Solarez' number on it and texts him.

Don't freak. I'm going to see my ex-boyfriend again and I don't want your agents following me.

Yes, it's a lie, and she knows they're monitoring her for her own good, but they can't know where she's going or who she's meeting. She walks into the kitchen in the back of the farmhouse, opposite of where the agent is most likely asleep in his car in the drive. She hits the send button on her phone, waits five seconds, turns it off, and leaves it on the counter. She softly opens and closes the door and runs through the woods toward Route 50. It's a beautiful morning, the sun is barely up. Not two minutes later, a black Ford pickup truck pulls up slowly on the shoulder of the road.

"How'd I know you'd be driving a pickup?" Amanda asks Ryan sarcastically as she hops into the truck.

"Morning. Let's get rolling." He shifts into drive and lifts his coffee from the console to take a sip.

"Solarez is going to have his minions searching for me as soon as he gets my text. You know that, don't you? I feel like he's my surrogate dad, always concerned about where I'm going and what I'm up to."

"I'll watch for a tail. We're going to the Golden Eagle indoor range because they've got a self-defense academy with training rooms too. I have all the weapons we need."

"You think I'm some kind of powder puff, that I don't know what I'm doing, and you're out to prove it today, right?"

"You said it, not me..."

"They weren't training us to be wusses the two weeks I was there."

"Yeah, but you weren't qualifying for anything. Solarez pulled strings to get you into the training."

"So what's your point?"

"I'm pretty sure I just made my it. My main goal is to keep you alive. Well, both of us actually. I'm friends with one of the owners, so he's getting us in early."

"What kind of weapons did you bring?"

"Glock, sniper rifle, and KA-BAR knives."

As they drive the two-lane highway, both of them occasionally check the side-view mirrors, but they don't see anyone following them.

A guy stands behind the check-in counter, with a Remington logo T-shirt when they walk into the training facility. Ryan knows him.

"You got a visitor with you, huh? What're you gonna need this morning?" The guy is asking Ryan the questions but looking at Amanda curiously.

"I've got eyes and ears. How about a box of 50 rounds, 9 mm. We'll start on a couple 25-yard lanes before we move to 50."

The clerk hands Ryan the ammo and he carries it, along with two bags—one short and one long—over to the 25-yard ranges. Ryan lifts a case out of the smaller bag and gently places it on the countertop in one lane. After opening it, he lifts one Glock out and puts it on the counter, pointing down the range, with a magazine and ammo, then does the same in the second lane. He positions a target in each lane and finally steps back several feet.

"Okay, why don't you go ahead and show me your stuff."

Amanda is annoyed by his chauvinistic, condescending attitude as she approaches the gun, but she doesn't say anything. She realizes he may have her back one day soon, or vice versa. She opens the box of ammo and places five rounds into the magazine. Watching her every move, Ryan can tell she isn't a complete beginner when she places her index finger along the upper shaft instead of on the trigger. He wonders why she only placed five rounds in the magazine since it holds fifteen, but decides not to press the issue. Amanda places the pistol down on the counter and toggles the target out as far as it will go.

"Now what, just fire?"

"Sure, aim for the head."

Amanda lifts the Glock, points down range toward the target, slides the safety, places her index finger on the trigger, and fires. Within a number of seconds she exhausts the five rounds with the brass casings skittering to the right of her on the floor. She reels the target back in after placing the pistol back down on the counter. Four of the rounds are within the perimeter of the head, one is wide.

"Not bad. Why'd you only load five rounds?"

"My instructor at Quantico said to do it that way because it's easier to keep track of what's in the magazine. He said it's fine to load the whole magazine in tactical settings but to stick with five on the range."

No longer feeling the need to test her, Ryan walks over to his lane and begins firing as she reloads and sets up a new target.

Several minutes later they move to the 50-yard range with his rifles. He watches her technique again before he starts shooting, not giving any indication of how he thinks she's doing. When they finish, he asks the clerk to watch his shooting gear.

"Let's go over to the self-defense academy." He slings another small bag over his shoulder and they head to a room with a large padded mat on the floor. "You were trained in martial arts and defensive maneuvers, right?"

"Is this another test?"

"Look, if I'm going to manage this crazy-ass mission, I need to know who I've got as my wingman, or should I say, wing person." Ryan smirks.

"I haven't trained since my time at the academy, but let's go."

Ryan rummages through the bag, turns away from her, and inserts a protective cup into the front of his pants. He looks in the bag again and takes out two sets of headgear, one of which he tosses to Amanda, and they put them on and strap the chin guards in place.

"Let's do some defensive hand-to-hand combat. When I approach you, see what you can do to repel me."

He moves toward her on the center of the mat, she thrusts her left arm forward and tries to trip him by wrapping his body over her thigh. He counters her maneuver with a quick stroke of his arm that takes both of her legs out from under her, landing her flat on the mat.

"Okay, you got me that time. Let's go again."

On the second approach, she rapidly kicks toward his head and he moves back a split second before contact. As she retracts, Ryan grabs her raised leg and turns it, making her lose her balance, then releases it, having made his point. Amanda grimaces with frustration.

"Did they teach you Krav Maga, jujitsu, or Yugo?" he asks her.

"I don't remember the names of everything, I just know the maneuvers."

"This time, as I come in, I want you to knee me in the groin like you're going to flatten my nuts into pancakes. I have a cup on, so don't hold back."

Ryan approaches her and attempts a backhand chop towards her torso. Amanda repels that maneuver and brings her leg up swiftly, smashing it into his crotch. Ryan winces.

"Damn, that's what I'm talking about. That's your best move."

They walk off the mat and into an adjacent room, where Ryan slides back a mirrored closet door. He brings out a base-mounted foam rubber dummy wearing ripped clothing and pushes it to the center of the room.

Amanda warily eyes the dummy. "We didn't have knife training."

"Didn't have it during SEAL training either. I learned it while I was with a contractor after I left the military."

He heads over to his small bag and brings out two long KA-BAR knives. He hands one of the knives to her by the handle and keeps one for himself.

"Let me guess, you want me to try to kill you by stabbing you in the torso?"

"You can try, but you won't get very far since they're rubber."

Ryan hands her a lower leg holster that she puts on after watching him strap his around his calf.

"First I want you to work on grabbing the knife from the holster, then we'll use the dummy to practice thrusting."

Ryan demonstrates how to remove the knife rapidly from its position on his lower leg and thrust it into the torso of the dummy. He repeats the motion three times, each time taking only a second. Amanda tries to emulate his technique and manages to improve a little each time, but can't quite match his speed.

"Keep trying. Every second counts," he tells her.

Next, he teaches her how to throw the knife into the dummy from several feet. She's able to cover the distance, but the knife drops to the ground instead of sticking into the dummy about half the time, so he re-positions her hands on the weapon and has her flick it differently. As she gets the hang of it, the knife sinks into the dummy three out of four times.

Then he explains the importance of stealth. "Let's say you're feigning injury, you're coiled on the ground, and the hostile doesn't know your knife is strapped to your leg. When he moves toward you, thrust your knife as deep as you can, pull it out, and thrust it again."

He instructs her to curl up on the ground and he approaches her. She thrusts at his torso twice and he retreats and approaches her again several times.

"Your chances of using hand-to-hand combat or your knife are higher than using a pistol or rifle, at least on a mission like the one we're planning," Ryan tells her.

After another half-hour of knife practice, Ryan loads the equipment into the back of the pickup and they head back toward Crossroads Farm. As he drives, Amanda peppers him with questions.

"Have you talked to your Chinese contacts? Any confirmation that Justin's in Beijing? What about my dad?"

"Nothing on your dad. My contact is working on tracking down Justin, and some other plans I've devised."

"You've devised? What's that mean?"

"I don't have enough intel to discuss it yet." Ryan explains some of the logistics of getting out of the U.S. and getting into China. "I'm working on our fake passports and visas. We'll also have letters of introduction in case we get stopped and are pressed for details about our business in China."

"What will our business there be?"

"Dunno yet. But our back story will be we're meeting with Beijing business contacts on behalf of our company. I'm meeting with a buddy in logistics soon to iron out the details. Right now we're stopping at the shop of another one of my buds so he can take some measurements."

"Measurements of what?"

"You'll see."

"How many of your *buddies* will be involved by the time this is all over?"

"Enough to give us a fighting chance to survive."

CHAPTER 69
PURE GENIUS

AMANDA STANDS in the center of the room while Ryan's friend gradually moves the camera mounted on a dolly a full 360 degrees around her, stopping periodically to take more pictures. Next, he tells her to place her chin on the ledge of another piece of equipment. It makes a slight whirring sound as it captures the contour and dimensions of her head, including the fine details of her face. Ryan goes through the same process before he thanks his friend and they leave.

"That guy is pure genius," Ryan tells her once they're back in his truck on the road. "No telling how many unbelievable disguises he has created. The CIA is his biggest client."

"He doesn't know anything about our plan, right?"

"Only that we needed some disguises, off the books. I did mention I wanted Chinese ones, so he may guess we're headed to China, but it could be Taiwan, Japan, he won't know. He's also lining up some surveillance equipment for us. Oh, and before I forget, I need your sizes—underwear, bra, shirt, pants. I know it's kinda personal, but you're gonna need clothes to complete the different looks. Jot 'em down on that notepad."

He motions toward a pad of sticky notes and a pen in the center console before continuing. "I think we're going to pose as Canadians first. They sound pretty much like us, so we won't have to worry much about accents. And we'll be from the part of the country that doesn't speak fluent French so that doesn't become an issue."

"Sounds like you've been busy planning." She writes down her sizes. "Are we getting cool secret agent toys too? Fountain pens that fire bullets—"

"Nothing that high-tech. Lightweight kevlar vests and caps. We'll have weapons, a small drone with a night-vision video camera and joystick controls, not much more advanced than the off-the-shelf ones. I'll also need some remote-detonating explosives, a few small aerosol spray containers, and some blow darts."

"And we're smuggling this all in with us?"

"Nah, I'll carry some of it, but the rest I'll ship to my contact who will already be there."

"What's your plan for getting us out of the U.S. and into Beijing without Solarez and the FBI stopping me?"

"We'll go over that later. You need to wire the agreed money into an offshore bank account I set up. I gotta pay some of my buddies in advance for their help."

"Okay, I'll do that the day before we leave so my uncle doesn't catch wind of it and shut us down. I don't know how he would, since it's my money, but I don't wanna take any chances."

"That won't work, they want to be paid now."

Amanda glares at him. "Guess I'll have to risk it. I'll do it when I get back to the farm."

"You should learn some Mandarin too."

"In a few days? Oh sure, no problem."

"You won't be fluent. Common phrases, numbers, that kind of thing. Here's a book."

He reaches into the pocket on the back of her seat and gives her a well-worn, palm-size paperback. She picks it up and leafs through a few pages.

"Looks like someone got a lot of use out of this. You, I'm guessing?"

"Yep. You can get a small digital translator too, if you want.

You say something in English and it'll say it back in Mandarin. You just need to learn the basics, like, 'Do you sell C-4 here?'"

"What??"

"I'm kidding."

Solarez receives the report from his agent who tailed Ryan and Amanda.

"You need to take her into custody for her own good, sir. Ryan is in contact with her. What if he was hired to get to her? Why else would he be interested in her?"

Solarez runs the fingers of his right hand along his solid cherry desk as he thinks.

"Harming her obviously isn't part of his plan. If it was, he would've done it by now. He's either working for the kidnappers and is planning to deliver her to them alive, or he somehow got his hooks in her. I'm not sure which."

"But sir, Ryan was working with Franklin, and Franklin's dead. What if Ryan was involved? The girl could be next."

"Instead of messing up his plans, whatever they are, let's use Ryan to our advantage. If he's working with the kidnappers, he may lead us to them. I'll reach out to Braningham, maybe we can convince the Foreign Intelligence Surveillance Act judge we need a bug on Amanda Michaels so we know where she is at all times, and a warrant for Ryan's international calls and internet activity, so we know who he's talking to. In the meantime, stay as close as possible to both of them."

CHAPTER 70
TRACKING RYAN

THE CHINESE ANALYST tracks the location of the Ryan's pickup on his monitor through the tiny device magnetically attached to the undercarriage of the black Ford. First, Ryan visited a shooting range for a number of hours. Afterward, he travelled to a non-descript facility in a shopping center. The analyst later did a background check on the business but still wasn't sure why Ryan went there.

He types up his report to his supervisor in the Chinese embassy, recommending personal active surveillance of Ryan.

CHAPTER 71

DROPPED

BARBARA GROFELT and a young associate from her law firm, Andrew, enter the lobby of the high-rise. As they approach the elevator bank, the doors are closing on a crowded car. Grofelt knifes her hand through the narrow slit between the two doors, forcing them to reopen, and they squeeze in. Moments later they are standing at the large horseshoe-shaped receptionist station at Franklin's law firm.

"We're here for a meeting with Mr. Lyle about the Hemispheres versus Michaels case."

The receptionist speaks into the small mouthpiece on her headset. "Barbara Grofelt is here for Mr. Lyle."

A few moments later James Lyle walks into the reception area to greet them. "Barbara, so good to see you, even under these terrible circumstances."

He ushers her and the associate into a large conference room with an expansive wooden table, numerous chairs, and a wall of windows overlooking the street below. Another attorney from Lyle's firm is already there. As soon as they have been introduced and are seated, Grofelt begins.

"Your former partner convinced me to join this high-profile case, and I was relying on your firm to do the heavy lifting. How is this going to work now that Paul is dead?"

"We were planning on pressing forward, with the two of us taking the lead in Franklin's place."

"Well I want out." The two attorneys replacing Franklin look at Grofelt in disbelief as she continues. "I came here as a courtesy. I can file a motion to withdraw from the case without your consent, but I didn't want the press to hold anything against you if you decide to carry on without me. I don't feel comfortable continuing. I'm not trying to cast any aspersions against either of you, but I don't know you from Adam. I only agreed to work on the case because of my relationship with Paul."

"Let me know by tomorrow afternoon if you want to move forward. I'll file my own motion to withdraw and won't make any court pronouncements that would adversely affect your case."

The two attorneys look at each other incredulously.

"There's nothing we can say to convince you—?" Lyle begins.

"Not unless you can bring Paul Franklin back from the grave. I'll wait to hear from you tomorrow."

With that, Grofelt stands and starts for the door with young Andrew looking feebly at both of the attorneys as he grabs his expandable file off the table and stuffs it into his oversized brief-case on his way out.

At 4:00 p.m. the next day, Lyle calls Grofelt at her office.

"We had a partner meeting this morning and we're requesting that you wait a couple days to file the motion. We'd like to go to the government and see if we can get them to pay us nuisance money, even if it's just case expenses, so they won't file for attorneys' fees against us if we seek to dismiss the case. Remember, since you were part of the case, your firm could be held responsible for reimbursing their potentially massive fees too."

Grofelt hates being told what to do, but she hates the thought of paying thousands of dollars to the government even more. "Fine, I won't file, but I don't want the press getting wind of any of this. This has to be handled in a private discussion with the assistant U.S. attorney representing the government. I'm not so sure I shouldn't be the one negotiating the issue."

"Oh no, we brought you in on the case, we should be the ones to negotiate. Please don't file anything until we get back to you."

CHAPTER 72

SOUTH BEACH

RYAN TEXTS LIZA:
Hey - How u been?
Fifteen minutes later he gets her reply.
Surprised to hear from you. Whassup?
Let's get together. Will be coming to NYC, can we meet?
Her response is nearly immediate.
Can't meet in NYC. At fashion trade show, South Beach, FL. Two more days left.
South Beach sounds appealing. Some sunshine would be a nice complement to getting together with Liza again.
I can be there tomorrow. Just need your hotel.
He smiles and hopes she bites. If there's one thing he's come to enjoy about Liza and their relationship, or the lack thereof, it's the adventure, unpredictability, and intensity of it. He tries to recall how long they've been doing this as he waits for her to answer.
The reply comes five minutes later. Did she wait to send it on purpose?
The Rendezvous Hotel, South Beach.
He texts back immediately.
I'll be there tomorrow. Won't have this phone, look for a 202 area code.
Ryan hops online and books a flight and hotel under an alias supported by one of his many fake driver's licenses.

When Ryan arrives at his hotel room the next morning, he opens the sliding glass door on his balcony and scopes out the Olympic-size pool, which is very enticing in the 91-degree heat of south Florida. After slipping on his trunks and t-shirt, he strides toward the bank of elevators and texts Liza from his burner phone.

Arrived.

Liza talks to one of her inside sales assistants at the company's New York sales office. "We've got to ship the new line of dimpled leather handbags to Macy's by the end of this week, Albert. I've been promising their buyer for weeks. There will be hell to pay if we don't—"

"I don't have confirmation that the container hit the port yet," Albert counters.

"That's insane. Talk to the freight forwarder and get that container unloaded. Call me back this afternoon."

Liza hangs up and stares down at the pool through the sliding glass door of her room. She notices a guy swimming laps and one or two people hanging out in the chaise lounges on either side. Not much of a crowd since it's only 9:15 in the morning. *Is that Ryan?* She thinks to herself. She walks out on the balcony, cell phone in hand. She looks again, but still can't tell for sure until he pulls himself out of the water and walks the short distance to pick up his towel off a chair. It's him, she'd know that gait anywhere.

She scrolls through her messages, sees a new one from the 202 area code, and decides to call instead of texting.

Down at the pool, Ryan hears a phone ringing. At first he ignores the unfamiliar ringtone, then realizes it's the burner phone. He looks at the number and sees the NYC area code.

"Hello?"

"Hey, it's Liza. Was that you who just got out of the pool?"

He looks around in several directions, but doesn't see her. "I guess so. Where are you?"

"Look south. I'm on a balcony on the 10th floor, waving."

Ryan spots her and waves back. "There you are. I thought you were in meetings today."

"I'm supposed to be there by 10:00, but I could spare a few minutes. I'm getting in the shower, care to join me? Room 1016, I'll leave the door open a crack."

"On my way."

Ryan approaches the door to Room 1016, pushes the door open, and walks inside. He hears running water through the slightly open bathroom door. As he tries to make out her nude body through the steamy glass shower walls, he unties the drawstrings of his trunks, which drop to the floor, and he takes several steps toward the shower stall. Instead of opening the door, he presses his body against it so she can see every part of his taut body.

"What took you so long?"

Ryan says nothing as he pulls the door open and steps in. He presses his body against hers and their tongues meet as their arms intertwine. Her hands drop to his ass and pull him toward her. Neither notice the water pulsating against their heads.

Ryan dries off on the mat outside the shower and walks out of the bathroom with his towel draped over one arm. Liza admires his strong body. She wraps a towel more demurely over her breasts and it barely covers the V at the top of her thighs. Ryan notices a few beads of water still collected in her cleavage above the towel that is begging to be ripped off of her. He flops face-down on the bed and she slaps his ass.

"I know you want something. Ty Ryan would never fly down here just for good sex."

"What makes you say that?"

"I know how you operate."

"Let's talk this afternoon. What time do you think you'll be done with your show, or sessions, or whatever you do at these events?"

"Why don't we meet down by the pool at 4:30?"

"Sounds good. Guess I'll go work out, I don't exactly have a busy agenda. I'll meet you at the swim-up bar and we can talk over a drink."

He picks up his wet trunks and slips them on, ignoring the cold, wet fabric. Years of SEAL training make that minor inconvenience, well, a real minor one. For a split second, he flashes back to his ice-water training in Kodiak, Alaska, where purposely wading into freezing arctic waters was a daily training ritual.

"See you later," he says and walks out.

Liza goes into the bathroom to take care of her makeup, wondering what Ryan's up to and how he thinks she's going to be involved.

CHAPTER 73

LOGISTIX

AT 4:20, Ryan wades into the shallow part of the pool where a series of round, concrete stools line the swim-up bar.

"Jack Daniels, on the rocks with a splash. Oh, and I'll need a margarita for someone who's joining me." He admires the female bartender who wears a bikini top and her hair pulled back in a high bun as he places his order. *I could live in South Beach, no wonder people love this place.*

Liza wades toward him a few minutes later wearing a tiny red, white, and blue bikini over her thin frame. Her eyes hide behind brown Michael Morse wayfarer sunglasses. Ryan looks at her and admires her youthful, athletic shape. The split second of lust passes.

"Okay, now tell me the real reason you flew down to see me." She places the swizzle straw on the stone bar and takes the first sip of her margarita.

"I have a sensitive but lucrative contract mission. I'm going to Beijing and need help with logistics. My entry will be through southern China."

"Just logistics? What does it involve?"

"We're going to be doing some surveillance, but the less you know the better."

"Of course. But our factories are in Dongguan, not in Beijing."

"Then I need you to come up with a reason to be in Beijing, and soon."

"I'm assuming if I ask who our client is, you're not going to tell me."

"You assume correctly."

"What's the rush? This takes some time."

"There's an event taking place."

"How many on your team?"

"Two."

"No one's being eliminated?"

"No. I'm offering you $200,000.00 for what I need."

"Wow, keep going."

"Lawyers, guns, and money. Just kidding. No lawyers. I need specific weapons in a duffel bag in a locker in Shenzhen, along with cash, which I'll provide on top of the $200,000, and two burner phones. You'll need a phone too. I need two adjoining rooms in two Beijing hotels, close to Tiananmen Square. A rental car, or any car that is untraceable."

"This is too easy, what else?"

"I need you to buy a commercial drone before we arrive and get us video of all persons coming and going at a certain residence. This is where you earn your keep. It needs to look legitimate, like you're doing it for a real estate company, surveyor, or contractor. Then have the drone in the duffel with the other supplies."

"Here we go. There are some high-value targets in this residence, right?" She asks.

"Nope, no high value targets."

He takes a healthy swig of his drink and runs his finger down the condensation clinging to the exterior of the clear plastic bar cup.

"Who's 'us'? You said 'get us video.'"

"Again, the less you know, the less you can spill under, um, duress."

Liza sips her drink a few moments. "I could be some kind of utilities inspector or government employee shooting the footage for a new sewage project. We're adding so many new apartment buildings we have to lay more pipe."

"I like it."

"Anything else?"

"Yeah. Once we get to Beijing, I want to be able to reach you in case something else is needed. We won't plan to meet, but I may need more support if we run into a problem."

What else?"

"The car needs to be at the Beijing train station, and we'll be using it for several days."

"And?"

"You may need to plant some items on the ferry between Hong Kong and Shenzhen. I might think of some other stuff, but that's it for now."

"$200,000.00?" she confirms. "What weapons?"

"I'll make a list. You told me before you have a weapons source. Reliable?"

"Very much so under normal circumstances, but you're giving me no time at all."

"I know. I'll need your wire transfer info. Can you get on this by tomorrow and be in China in two days?"

"My great aunt lives in Beijing, and I haven't seen her in like seven years. And now they allow you to visit other parts of the country as long as you have an approved travel visa."

"So, you're in?

"For that kind of cash, I'm in. You must be getting paid well too, Ty, which usually means there's a lot of risk involved. Should I be worried about you?"

Ryan smiles, knowing he has just the right person inside to make the operation come together, but he says nothing. The movement of the bartender's breasts—barely covered by her hot-pink fringed bikini top—while she shakes a martini a few feet away distracts him for a moment.

"No, you don't have to worry. I don't take on suicide missions."

"I'm not sure if that's reassuring or not. When will you be in Beijing?"

"Soon. I'll include the exact dates on the weapons list."

"I take it you have the visas lined up?"

"Yep, along with our Canadian passports. We're going to be from Toronto."

"I can have your letters of introduction to you tomorrow. I'm thinking you'll be IT specialists designing the software to interface with a Chinese factory's large Canadian customer. Can you build out that role?"

"Sure. We'll need to have some markers that you don't place until you've accomplished the logistics, like the rooms and cars."

She looks at him with a frown.

"I know it seems stupid, you would never get compromised, right? But I've gotta have some way of knowing if something goes wrong. I don't wanna use the burner phones except as a last resort."

"Okay, the Beijing train station can be the first place. Then you pick a place close to one of the hotels. How about a pink peace sign? We can pick the exact spots later, in my room."

"Let's use the lobby computer instead."

"Fine. How are you planning on getting back out?"

"Same way we got in."

"That sounds too easy."

They both take a sip of their drinks. Liza lays straight back from the concrete stool and submerges her torso and head in the pool to cool off. As she sits back up and wrings out her hair, Ryan watches and hopes for another encounter with her later.

"A toast." He holds his plastic cup toward her.

"To the Chinese version of capitalism," she responds, pressing her drink to his and leaning in for a deep kiss.

CHAPTER 74

DOPPELGANGER

HEATHER LASTING'S daily existence mainly consisted of competently handling her administrative assistant job at a Manhattan bond trading firm, dealing with type-A traders, without going off the deep end. But her daily routine was turned upside-down about a month after the Hemispheres crash. With Amanda Michaels' photo splashed over the cover of so many magazines and newspapers, it wasn't long before the similarities between her and the famous survivor started being noticed. It began when Heather hit a nightclub with her friends and the bouncers and other patrons mistook her for Amanda.

"Ms. Michaels, thanks for coming. Folks, let her and her friends through. Right this way, please."

When she and her two girlfriends left an hour later, there were several paparazzi snapping photos as they walked down the sidewalk. The pictures were published online the next morning and in the *New York Gazette*, the first of several Amanda Michaels sightings in Manhattan. But a week or so later the truth came out: it was Heather Lasting, Amanda's doppelgänger.

At Sunset Cafe, where Heather and her co-workers sometimes headed for lunch, patrons would lean in and provide encouragement.

"I believe in you, Amanda."

"So glad you bounced back."

"I love your charity page on Facebook."

A graduate of NYU, Heather was three years older than

Amanda, but that never mattered, the resemblance was uncanny. Heather kept her hair in the same style as Amanda's because, why not? May as well enjoy her few minutes of fame.

David suggested a Doppelgänger rendezvous for charity. They could appear together on one of the local talk shows in DC. The idea started to grow on her. David mentioned the plan to Solarez, who was concerned about Amanda's security, but didn't say "no." He told David as long as he was provided all the details no less than seven days in advance, he would make sure Amanda was safe.

However, all of this negotiating had taken place before Ron Michaels vanished. And in light of that, Solarez wanted to veto what he had previously approved. He called Andy Michaels and asked him to break the news to Amanda, but Andy was having none of it.

"This is a big fundraiser for Broken Halo. We've spent all the promotional money, or nearly all of it. There's no evidence that Amanda's at risk. You're having her tailed 24/7, right?"

"Right, but in light of your brother's disappearance, I don't think it's a good idea."

Confident he had inside information about Ron that Solarez didn't, Andy again refused to tell Amanda or cancel the fundraiser. Ultimately, Solarez caved. He increased Amanda's detail from two to four agents and told them to escort Amanda to the TV studio, the Washingtonian Hotel, and back to Crossroads.

Naturally, the production staff of Daytime DC knew this was

a prime opportunity to get picked up by network news, so their staff reached out to Heather and offered to pay for her flight to Washington, where she and Amanda would appear on their local afternoon talk show. Amanda also wanted Heather to appear with her that night at a fundraising dance to benefit her Broken Halo rehab facility and Healing Heroes, the charity that had featured her at their annual Kennedy Center event the first year after the crash.

The producers asked Amanda and Heather to wear matching black skirts, white blouses, and black pumps. The network would provide hair, makeup, and matching purses from a local boutique to make the women look as much alike as possible.

Amanda publicized the fundraising party through social media on the charity FB page, Instagram, and word spread, including to everyone who currently attended or recently graduated from Middleburg Academy. With social media and the students alone, the party tickets sold out days before the show even aired, and including charitable sponsorships, donations were expected to hit $75,000.00.

Amanda texted Heather in advance and offered to pay for her hotel room for the weekend so she could enjoy the party and do some sightseeing. Heather graciously accepted and decided she would fly in early Friday morning before their appearance that afternoon and fly back to New York on Sunday. Heather was both excited and anxious about meeting Amanda before the show.

While Amanda knew many MA alumni were attending, she had no idea that Jonathan and Amber would attend, much less Charlyne, Iris, and several other high school friends, until David told her it was going to be like a high school reunion when they talked on the phone the day before the event.

After the countdown from the production assistant, Amanda and Heather walk hand-in-hand onto the stage and stand in front of the couches beside the show's host, Rachel McKnight.

"Okay ladies and gentlemen, all of you who think the young lady on your left is Amanda Michaels, please raise your hands."

About half of the 100 or so studio audience hands go up.

"I assume the rest of you think the young lady on the right is the real Amanda Michaels?" Heads nod and hands raise in the audience as the TV camera pans across the studio. The host asks Heather and Amanda to walk off the stage and come back. She repeats the exercise and the audience is split 50/50 again. The real Amanda Michaels is revealed, and the conversation between the three women on the stage becomes fun and spontaneous. Heather tells her funniest stories of mistaken identity in Manhattan and sheepishly admits she enjoys "being Amanda."

"I think we're sisters from different mothers!" Amanda says.

"I can't imagine what she went through, with the crash and all," Heather admits, "but I told Amanda I'd like to try being her now for a few days to see if I could pull it off."

"You could easily be me, Heather, but I couldn't fake being a bond trading assistant, even for five minutes," Amanda laughs.

McKnight then adopts a more serious visage. "I need to ask you about your memory, Amanda. Has any of it returned from before the crash?"

"Unfortunately no, although I'm continuing to work with a professional."

"I'm so sorry to hear that. One more thing, I read an article online recently by Lorainne Townley of the Washington Inquisitor. It seems to be getting a lot of buzz right now, and it suggests that—"

"That I have magical powers? Or does this one that say I'm an alien?" Amanda finishes her question, and loud laughter from the live audience erupts.

"Did you receive any experimental treatments from your late

father, as Lorainne suggests in her article?" McKnight looks down at some notes on her desk, lifts the notes up to be accurate. "She says her sources claim he gave you experimental treatments for your cell telomeres, and that it may delay the natural aging processes."

Amanda laughs, but inside she's ready to explode. *How could this information have gotten in the hands of a reporter?* "Rachel, I told you I don't have any memory from before the crash and I don't know anything about any kind of treatment on my cells, but, really, I wouldn't mind staying right here in my 20's.""

Amanda, Heather and Rachel all laugh and gesticulate together.

"Stay right there, we'll be back after these messages." McKnight tells the television audience before the live cameras cut away.

For the charity event in Georgetown, Amanda and Heather agree to remain dressed alike for the first hour so visitors can have photos taken with them for a fee, which will raise money for Healing Heroes. They both plan to change for the rest of the festivities. The party will feature a popular DJ known for providing solid dance music.

"Heather, I want to prank some of the staff at Broken Halo. Would you help me pull it off?" Amanda asks her before they leave the TV studio.

"How so?"

"I'll have a limo service waiting at the hotel to take me back to Crossroads on Saturday morning. What if you—"

"Get in the limo instead and see how long I can keep people fooled?"

"Yes! I'll show up an hour or so later at the farm and you can head back to D.C. after we punk the staff."

"That'll be fun! When do you want me to head out in the morning?"

"Let's say about 11:00. We'll wanna sleep in before we head back. I'll buzz your room and have the limo service all arranged. Not a word to anyone, got it?"

"Not a word."

Amanda never mentions the "limo service" is being provided by four FBI agents.

CHAPTER 75
JUST DANCE

WITH THE PHOTO SHOOTS OVER, both Heather and Amanda stand in front of the mirror in Amanda's hotel room on the ninth floor, high above the ballroom where the dance has started. While Amanda touches up her makeup, Heather pulls a piece of candy out of her bag.

"Wanna gummy bear?"

"No thanks, I'm not into candy."

"You sure? My friend gave me a bunch of them. They're pot gummy bears."

"I've never had one before. Is it strong?"

"Nah, not if you just do one. C'mon, it'll be fun." Heather pops a raspberry one into her mouth, then unwraps the other and hands it to Amanda, who stares at it.

"I'm not sure..."

Heather doesn't press her, she just reaches inside her little bag for her mascara and starts touching up her makeup. Out of the corner of her eye, she sees Amanda pop the edible in her mouth.

"You won't notice it for at least a half hour, maybe an hour."

"I may need it by then. My old boyfriend from high school is going to be here with his new girlfriend, who we both graduated with."

"That sounds awkward."

"Everybody says Jonathan and I were inseparable before the

crash, but I don't remember any of it. Can you imagine having no memory of a guy you were once joined at the hip with?"

"I've only had one or two binges where I don't remember what happened. I can't imagine losing all of my memories. Who's the girl he's with now?"

"One of my teammates from soccer. She made her move on him after everything happened, which at the time didn't bother me since I didn't have any feelings for him. But we hooked up again not too long ago."

"No way. Didn't you feel bad, I mean for the other girl?"

"Not really," Amanda says, applying some lip liner. "I mean, he was mine before he was hers."

Heather sprays a little perfume as Amanda notices a text on her cell phone.

When are you guys coming? This place is packed.

It's from David. He sends another one before she can respond.

Half of our class is here, including Jonathan and Amber. Hurry up!

Amanda texts him back.

Be down in 5.

"That was David, another friend from high school. He was one of Jonathan's best friends and he just told me Jonathan's here."

Heather has music playing through her phone. A few songs are by the Chainsmokers, up-tempo electro pop. She starts dancing and Amanda joins her. Then Heather stops and takes a few sips from her wine glass.

"Thank you so much for inviting me to do this, I'm really having a good time."

"I'm glad you came down. It's been fun for me too, and it's helped me take my mind off some stuff that's been going on."

"Like what?"

"I feel like I can trust you. I have a baby brother who's been kidnapped, and I have no idea where he is."

"Oh my God! Kidnapped?"

"I just found out a few days ago. I can't tell you anything else."

"The cops are trying to find him, right? Why didn't you cancel this?"

"The FBI, they're looking for him. But no, I would never cancel, and I can't let on anything happened either. Please, you can't breathe a word about this to anyone, not even that I have a baby brother. Let's go down and dance. Are you ready?"

"You poor thing. How can you even think about partying?"

"It's keeping me from obsessing about finding him, for a few hours anyway."

Amanda drinks the rest of her wine and puts the glass down on the dresser near the TV. A minute later, they're getting off the elevator on the ballroom level.

Together they enter the ballroom, passing the table where the ticket-takers sit. Two attractive women in their 20s smile at them as they pass, and a photographer at the door snaps another picture of them. Once inside, Amanda sees David talking to Adam and Taylor, two other guys who graduated in Amanda's class. They greet Amanda and she introduces them to Heather.

"Here's my twin sister, Heather. She came down from New York," Amanda shouts as the DJ's sound system pumps out the bass.

Taylor says, "Yeah, we saw you two before when everyone was taking pictures. Nice to meet you, Heather."

Amanda scans the throng of attendees until she spies Jonathan standing on the edge of the dance floor. She figures the blonde next to him with her back to her must be Amber. At that moment, Jonathan sees her too, so she turns back toward David and the other guys. The music pulsates and the lights on the stage project blue and red shades across the room.

"Don't Let Me Down" by the Chainsmokers and Daya begins playing and Amanda grabs Heather's hand and starts dragging her toward the dance floor.

"Don't ya know, I'm losing my mind about now!" Amanda yells at her, feeling the pot kicking in.

"You're just playing, right?"

"Of course! It's just a line in the song."

As they dance, David joins them with Adam and Taylor. The entire room is a sea of bodies moving in hypnotic motion to the song, and the vibration of the bass pulses through Amanda's body like seismic waves. When the song ends, the DJ kicks right into Calvin Harris' "This Is What You Came For."

Across the room, Amanda sees her uncle and his girlfriend standing at a high-top table not far from the packed dance floor. She breaks away from the group and makes a beeline in their direction. Becca sees her and walks toward her with open arms.

"What a great dress, you look fantastic!" They embrace.

"Thanks so much Becca. I'm glad you're here."

Uncle Andy stands and hugs her. She notices her other uncle and aunt, the Simons, as well.

"Aunt Barb! Haven't seen you in so long."

They hug briefly. Amanda still bristles when she remembers Aunt Barb is the one who signed the papers that landed her in the psych ward after Kent's death.

Amanda doubles up on the B.S. as she shakes her uncle's hand, "Uncle Steve, missed you too."

"This is quite the fundraising event, what a great idea. I saw Heather a little earlier, you guys truly are twins!" Uncle Steve says.

"She's so much fun, I've enjoyed getting to know her."

Amanda notices David, Jonathan, Amber, and Charlyne all chatting and having a drink together.

She pulls Andy aside for a moment, "I need to tell you something. It's pretty important."

"Okay, go ahead."

"I may have a lead on getting Justin back."

Amanda only has the detailed plan from Ryan, not an actual lead, but it could result in them locating Justin. And it's a good way to clue her uncle in so hopefully he won't be completely shocked if she disappears for a few days.

"Tell me more."

"Not a lot to tell yet, just a lead."

"Did you call Solarez?"

"No, not yet. Hey, I gotta go talk to some of my old school friends."

"Sure, keep me posted as you get more info."

Amanda heads for ex-classmates.

"Charlyne, I'm so glad you're here. Amber, nice to see you," Amanda lies. "Hi Jonathan."

She gives him a partial hug, knowing Amber is watching her carefully. They all engage in conversation about the charity and how everyone has been doing over the summer. Amanda whispers with Charlyne for a minute or two. She's feeling mischievous and leans over to ask Jonathan if he would like to dance. He takes a quick look over at Amber, who is talking to Charlyne, before they head to the dance floor, where Jonathan wedges his way into the middle, holding Amanda's hand to guide her.

Amanda wonders how long it will take Amber to figure out they are on the dance floor together. She and Jonathan begin dancing, and she sees Heather not far away, dancing with both Adam and Taylor. She looks back at Jonathan, whose stare sears through her, making her body tingle. Impulsively, Amanda kisses him, and he instinctively encircles her in his arms, both knowing many of their friends have seen this PDA. They put a little distance between themselves and continue dancing.

Almost immediately, Amber appears between them and faces Amanda.

"A mind is a terrible thing to waste, unless it's yours, bitch," Amber sneers, just loud enough for Amanda to hear, then turns back to dance with Jonathan as if nothing had happened.

Amanda decides to find Heather and get back to being happy. As they laugh and dance, one song segues into another and they lose track of time.

At about 11:15 p.m., Amanda says goodbye to David, Uncle Andy, Becca, and everyone else she sees in the immediate area, explaining she is totally exhausted and going to head to her room. She finds Heather before she heads to the elevators.

"Remember, be ready at 11:00 tomorrow morning to head to Crossroads. I'll show up shortly after you do."

"Got it, although I don't know how long I'll last before they figure it out."

They hug and Amanda takes the elevator to her room as Heather returns to the party. She gained some new admirers throughout the evening, including David, Adam, Taylor, and some other Middleburg Academy graduates from the year ahead of her class, whose names she can't recall. At about 1:00 a.m., the DJ announces the final song and they close down the party. They all say their goodbyes and invite Heather to meet them for Sunday brunch.

Heather is thankful she only needs to remember her room number and find the elevators.

THE TWO BLACK Escalade SUVs occupy the middle of the covered hotel portico, awaiting Amanda for the trip back to Crossroads. One undercover FBI agent stands waiting, his ubiquitous earbud and clear coiled wire visible from his left ear, two others wait in the driver's seats.

Amanda opens her hotel room door around 10:45 a.m. and nods at the FBI agent down the hall, perched in an uncomfortable chair near the elevators. Feeling casual after the night of formality, Amanda is wearing a pair of large sunglasses, a worn UVA hoodie, gray leggings, and the cross-body purse Daytime D.C. provided, and she is carrying a small duffel for her clothing. She and the agent ride the elevator down to the lobby and walk out under the portico. She says hello to the other agent who opens the rear door for her.

The two SUVs pull away from the hotel and down the horseshoe drive, but suddenly the entourage slows to a crawl and stops on the right side of the street, hardly a block away.

The driver turns to the agent in the back seat of the SUV beside Amanda.

"Solarez wants us to check her for identification. Let's have a look at your ID."

"That's ridiculous," Amanda replies, and clutches the purse lying next to her with the strap still over her shoulder.

The agent in the back seat says, "Can you please show us

your ID? We have direct orders not to go any further until you do."

Amanda grasps her purse now with two hands, but the agent beside her reaches for it also. They momentarily tussle over it before the agent wrenches it away from her and unclasps the top. He digs through its contents and locates her driver's license, which he pulls out and reads aloud, "Heather Lasting, from New York."

"Dammit, Solarez was right." He presses on his earbud, "Code red, we're heading back to the hotel with Heather Lasting. We need to find Amanda."

Both SUVs turn on their blue and red grill flashers and do 180s, tires screeching.

"It's just a prank, we were going to fool the Crossroads staff," Heather tries to explain, but the agents are not buying it.

As soon as their vehicles squeal to a stop, all four agents burst out and sprint toward the hotel. The one who rummaged through her purse for the ID yells to her over his shoulder, "Sit tight!"

She waits for a moment to make sure no one is coming back for her, then stuffs the purse in her duffel bag and runs full tilt toward Foggy Bottom.

CHAPTER 77
EXITING

OUT OF BREATH from the dash away from the hotel, Amanda pulls open the heavy glass doors at the Executive Board Company office building on the corner of M Street Northwest and 25th. She's not sure why Ryan picked this place. As she approaches the banks of elevators on both sides of the lobby, she sees a man sitting on a padded bench on the opposite end. It's Ryan, but he looks decidedly different in a tan sports coat and off-white button-down shirt, and his hair is now jet black rather than dirty blond. As he directed, she's wearing a sweatshirt with the hood up and a pair of sunglasses. He's on his feet by the time she nears the bench, walking down the hall to the left, and she falls in step behind him. He pushes open the door to the women's room and she follows him inside.

"Anyone in here?" His male voice sounds out of place echoing off the walls of the women's restroom.

No response. He turns the thumb bolt on the door and drops a small duffle bag on the floor at her feet.

"Change into these. They've had too much time to mark you in what you're wearing."

"Who?"

"The FBI, your brother's kidnappers, whoever is after your dad, take your pick."

She picks up the duffel and heads toward one of the two stalls, but Ryan stops her.

"Nope, change right here. I have to study every part of your body."

"Are you serious?"

"Dead serious. Do it."

She gives him a stone-cold stare before reluctantly taking off her hoodie and short-sleeve shirt. Then she unbuttons her jeans and wriggles out of them, leaving her completely exposed other than her bra and pink thong. He pulls a pair of jeans, bra, shirt, and shoes out of the duffel and looks at her.

"Take your bra off."

She unhooks the front clasp between her breasts and the bra drops to the floor with her other clothes. He examines every part of her body like a dermatologist doing a complete cancer scan, walking behind her, lifting up her hair, looking carefully at her neck, inside and behind each ear. He searches her scalp with his fingertips for any raised surfaces and finds none. Then kneels down and studies her bottom half just as thoroughly.

Amanda is shaking, both from the cold and the humiliation of being subjected to Ryan's obsessive inspection.

"The shoes and the socks need to go too."

"You do it," she insists, trying to regain at least the slightest control of the situation. She lifts one foot followed by the other and he pulls off her socks and shoes.

"Slide the thong down so I can see all the fabric."

She slides the thong partially down her thighs, holding both sides.

"Satisfied?"

He feels through the fabric in the crotch and finds nothing.

"Okay, it's fine."

She slides it back up. "Happy now that you sexually harassed me for no good reason?"

"Trust me, it *was* for a very good reason."

He sees the hamsa necklace around her neck, the only item of jewelry she is wearing.

"You can't bring that. Could be tracked."

"I have to. You don't understand—"

"What I understand is it could be used as a tracking device. The tiniest sliver of metal can be used by someone who knows what they're doing. It can't come."

"My dad gave it to me, and it's how they identified me after the crash. It would be seriously bad karma not to bring it."

"Bullshit. I don't believe in karma, we determine our own fate. Hide it in here somewhere, and when we get back from the mission you can come get it."

He fishes around in his duffel bag and finds a small baggie and hands it to her. She grudgingly removes the hamsa and puts it in the bag, then surveys the bathroom for a spot to hide it. She opens the cabinet under the sink, feels around, and finds a little crevice where she can leave the necklace.

"Okay, its hidden."

"The clothes should fit." Ryan says, trying to be more accommodating after making her strip down and leave her necklace behind.

Amanda gets dressed in the new outfit. Ryan hands her a pair of slip-on lightweight running shoes with no laces.

"Not bad on the shoes. Did a woman pick these out for you?"

He doesn't answer her. "There's a surveillance cam in the lobby, so we're going to walk out separately. I'm going to dump your old clothing in the trash can in the men's room and we'll meet down the block toward 25th."

Ryan's arm is up as soon as they meet on the corner, and within 30 seconds a cab pulls over. He opens the door for her and slides in next to her.

"McKee's American Pub in Manassas, 9812 Main Street."

The cabbie plugs the address into his GPS.

"Got it man," the cabbie says, then finds the local news channel and puts his ear buds in.

Ryan whispers to Amanda, "This pub is less than a mile from the airport. We're taking a charter jet from here to Toronto. If the pilot wants to chit chat, we're scouting locations for a movie. You shouldn't have trouble remembering what it's about. It's about a girl who has altered genes and may be immortal."

"Very funny."

"Anyway, I'm Roger, one of the executive producers, and you're my assistant, Rachel."

Amanda rolls her eyes and looks at the fake passport he hands to her.

Ryan continues in a low whisper, "We'll be going from the municipal airport to Toronto Pearson International. After changing disguises, we'll board a Cathay Pacific jet with our Canadian passports and visas to Hong Kong. We're IT techs, we design server networks, and are in China to help coordinate the servers between a Beijing company and its subsidiaries in other parts of China. Once we arrive in Hong Kong, we'll take a passenger ferry, where you normally need to clear customs, but most likely, we're going to jump ship and swim to a dock. This is one of the riskier parts of the operation. Once we're back on land, we'll have supplies in a locker that my contact left for us, including additional clothing and weapons. Questions?"

"Plenty, but I won't start asking them yet."

CHAPTER 78
MANASSAS REGIONAL

THE CHANTILLY AVIATION DASSAULT FALCON 10 streaks down the municipal runway and lifts off from Manassas Regional Airport. The flight attendant asks Roger and Rachel if either of them want a drink. She and the pilot form the entire crew.

"I'd like a cup of tea, any hot tea you have," Ryan looks over at Amanda.

"Just a water for me."

As the attendant walks toward the plane's tiny galley for their drinks, Amanda reclines her chair and falls asleep within seconds. The charity event and the stress of the mission have drained every bit of energy from her body.

"Don't tell me she disappeared! She can't vanish!" Solarez shouts at the analyst.

"She was at the charity event where our agents were on her around the clock. She went to bed at the hotel that night and got in our car the next morning to head back to the farm. When you contacted us with your suspicions about her being the doppelganger, we found the ID for Heather Lasting in her purse and returned to the hotel to find Ms. Michaels. But they had switched IDs, and the person we had in the car was the real Ms. Michaels. By the time we located Ms. Lasting in the hotel and realized our mistake, Ms. Michaels was gone."

"Incredible. How could we be so inept?"

"Sorry sir, she pulled a fast one on us. At least we can track her."

"Right. How long will that take?"

"A matter of minutes. I'll get some analysts on it."

Solarez storms into the ready room.

"What've we got on Michaels?" he roars.

"We've tracked the signal to an office at 25th and M Street, sir."

"Okay, send two plainclothes agents to that building pronto. What's in there?" he asks, peering over the analyst's shoulder at a bird's eye view on his monitor.

"The Executive Board Company, some kind of think tank or professional advisory firm."

"Connect me with the two agents on site so we can communicate as soon as they enter."

Five minutes later, the agents arrive. One provides real-time video feed through a small recorder attached to his lapel as they walk through the lobby. The other agent holds a device that he studies while they walk past the elevators and head to the left down a hallway.

"It looks like she's in the ladies' room."

They knock, announce their intent to enter, then open the door. The video shows two stalls, two sinks, a soap dispenser, and a hand-dryer, but no one inside. The agent checks the tracking device again and opens the cabinet under the sinks. He feels around and finds the baggie with the hamsa. Solarez sees it on the monitor and sighs.

"Well, we know they were here. And with the way the neck-lace was hidden, it looks like she had plenty of time to think about it, so this probably isn't a kidnap situation."

Solarez studies a map on another monitor.

"What's near there, a subway or train station?"

"The Foggy Bottom Metro Station is closest," one analyst replies.

"Send two more agents. I want you two to canvass every taxi cab company that services DC to see if any of them picked up a man and woman fitting Ty Ryan's and Amanda Michaels' descriptions. They would never use Uber since it requires a credit card. Cash-paying customers, that's who we're looking for."

Solarez paces back and forth. Where could they be headed? He thinks. No. She wouldn't be crazy enough to try to travel all the way there, would she?

"Put agents at Washington Reagan National Airport, Dulles, and Baltimore Washington International. Make sure they have photos of the targets. All TSA agents should be alerted as well. And I want twelve analysts working on this."

Solarez rubs his thumb and fingers over his chin. "Does Amanda Michaels own a U.S. passport?"

"Yes, but it hasn't been used, at least not yet."

"Well that's not reassuring."

"Sir, she wouldn't be dumb enough to use it, would she?"

"True, especially if she's with Ryan. Contact the CIA director and ask him to send an agent to Beijing."

"Sir, in three days the North Korean leader is visiting China's President in Beijing. You don't think—?"

"The timing is significant?"

"Yes sir."

"I certainly hope not."

CHAPTER 79
SHERWOOD

GUARDS on either side of the convoy clear the three vehicles through security and allow them entry to the compound grounds. In the back seat of the last black bulletproof limousine, CIA Director Isaacson turns to look at Solarez.

"I want you to stick around after my talk today and meet with these guys individually. This is where we'll get our leads."

Isaacson stands beside the small speaker's lectern in the room where the Dirty Dozen presents their lab findings each week. He hopes his more casual stance will personalize his message and make this highly-intelligent but socially awkward group of researchers more comfortable with having the director of the CIA in their meeting room. He also knows they consider Ron Michaels a friend in addition to being their boss and are highly concerned about his disappearance.

"I'm sure you're worried about Ron Michaels, and I want you to know we are mobilizing at every level of the agency and working with FBI counter-intelligence to find out where he's been taken. And I say 'taken' because I'm sure he didn't leave on his own volition. He disappeared during a special outing with his son and their nanny in Annapolis, actually, it was the Disney Day parade, and he hasn't been heard from since."

Isaacson knows about Justin Michaels too, but doesn't think Ron's employees need to know about that troubling part of the investigation.

"You realize he was coordinating all the work we're doing, right?" Fletcher asks.

What Fletcher doesn't mention is his evening rendezvous with Monica at the hotel. He's starting to freak out about his secret transgressions, especially now that the government will likely be examining everything with a fine-toothed comb. He's been ultra-careful and doubts any investigation would ever detect the minuscule amount of blood he's been 'borrowing' from the lab, but he's still worried to death.

"Yeah, Ron was the glue here." Kabo adds.

"Which brings me to the next piece of business. We're placing Walston in charge of your research. He will be your glue, until we can bring Ron Michaels back."

Like a half-listening, half-dozing kid in class who gets called on, Walston jerks to attention, a reddish tint spreading over his cheeks.

"Huh?"

"Yes Walston, you now hold the reins, and we'll give you access to Ron's data. All of you need to pull together. The work you're doing was approved by the president, and he's expecting me to provide regular progress reports to his national security team."

Walston thinks to himself, *No one asked me if I wanted this assignment,* before responding. "But once you find Ron, he'll return and lead the remaining testing, right?"

"Of course. Now, you're probably wondering about this gentleman beside me, so let me introduce him." Isaacson gestures toward a chair at the front of the room occupied by Steve Solarez. "This is Agent Solarez with FBI counterintelligence, and he's heading up the investigation into Ron's abduction, which is going to involve all of you. There might be something you know or something you saw that could help lead us to his abductors. So, I'm going to ask you each to talk to him informally after this meeting, and he'll follow up with you as necessary. Would you like to say a few words, Agent Solarez?"

Solarez stands up to address everyone. "I want to echo what Director Isaacson just told you. You guys might hold the key to a lead. No tip, no unusual detail, is too minor. We want to consider everything, no matter how small or trivial it seems. This is the preliminary phase of the investigation."

"Are you going to subject us to polygraph tests or something?" Fletcher is half-joking, half-terrified.

"We're not intending to polygraph everyone at this time. However, as you were advised when you accepted this classified work, you can all be subjected to polygraph at any time."

Solarez sits in the small conference room at a round table in one of the four chairs. The walls are bare, except for a single picture of Albert Einstein standing at a lectern, delivering some famous lecture, he presumes. He looks back at Walston, the first researcher he's questioning.

"That old photo of Einstein, where was that taken?"

"I have no idea." Walston is way more nervous about his new "acting chief" role than Solarez recognizes.

"It appears to the intelligence agents and analysts who reviewed the data, including emails here at the lab, that you enjoyed a relationship with Ron Michaels. Would you agree?"

"We got along fine. We weren't close friends, but we got to know each other pretty well. I'm trying to stay positive, but I'm worried about him and I hope you guys find him soon."

"Well, I'd be lying if I told you there weren't a lot of foreign governments after this telomere research. "How am I supposed to carry on this research without being Ron Michaels?"

"We're going to give you access to the data, including Ron's personal materials. Did he ever say anything to you or give any indication of trouble with regard to his research?"

Walston thinks but can't come up with anything. "Not that I

recall. He's a big brainstormer though, and he encouraged me to apply other biological breakthroughs to our telomere research."

"Okay, keep me posted if you think of something." Solarez stands to open the door and find the next member of the research team.

Walston follows his lead and gets up from the table. "Actually, there was one thing, but it's probably nothing."

"What's that?"

"He had me drop a folder off at his brother's Georgetown law office when I was going to visit my folks one time. I just dropped the folder off, but he was insistent that I slide it through the mail slot over the weekend. I mean, I was going over the weekend anyway, but it seemed, I don't know, like it was very important that I did it just like he wanted." Walston shoves his hands into his pockets and starts to walk down the hall.

"That seemed unusual to you?" Solarez calls after him, and the researcher turns back around.

"Yeah, a little. Just because that was the only time he asked, and I couldn't figure out why he didn't overnight the papers to him."

"Okay, thanks for that."

Solarez makes a mental note to follow up on that information.

"So, you've finally made your way to the lowly administrative assistant. You know, we tend to know more juicy stuff than the researchers. But you knew that, that's why you wanted to talk to me last, right?" Randi Middleton teases.

"Sometimes that's true." Solarez smiles.

Randi doesn't return his smile. "You'd better find Ron. And in one piece too. I've got one thing to tell you. I don't know if it means anything, but he borrowed my laptop because he had something he wanted to type. He gave me some reason why he couldn't use his own. I thought it was strange."

"How long did he borrow it for?"

"He took it home one night and brought it back to me the next morning. He said he didn't have Excel software on his Mac, so he needed to borrow mine, cuz it ran Microsoft."

"Do you still have the laptop?"

"Yeah, at home. Are you guys still gonna be here tomorrow?"

"I won't, but a couple other agents will be here following up. So yeah, bring it in and my computer people will look at it." Solarez decides there's a lot of fertile ground to be plowed here at the lab, and maybe the laptop will provide a solid lead.

CHAPTER 80

CHEATING

THE MAN SURVEYS the area below from the roof of the hotel, his earbuds pumping a dance track into his ears. The north and east sides won't do, with lush grass close to the building. The west side is a parking lot, but shrubs line the foot of the hotel. The southern exposure is perfect, a solid concrete parking lot. He walks back to the metal door leading to a stairway that is rarely used, but mandated by the building code. The door is propped open by a shim he placed in the hinge on his way out. He checks it behind him after he walks through to confirm it stays slightly ajar. He descends the stairs, checking the exit doors at each landing before he arrives on the seventh floor, then leaves the stairwell and returns down the hall to Room 732. After he looks both ways for surveillance cameras, he slides a keycard into the door and enters.

Fletcher's favorite night has arrived. He exits the elevator with the vial of Amanda's blood stashed in his inside jacket pocket and a small bouquet of red and white roses in his left hand. After knocking lightly, he waits for Monica to open the door and hopes he can talk her into spending a little time in the hotel room before they head out for dinner and drinks. The door opens and Fletcher eagerly enters, but when he notices the muzzle of the pistol aimed right at him, his face turns ashen.

"You didn't know Monica was my wife, did you, you punk bitch!" the gunman seethes through clenched teeth.

Fletcher knows better than to try to run. He freezes in place, the flowers still in his hand.

"Take a seat at the desk, Fletcher, and don't even think about yelling, you damn house wrecker." Charon keeps the gun trained on the scrawny scientist as he creeps to the chair and slinks down in it. "Bet you're sorry now, aren't you?"

"She never said a word about being married."

"You write down on that piece of paper your apology to me."

Fletcher looks down at several sheets of hotel stationery and a pen. He tries to pick up the pen, but his hands are violently shaking.

"Write something like, 'I'm overcome with guilt. I'm so sorry about what I've done.' Then sign it."

Fletcher doesn't ask questions, he just starts writing: *I'm overcome with guilt*. "I wrote the first part. What was the rest?"

Charon looks over his shoulder.

"I'm sorry about what I've done." He watches Fletch writing. "Now you sign your name and date it."

Fletcher complies.

"Where's your wallet?" he demands.

Fletcher pulls it out of his pocket and holds it up in his right hand. "Right here."

"Put it on the desk next to the note, I want to check something. Now, stand up and put your hands behind your back."

"What for?"

"Shut up if you know what's good for you."

Fletcher stands up with his hands behind his back and feels the man putting thick plastic zip ties around his wrists. After that, the man pulls out a small roll of duct tape and rips off a piece to put over Fletcher's mouth.

"Hey, I don't know what you think you're doing—" Fletcher protests.

Charon backhands him with the gun across the back of his head. Fletcher falls to one knee, but gets back up.

"Follow my orders." Charon presses the strip of duct tape across his mouth. "I'm taking you to the top floor where Monica is waiting, and we're going to chat." He grabs Fletcher's bound wrists. "My Glock is going to be right here in my jacket pocket pointing into your back, so don't try to be a tough guy. If you follow my instructions, you'll be walking out of here after we all talk this out."

Charon puts his ear to the door to listen for any noise in the hallway, then he jerks Fletcher behind him, opens the door, and edges out into the hall. He positions Fletcher in front of him and they head toward the emergency stairwell where Charon pulls the door open and shoves Fletcher through. They start trudging up towards the rooftop.

Fletcher's mind whirls. Why is this guy setting up a confrontation between me and Monica? I wrote his stupid apology note. Wait, did Monica set me up? Fletcher can't bring himself to believe Monica was involved. We were in love, right?

As they pass the ninth floor and a sign stating, "Roof: authorized access only," Fletcher finally stops obsessing about Monica and concludes he isn't coming back down alive if they reach the roof. He jerks his entire body around and breaks away from his captor. He hauls ass toward the ninth-floor door and reaches it before he realizes he can't turn the round knob to open it since his hands are bound behind his back. This brief hesitation allows Charon to get within a few steps of him. Charon lunges toward him and plunges a needle into Fletcher, just below his right shoulder blade. Fletcher collapses on the concrete stairs, unable to move due to the paralytic agent.

Charon takes stock of the situation. Fletcher appears to be 5-foot 8-inches tall and must weigh no more than 125 pounds. Charon removes a small pocket knife from his back pocket and cuts the zip ties holding Fletcher's wrists. Then he flips him onto his back and begins pulling him by his arms.

"We found love in a hopeless place—" Charon sings almost to himself but loud enough that Fletcher can hear his depraved, twisted voice. "You shoulda never fallen for that booty, Fletcher. Sex is the downfall of so many a man."

Fletcher's eyes are wide open in terror, but Charon doesn't notice. He pulls him one step at a time, back up past the ninth-floor landing and toward the rooftop, taking a few breaks along the way, complaining about how damn hard his work is. Fletcher feels the concrete scraping against any skin that is exposed on his body, but cannot express his discomfort.

Stooping and grabbing Fletcher's body, Charon forces his torso up against the edge of the four-foot wall surrounding the rooftop's perimeter. After he leans over and sees no movement, he puts both hands around Fletcher, half-lifting, half-rolling him on to the top of the stub wall. He gives his victim's body a powerful kick to launch it away from the edge of the building. For a split second, he thinks about Fletcher's too-short life, but quickly recovers.

Charon sprints as fast as he can to the rooftop door. He pulls the shim out and shoves it in his pants pocket as he goes, taking two to three steps in the concrete stairwell at a time until he reaches the fifth floor. Opening the door, he composes himself and walks toward the elevator with his sunglasses on and the hood of his hoodie placed close to his face, trying to conceal his identity while looking like just another guest. He descends to the basement level, where the laundry, fitness room, and his car are located. He gets in his car and slowly drives out of the lot.

CHAPTER 81

FERRY

AMANDA TURNS around in her seat to make eye contact with Ryan about eight rows behind her on the opposite aisle, disobeying his rule that they never acknowledge each other on any leg of their journey. When he ignores her, she faces the front again and reads the small handwritten note she'll soon be throwing out.

D Concourse. To South China Ferry Station, ferry ticket, HK-Shen Zhen. Meet highest level of ferry 10 minutes following departure. Discard note.

She closes her eyes and takes several deep breaths to calm herself. *You've got this*, she keeps repeating. *It's the best way to get Justin back, maybe Dad too.* And to succeed where the CIA failed —that would make quite a story someday. If she lives to tell about it.

She looks down at her almost non-existent carry-on bag that Ryan insisted was all she could bring. She tries to think of a trip where she brought such few belongings but can't. The contents aren't even hers, they were bought for her by Ryan. She wonders what she packed for the New York trip when the plane went down, then pushes the idea out of her head before it can bring back distracting thoughts of her deceased mom and the fact that she can't remember anything about her. She digs into the small duffel past a shirt and pair of pants, locates the sealed bag with the pill bottle, and glances at the disguises, also in large plastic bags. She fishes one red pill and one blue one from the bottle and downs them. She's a day or two behind in taking them, but they don't seem to be doing anything anyway, she just takes them because her dad asked her to.

After they exit the plane at the airport in Hong Kong, she and Ryan are heading directly to the ferry to avoid customs inside the airport. They'll deal with it when they reach Shen Zhen, a busy industrial city full of factories and warehouses packed with workers building products to ship to the rest of the world. The Chinese and English instructions to prepare for landing are announced, and the jet bounces a couple shorts hops before settling on the runway.

Once off the plane, Amanda finds a restroom in the airport concourse and changes into the disguise Ryan instructed her to use for this leg of the trip. Exiting moments later, she follows the signs written in multiple languages toward the ferry station.

Amanda finds a seat on the top deck of the ferry under the overcast sky. Her internal clock tells her she should be asleep, even though it's only late afternoon in Hong Kong. The sun, wherever it is behind the clouds, is sinking closer to the horizon.

Within a minute of sitting down, she hears a voice from behind her.

"Everything good?"

She doesn't turn around.

"Fine."

"Excellent. About five minutes before the arrival time, they'll announce we're approaching the dock. That's our cue to head to the lower deck. Find me at the rear of the ferry and follow."

Amanda nods slightly, then looks out the window at the lights from distant buildings along the starboard side. She uses her finger to draw her initials in the condensation, a cursive "AM." Then she traces a rectangle around them. Her near meditative state gets interrupted by someone speaking Chinese over the loudspeaker, followed by the English version. She slings her bag over her shoulder and heads for the stairway. *This better work.*

Arriving at the lower deck, she finds Ryan standing near a door, which he pushes open as soon as she approaches. As they rush down a short staircase to another door, Amanda notices a sign showing a circle with a red line through it. *Okay, pretty clear we aren't supposed to be here.*

The strong, musty smell of moisture envelopes them both as Ryan opens the next door. They make a right into a narrow hallway, then another right, and he finally opens a third door to reveal a small, dark mechanical room.

"We'll be staying here at least fifteen minutes after the ship docks so we can exit after the crew and the passengers. This is going to go one of two ways. We're either going to steal down the gangplank if we can do it without being noticed, which is the easy way, or we're going to navigate our way through the crew hallways to the stern, lower ourselves into the water, and swim to one of the piers. That's obviously the harder way, but we can't risk being seen if the gangplank is brightly lit. I've got rope in here and some other equipment, just in case. If this goes the hard way, ditch the duffel bag. There's nothing in it identifying you, right?"

"Nope."

"Perfect."

"What if something goes wrong? We don't have any weapons. What'll we—"

"I've got a weapon, right here." Ryan draws a gleaming knife out of a scabbard. The shiny surface catches tiny rays of light and glints in the near darkness.

"How'd you get that on the plane?"

"I didn't, it was hidden for us on the ferry. You didn't think we could pull off this operation without any inside help did you?"

"I guess I figured you'd know someone, but—"

"You'll meet her at some point," Ryan assures her. "Our

weapons and supplies will be in two duffel bags in lockers once we get to the dock."

A few minutes later the ferry engines change, the hum and vibration reduces to an idle, then they rev again and Amanda feels the ferry slowly reverse direction. As the engines die down again to a murmur, Ryan checks his watch while reviewing the details of the Beijing bullet train with her. They'll each be sharing sleeping berths with strangers, and she is not to try to contact him. If things go well, he'll be the one to come to her berth or find her in the dining car during the eleven-hour trip across the hinterland of China. They will each have two burner phones. He goes over several back-up plans that entail splitting up and finding each other at specific times and locations.

"We gotta see Liza's mark in the Beijing train station. If it's not there, we separate."

"So, Liza's her name. What's the mark?"

"In the main terminal is a coffee place with a board for messages and business cards outside the women's restroom. If everything is cool, there'll be a peace sign in pink on the board."

"Um, okay, not quite what I was expecting," Amanda says, slightly disappointed the sign isn't more spy-like and less feminine.

"Try to sleep on the train," Ryan advises. Amanda figures she has a lot more than sleep to worry about.

CHAPTER 82

BACKTRACKING

"SHANNON, find David Carter, the intern, have him report here to the ready room," Solarez barks to one of his trusted analysts already working at her terminal. When David appears, Solarez asks him and Shannon to follow him to the nearby conference room. They enter and he closes the door behind them.

"Shannon, we've been tracking this guy, Ty Ryan, and Amanda was with him several times before she disappeared. I now think they're together, and I need you to track what he's done in the last week. I mean everything, figure out where he's been, who he's seen, every detail. Report back to me within two hours."

"David, here's what I've got for you. We've searched Crossroads Farm, and we know Amanda was using her laptop recently, but now it's gone. It's either with her or was discarded somewhere. I want you to recreate every internet search she's done on that laptop."

"But sir, don't we need a subpoena to legally do this search?"

"That's a technicality, David. I can get one from the assistant U.S. attorney or from the FISA court. This is part of a counterintelligence operation involving whatever the hell the Chinese have done with her dad, and has international reach. Assume it falls under one of the open warrants we already got."

"Well, shouldn't I wait until—"

"No, I want you to start on it right away. You let me worry about the legal stuff. We're on the schedule to present an extension request to one of the FISA judges." Solarez stares at David until he nods. "Alright then, both of you get busy. And please send Anita in to see me."

Moments later Anita enters and sees the papers in organized rows in front of Solarez. She knows the drill, but Solarez briefs her anyway.

"Anita, we need to go over the CIA reports on the summit between the North Korean and Chinese presidents. Call our Chinese embassy agents and convey to them that this is a volatile situation. We don't know what Amanda Michaels plans to do, but we are concerned she may be planning to disrupt the summit. Don't mention a plot, just tell them counterintelligence needs every detail about the summit—times, places, locations—and we want some assurance that they are assigning several agents to scour all major entry points into Beijing. We'll continue to update them and we expect them to do the same for us."

"Yes sir."

Solarez wanders back to his office and tries to focus on various files on his desk, but can't. He's thinking about how to get ahead of Amanda and Ryan, especially because he refused to put Amanda into protective custody before her disappearance. Shannon buzzes him and says she has information relating to Ryan's whereabouts over the last several days. He asks her to come see him immediately. With only two years in counterintelligence, Shannon's sleuthing skills never cease to amaze him.

"So, we figured out he took a short trip to South Beach, Miami. Besides being at the hotel we didn't have anything at first. He only stayed about twenty-four hours, so I asked the hotel for all their surveillance footage, which included a camera with a good view of the pool area. I pulled in two other analysts to review the footage, and we found Ryan at the pool the day he arrived. He spends some quality time with a female he was obviously acquainted with before the trip. Our facial recognition team identified her as Liza Zhang. Get this: she's former CIA, retired from the agency after a short career, no black marks against her. Her exit interview indicates she just burned out on intelligence work. Now she's working for Michael Morse, and—"

"The clothing line?"

"I know, pretty weird, right? She's Chinese-American and speaks fluent Chinese, so she acts as a QC rep for Morse and travels to China often."

"And you're thinking Ryan knows her from their CIA days and they're up to something in China?"

"Yeah, but I'm not ruling out that she's been recruited by the Chinese either. Here's where it gets even more interesting. She flew back to New York City the day after their rendezvous, and within a number of hours left again for China, using her own passport. She stayed in Beijing for a day and a half, then went to Guangzhou."

"Where the hell is Guangzhou, and why was she there?"

"Guangzhou is in southern China, not too far from Hong Kong. Michael Morse has factories in nearby Guangdong Province, about an hour from the airport. But Morse doesn't have a factory or office in Beijing, so what did she do there? Or who did she meet? Maybe she's working for the Chinese? We're going to need the embassy's help on that part."

"Excellent work. Where is she now?"

"We assume she's still in Guangdong Province, perhaps at the factory or staying in a hotel nearby."

Solarez leans over, stabs a button on his phone, and talks into the speaker.

"Paula, connect me to Brittney Hayes." He releases the button. "Shannon, good stuff. Find out where Liza Zhang is and tell me the moment you do."

David takes a seat in Solarez' office and sets his manila folder full of papers on his lap.

"It looks like Amanda was extensively investigating the

Chinese government, their president, and the announcements relating to the North Korean ruler's first visit to Beijing. I compiled a list of the websites she looked at and it takes up about two pages, single-spaced." He places the papers on the desk facing Solarez.

"Then you would agree it appears she's headed to China?"

"I can't say for sure, but she was researching the area and the President's visit."

"She never intimated to you she was considering something like this, did she?" Solarez doesn't quite believe David has told him everything.

"No sir. I'm baffled about this, she never said a word to me."

"I have intel suggesting Ryan and Amanda both left the U.S. for China, and I think he's helping her plan something. I'm not sure whether she approached him or vice versa, but we're pretty sure they're together."

Solarez runs his hand along the edges of the paper David gave him, pondering what to divulge to David, and decides to hold back that Justin Michaels was swapped with another baby immediately after birth.

"Is there anything else I can research for you?"

"Not right now. Thanks for this material."

CHAPTER 83
HARD WAY

RYAN PEERS through the small porthole mounted in the metal hatch door, providing a partial view of the pier. The walkway along the warehouse area appears mostly dark; a couple low-watt bulbs on the corners of the building make dim puddles of light.

"Let's go!"

They make their way toward the passenger gangplank on the starboard side of the bow at the same time a figure comes around the side of the warehouse and shines a flashlight in their direction. They back away just as the ray of light approaches and trot back towards the wall of the hallway where they had been hiding.

"Looks like we're doing it the hard way," Ryan says, never turning around. He pushes open a door to the left, then kneeling on one knee, hurriedly fishes two sets of swim goggles out of the duffel. He tosses one pair to Amanda and straps some kind of tool belt around his waist.

"Ditch the duffels in here." He points toward a dark corner in the utility room and grabs a length of dock rope looped like a figure eight. "We'll wear our shoes for now, but if you feel they're weighing you down, just kick 'em off."

Ryan takes off again running and Amanda follows. Ryan has become her fearless leader, almost like her *spirit guide*. They both hear the distant whooping sound of an alarm, which gets significantly louder when they emerge on a small rear deck. The alarm is coming from somewhere off the boat.

"We've got to get off this boat, someone is bound to be

searching it." Ryan loops one portion of the rope around a metal cleat mounted on the waist-level wall of the ferry. He pops his goggles on and she follows suit.

"You climb down first, when I hear you hit the water I'll start climbing down," he instructs.

"Are you sure you don't want to be first?"

"I want to make sure you're in safe before I drop down. I can swim ahead of you and lead the way once we're in the water. Liza said there are some ladders along the pier we can use to climb up. Lower yourself down slowly."

Amanda climbs up on the short wall and starts to descend into the blackness off the rear of the ferry. Using her sneakers to glide down the stern, she reaches the waterline and feels the cold water soak into her shoes as she sinks down into the water. She glances toward the pier, getting a fix on the direction, then she notices a moving flashlight beam cutting through the darkness and paddles back into the shadow of the ferry. Once she sees Ty's silhouette sliding into the water and swimming just below the surface, she lowers her head and mirrors him, seeing nothing except his amorphous figure ahead, even with her goggles in place.

As they approach the pier, Ryan slows down and signals with his hand for her to do the same. He holds a finger in front of his mouth, indicating not to speak, and points toward the pier. The guard stands no more than twenty feet away on the sidewalk, his flashlight shining downward. Ryan disappears, and Amanda maintains her position, treading water, assuming he has a plan. The ray of light starts scanning the water in her direction so she pushes her arms up and silently lowers herself underwater. From below the surface she watches the light shake spastically, then hears a loud splash.

He's coming for me, she thinks, and begins swimming away frantically. The thrashing sounds, which come closer for several seconds as she strokes toward the ferry, suddenly stop. She turns and looks back, but sees nothing.

Now what? Ryan didn't tell me what to do if someone came after me in the water. Since there is no sign of the guard in the water, she decides to try to find her way back to the pier and hopefully get out of the cold water.

She begins swimming under the surface, coming up for air for a split second, and wondering if another guard will be waiting for her on land. A few feet away from the pier, she starts looking for one of the ladders Ryan mentioned when something on her left touches her torso. She jerks away, like a fish instinctively leaping to avoid a shark attack, and prepares to slam her fist down on the top of the guard's skull.

"It's me," Ryan hisses, just before impact.

Amanda lowers her arm and lets out a shaky breath.

"I had to take out the guard. C'mon, there's a ladder over this way."

He doesn't even sound winded, Amanda thinks to herself, her heart thumping inside her chest. They climb a metal ladder to a flat, concrete walkway. They run through the darkness into an alley behind a warehouse where Ryan climbs into a large dumpster and searches through it. He drops back down, holding a couple small, dirty towels. Amanda wrinkles her nose as he offers her one.

"Sorry, but this ain't the Ritz. Dry yourself off with this," he orders, pressing the other towel against his clothes. "Here is a dry top, I brought one for each of us in a dry pack."

"Where was that?" She asks.

"Tethered to my pants just above my butt."

Amanda takes the dirty towel with two fingers and begins dabbing at her wet clothes while Ryan combs his hair.

"Where'd you get that?"

"Same place, the dry pack. When you spend as much time in H_2O as I have, you learn how to carry the bare necessities. Here, it's yours now."

Pulling the basic black men's comb through her tangled hair, the only positive thing Amanda can conjure about her appearance is that no one knows her in China. She modestly turns her back to Ryan and slips on the long sleeve shirt, grateful one article of clothing will be dry.

"Next stop, the locker in the ferry station," Ty says. "Now that we've gotten past customs and immigration, we can carry baggage like everyone else. I'll get the luggage, and you'll follow me to the train station a couple blocks away. I'll wheel both of the suitcases to the restrooms and put one in front of the women's, which you'll take in with you a few seconds later. Your Canadian passport will be in a purse stowed in your backpack, along with all kinds of supplies, including other dry clothes and a modest disguise. You can dry your hair with one of the hand dryers. Liza bought us tickets, yours should be in the purse with your money and passport. We won't talk again until I find you on the train, and only if it looks like the coast is clear."

The large, wheeled piece of luggage stands upright in front of the women's room. Amanda casually walks up, grasps the handle, and wheels it into a spacious handicap stall. She unzips it and flips open the top, revealing a gray backpack nestled in some clothing and other items. Inside she finds a small purse, a KA-BAR knife like the one Ryan trained her with, and a sheath with a Velcro strap, which Amanda straps to her leg below the knee before she slides the knife into it. A pair of sweatpants with a matching top are neatly folded under the backpack. *Thank God,* she says to herself as she kicks off the sopping sneakers and sheds her wet clothing, tossing the items in a pile on the floor. Using long pieces of toilet paper, she dries her skin as best as she can before putting on the clean clothes.

Now that she feels a little more human, she investigates the contents of her suitcase a bit closer. She leaves the pistol with the loaded cartridge in the backpack and sets it to the side. Underneath is more clothing packed by outfit in vacuum-sealed bags. She also finds a long, hard case and assumes it contains more weapons, along with some other unfamiliar items in soft, black cases. She opens the purse, which is full of Chinese yuan and Canadian dollars.

Shoot, what's my name again? She looks at her Canadian passport. Rachel Michelin, right.

CHAPTER 84
FLY LIST

IT'S 10:42 a.m. as Andy Michaels stands in the TSA line at Washington National Airport. He glances at his phone and happily notes it's more than two hours before his departure time to Beijing, China. Using his contacts, it had taken him less than a week to arrange for his Chinese visa. He inches forward in the TSA line carrying nothing more than a small satchel with a tablet and his necessary travel information.

Andy hands his passport and his phone with his mobile boarding pass to the TSA clerk, a guy with a smoothly shaved head. The agent dutifully hands him back his phone but he makes a face after he scans his passport.

"Uh, Mr. Michaels, step off to the side a moment, my supervising agent needs to speak with you."

"What's the matter?"

The TSA agent calls up the next person and doesn't answer him. Within moments the supervisor, a heavyset woman with salt-and-pepper hair almost to her shoulders, saunters over to Andy.

"Please follow me, Mr. Michaels, and I'll explain everything." She leads him to the side of the busy TSA checkpoint.

"Mr. Michaels, you're on our do-not-fly list. Our instructions are to contact the federal government if you try to board a plane. Just wait right here while I make a phone call."

She takes her phone out of a small pocket on her uniform and dials.

"This is TSA supervising agent Jennings, Mr. Andy Michaels just came through security and came up on the DNF list with instructions to contact the FBI at this number. Yes, I can hold for a moment." She shrugs apologetically toward Andy. "He's right here, I'll hand him the phone."

"Andy, this is Solarez, you're on the do-not-fly list."

"Yeah, that's what she said. What the hell?"

"Why are you trying to go to Beijing?"

"To find my niece, and maybe my brother too, but you knew that."

"Look, leave this to us. If we're busy worrying about your safety too, we have fewer resources to commit to finding Amanda. If you want, we can meet somewhere and I'll give you some idea of what we're working on, but I cannot let you go to China now. You could be additional abduction bait."

"How is this legal? You have no justification." Andy says.

"Really? You haven't thought about that last blanket declaration."

"Is the CIA doing everything imaginable to bring her back safely."

"Believe me Andy, we're doing our best to find all your family members. I will direct TSA to escort you to the nearest exit and we can meet as soon as you'd like."

CHAPTER 85

SLEEPER

AMANDA MAKES her way down the platform, weaving in and out between the Chinese passengers, many of whom are wheeling large, heavy suitcases. She smiles inside because she has nothing more than a duffel bag, but knows that this is no way to pack. She's got more weapons than she does clothes. She glances over her shoulder for Ryan, who is nowhere to be found, and hopes it will be safe enough for him to find her on the train.

Once aboard, she shows her ticket to a uniformed attendant who she assumes is a conductor. He points in the direction Amanda needs to head. She walks through a couple vestibules and arrives at a sleeper car. Luckily numbers are universal, even the Chinese use 1-10, just like Ryan told her. The door is ajar, so Amanda pushes it open the rest of the way and walks through. One passenger is already inside, a young Chinese girl who laid claim to one of the lower bunks. Amanda doubts the beds are assigned and claims the other lower bunk. An older passenger makes her way into the car, and then another. All four bunks are soon claimed.

Amanda hears the Chinese, then English, announcement of their impending departure. Within ten minutes, the train is knifing through the air with an occasional slight undulation that soon becomes familiar to Amanda. Lying on the lower bunk, she stares at the underside of the one above her. At some point her eyes open, and she realizes she fell asleep, but is unsure of how long she was out.

She thinks about how she ended up on this bullet train.

What kind of scum-sucking cockroaches kidnap a defenseless baby? She will make them regret that decision.

She feels with her fingertips along the thin foam-rubber pad masquerading as a mattress. There it is. She tugs on the lower portion of her backpack hiding the loaded pistol with the customized silencer, nestling what constitutes all her belongings in the crook of her right arm. The sheath strapped under the left pant leg of her jeans secures the long-bladed knife that was hidden in her duffel. And in the right pocket of her hoodie are two identical burner cell phones, one of which is her only means of communication with Ryan, the other to communicate with his logistical person inside China, but only in case of emergency.

Imagining the linen scent of her favorite candle briefly tricks her olfactory glands into ignoring the foul odors. The elderly Chinese lady on the bunk overhead smells like mildewed clothes. On the lower bunk an arm's length away, the Chinese girl sleeps with her jacket over her head. The sleeper car's other occupant, a tiny woman who barely stands five-foot tall and can't weigh 100 pounds, presses her torso against the tiny sink, paper towels surrounding the collar of her shirt, while she works some type of soapy liquid through her dark brown shoulder-length hair. Amanda decides to pass on that shower.

All I want is to get my brother back, she thinks. If captured, what could they possibly "get" out of her? To study her telomeres, maybe that's what they would want? Or maybe they would torture her to learn whatever she knows.

The bullet train hurtling northbound towards Beijing at 180 miles per hour suddenly lurches, causing a metallic screech that soon fades.

Amanda thinks for a moment about a family photo. Of her dad, her, and her mom, sitting on the front porch of the house they used to live in. The one her Uncle Andy showed her, the one she hopes to recall on her own someday. She mentally photoshops her baby brother, Justin, in too. Nothing can stop fantasies no one else can see.

The sink-showering lady climbs back up to her top bunk and talks in Chinese with the other older lady.

If our plan fails, I won't have to worry anymore, Amanda decides, because I'll be dead. So will Ryan. And Justin? She's not even sure he's in Beijing, but if the Chinese government is behind the kidnapping, there's a good chance that's where they're hiding him. Ryan's plan is solid.

Amanda gets up and walks over to the now available sink. It's tiny, like everything else, which allows four occupants to share this sleeper berth. There's no mirror, just a small metallic plate that offers a little bit of a reflection, gives you the idea that you're looking back at yourself.

What's the point, you can't make out any detail?

CHAPTER 86
HARBOR RAT

BRITTNEY HAYES, aka Elizabeth Gardner, listens intently to the CIA analyst in the small conference room at the U.S. Embassy in Beijing.

"Our informant at the Shen Zhen Harbor reported one of the harbor security guards turned up dead. His wallet and money were missing, which made it look like a robbery, but we sent an asset to check it out. He searched the last ferry to arrive and found two small duffels in one of the utility rooms below deck. Here are the pictures."

He slides the laptop closer to Britt and she scans the photos. One shows female clothing spread out beside a duffel along with a small, plastic bag with pills inside.

"How do we know that's Amanda's bag?"

"Solarez looked at the pictures and said those meds are Amanda's. He compared them to images of some pills Ron Michaels had on his laptop in a file labeled 'Amanda.' His laptop was confiscated and combed through when he disappeared."

Britt stares at the picture a moment. "So what's this do for us? I guess I'm missing something."

"According to her dad's notes, Amanda needs these meds. You know he gave her treatments, right?"

"Sure, I knew he treated her when she was younger, but why would she be taking these pills now?"

"Because she can have all kinds of side effects if she doesn't. We don't know for sure if she has more with her, but we have these." He sets the bag of pills from the photo on the table. "We had them overnighted here."

Britt lifts the bag and surveys the pills. "We've got to find her, which involves tracking down Liza Zhang first. She'll lead us to them, or we'll extract the information from her."

"Let me run down what we've got on her and where she's been since she arrived in China," the analyst tells Britt.

"I need that stat." The Chinese-American analyst looks at her quizzically.

"That means now. I'll be here working, get me what you can, and fast."

CHAPTER 87

CHECKERS

AMANDA WALKS through several cars before reaching the dining car. As she makes her way to the counter to order a cup of hot tea, she passes several tables and notices a family on her right —a dad, mom, and what appears to be about a 10-year-old boy and teenage girl. The kids are playing checkers.

The female behind the counter hands Amanda the tea and Amanda hands her a Chinese bill from the wad in the purse she acquired at the Shen Zhen station. She figures it also from the large sum of money she paid Ryan to help her on this mission. So far, she doesn't have any regrets, Ryan has proven himself to be ultra-careful and well-prepared.

She walks back through the dining car to find an empty table and notices the game board still sitting where the girl and boy were playing, but the brother is gone, and a thin novel lays on the table beside the board. It's *The Catcher in the Rye*, and the cover is in English, which strikes her as odd. Amanda stops impulsively.

"Are you studying English?" She asks the girl.

The Chinese girl gives Amanda a funny look, then glances down at the paperback.

"Yes. This is my current assignment in English class. Do you know this book?" the girl replies in slow, but appropriate English.

"Of course. I mean, most people know that book in the U.S. Holden Caulfield is one of the greatest characters ever written." Amanda doesn't mention it was on the bookshelf in Kent's room, or that she read it after Kent died, taking notice of the sections he had highlighted with a yellow highlighter. Kent even talked about it once when they were together. Amanda has no idea if she had also read the book before the crash, but suspects she did because Kent said every U.S. high school English class does.

"Do you want to play checkers with me?"

"Sure." Amanda sits down. "What page are you on in the book?"

The girl opens the paperback to a dog-eared page. "Page 79."

"May I?" Amanda takes the book and flips to one of the parts she obsessed over and memorized in Kent's room.

"'I have to be the person watching them like if they're going to go over the cliff. I have to catch them before they do it. I'm like a catcher in the rye.'"

The teen looks at her quizzically.

"That's one of the best parts in the book. Holden feels like he must save all these young people before they go walking off a cliff. Anyway, what's your name?"

"An Ling."

"Nice to meet you, An Ling. I'm Rachel Michelin. Why don't you go first?" Amanda places her black checkers on the board; An does the same with the red and makes the first move.

In the middle of the game Amanda asks her whether those were her parents she was sitting with earlier. An says they were and that her brother is 10 years old, in admirable English. They're all sharing a sleeper berth. She tells Amanda she hopes to come to the United States in the future and asks Amanda what the large letters mean on her shirt.

Amanda explains the "UVA" stands for University of Virginia and launches into the cover story Ryan went over with her until she was confident about it. The part about going to UVA for college is true, because she was a student there, but that's pretty much it. Her fake persona is now employed by a computer company and is working on a contract involving server networking. An Ling turns out to be an excellent checkers player and handily defeats Amanda. As they set up for the next game, Ryan walks through the dining car and glances at Amanda with a disapproving look. Pursuant to his request, she does not acknowledge him as he walks by.

"If you ever come to the United States, you should visit Washington, DC and Charlottesville, Virginia, where I attended college. There are beautiful rolling hills there, horses, horse farms, and many things you would enjoy." Amanda is careful with her English, knowing An is hanging on every word in an attempt to understand. She momentarily thinks to herself how it is unfair that most Americans have not even grasped a second language, while the Chinese people can not only speak English, one of the most difficult languages to learn, but many of them also learn a third language or several Chinese dialects.

An tells Amanda she should visit the Great Wall of China and Tiananmen Square while she's in Beijing. The girl's parents return to the table and introductions are made. Both of them speak excellent English and are professors at the Graduate School of Tsinghua University in Beijing. An's father has been teaching there for more than ten years in the division of life science and health as a chemistry professor. Her mother works in the same program, but in biological life science. They met in college. They engage Amanda in conversation about the University of Virginia, knowing that it sits in the foothills of the Blue Ridge Mountains in Charlottesville. They ask her about one colleague from China who is a professor at the undergraduate government school there, but Amanda doesn't recognize the name.

An's parents move to another table and she and Amanda continue to play. An begins to confide in her new American friend.

"I went to a program in London last summer, offered through Oxford."

"Oxford? No wonder you speak such good English!"

"Yes, that was when my studies of English helped me the most." Then she leans closer over the white tablecloth. "I met a boy there too. He's from China, but he lives in the United States now. I told my parents I want to go to university there, but they want me to go to Tsinghua in Beijing because they both teach there. I argue with them, they do not understand."

Amanda studies her face for a moment, then looks back down at the board and double-jumps one of An's pieces, one of the first times she manages to do that. She figures the teen is distracted by thoughts of the boy she met, but only feels slightly guilty about taking advantage of it.

"Do you keep in touch with him?" Amanda asks while An makes her next move. "Are you friends on Facebook?"

"We cannot have Facebook in China, not allowed."

"Really? I didn't know that. Why not?"

"You will have to ask our president or the government that question. Maybe they think we will become too much like Americans."

About that time, Amanda feels the train slowing down. She decides it's time to head back to her berth. She tells An and her parents how nice it was to meet them and starts walking toward the sleeper car.

Moments after Amanda closes the door to her room Ryan knocks on the door and she joins him in the hall.

"What are you doing talking to random people on this train? We have to maintain the absolute lowest profile possible," Ryan whispers.

"She was just some teenager playing checkers in the dining car. What, do you think she's a teenage Chinese secret agent or something?" Amanda notices Ryan still wears the same beanie hat embroidered with a few Chinese letters that they picked up from the disguise genius back in Northern Virginia.

"Of course not, but you can't draw attention to yourself. And remember, thirty minutes before this train pulls into Beijing you have to change disguises. Put on the one with the face mask. You can take it off in the train station restroom when we get there."

Ryan had consulted with one of his former CIA agent friends about disguises that would be well-received in China. His friend said it was not uncommon for the Chinese to wear face masks or respirators because of the poor air quality in their country, and, unlike Americans, they did not hesitate to protect themselves from germs that are easily transmitted on public transportation. As a result, Amanda's departure disguise is straight, shoulder-length black hair, a mask with Chinese features, and a surgical mask to further hide her American features. Her shoes are a popular brand known to the Chinese, a pair of modern workout pants, and a loose-fitting hoodie.

"So, no more chatting with strangers, got it?"

Amanda nods and Ryan walks back toward his berth.

CHAPTER 88
VESTED

THE TALL MAN with the charcoal-gray overcoat is one of 20 or so passengers who boards the train at Zhengzhou East Station, and is the only non-Asian boarding. About 45 minutes later, while half-reading a book on his tablet, he spies his mark walking through the café car. Ryan hits the button that opens the sliding doors between the café car and the next one. Charon gets up and follows him, staying ample distance behind him, but near enough to watch him stop in front of a door in the sleeper car.

Ryan, ever vigilant, looks left, right, and down at the foot of the door before placing the small key on the elastic loop into the lock and stepping into the room. Charon nods slightly to himself and retreats from the vestibule back to his seat; he has the information he needs.

Ryan looks at his watch and figures the train is about an hour outside of Beijing, leaving only one stop before their destination. He makes his way from his room to the café car again. Two women are in line ahead of him, so he waits, albeit impatiently. When he reaches the counter, he points to the espresso picture on the small laminated menu. After paying with exact Chinese coins, he walks away and takes a seat at a built-in table for two at the opposite end of the car. The train, moving at over 200 miles an hour, presents nothing more than a whirl of countryside through the windows. He indulges himself in a Tetris-like game on his burner phone for a couple minutes, never losing sight of everyone passing.

Ryan runs through his and Amanda's first several moves once they arrive in Beijing, knowing their mission relies on Liza. So far, everything has gone well. *Maybe I'll give up the investigator gig once I get back to DC, start my own business.*

Having finished his drink, he tosses the cup in the tall trash can beside the snack counter. Returning to his room, he again checks in all directions before opening the door. The first shot hits him in the back just as he unlocks the door and turns the handle, pushing his body forward. The second jolt whips his head sideways, sending the beanie cap with it while he lunges, turning his body like a running back dodging head-on contact. But he's not quick enough, and the third bullet also strikes his back. He slides along the floor into the room, kicking the door closed as two more bullets tear through it. *Damn, Kevlar saved my life.*

In the room across the narrow hall, Charon pauses a second or two before retracting the silenced pistol projected through the slight opening in the door. He knows no one can survive that many bullet wounds at close range.

Ryan lays flat on the floor of the sleeper berth, pistol trained toward the now bullet-pocked door, ready to fire at any sign of motion. *Whoever shot me assumes I'm down. Even though he's wrong, the operation is still compromised.*

As he reaches around and feels the holes where the bullets hit his Kevlar vest, the door to his room jolts as if someone kicked it. Ryan fires two shots through the door and hears them strike something in the hall. Charon, standing just to the side of the door, now knows Ryan's alive, but assumes he's mortally wounded. He bolts down the narrow passage and hits the button on the vestibule door. He continues running through the cars, brushing past other passengers, never looking back.

Ryan leaps to his feet, still holding his pistol in front of him, and inches toward the wall beside the door. In one swift motion, he reaches his left hand out, turns the knob, and pulls the door inward, squeezing himself against the wall. No return fire. Ryan extends a short-handled mirror into the hall, but sees nothing except a mom and her young daughter now walking toward him, hand-in-hand, from the end of the sleeper car. He waits until the woman closes her door a few rooms down from his, crosses the hall, and kicks down the door the shooter must have been hiding behind. Hearing nothing from inside, he enters, pistol drawn, but finds no one. He backs out, pulling the door shut behind him, and re-enters his berth. There is an announcement in Chinese, then in English: "Baoding East Station stop. Passengers disembark for Baoding in one minute."

Ryan has no clue which direction his assassin went. He reaches up to the top bunk and feels for his duffel bag. He lifts it without unzipping it and gives it a shake—all his gear is still there, then he slings the strap over his shoulder. Ryan darts back out into the hall and with no more than a coin-flip of odds, heads to the right and hits the vestibule door with his left palm, keeping his other hand on the pistol in his jacket pocket.

The train slows with a faint but increasingly louder high-pitch screech; they are nearly at Baoding East Station. Ryan walks through the first car, and again into the café car. He stares through the large windows facing the unfamiliar train station platform. He vigilantly watches the passengers exiting the cars, a husband and wife with two small children, an elderly man, two girls. No one of interest.

Two train conductors and the woman who Ryan had seen with her daughter now stand outside the door to his berth. The woman points to the bullet holes in the door and another in the hallway wall. The conductor raps on the door to Ryan's berth. When no one answers, he lifts his passkey to unlock the door, but it's ajar. Both conductors cautiously enter the room, and one immediately calls his supervisor on the handheld radio when they see it's empty.

Just as he hears an announcement he assumes means the doors are preparing to close, Ryan sees a tall man in a charcoal overcoat exiting about two cars to his right. The man strides away from the platform carrying no luggage, just a backpack slung over one shoulder. Ryan can't make out his face, only notices his lanky height and brisk gait. Something tells him this is the guy who left him for dead.

Ryan rushes out through the closing doors, almost entrapping his duffel bag between them. He jogs along the platform and bursts through the double doors into the waiting area of the train station, but his assailant is nowhere to be found. *Damn.*

He examines the map to see how far he is from Beijing. Since the train left the station without him, he and Amanda will have to use their back-up plan. He'll contact her on the burner phone once he finds a secure place to make the call.

How were we compromised?

CHAPTER 89

IRIDESCENT

TWO-HUNDRED ANALYSTS WORKING three different shifts with multiple computer monitors on their desks tap on keyboards inside the Chinese cyber-intelligence unit in Beijing. Dozens of hidden video-surveillance units dot every major international travel facility, including the Shen Zhen ferry terminal and the train stations. Local police descended on the area once the ferry agent was found dead. Given the heightened security due to the upcoming summit, they were soon joined by Chinese intelligence agents. Facial recognition algorithms run on the video footage identified Ty Ryan, a former U.S. Navy SEAL, and Amanda Michaels, a civilian, entering the ferry terminal, and later, entering the train station in disguise.

Given the Chinese government's high concern with the possible disruption of the summit, the intelligence is transmitted first to the highest echelons of the Chinese Embassy staff in Washington DC. Birdie knows this information is also exceedingly valuable to Lu Li Xi, and that the company will be willing to pay handsomely for it.

Ryan and Amanda Michaels in China. Uncertain of their mission, probably to locate Justin Michaels. Will send coordinates on Ryan for $300,000 USD. Use same wire transfer.

The deposit and subsequent sharing of Ryan's approximate location is completed within 45 minutes of the message's receipt. The Lu Li Xi "contractor," already in China, is dispatched.

Also, Birdie knows Lu Li Xi isn't the only one willing to pay for this intel. He shoots off another email and awaits his second payment.

The email in Solarez' inbox from Birdie might as well be iridescent, that's how easily Solarez spots it.

Have information about the China/North Korea meeting. Ryan and Amanda Michaels in China. Wire $100,000.00 USD to my account for more info. I need a favor too this time.

Solarez reads the email again, then checks the time at the top of his screen: 1:00 a.m. Knowing he can't complete the transfer without approval, he dials the CIA director's home phone number. After the third ring the director answers.

"Sir, I'm sorry to bother you so late, but Birdie claims to have information pertinent to the Chinese-North Korean summit tomorrow. He also knows about Ty Ryan and Amanda Michaels. He wants $100,000. I need your approval for the wire transfer."

"You're in favor?"

"I don't think we really have a choice. If we don't pay for the intel and Ryan somehow manages to disrupt the summit, it'll wreck our diplomacy and cause increased tension between us and China. As for North Korea, their dictator is so volatile, who the hell knows. Plus, we need to get Amanda back to the U.S. safely and as soon as possible. So, yeah, I think we need to pay for whatever he knows."

The CIA director gives his approval and Solarez contacts his assistant to complete the transfer. Once he has the confirmation, he emails Birdie.

Wire is complete. Need info ASAP.

Solarez nervously taps the desk next to his laptop. When a response doesn't arrive right away, he gets up and walks over to his bar where he pours two shots of Jack Daniels in a cocktail glass before carrying it to the kitchen to add some ice from the dispenser on his refrigerator. He downs a couple swallows as he paces for a minute or two. Hearing the familiar ping, he returns to his laptop to read the message.

Lu Li Xi holding Justin Michaels but I don't know where. Contract out on Ryan. China believes he is plotting to disrupt the summit, but not how he plans to do so. Need to ask favor over secure line. Send number and I will call you, noon your time tomorrow.

Solarez provides his encrypted satellite phone number and tracks down Britt Hays in China.

CHAPTER 90
INTERCEPT

THE BLACK LIMOUSINE approaches the entrance to the United States Embassy in Beijing; the first black iron gate swings open, and the guard with a semiautomatic weapon over his shoulder steps toward the driver's side of the vehicle and peers inside. He nods, waving him forward with his free arm; a second iron gate swings open, and the limo continues driving to the embassy.

Britt Hayes meets with the CIA station chief and a state department officer under diplomatic attaché cover. They review the information obtained in Guandong Province, tracking every significant move of Liza Zhang. The dossier reveals Zhang visited a factory operated by Morse Clothing, then within the next 24 hours boarded a jet and flew to Beijing, where she rented two cars from different rental agencies under aliases and had them delivered to the guest parking lots of two separate hotels. Zhang herself got a room at the Emperor's Plaza, a hotel within blocks of the Beijing International Airport. An advance team of two agents shadowed Liza and surreptitiously confirmed the location of her seventh floor room.

The CIA director provides Britt the assistance she requests: one agent for the interception of Liza Zhang, and two inside analysts at the embassy. Given Zhang's prior CIA training and the uncertainty of whether or not she is working alone, the details are run through a second time. Amanda Michaels and Ty Ryan have disappeared; while the CIA is fairly certain their goal is to disrupt the North Korean-Chinese summit, none of the intelligence channels have located them. Britt still hasn't figured out their plan, but she's confident Zhang is the best way to find them.

The Emperor's Plaza Hotel lobby is sparsely furnished with contemporary white plastic couches topped with orange cushions and a few matching end tables. The center of the lobby features a long rectangular table with numerous large computer monitors for guest use. After she arrives and confirms the lack of surveillance cameras, Britt settles on one of the couches and pretends to browse the internet on her tablet computer. Her associate has been shadowing Liza Zhang for the last hour and just messaged Britt, she is returning.

Liza feels satisfied with the way the plans are coming together. She daydreams about the $200 K landing in her secret bank account. Maybe after this mission Ryan would join her for a vacation to New Zealand and Australia, two places she has always wanted to tour. The hotel rooms are secured, the rental cars placed, the weaponry she managed to secrete onto the ferry was stashed in the lockers. In about an hour, she will walk to the Beijing train station to pin the pink marker on the bulletin board, notifying Ryan the operation is on. Until then, she needs to bide her time. Assuming Ryan doesn't lay any additional tasks on her, this is the easiest several hundred thousand dollars she has made in her clandestine career.

She stops at the Starbucks attached to her hotel, one of several that have sprouted up in Beijing over the past few years. The décor is remarkably similar to those at home, with the exception of the signs hanging over the cashier being in Chinese. A café Americano espresso, no sweetener, just the jolt she needs. As she swings the doors open to the hotel lobby, she takes a look around, assessing the various international visitors hurrying in different directions.

Spying Liza over her screen, Britt closes the laptop and slips it into her carry bag, which also conceals her weapon. Liza walks to the bank of elevators and Britt follows a few steps behind, relieved no one else is headed in their direction. Within a few seconds, the elevator doors open, and the two women enter. Liza presses the button for the seventh floor and Britt leans forward and selects 12. The elevator chimes softly as it passes each floor.

Just before they reach Liza's floor, Britt draws the pistol with silencer out of her bag and points it directly at Liza's back. "Liza, don't move. We know who you are, and we have some questions."

Liza was trained by the same organization as Britt, so Britt takes nothing for granted. "Well, I don't know who you are, who do you work for?" she inquires, feigning compliance. She turns as if to get a look at her captor, but instead tosses the hot coffee in Britt's face and backhands her in the torso. Britt recoils against the metal back wall of the elevator, her pistol now aimed at the ceiling. She kicks her leg forward to smash her heel into Liza, but it glances off her thigh.

On the seventh floor, the elevator doors start to open. As soon as her body can slide through, Liza bursts out, but her forward motion is met by an equally powerful motion—a punch in the gut from the operative working in tandem with Britt. Liza drops like a boxer down for the count, barely past the threshold of the elevator doors. Britt composes herself and steps out of the elevator, looking in both directions for witnesses.

Archer, her associate, says, "I'll get her, you get the door."

He slings Liza over his shoulder and carries her like an oversized ragdoll to the door, which Britt opens. Dropping Liza on one of the two beds, Archer cuffs her hands and zip-ties her legs. Britt rifles through Liza's pants pockets and finds her hotel key.

"Give me a minute, I'm going to see what else she brought with her."

Britt walks down the hall and enters Liza's room. She locates a laptop and tosses it toward the foot of the bed. The main part of the suitcase is filled with clothes and shoes, but in a side compartment Britt finds a phone, which she decides must be Chinese because it doesn't resemble any American model. *This may come in handy.* More clothes hang in the valet area, so she runs her hands through all the pockets. Nothing. Same with the clear toiletry bag on the bathroom counter. She scoops up the laptop and phone and heads back down the hall. A young couple approaches from the opposite direction, so Britt walks past her door and waits until the couple enters a different room before doubling back.

CHAPTER 91
FAMILIAR VOICE

AMANDA HEARS THE ANNOUNCEMENT, and waits for the English translation: "Beijing East train station, five minutes."

As the other passengers in the sleeper berth scurry to organize their belongings, Amanda turns on her burner phone. When it powers up, a message flashes on the screen.

Compromised. Meet at second location.

What the hell does that mean? She powers down the phone. Where is the second location? Yeah, in my cryptic notes.

Amanda considers going in search of Ryan before the train stops, but she doesn't even know where his room is. She feels the train changing speed. *Wait, the disguise.* Ryan said she should be wearing the young Chinese girl mask when they arrive in Beijing. Amanda rummages through her backpack, locating the items she needs, smiles a quick goodbye to the woman across the aisle, and bolts from the sleeper berth.

She finds the public restroom and locks herself in. She carefully rolls the thin, pliable silicone over the top of her head and face and under her chin, checking the fit in the mirror. *Halfway convincing.* Then she slips on the white face mask and adjusts the elastic behind her head so it fits over her nose and mouth. She still wears the orange UVA hoodie with the navy blue "V" logo. It looks a little strange, but who knows, maybe she visited Virginia, lots of foreigners do. Amanda turns on the phone again. Nothing since Ryan's earlier message. She shuts it off, a little voice inside telling her not to panic. But her adrenaline has amped up big time.

The train slows even more, creeping toward the South Beijing Railway Station. *Showtime,* she hears Ryan saying in her head. *How does he know we've been compromised?*

She peeks outside the bathroom and sees a number of people walking down the aisle toward the exit door. Ryan was going to find the rental car, and she is supposed to meet him at Concourse A. If he's not there in 10 minutes, she is to abort and go to the contingency location. *Is that what he meant by the second location?*

Masses of people exit the train cars. As she hits the concrete platform, Amanda looks left and right, but doesn't see Ryan. She follows the crowd, pretending she knows where she's going. She takes the escalator up and sees the Concourse A sign, which reminds her she needs to look for Liza's mark at the coffee shop. She stops at an information desk in the middle of the terminal to ask for directions, then realizes how strange it would be for a Chinese woman, which is who she is supposed to be, to speak in English or very broken Chinese. Instead, she finds a map of the station and searches for the nearest coffee shop. A mug with a swirl rising from it shows it is to her left, a few hundred feet away.

She quickly heads toward the Starlings Coffee Shop. Past the front counter, down a short hallway, she finds the women's restroom and the bulletin board. Business cards and all kinds of little notes covered with Chinese characters remind Amanda how far from home she really is. She frantically scans the board and lifts up some of the overlapping papers, but there's no trace of a pink peace sign.

Amanda wheels around. She foolishly entertains the idea of getting a cup of coffee for about half a second before coming to her senses. The mission has definitely been compromised, maybe even more than once, based on Ryan's message and now the missing peace sign from Liza. She dashes away from the restroom area and out into the main concourse. If Ryan did get a rental car, she needs to get to arrivals. Several uniformed guards with submachine guns run past her and across several lanes of traffic as she makes her way through the automatic doors to the passenger pick-up area. *No, they couldn't be looking for us, could they?* She adjusts the white face mask, assuring herself it's in place, and watches for Ryan and a rental car. Instead, she just sees more armed police running her way.

Rows of taxis and cars slowly come and go. Amanda turns on her phone, twelve minutes have passed. Remembering Ryan's instructions to only wait for ten, she gets a sinking feeling in her stomach. *Ryan thought of everything. How could he not be here to pick me up? I must be at the wrong place.* She scans the cars one last time before trotting back inside to check the signs, which show the familiar Hertz and Avis logos Ryan specifically mentioned. She glances back at her phone, 15 minutes. *I've got to text him,* she decides.

Concourse A. Are you coming?

The phone vibrates.

No. Second meeting place.

No? She finds herself feeling light-headed and gasping for breath, the corpuscles of blood pulsing violently through her temples.

This is exactly why Ryan had concerns about me as his mission buddy. I refuse to prove him right, I need to calm down. Think. She reaches into the pocket of her hoodie and pulls out a wad of Chinese currency. *I have yuan. I can pay my way, I just don't know which way that should be.*

Amanda looks up and again sees several police officers, this time standing guard outside the terminal. She pushes her hoodie up over her head, paranoid her disguise may not be enough, and walks purposefully through the doors, past the officers, toward the long line of taxis.

It dawns on her she doesn't know the name of a single street or hotel in Beijing, but now that she has her wits about her, she remembers she is to meet Ryan tomorrow at 11:00 a.m. if they don't find each other at the station. She'll scroll through the notes on her phone to find their rendezvous point later, but right now she's on her own. As she goes through the list of American hotel chains in her head, trying to decide which ones might have hotels in Beijing, she swears she hears a voice speaking English from behind her.

"Rachel? Rachel Michelin?"

She is momentarily blindsided. *They know I'm here, and why.*

She doesn't turn to face the voice right away; instinctively swings her backpack off her shoulder, to reach for the pistol in her backpack. Then she freezes. *I know that voice.* It's An Ling, her checkers opponent. She slings the pack back on to her shoulder and with her other hand stealthily removes her mask and stuffs it into the front pouch of her hoodie before turning around a second or two later.

An is leaning out of the rear window of a bright red compact car a couple lanes of traffic away.

"I thought that was you, Rachel, I saw your hooder. Do you need a ride somewhere?"

Amanda knows An Ling means "hoodie" but decides now is definitely not the time to correct her English. Amanda can see the car is driven by her father, and her mother occupies the front seat. She walks across the two lanes of stopped traffic to her newfound friends.

"I was supposed to be picked up by a tour guide driver, but there must've been a mix-up. I waited for them for a while and finally just decided to take a taxi to the hotel."

"We can give you a ride. Or, wait one minute." An Ling pokes her head back inside the car and Amanda can tell she's talking with her parents. She reappears with a smile on her face.

"We have a room, you can be a visitor at our home tonight. We do not live far from station. Then you can get a taxi ride tomorrow. My parents said this plan okay."

A horn blasts behind An Ling's dad; he moves a few feet forward and partly onto the raised median to allow the impatient driver to go around him.

"Rachel, it is fine, we give you a ride and you may stay with us one night," An Ling's mother confirms. The trunk opens to reveal several suitcases, and An's dad gets out to help her squeeze her duffel into the tiny space.

Amanda considers the weapons she is carrying. "Not a problem, I'll hold my everything on my lap," she says, and walks toward the rear door. She climbs into the car on the right, An's brother sits on the hump in the middle, and An Ling sits on the left.

"I never thought I would see you again, what do you call it in English, when you are, uh, surprised?" An asks Rachel.

"A coincidence."

"That's it, co-in-ci-dence. You can teach me more about American music," An says, and her dad, makes a strange face that Amanda notices in the rearview mirror.

Amanda feels safe, at least temporarily.

CHAPTER 92

AN LING

THE CAR PULLS into a driveway in a residential neighborhood, which An's dad explains is called the Baizhifang residential district. Amanda notices the home is a detached two-story building, not an apartment, and assumes An Ling's parents must be paid well as university professors. There is a small patch of a front yard with some shrubs and a pebble walkway from the driveway to the front door. Mrs. Ling shows Amanda to a guest room with a simple fold-out bed and a hall bathroom. There are a couple paintings, which appear to be of Chinese temples.

"We are pleased to have you as our guest, Rachel. If we can drive you to meet your tour tomorrow, please let us know in the morning."

"I'm sure I can find transportation. Thank you for having me. Can I pay you for—"

"No, no. Please." An's mom walks back downstairs.

Sheets lay on the couch, waiting to be put on that evening. An Ling sits on the floor next to it, showing great interest in everything American and revering every word that comes out of Amanda's mouth.

"Do you listen to Beyoncé? I also listen to Jay Z, but we do not receive best music in China. We receive it years after you do."

"I like Jay Z," Amanda offers. "I've got *Run This Town* with Rihanna on one of my playlists. Have you heard *Bitch Better Have My Money?*"

"Oh no, that is a U.S. obscenity word. China does not allow

bad U.S. words in songs. We have to get those on uh, unauthorized website. Chinese government deletes websites, then they come again, then they delete. That is what it is like here. Scared Chinese minds get poisoned by American culture."

Amanda shakes her head.

"We have lots of problems, but artists say anything they wanna say."

As An gets lost in her music again, Amanda's mind turns back to the mission. *How will I make it to the rendezvous point? Is the mission still a go?*

The news on the TV opposite the couch catches her eye. It's showing the Chinese President, followed by clips of the North Korean dictator. An Ling looks up and stares at the screen too.

"This is first visit from the North Korean dictator to Beijing, we should not invite him. News all the time. The parade will be on Chang'an Avenue. The Chinese President closed businesses and invited all the Beijing people to attend." An explains.

An's parents leave early in the morning, before Amanda awakes. She groggily opens one jet-lagged eye to find An sitting on the floor beside the couch, staring at her phone. Even though her eyelid barely flutters, An notices and starts talking immediately, eager to make the most of her time with Amanda before she leaves.

"At last, you awaken! My parents left instructions on how to obtain taxi driver, and here are telephone numbers. I can make phone calls for you. Do you know the song *Royals* by Lorde?"

"Sure."

"Do you like it?"

"I dunno, I guess, I don't dislike it."

Amanda's thoughts are far from song choices, getting a hot shower is front and center.

"I'll talk to you after I'm out," she tells An before trudging toward the bathroom and softly closing the door. Not sure what to expect, Amanda is relieved to find the shower operates like the ones in the U.S., and she turns on the water to let it warm up. She finds a bottle she hopes is shampoo and washes her hair. The bar of soap is readily apparent, and she lathers herself from top to bottom, appreciating being clean more than ever before.

While Amanda enjoys her shower, An's curiosity of all things American makes her visitor's unusually large backpack irresistible. The running water can be heard through the thin walls beside the couch, so Amanda won't be coming out for a while. She flips open the canvas top and loosens the pull cord on the main compartment. Reaching into the pack and pushing some clothes aside, her hand touches something cold and metallic near the bottom. She pulls the object upward and recognizes the muzzle of the pistol, then immediately shoves it back down, her hand trembling. Scared, but even more curious now, An leans in closer and gingerly lifts up a clear storage bag containing a silicone face mask and a white dust mask.

Feeling the long, thin outline of what appears to be a knife in the exterior vertical pouch pushes An over the edge. She leaps off the couch to find her mom or dad, but remembers they have left for the day. *Americans own guns, yes, but how did Rachel bring these weapons into China, and why?* Her teenage mind throbs with uncertainty. Is her new American friend here for something other than sightseeing?

She remembers Amanda's interest in the President and dictator on the news the night before. Could she be here because of that? Had her family unwittingly given refuge to a criminal? The bathroom door opens, and An jumps.

"Sorry to scare you." Amanda pulls a brush through her damp hair. "I feel so much better now."

An glances at Amanda and turns to the TV, avoiding eye contact. "Did you plan to watch the parade?"

"No, I didn't know it was happening until I saw it on the news with you this morning."

An doesn't believe her. This meeting had been discussed for weeks around the world, and if she knew about it in China, any American, with their open news sources, must have been aware.

"Are you here as a tourist, or for some other reason?"

"What do you mean?"

"Did you come because of the North Korean dictator visit?"

"No. I always wanted to come here, China is fascinating. I want to learn about your history, visit Tiananmen Square, go to the Great Wall. Which reminds me, I'll need that taxi ride to meet my tour guide later this morning."

Amanda realizes An suspects something. She wonders what tipped her.

"I can make the phone call for you. First I'm going to the, uh, restroom. Is that how you say it in English?"

"Yeah, restroom. Or bathroom."

An leaves, but doesn't go to the closest restroom, she goes downstairs instead. This confirms An's change in attitude toward her, and Amanda quickly debates how best to handle it.

CHAPTER 93
LIFELINE

AN CLOSES the bathroom door and softly turns the lock before shakily dialing her mom's number on her cell phone. As it starts to ring, the door crashes in and Amanda storms in with a long knife in her right hand. She swats the phone out of An's hand and it clatters to the tile floor. She grabs An around her neck, positioning the knife just below her chin. When she hears the phone ringing, she pulls An downward with her and picks it up.

"Cut it off, now!"

Before An can hang up, they both hear her mother's panicked voice.

"An! An!"

"Hang it up!" Amanda hisses, moving the knife blade closer to her chin. An presses the button.

"That was a very stupid idea, An."

"You are not a tourist. You are here to kill someone. Why else would you bring a knife and gun?"

"Oh, I see, you went through my bag. No, I'm not here to kill anyone."

"I don't believe you. Now you kill me?"

"Not as long as you don't do anything else dumb. But since you have now involved yourself by snooping through my stuff, there's a new plan—we are driving into town together."

"I'm not going to help you kill," An says defiantly.

Amanda slides An's phone into her back pocket. She thinks about taking the battery out, but she decides not to.

"Let's go find the keys to the car." Amanda keeps her hand on An's back just above her jeans and propels her forward.

"I cannot drive yet. You must be 18 in China. I only have training permit."

"But you speak perfect Chinese, and there will be roadblocks leading into downtown. I need someone convincing to talk our way through."

An takes the keys from a small basket on the kitchen counter. Amanda grabs them from her hand.

"Let's pretend. I'm your aunt visiting from the United States, your mom's sister married an American. I'm your adult for driving the car. Do you understand that?"

An doesn't answer.

"Call me Aunt Rachel. Do you understand?"

"Yes, I understand."

Tears pour down An's cheeks while Amanda guides her back upstairs to her backpack. Amanda regrets scaring the girl, but she's come so far and worked so hard to find Justin, she can't let anything keep her from completing the mission, including An Ling.

CHAPTER 94
JOYLESS RIDE

BACK IN THE GUEST ROOM, Amanda guides An to the couch, still made up with her sheets and blanket. Again, she feels a twinge of guilt about not being a gracious guest.

"Sit down and don't move."

Amanda turns on her phone to check for messages from Ryan. There is one text, but it's from an unfamiliar phone number.

New instructions. 11:00 a.m. Vista Hotel, 814. —L

Liza is the only other person with her burner phone number, and Amanda presumes the liaison coordinates changed because the mission was compromised. But to be sure, Amanda texts the information to Ryan for confirmation.

11:00 a.m. Vista Hotel, 814 per L text. Confirm.

Amanda waits a minute, then another. Finally, a text appears from Ryan's number.

Yes.

Amanda breathes a sigh of partial relief. The three of them will meet and Ryan can put all the pieces back together.

She turns off the phone, slips the hoodie back on, and with her back to An, slides the pistol in the front pouch of the hoodie to avoid scaring her further.

"An, I really do like you. But if you try anything, I will use my gun. Got it? Now, let's go to the car."

"I do not drive well, I am still beginner."

"Consider this an opportunity for more practice."

Amanda unlocks the car doors with the key fob and puts An in the passenger seat while she backs the car down the driveway. Then they switch places. After An confirms her lack of driving skills by unnecessarily slamming on the brakes two or three times and veering over the center line in the first few blocks, they switch places once more and Amanda drives until they see the roadblock ahead of them. At a stop sign, Amanda gets out and An slides across and back into the driver's seat.

While they sit in the line of traffic waiting to have their ID and passport checked, Amanda falsely warns An, "I can't speak Chinese very well, but I can understand it. All of it." In fact, she only recognizes a few very common words, like "stop," numbers one through ten, "yuan," "hello," and "goodbye."

"Why don't you drive the car to the roadblock and I can do the talking?" An suggests.

"You know tourists aren't allowed to drive here, even with an international driver's license. Don't play games with me."

Suddenly the driver's door bursts open. An grabs Amanda's backpack and bolts out of the car, then runs down an empty side street. Amanda leapfrogs into the driver's seat and pulls the door shut while the car ahead of them moves up a car length. She makes a hard left turn and follows An, who's running as fast as she can with the backpack now over both arms. Fortunately for Amanda, the block she chose is blanketed with tall office buildings jutting upward, cutting out the sunlight along the narrow two-lane street. Amanda floors it, catching up to An halfway down the second block. She jams the car into park and launches out of the driver's side to catch An, who turned down a perpendicular street block.

Several shocked tourists and office workers move out of the way of the frantic Chinese teen with the Caucasian woman chasing her. Amanda hears An yelling two words in Chinese she understands: "Help! Help me!" After running past several pedestrians, Amanda loses An for second, looks right, then left to see

An running down a deserted alley. Amanda easily closes the gap between them and leaps onto An's back, throwing them both to the ground in a heap. Amanda strips the backpack off An's arms while the girl yells at the top of her lungs. Amanda reaches to cover her mouth, but she's too late.

Amanda looks over her shoulder and spies a police officer trotting toward them in his long, forest-green overcoat; a billy club hangs from his black belt, and what appears to be a rifle or submachine gun is trained on both of them. Amanda raises her arms away from An, clutching the pack in her right hand. An, still on the ground, turns and yells at the officer in Chinese, apparently telling him Amanda has a weapon in the backpack. He trains his gun on Amanda and with his other hand indicates for her to drop the bag.

Amanda contemplates trying to drop her left hand inside her hoodie to grasp her pistol, but decides not to risk it. She slowly places the backpack on the ground, her left hand still raised in the air.

The officer motions for her to step away from the backpack. Amanda moves on the sidewalk between the guard and An, who still cowers on the ground with her back to the pavement, frightened, crying, and screeching in Chinese:

"The American has a gun! She's wants to kill someone at the parade!"

Amanda watches as the police officer momentarily lowers the sub-machine gun muzzle toward the ground and takes a partial step toward the backpack to lift it off the ground. At that moment, Amanda drops her hands and slides the razor-sharp KA-BAR knife out of the leg holster strapped to her calf. She lunges at the officer and draws the blade across his neck, causing blood to spurt everywhere, then violently lifts her left knee and pounds it into his crotch. As he tumbles to the ground, Amanda wrenches the sub-machine gun off his right arm; it bounces to the pavement, where Amanda swipes it up and trains it on An Ling. She slides the backpack onto her shoulders.

"Get up, now!"

An stands up with her hands raised.

"Don't say another word. One more dumb move like that and you'll have your blood gushing like the cop." An's eyes remain unblinking, sheer terror seizing up her little teenage rail of a body.

Amanda realizes there is no good way to hide the long muzzle of the officer's weapon under her hoodie, and once they emerge from the alley, they will be around other people again. Noticing a dumpster several feet away, she walks over, keeping her eyes on An, and tosses the big gun inside.

"Smile like you're having a good time, and walk a couple steps ahead of me."

"I knew it," An says as they emerge from the alley, "you really are American assassin; I will not help you kill president."

"I'm not here to kill anybody. If you cooperate, I'll tell you why I'm here when we get to the car."

They reach the car, parked slightly askew by Amanda in her rush to catch An.

"Climb in the passenger side, I'm driving. We're going to drive away from the roadblock a few blocks to chat."

Amanda looks both ways, but doesn't see any police vehicles. She eases down the street to avoid detection and turns in the opposite direction from the roadblock traffic. After traveling two or three blocks, she finds a side street and parks the vehicle. An Ling recognizes the outline of the pistol in the pouch of Amanda's hoodie.

"I saw how you and your family enjoyed each other so much when we were on the train, and it made me hurt inside. Can you imagine what it would be like if your younger brother was gone?"

"Are you going to kill my brother?"

"No. I'm asking if someone kidnapped your brother and you never saw him again, how would you feel?"

"I would cry, I would be sad. You are telling me you will kidnap him unless I help you?"

"No! That's not what I'm saying. You wouldn't just be sad. You would think about it every day and you would want your brother back. Wouldn't you do anything to find him if the police couldn't?"

"I do not know...I think so. Yes."

"If you thought he was taken to another country would you go there?"

"I told you I do not know. What are you going to do to him?"

"Look at me and listen: I am not going to do anything to your brother. I have a brother, a little brother, he's about one year old.

Somebody kidnapped him and brought him to Beijing. That's why I came here."

"For your brother?"

"It doesn't matter, you won't believe me anyway." Amanda sighs and rubs her left hand across her forehead, feelings of hopelessness and heavy remorse for what she did to the police officer settling in. Amanda knows she's barely hold back her own tears.

An Ling looks over at Amanda, her deep sorrow and pain finally registering.

"Are you sure your brother is here?"

"I think so. I'm just not sure exactly where he is. Look, my dad is a U.S. scientist. His research is worth a lot of money. And someone from your country killed people trying to get his research."

"How are you sure China killed people?"

"Trust me, I just am. I believe it's the government or a large company that makes medicines. And the American government thinks that too. My mother died in a plane crash, it crashed because of sabotage by the Chinese government, but I survived. I was the only survivor."

"What? That is bad! Are you American assassin, you said you were not!"

"Oh. My. God. For the last time, I'm not a secret agent. I came here with another man to bring my brother home. My government doesn't know we're here."

"Tell me what your plan is."

"I can't, it could get you killed. But I promise you I'm not here to kill anyone."

"You just killed that policeman."

"That was only because you ran. I'm not happy about it. Look, I don't want to hurt you, or anyone else, but I can't let you interfere with getting my brother back. Will you help me clear the roadblock? If you do, I will be sure you get back to your house safely within a few hours. I am asking you, no, I am begging you, please don't tell the police why I am here, or what happened to the man in the alley."

"Why should I protect you?"

"Because I told you the truth. Think, what if it was your brother."

She looks at Amanda, then out the window, before almost imperceptibly nodding her head.

"Thank you. You have no idea what this means to me. Once we clear the roadblock, I will blindfold you and put you in the trunk. If you are not rescued within a few hours, I will come back for you myself and return you safely. And when you get out, please, keep my secret so I can find my brother."

An Ling and Amanda clear the roadblock with An Ling at the wheel. Several blocks later, Amanda finds a side road with very little traffic and tells her to park the car there. Amanda assures her she will leave the car in a busy area where someone walking by will hear her banging on the trunk. An climbs in the trunk, and Amanda blindfolds her.

"Don't start banging for ten minutes, I need to be out of the area first. Please. I'll leave the keys under the floor mat of the driver's seat. Thank you for helping me. I'm sorry our friendship has to end this way."

Amanda closes the trunk and drives to a street a few blocks from the Vista hotel. She has just enough time to park the car and reach the meeting place by 11:00 a.m. As she gets out of the car and walks toward the hotel, she figures it's 50/50 on whether An Ling will keep quiet. Amanda figures Ryan would never let An Ling live. Even if she talks, An has no idea what their plan is, so she shouldn't be able to compromise the mission.

CHAPTER 95

CASING

The Prior Evening

SUNLIGHT BREAKS through the cloud cover as Ryan exits the vehicle dressed like a Chinese utility worker, wearing the company's blue jacket Liza supplied him. Thanks to a wig, his hair is now straight, close-cropped, and almost the same color as the nondescript black knit cap covering most of it. He lifts a small plastic container from the backseat of the rental vehicle and places it on the sidewalk. Using a program on his tablet, he launches the drone, watching it rise vertically, and puts the container back into the backseat without looking away from the sky. His timing is perfect, as several young women walk past him and down the sidewalk a moment later, hardly paying attention to him and completely unaware of the drone.

The drone flies 100 yards, over the twelve-foot-high rust-colored masonry walls surrounding the residence on all four sides, lined on the inside with well-groomed hedges. Ryan rules out scaling the wall for his operation; he'll have to gain access through some kind of ruse. Another 150 yards, and the drone reaches its target. Ryan positions it over the rear of a main residence building, which takes up at least half an acre, and watches a guard emerge and walk the entire perimeter. Then he propels it a hundred feet in the air above the front of the building. A second guard is standing in the front of the building; Ryan dips the drone down another 50 feet and zooms in to find a holster holding what he assumes is a pistol on the guard's right hip. He returns the drone to its original height in the sky to watch the traffic. At 5:10 p.m. a Mercedes SUV pulls up to a pair of black metal electronic gates—the only opening a car will fit through. The other black metal gate, more like a tall door, appears to require the use of a keypad. The driver places a keycard reader into a slot and the large gates swing open from the center, moving inward. The tinted windows make it impossible for Ryan to see the occupants, even with the camera zoomed in.

Ryan flies the drone back and lands it in the plastic base that he returned to the sidewalk. Moments later his gear is stashed in the rental and he pulls away.

Around 10:15 the same evening, Ryan changes his disguise in the back of the car. He trades in his utility worker outfit for khakis, loafers, and a white lab coat with a Chinese name and logo embroidered on the front right side. He drives the small rental SUV about a mile and parks it on the street in front of the morgue, about a half a block from Beijing's largest hospital complex. Ryan enters the morgue through a service door and carries a small soft-sided cooler down a long hallway and flight of stairs into the basement. An elderly woman in a gray uniform and shoes with thick soles slaps a well-worn mop against the terrazzo floor, unaware of Ryan's presence. He ducks into another corridor before she sees him, relieved that there are no surveillance cameras mounted on the walls or in the ceiling. He continues down the hall until he finds what he's looking for—a room with large metal drawers holding the deceased. Within 5 minutes he is done, and exits the morgue without being detected.

Beijing's population in 2017 was estimated at 21.7 million people. That many people require a massive governmental infrastructure to support them, including many fire stations and rescue squads. For his third casing mission, Ryan chose the Han Lo fire and rescue station, not randomly, but because it is one of the newest in Beijing and boasts the latest in rescue technology.

Once Ryan arrives, he hunkers down behind some neatly stacked boxes of supplies with a nice vantage point of the entrance on the side of the facility. His interest lies not in the enormous firetrucks outfitted with hoses and ladders, but rather the paramedic's vehicles. This particular station appears to have three small modified vans, *like mini ambulances,* he thinks. *I need to see one of them in action.*

An hour passes before two paramedics—one female, one male —trot over to one of the vehicles, jump in, and pull out onto the city street, lights flashing and siren wailing. Ryan emerges from his hiding place and takes up pursuit. They park in front of an apartment building and run in without ever accessing the back of the little ambulance for a gurney, which disappoints Ryan. Within 15 minutes they emerge with their utility bags slung over their shoulders; apparently this call didn't require transporting the patient. The female driver pushes a button on a key fob as they approach the vehicle. He needs to share this intel with Liza, and propose the expanded role he has in mind for her.

CHAPTER 96

REUNION

ACCORDING to the map in Amanda's hand, she's within two blocks of the hotel. She checks the time on her phone—10:55—and a new text message arrives:

Room 814. Two hard knocks on the door. -L

As she makes a right-hand turn, she looks halfway down the block and sees the English translation below the larger Chinese lettering on the hotel sign: Vista Hotel. On the opposite side of the street, Amanda walks past the double doors of the main entrance and continues about 20 more yards, casually looking over her shoulder. She spends another 30 seconds or so pretending to look in a couple store windows as she surveys the other people on the sidewalk around her and near the hotel.

Seeing nothing suspicious, she jaywalks across the street, enters the hotel, and walks toward the chimes of the elevators. A couple with three kids are already waiting. She lets them take the first elevator and politely declines their offer to join them by shyly shaking her head. She enters the next elevator alone and exits on the eighth floor, checks the signs, and makes her way to the room.

Before knocking, she leans close to the door but doesn't hear anything from the other side. She raps on it twice, as directed. Seconds later the door swings open.

"Amanda, sorry about the change in plan," Liza says, not smiling and holding her hands behind her as she backs up to let Amanda in.

Amanda takes a few steps forward. "You must be Li—."

As the door swings closed a man appears, training his pistol with both hands directly at Amanda, who pivots and grabs for the doorknob. A familiar female voice makes her pause and turn once again toward the interior of the room.

"Take your hand off the knob and put both of them in the air."

"Britt? Where's Ryan? Why...are you...even doing this?"

Brittney Hayes doesn't answer as she begins to pat down Amanda. She removes the pistol in her hoodie pouch and stuffs it in her rear jeans pocket. Next she locates the KA-BAR knife. Sliding it out of the sheath she sees the traces of blood along the tip.

"Looks like Agent Down-Low here has used this knife already—and recently," Britt says to her colleague, walking away from Amanda and placing the knife on the round table in the suite. "Ryan has a standing invitation like yours, we should be seeing him soon. Then we can shut down whatever the hell you two are planning. I was hoping you would've learned something from the previous stunt you tried to pull with David a couple years ago in New York." Britt and Amanda have some serious history together, though neither plan to reminisce at this time.

"Sorry, Amanda, she sent you those text messages, not me, they took my phone and—" Liza starts to explain from her seat on the couch, her hands zip-tied behind her back.

"Liza, shut the hell up," Britt interrupts.

"—And they snatched me before I could place the mark," Liza finishes.

"I have to restrain you. Have a preference of front or back?" Britt approaches Amanda. "Solarez tells me you're quite the lethal weapon now, what with your Quantico training and personal training with Ryan." Amanda eyes Britt's colleague with the gun still trained on her, and any thought of an evasive maneuver vanishes.

"I'm not telling you anything. Why are you trying to stop us?"

"Because we're not gonna let you blow up U.S.-Chinese relations. Tell me what you and Ryan have planned. You owe it to Solarez, and me too, for that matter. If we know what you're up to, perhaps we can work together."

"C'mon, really? You know I'm here for Justin. Maybe my dad too."

"Partial disclosure doesn't cut it. But you're right, we already figured that. Tell us everything, and maybe we can provide some support."

"We're not gonna interfere with the summit."

"If you're not willing to cooperate, Solarez will order me to detain you until the summit's over."

"Let me talk to him."

"Maybe after Ryan gets here. Oh, and here's your meds, compliments of Solarez. Do you have a supply of them with you?" Britt tosses a couple small bags containing various-colored pills onto the coffee table.

"Nope, had to leave them behind. We had a few problems, and I had to lighten my load."

"What are those for? Are you sick?" Liza asks from the couch.

"Telogurl 13 has some special genes," Britt says, surprised Liza has no idea about Amanda's tweaked telomeres.

"Wait, how did you know that phrase?" Amanda asks Britt.

"Every communication your dad had with you, or anyone else, has been reviewed since he vanished. Once we realized Ryan met with Liza in South Beach, we tracked her to China, and well, you get the rest."

"Her dad? Now I'm even more lost."

"Obviously, they didn't fully brief you, Liza, and I have no intention of doing it either." Britt looks down at her mobile phone.

12:30 p.m. and Ryan is still a no-show. Britt confers with her colleague in a whisper on the other side of the suite. "Where the hell is Ryan?" She asks him.

"Don't know. Could he have been tipped off?" He answers.

Liza chimes in sarcastically from across the room. "How about some lunch, and maybe a decent movie on the TV? Looks like we're gonna be here a while."

"Ryan either got a better offer or was detained. Liza, you may need to send him another text," Britt replies cynically, returning the barb, they both know any text will really come from Britt posing as Liza.

The agent working with Britt begins changing channels on the television. He comes across a Chinese news station and Liza swears she glimpses a picture of Amanda.

"Wait, go back to the last station." Liza says. Amanda's face appears in the top right corner of the screen as the reporter talks to a teen girl. "Um, we have a problem, Amanda. You're being featured on a Chinese news show. Any idea why?" Liza asks.

Amanda looks at the screen too. "Oh crap, that's An Ling."

"Mind explaining?"

Amanda leans her head against the wall behind the bed and looks at the ceiling, thinking.

Liza listens to the teenage girl and translates. "She's saying, 'I met this girl and she said she was an American college student sightseeing in China and was excited about seeing the Great Wall. But, she wasn't a student.' Now she's saying she thought you were going to kill her, but instead you locked her in the trunk of a car."

"I had a feeling she'd talk, I mean she's only 15. I met her on the bullet train." Amanda says.

"There's more to her story than that," Britt says, after listening to the last part of the interview.

Amanda doesn't want to explain why she locked An Ling in a car trunk, and no one pushes the issue.

"Amanda, at some point you will be explaining your master plan to Solarez." Britt says. Amanda says nothing.

"How about that movie now?" Liza again requests.

Britt's colleague surfs through the Chinese stations again.

"Stop right there," Liza barks all of a sudden. It's an older American movie with subtitles.

"Hey, Freaky Friday. I love Jamie Lee Curtis. And I love strange juxtapositions."

CHAPTER 97
BALCONY

IT'S ABOUT two hours before dawn. A man in all black slinks across a balcony, then leaps several feet over the railing onto the balcony of the next hotel room. He checks for witnesses of his leap down on the ground but there are only the headlights of an occasional vehicle on the street eight floors below him. Striking before sunrise has helped him remain undetected, but the blackout drapes drawn for the night in the room afford him no view inside. He presses his left palm on the sliding glass door to see if it's locked. To his surprise, it moves a millimeter or two.

A light sleeper ever since the plane crash, Amanda senses something. She opens one eye and see a couple slivers of light along the edge of the window near the bed where she, and she assumes Britt, lay. Before the lights were turned out for the night, Britt had propped herself up on two pillows with her pistol in her hand; her partner had left at midnight and Liza laid across the couch she had been occupying all day.

Suddenly a flashbang grenade illuminates the entire room in a flood of blinding white. Britt raises her pistol and points it directly at the outline of the figure standing inside the partially opened balcony door. Ryan's gun is also pointed at Britt as he declares his identity in hopes of avoiding shots being fired.

"It's Ryan!" Liza gasps from the sofa.

In an attempt to take advantage of the confusion, Amanda launches herself across the bed with her tied hands in front of her to deflect Britt's pistol, but her plan fails. Shocking pain sears through her right shoulder, and both she and Britt go tumbling off the bed to the floor.

"Amanda, move away from her!" Ryan leaps on top of the bed and points his pistol down at the two of them tangled together in the gap between the wall and the bed.

"She's CIA! I know her!"

"I don't care who she is, she was going to shoot me! Put both your hands where I can see them!"

Britt complies and Ryan leans over the foot of the bed and picks up her weapon.

"Amanda, are you hit?"

"Yeah, my shoulder."

Ryan flips on the light. Blood seeps through Amanda's T-shirt.

"Amanda, if you can, get up and move off of her slowly." He keeps his pistol trained on Britt as Amanda inches off of her, trying not to wince in pain.

"We weren't going to harm them, we just need to know what you're planning," Britt explains.

Liza now stands beside Ryan. "They detained me, figuring they could use me to catfish you. She's got other agents working with her too. How'd you know the text wasn't from me?"

"Tell ya later. Let's get her restrained and triage Amanda first."

Ryan orders Britt to roll over onto her stomach. He zip-ties her arms behind her back and places a pair of ankle-cuffs around both of her ankles, leaving only a few inches of chain between her legs. He lifts Britt by her belt with one hand and drops her on the bed, then takes his knife from its holster and cuts the zip ties off Liza and Amanda.

"Where are the other agents, and how are you communicating with them?" Ryan asks Britt, but she remains silent.

"Look, something tells me we need each other," Ryan tries again, "and we might need someone to tend to this wound."

He leans over and inspects Amanda's shoulder, where there appears to be one entrance wound. "Can you pull that top out of the way so I can get a better look?"

Amanda slowly peels her shirt off her shoulder using her left hand. There's a puncture wound a few inches down from the top of her right shoulder, but there's very little fresh blood.

"I told you before, I don't bleed." Amanda says before Ryan can comment.

"I remember now. Can you move your right arm?"

Amanda lifts her right arm almost level with the top of her shoulder.

"I get some pain right about there. I'll be fine."

"Can you fire a weapon?"

"I don't think that'll be a problem."

"If you can wait an hour, I know we can get medical help without drawing attention."

"I told you, I won't bleed out. Britt, what's the surveillance situation in the lobby?"

"It's not even 6:30, he's not out there yet."

"Where's he staying? The next room, down the hall?" Ryan asks her.

Britt remains silent, so Amanda tries again. "It's not like we're enemies, Britt. I'm here to get my brother back, and my dad too. We might not be on exactly the same page, but come on."

Britt relents. "He's based here in Beijing. He sleeps in his own apartment." She turns to Ryan. "We can get her seen by a trustworthy doctor. To let her leave here without getting medical care is bad planning. You don't have any idea what type of internal bleeding she has."

"Don't listen to her. We need to get out of here before they throw us in some U.S. Embassy holding cell and send us back to the U.S. Who knows what they'll charge us with," Liza interjects.

"The best thing would be for all three of you to let me extricate you out of Beijing in one piece. If the Chinese get a hold of you, you'll either all be dead or rotting away in a Chinese labor prison. I'm your best opportunity to get outta here alive."

"Let's talk, Ty." Liza motions to Ryan and the two of them step away.

"Amanda, keep an eye on her."

Britt sits up on the side of the bed and looks at Amanda standing in the center of the room, training Britt's pistol back on her.

Britt whispers, "Amanda, you need me, but I don't need you."

"What the hell does that mean? I probably saved your life. I think you and I are finally even now. I'm going to get my brother back, whether you help us or not."

"You'll never get out of China alive. That's where I come in. I can get you out."

"How?"

"Through an embassy, although not necessarily ours. We have friends here, and sometimes we extricate through a friendly embassy. Just how are you planning to get your brother back anyway? The North Korean prime minister is—"

Amanda cuts her off. "Prime minister? You mean dictator."

"Who cares what we call him. I don't know what you're up to, but if you disrupt his meeting with the president today, you'll never have our support again. We'll disown you, and you'll probably get executed by the Chinese."

Liza and Ty emerge from the bathroom.

"Amanda, I need to talk to you a moment," Ryan says, and Amanda joins them.

"Do you think we can trust her at any level?"

"She helped me get through a lot stuff after the jet crash. She was basically embedded with me the entire time. She says she can get us out of Beijing using embassy contacts, which'll be easier than working our way to south China. "

"They may have the means to get us outta here, but they won't approve any part of our plan. Trust me, I know how they work. I can get you the medical care, and get us in the compound." Ryan says.

"How?"

Ryan whispers his plan out of Britt's earshot, including how Liza will be critical.

"Hmm. Got it. It's our only chance. So, what the hell happened on the bullet train Ryan? I'm lucky to be in one piece. Didn't get shot till you got here." Amanda whispers looking towards her wounded shoulder area.

"Almost got my head blown off. A pro using a silencer.

Remember the kevlar beanie. It probably saved my life. I chased him, he bolted off the train before Beijing. Never found him, and I'm sure he's still looking for me."

"So you weren't even on the train when I got off?"

"Roger that."

"Where'd *you* go? Liza now interjects, asking Amanda.

"I befriended a Chinese family for a night, then bolted."

They go over some other details and collectively agree to give Britt a burner phone in case they need to get in touch with her.

"We'll call you if we need your help," Ryan tells Britt.

"I'm your ticket out of China. I'll report shots were fired, I was overpowered, and there was nothing I could do to stop you, which is true. I'll say it again, we can safely exfiltrate you back to the U.S. But, assure us you're not here to disrupt the summit."

Ryan looks at Liza and Amanda. "You'd better not be sending us into a booby trap. If we take off out of this hotel and something happens to us—."

"You wouldn't do that to us, would you Britt?" Amanda asks.

"No. Don't forget your meds."

"Already got 'em."

"If you find your brother, how are you going to I.D. him, anyway? You haven't seen your real brother, like ever. We have the world's most sophisticated facial recognition software, its like Facebook times a thousand." This gets Amanda's attention fast.

"So, how would you help us?"

"The CIA has a handheld satellite phone that can snap a photo, and in a second we can verify if Justin is really Justin by comparing to your parents, to you, etc."

Ryan grabs Britt's phone and puts it in the bag with the rest of his gear. "Interesting. We'll call you on the burner phone if we need you. Sorry we didn't get more bonding time." Ryan starts to walk away, then turns back. "I'm sure your contact will come looking for you when you don't answer his texts. Prepare exfiltration plans for a party of four, but don't expect to see us again anytime soon."

He examines the bed frame and notices it's bolted to the floor. He takes out another metal cuff and connects Britt's existing leg cuffs to one of the corner bedposts. As the three of them exit, Amanda turns back and makes eye contact with Britt.

"Good luck, Amanda."

"We're going to need it." The door closes softly behind her.

While she waits for her contact to free her, Britt wonders what Amanda and Ryan have up their sleeve. Amanda said they weren't there to assassinate anyone, and despite their rocky history, Britt doesn't think she'd lie to her about something like that. Killing someone wouldn't get her brother back anyway. They probably have good intelligence on where Justin is being held and are planning a daring rescue effort, which is not of Britt's concern. Her directive is to assure they do nothing to interfere with the meetings currently being held between the world's most hated dictator and the Chinese president. The CIA has surveillance devices in place for the meetings, but it will not countenance any American involvement with any attempted or actual assassination of either leader.

CHAPTER 98

FIRE & RESCUE

USING THE BURNER PHONE, Liza calls the fire department's central dispatch number. In Chinese, she frantically gives the address of the apartment complex where flames are pouring from a rear third-floor unit and people are trapped. Within five minutes the lead paramedic's vehicle screams up to the street in front of the main building, arriving first before an ambulance, or a fire truck. The female paramedic jumps out of the vehicle and trots to the set of doors at the front of the building to assess the situation. She meets Liza in the entryway between the outer and inner doors and asks if she is the one who called in the fire.

"Yes, I called, but there is no fire."

The paramedic appears angry about the false alarm, then her expression turns to confusion as Liza draws her pistol from the pouch of her unzipped, lightweight jacket.

"If you follow my instructions, you won't get hurt. If you don't, I'll kill you. First, you're going to report this as a false alarm, to call off the fire trucks. Then, we're both going to walk out of here and get in the back of your ambulance."

The young paramedic pales.

"Tell me you understand!" Liza says.

"I understand."

"Good."

Then, with Liza's pistol inches from her skull, she uses the belt mounted radio to call in the false alarm and reverse the fire engines. As they walk toward the paramedic's vehicle, they see the ambulance behind it. Liza catches a glimpse of the unfamiliar driver, then sees Ryan already in the passenger seat.

"Open the doors and get in," Liza directs her hostage as they walk the short distance from the apartment building to the rear of the ambulance. Once inside, she orders her to shut the door.

Seconds later there are three taps on the doors. Liza opens one of them and Ryan, Amanda, and another paramedic are standing outside. All of them climb in and Ryan directs Amanda to lay on the gurney. As she gets settled, Liza explains in Chinese that Amanda has been wounded and they are going to remove the bullet.

The female paramedic begins to protest, "We do not remove bullets, we transport the patient to the hospital and—"

"I don't care what you usually do. You're going to remove the bullet right here if you and your coworker want to live," Liza orders.

Liza hands her gun to Ryan and helps Amanda take her shirt off over her head. She has her turn on her left side to expose the area where the bullet entered at the rear of her right shoulder. A small amount of dried blood marks the exact point of entry.

"Get busy!" Liza barks.

The paramedics flip open one of the compartments next to the gurney and pull out a pair of tweezers, a tourniquet, a scalpel, plenty of gauze, a metal tray, a small bottle, and a long syringe.

The male attendant looks at Liza, "We need to give her a shot for the pain."

"What is it?"

He explains it's a synthetic drug similar to morphine. Liza translates for Amanda, who nods her head. A few minutes after he administers the injection, he uses the long, narrow tweezers to examine the entry wound area.

Ryan has seen this exercise too many times, but he's also seen much worse—friends blown to pieces by IEDs, skin burned beyond recognition by incendiary mortars, guys dying while the medic tries to save them. He turns to look out the small window of the ambulance, under the guise of watching for anything suspicious.

"I've never done this before," the nervous male attendant tells Liza.

"Guess there's a first time for everything."

Ryan turns back to face Amanda. "I need to tell you I'm sorry. This is my fault."

Thanks to the shot, Amanda doesn't feel any pain, but she knows his tweezers are working inside her shoulder.

"Ty, I know. I owed it to Britt. She claims she saved my life before, and maybe she did."

"How so?" Liza asks.

"That's too long of a story."

About a minute later the paramedic withdraws the tweezers from Amanda's shoulder and drops what appears to be the bullet with a clatter on a metal tray. He and the female attendant dab an antibacterial ointment on the wound, then fashion a makeshift bandage with gauze and medical tape.

Liza first thanks the paramedics, then tells them to take off their uniforms. They hesitate, but Liza gives them a death stare and they get busy. She scrounges up a third uniform from another compartment and she, Ryan, and Amanda put them on. The paramedics don their ill-fitting discarded street clothes before they are bound in the back of the ambulance.

"Do either of you speak any English?" Liza asks in English. No response. She repeats the question in Chinese. The man says he understands a few words, but can't carry on a conversation. Liza tells Ryan and Amanda it'll probably be okay to talk in English, especially since they plan to keep them hostage until the mission is complete.

Ryan turns to Amanda as they stand with Liza outside of the ambulance. "We have a big decision to make. We don't have to tell the CIA what we're doing, but we could take them up on extrication from China. We'll either have succeeded or failed by then. Or Liza can disappear on her own and we can use our disguises to try to make it back to Shen Zhen. If we want Britt's help, we'll need to call her and suggest a meeting point. We'd dump the ambulance and have her transfer us to a safe vehicle for the exfiltration.

"You didn't ask me," Liza interjects, "but I'd use the agency. A million Chinese citizens will be looking for you. Besides, it sounds to me like the agency has a special interest in Telogurl here."

Ryan holds up the burner phone and the battery. "Well, is it a yes?"

"Yeah, if you and Liza both think it's the best way. I don't care what they do to me if we get Justin back."

"Justin?" Liza asks.

"Well, the cat's outta the bag now. You may as well fill her in." Ryan says.

"Justin's my one-year-old brother. He was kidnapped, and we think he's here."

"That's the mission? To find your brother and kidnap him back? Ryan you never told me this."

"Oh well. That's part of it. There's another part too, but we can tell you that later." Ryan says, then dials Britt's number on the phone.

"Elizabeth Gardner here." Britt answers, relieved they called. She assured Solarez they would call, but she was not really as confident as she made it seem.

"Okay, we want to rendezvous and have you help get us out."

"The offer still stands, but only if you aren't tampering with the summit today. Do I have your word on that?"

"Yep. We'll be a party of three, maybe four. I'll call you five minutes before our arrival. We'll meet at the Guanzang office building on Chai Ling Boulevard, underground parking Level 2, the westernmost corner. We'll be in an ambulance."

"Creative transportation. Okay, we'll have a large black SUV, diplomatic plates. We'll flash our lights twice as we approach."

"Okay, we'll be counting on it."

"How's Amanda's bullet wound?" Britt asks him.

"We got it handled, she's doin' great. Gotta run, thanks." He ends the call abruptly and looks at the panicked paramedics in the back of the vehicle.

"Liza, tell them we aren't going to hurt them. Amanda, we need to get our disguises on now."

Within minutes Ryan drives off in the smaller paramedic SUV and Liza takes the wheel of the ambulance.

"I don't think I could ever be a paramedic," Amanda says to Liza. "I don't like seeing people with bad injuries or people taking their last gasps, it gives me the heebie-jeebies."

As they follow Ryan, Liza can't resist asking, "How long ago did you meet Ty?"

"He came to the rehab center I help run outside of DC and offered to devise this mission, with my input. It was just a few weeks ago. What about you? Where do you fit into all of this? He didn't tell me anything about you."

"I used to work for the CIA. I met Ty when he was special forces and I was embedded in Iraq. We handled missions together."

Amanda lets that sink in for a few seconds and decides not to pry into their relationship. "So, what are you doing now?"

"I work as a quality control rep for Michael Morse."

"Wait, you're a part-time undercover agent and full-time with a clothing line?"

Liza laughs. "Strange mix, I know. But when the price is right, it's hard to resist."

CHAPTER 99
NABBED

4:00 a.m.

Ryan pulls his night vision goggles on over his black ski mask and kills the lights on the paramedic vehicle before getting out. Barely any signs of life can be seen along the two-lane street, though it bustles with activity during daylight hours. Leaning into the rear of the SUV under the raised rear door, he connects the payload under the drone with a J-hook.

The nearly silent drone rises into the night sky following the GPS coordinates. Within seconds the drone hovers above the high wall surrounding the compound, and, on Ryan's command, drops the incendiary device into the leafy hedge near the interior base of the wall.

He directs the drone back toward him, landing it softly on the deserted sidewalk, then packs it back inside the duffel bag in the rear of the vehicle and returns to the driver's seat.

Ryan pulls the SUV into position on the opposite end of the compound, closer to where he has dropped the payload, and turns off the lights again. *So far so good.*

He texts Liza, and the full-size ambulance rolls up behind him, also without lights. Approaching the driver's side, he sees Liza behind the wheel and Amanda in the passenger seat, both still in the EMS uniforms, and Amanda wearing her Asian mask and wig with straight black hair. No matter how many times Ryan has used disguises created by his contact in the States, it still amazes him how realistic they are.

"Amanda, you could easily pass as a 22-year-old Asian, seriously. Liza, once we get into the compound and head to the back, you'll operate the fire extinguisher and I'll take care of the security guards. Then follow my lead, I'm going to locate the kid and we'll extricate him to the ambulance."

"Amanda, you stay out front and monitor the street and the door. We'll all be on the closed walkie-talkie system. Let's try them now." All three confirm their audio. "All right, I'm going to start the fire and we move out once we see flames from the back of the compound."

Ryan presses several buttons on his small remote control, then puts it in his pocket and walks back to his vehicle as he buttons up the front of his paramedic uniform. About 30 seconds later, flames rise from the rear corner of the compound.

Tapping her fingernails on the top left and right of the steering wheel, Liza turns to Amanda. "How did you figure out your brother was being held here?"

Amanda starts to answer. "It's not that..."

"It's not...what?"

"Nothing. Look, Ryan is getting ready to pull out. We can explain later."

The lights and siren have activated on the SUV, and their ambulance follows. Both vehicles make a left turn and travel half a block past several large residences, until they arrive at a U-shaped driveway in front of the compound. Ryan exits the SUV, his Asian disguise in place and cartridge respirator over his mouth. He leaves the red emergency lights whirling, and Liza and Amanda follow suit. Liza will enter first to communicate with the guard.

She and Ryan both hold large fire extinguishers found in the rear of the ambulance, and they walk urgently toward the guard standing just inside the metal gates.

"What is the nature of this?" the guard asks Liza.

"You have a fire in the rear of the compound. We received the emergency call, open the gates."

He presses an unseen control, swinging the metal gates inward. Liza and Ryan rush through the gates and toward the front door, where another guard ushers them in. Liza's gaze first takes in the large watercolor paintings along both walls, then she looks upward at the vaulted alcove just inside the door of the majestic residence. A long hallway stretches from the foyer to the rear of the compound.

"What's the best way to the gardens in the rear where the fire is?"

"Straight back this way. Follow me."

"If anyone is here, awaken them now and evacuate them to the front alcove," Liza directs the guard as they trot toward the rear of the compound.

The guard lifts a radio from his waist and begins barking directions to another guard. After about 50 yards the three of them arrive at a set of doors that the guard unlocks. Through the thick glass they can see the fire, probably 50 yards away, toward the rear of the long, open gardens.

"I'll see if I can get it under control," Liza says. "Go back inside and make sure everyone has evacuated."

Liza trots off toward the flames and the security guard reenters the compound. At that moment, Ryan hits him with a Taser charge. The man jerks involuntarily as if stricken by a seizure, then falls to the ground, his limbs twitching. Ryan jabs a hypodermic needle into his left buttock, grabs both of the man's wrists, and drags him off the paved path and around the corner of the building, out of sight.

Liza extinguishes the flames and runs back in his direction. They both re-enter the compound.

As they make their way back down the hall to the front of the home, one of the security guards approaches Amanda waiting outside. He is demanding something in rapid-fire Chinese, and she struggles to understand what he is asking. Very few of the words make sense to her, but she is sure it has something to do with why she is there. Unable to put together an appropriate response, Amanda pulls the Taser out of her pocket and fills the security guard with electric current until he jerks and falls to the ground. She has a syringe identical to Ryan's in her other pocket, which she withdraws and sinks into the guard. She quickly surveys the area, to make sure no one saw what just happened. Seeing no one, she drags, then partly rolls his body closer to the driver's side of the ambulance out of the light.

Back inside, Liza and Ryan come upon a 30-something-year-old man and a woman who appears to be his wife, both in their pajamas. The wife is holding a small boy, maybe a year or two old.

"There is a fire in the rear of the property, and we are trying to control it," Liza tells them both.

The man, eyes wide with concern, asks, "Do we need to evacuate?"

"Not sure yet. Stay in this front room until we can fully assess the situation." Liza points toward a nearby door, and the man dutifully walks toward the room, followed by his wife who still carries the boy. As soon as the man enters the room, Liza brandishes her pistol and pulls the door shut behind her.

"But, my wife is still—"

"Remain silent and you won't be hurt."

The man instinctively yells his wife's name.

"You don't listen very well." She pulls the Taser from her pocket and he goes down in a heap. She jabs her syringe into the top of his left thigh, watching his face to ensure he loses consciousness.

On the other side of the door, Ryan pulls his pistol on the wife. "Give me your baby," he demands in passible Chinese.

She grips the baby tighter, indicating no intention of complying.

"Give me your baby," he repeats as Liza exits the room without the husband.

Instead of complying, the mother turns and begins running down the hall with the child clutched to her chest. Ryan takes off after her and in less than 10 yards has caught her. He ruthlessly pushes the gun's silencer against her head and she freezes.

He strips the baby out of her hands with one powerful arm. The boy begins crying, his eyes trained on the mother, arms outstretched trying to reach her. Ryan hands the child off to Liza and tases the mother. Once again, he pushes her over onto her stomach and jabs the hypodermic needle into her buttock. He binds the hands of the mom but doesn't bother binding her legs since she'll be out cold for a couple of hours.

Liza looks at the screaming child in her arms. "Um, Ryan, this baby is Asian. I thought we were rescuing Amanda's baby brother."

"Not exactly," Ryan responds cryptically, taking the child from her. "Where's the dad?"

"He's out cold and bound in the front room."

"Good. Let's get outta here."

Ryan removes a cloth from a plastic bag in his pocket and loosely holds it over the nostrils of the child, who loses consciousness in a matter of seconds. Both of them run to the front door, with Ryan carrying the precious cargo. They stop and peer out the door and see Amanda, already seated in the passenger seat of the ambulance, the lights outside still swirling. Ryan notices a few curious onlookers, an older man and woman on the sidewalk near the electronic gates, outside the walled compound. He has no idea where they came from, but figures they are just rubber-neckers and ignores them. They run out of the house and open the rear doors of the ambulance, putting the baby boy on the gurney and strapping him in place. The real rescue squad personnel sit on the floor, knees up, packed closely together.

"Liza, you stay back here with the boy. I'll drive the SUV and Amanda will drive the ambulance. I'll message Britt we're on our way. Amanda, no siren, just lights."

Just then, Ryan notices the body next to the ambulance. "Amanda, there's a guy laying halfway under your vehicle."

Amanda leans out of the driver's door window. "Oh, yeah, I had to knock him out. He was acting hostile and asking questions in Chinese I didn't know how to answer."

Ryan goes back to the rear of the ambulance and opens the doors, startling Liza. He asks for the backboard and she takes it off the interior wall hooks and hands it to him.

"Stay with the kid. Amanda will help me, we've got one more body, leave the doors ajar."

He taps on the window, Amanda gets out, and together they lift the compound guard onto the backboard and maneuver him into the back of the ambulance with Liza, contributing one more unneeded body to the overcrowded situation.

He exits the ambulance, and Liza bolts the doors from the inside. She sits in a flip-down seat bottom beside the baby and fastens her shoulder harness.

Ryan walks over to the driver's side and Amanda lowers the window.

"All set?"

"Roger. Just follow a couple car lengths behind me."

As Ryan walks to the SUV, he pulls the burner phone out of his pocket and texts Britt, confirming the countdown.

CHAPTER 100

PLUS ONE

THE SUV and ambulance turn into the parking garage. Both drivers shut off their emergency lights and proceed to the lower level as directed by Britt. In less than five minutes, a black stretch SUV pulls in, flashes its headlights, and stops near the ambulance.

Ryan, with his hand on his gun, opens his door and slowly exits, eyeing the driver of the limo.

Britt emerges from the front passenger seat and stands where he can see her. Liza exits the ambulance through the rear doors with the baby. Amanda also gets out and steps away from the driver's door of the ambulance. All three of them now stand near the open limo door just behind Britt's door.

"We have an extra passenger?" Britt leans close to examine the child, who is still sleeping.

"He's collateral," Ryan says. Britt closely inspects his features, which are distinctively not caucasian.

"Who is it?"

Ryan and Liza both look at her but don't answer.

Finally, Amanda speaks up. "It's the Chinese president's grandson."

Britt rolls her eyes and stares upward. "Of all the crazy, no, insane plans!"

Amanda, Ryan, and Liza, holding the sleeping boy, all slide into the limo, and Ryan closes the door behind them. Britt stands beside the front passenger door and shakes her head.

"Oh my God," she whispers to herself, then finally gets in and closes the door.

"Let's go," she tells the driver.

The limousine pulls up to the gated entrance to the Embassy of Singapore. Two large metal gates swing inward and the limo pulls through as the gates close behind it. The limo stops under a covered portico, a common fixture on foreign embassies designed to keep prying eyes from knowing who is entering and exiting. The entourage exits the vehicle and enters the embassy. An administrative assistant greets Britt.

"Right this way, Ms. Gardner, we've been expecting you."

CHAPTER 101

NEXT MOVE

THE AMERICAN ENTOURAGE follows the Singapore Embassy aide past the guards and through a locked door as she explains to them all of the staff speaks English. She leads them into a wing of the building comprised of a number of small rooms set up like an extended-stay hotel. Each has a kitchenette, bathroom, and sitting area, and Amanda's room is equipped with a crib for the baby.

Liza holds the child, now swaddled in a blanket and still sleeping soundly. "Does anyone know more about this than I do? Because I'm kind of clueless about babies and toddlers."

"No, but between all of us we should be able to figure it out. Besides, it will only be for a few hours, maybe a day," Ryan reassures her.

"You don't know that," Liza replies.

"Let's all hope he's right though." Amanda says.

Britt stands down the hall just out of earshot, talking to the embassy staffer.

"My friends here will need diapers and some baby food. Do you have any supplies? I will ask our embassy to bring some things, but in the meantime, if you—"

"We will get them what they need for the child, and there are some necessities in the rooms. How long will they be staying?"

"Two days, maximum."

The staffer nods and walks in the opposite direction, and Britt rejoins the group.

"They have some supplies here, and we can get the other things you need, like clothing. There are toiletries in the shower in each room, as well as a little food." Britt looks directly at Amanda. "Keep the kid in your room. Don't let anybody here see his face. Avoid any surveillance cameras too."

"Okay," Amanda replies, "but I still don't understand why they're willing to help us."

"We have longstanding relationships with a number of countries. As long as what we ask of them doesn't affect their standing with other nations, they don't ask us any questions. But if they find out who the baby is, they will not protect you, who knows, they might even notify the Chinese authorities. We understand your plan now. In fact, Solarez is now in Beijing, at our embassy. But our government can't appear to be even remotely involved in anything you're doing. Now, do you know where Justin is being held?"

"We think he's in this area, but we don't know the exact location," Ryan answers.

"You *think*? That's all you've got?"

"It doesn't really matter where he is. They'll produce him, especially if they think we might harm the president's grandkid."

"This doesn't sound sane, or safe. How will you establish contact with the Chinese government?"

"Through Liza."

"Solarez says he has intelligence from someone who might help. Perhaps he or she can be your intermediary, like your mediator."

"I want to talk to Solarez," Amanda says.

"Like I said, we can't be much more involved with what you guys are planning than we already are, so I'm not sure I can make that happen. But I'll see what I can do."

CHAPTER 102
SUMMIT INTERRUPTUS

THE NAME of the Zhongnanhai complex, located west of the Forbidden City and Tiananmen Square, refers to the two lakes inside the sprawling government compound. The Chinese president and North Korean dictator walk from Tiananmen Square to Zhongnanhai with pomp and pageantry after the massive parade, as live coverage of this historic event is broadcast throughout China and North Korea, and to many other nations.

The leaders and their delegations walk beside one of the lakes, then pass through Xinhua Gate, otherwise known as the Gate of New China. "Long live the great Communist Party of China," states the wording in the wrought iron above the entrance. The formal talks between the two countries will take place in the Regent Palace during the afternoon.

Two hours and fifteen minutes into the meetings, one of the Chinese president's aides enters the cavernous room. He crosses the parquet floor and passes a small note to the president, who reads it and looks up with a serious, slightly pained expression on his face. Immediately excusing himself, he asks the delegates to carry on and promises he will soon return as he walks out with the aide who brought the message. Two guards close the sixteen-foot-tall doors behind them. Once they are standing in the large outer hall, they are joined by two other men in black suits and thin black ties from the Ministry of State Security, the Chinese equivalent of the CIA.

The MSS director and agent fill him in on the kidnapping of

Bin Lai in hushed whispers. The director reassures him his daughter and son-in-law are currently in a safe location with MSS officials.

"But where is the child? Have you located the criminals?" the president demands.

"Not yet, Mr. President. We have not heard from the abductors yet."

"I would like to speak with my daughter."

"Absolutely Mr. President, let's step into this conference room to make the call." The men hurriedly walk through a nearby door, and the MSS director dials a number on the phone in the middle of a large round table. Several Chinese police officers have taken up posts outside the door. Once contact is made, the director hands the phone to the president.

"Zhu, you are safe?" he asks.

"Yes father, but they have Bin Lai. They have Bin Lai!" she says, nearly shrieking the second time she says her son's name.

"Did you see them? Are they foreigners?" the president, now a concerned father and grandfather, asks.

"We've told the men everything. The female spoke very good Chinese. I'm not sure about the man. He may have been in disguise, and I did not hear him say more than a few words, so I couldn't tell what country he was from."

"They did not harm you or Liu?" her father asks.

"No, they drugged us but we weren't injured."

"What would they want with Bin Lai?" the president asks, mostly to himself, but his daughter responds.

"I don't know, but do everything you can to get him back, Papa."

"I will Zhu, and I'll contact you when I hear something," the president promises before ending the call and looking at the director of the MSS.

"Mr. President, I assure you, dozens of our operatives are searching every possible avenue to find him."

"I can't imagine how this would be related to the summit, but the timing seems more than coincidental," the president says. "Don't let them leave our country with my grandson."

"I thought that too, Mr. President. As soon as we locate the kidnappers or make contact with them, I will notify you."

"There is to be no word of this to any media representatives at the summit. Do I make myself clear?"

"Yes sir."

The president rises from the table and the others in the room follow him. Moments later, he walks back into the meeting and assures his North Korean counterpart that everything is fine, there was a family matter needing his immediate attention, but it has been handled.

CHAPTER 103
BACK CHANNELS

INSIDE THE UNITED STATES' Beijing Embassy, Solarez is ensconced in a room with six staffers, each with triple computer monitors on the desks in front of them. He slowly swivels to view the different screens, but stops when his phone rings and he sees Britt's number.

"Our monitoring indicates their president was just advised of the kidnapping," Solarez reports before Britt can get a word out.

"Okay. We took them to the Singapore Embassy—Ryan, Liza Zhang, Amanda, and the president's grandson. Are we going to intercede and return the kid?"

"Depends. Let me see if my Chinese connection can mediate a trade. If not, we may have to."

"Wait, do you know where Justin is?"

"No, but I have some thoughts on who might have him. I'll reach out to my contact and see if he wants to deal with Ryan and Amanda."

"I doubt it. What if he refuses to cooperate?"

"We'll cross that bridge when we come to it. I'll send over some supplies, including a laptop to make the connection on if he agrees. The signal will be masked through our servers and we'll monitor the conversation."

"Amanda wants to talk to you," Britt casually mentions.

"No way. I have to keep my distance, especially if we end up having to abort her mission."

"Alright, tough love it is," Britt says and ends the call.

~

The staffer hovers beside Solarez, a small laptop tablet in her right hand.

"Sir, we have analyzed footage

Solarez swivels back around to one of the computers and begins typing a message to Birdie.

"You know that favor that you needed? There's a chance I can deliver. I'm in Beijing. Your president's grandson has been kidnapped. Let me assure you the U.S. government is NOT responsible, but we can put you in contact with the kidnappers. We have an email address for them, nothing else.

So I will get you what you wanted, but only if you can make a deal that involves Justin Michaels."

Solarez hits the send button and pushes his rolling desk chair back to the middle of the room. One of the female agents turns and addresses him.

"Sir, the Chinese president went back into the room with the North Koreans. We'll be keeping tabs on his whereabouts and will let you know if he leaves again."

"Sounds good."

Less than five minutes later, a message from Birdie arrives.

"This is a most serious threat to Chinese-American relations. We know Amanda Michaels is in China with a former SEAL, Ty Ryan. The Chinese Ambassador is requesting an emergency meeting with U.S. ambassador in Washington. Maybe I will attend, maybe not. If I make a successful deal, you will provide me assurances on my request?"

Solarez studies the message and knows Birdie must be worried, when he notices the first typo his connection has ever made in the messages between them, misspelling *Ambassador*. He picks up a satellite phone and contacts the director of FBI counterintelligence to explain the situation at hand.

"Yes, we can make the necessary arrangements if he facilitates the return of Justin Michaels. However, if the MSS believes our agency is behind this kidnapping, we'll have hell to pay," the director says.

"Hell to pay? The Chinese didn't exactly ask permission to kidnap the Michaels kid either."

"We still don't know if the MSS or the government was responsible."

"Sir, no one else has been all over the telomere research more than MSS. And this is their crown jewel of foreign intelligence: hacking and purloining. The Russians are a little sloppy, but the Chinese know how to be discreet and virtually invisible."

"I hear you, but I'm being told the Ambassador from China is contacting my office. I'll get back to you after I take this call."

The FBI director calls Solarez back a few minutes later.

"A Chinese delegation is arriving at the old executive office building. I'll be there, along with officials from the Department of Justice."

"Is Stein going to be there?" Solarez asks.

"I'm not sure who all the participants are, but I imagine he'll be there. Any idea who the kidnappers are? Please tell me they aren't Americans."

Solarez pulls the phone away from his cheek for a moment and pretends to cough, not wanting his pause while he's deciding how much information to share, to clue the director in on what he knows.

"Our agent, Britt Hayes, believes she located them, but I'm waiting for her report. I'll forward it to you as soon as possible," Solarez fibs.

"It would help if I had it before our meeting."

"I understand. Oh, one more thing. We may need collateral to keep the Chinese honest during the negotiations."

"Collateral?"

"Yeah, it might be beneficial to hold some citizens so they don't try to seize or kill Amanda Michaels."

"You mean take hostages? Are you kidding?"

"I wouldn't call them hostages, they're more like temporary bargaining chips. I'll explain it to Stein."

"If he approves some temporary detention, and I'm talking a matter of hours, I'm okay with it. If he won't agree, forget it."

"Yes sir."

∾

Solarez pushes himself out of the chair after ending the call and exits the ready room to search for an Embassy agent he can use as a messenger. When he locates one, he hands over a laptop in a metal case and writes an email address on a memo pad.

"Give these to Britt Hayes. She'll know what to do with them." He then reviews some other details that Britt is to impart to the new guests ensconced in the Singapore Embassy.

CHAPTER 104

CYBERSPACE

THE UNITED STATES EMBASSY attaché drives through the gates at the Singapore Embassy and parks under the portico. The attaché walks inside, past the security guards, and meets Britt Hayes in the conference room where she waits.

"This is the laptop and satellite phone with facial recognition tech from Solarez. He said you'd know what to do with it."

Britt opens the lid and powers it up to confirm the encrypted internet capability.

"Thank you, I'll take care of it." She says.

Britt watches the man leave before she strides back down the hall toward Ryan's room.

"Here's the scoop. Solarez provided this computer, which will encrypt your location when you use the internet connection. And this satellite phone, has our proprietary software on it. Amanda let me show you this." Britt says, holding it over in front of Amanda. "Once powered on, its programmed so when you snap a photo of the baby's face, click here to upload it, and it will return either a green confirm checkmark, or red 'X' within seconds, it's programmed to be used for Justin's image only." She hands the mobile device to Amanda.

Britt hands Ryan the laptop, and a piece of paper, on which he sees the email address and the word "Birdie."

"What's Birdie?"

"The name of the Chinese official you'll be dealing with. We aren't sure who he is, but we believe he's ranked pretty high in Chinese intelligence. Solarez has been dealing with him for some time and assures me he is authorized to make a deal, but he may be a double agent."

"Sound's dicey, but we shall see. What about transportation? If this works, I'm going to need some way to get us out of here, preferably something I can inspect before we leave to try to swap babies. And what about our exfiltration?"

"That depends."

"Depends on what?" Liza chimes in, now concerned.

"If we can transfer you to a diplomatic limo without you being tailed. If you're followed, we'll need to abort the mission. Solarez said we can't risk impairing our relationship with China."

"I still think our original plan will work," Ryan assures Liza and Amanda.

"I'll work on getting a vehicle and having it here when you're ready. Remember, under no circumstances can the personnel here find out you're holding the president's grandson. All bets are off if that somehow becomes known."

Britt gets up to leave, then looks back at Amanda. "Solarez said to remind you to take your meds. Says you could have a nasty seizure if you don't." Amanda doesn't answer.

"Are you taking them?"

"So, he's worried enough to nag me about taking some pills, but he can't talk to me?"

"You're radioactive Amanda, at least for right now." Britt answers, then looks at Ryan and Liza.

"Do you need any weapons? That's the other thing we might be able to help with."

Liza, standing against the wall closest to the window, turns to face her. "We could use a couple Glocks, two or three stun grenades. An invisibility cloak would be great too."

"I'll see what I can do. Don't hold your breath on the cloak." Britt turns and walks out of the room.

CHAPTER 105

BARGAINING CHIPS

SOLAREZ LOOKS at his watch and realizes the 12-hour time difference means it's the middle of the night in D.C. No matter, he's contacted Brett Stein at the Department of Justice at all kinds of odd hours. Stein is the DOJ's point man on sensitive intelligence matters. Virtually no one outside the intelligence community has ever heard of him, or if they have, they don't know what he really does.

The phone rings several times before Stein picks it up. Seeing the four-digit number, he realizes it's a secure call.

"Stein here."

"It's Steve Solarez, I'm calling from the Beijing Embassy. We have a situation involving the Chinese president's grandson."

"I can't tell you I knew he had a grandson. What about him?"

"He's been kidnapped, but the worst of it is our intelligence indicates the kidnappers are likely Americans. We're concerned the Chinese will believe it's been orchestrated by the CIA. It wasn't, in case you're wondering."

"I'd say that's definitely what I classify as a diplomatic problem. But what can I do at this hour?"

"The Chinese ambassador already contacted the director of the FBI and I don't know who else. They want to meet to discuss how we're going to help, today, like during business hours."

"Well, can't it wait 'til first thing in the morning here? I can put all the pieces together, but not in the middle of the night."

"It's, uh, messy. I believe the kidnappers are going to demand the return of Justin Michaels. You remember he was kidnapped, right?"

"Oh yeah, Ron Michaels' son. Now he's disappeared too. So these kidnappers are trying to exchange the grandson for the Michaels kid?"

"That's what it looks like. And I can't say for sure, but I think Amanda Michaels and Ty Ryan may be involved."

"What?? How could the two of them be working to pull something like this?"

"I can fill in those details later, but right now I think we need some *bargaining chips*. Their chances of getting out of China unharmed are slim. I'm not talking kidnapping, just temporary detainment—"

"Are you proposing we detain high-level Chinese diplomats or the Chinese ambassador as collateral?"

"Well, um, sort of."

Stein is incredulous. "This conversation just keeps getting better. Did you run this by the FBI director?"

"Yeah, he said if you agree, he agrees. So, I really need you on this."

"I don't agree. Can I go to sleep now?"

"Wrong answer. Just hold them, maybe an hour, just enough time for Amanda Michaels, the kid, and whoever else is with them, to survive the swap. If we don't help, they're going to live the rest of their days in a Chinese prison or be killed. Do you want Americans facing that?"

As the silence extends past a few seconds, Solarez gets nervous. "You still there?"

"Yeah, I'm thinking about it." The line goes silent again. "In the meantime, I'm get this meeting organized in the morning. I'll keep you in the loop."

"I'm in the Beijing embassy, get with me first thing in the morning your time."

Stein then hangs up before Solarez can plead any further.

CHAPTER 106
BIRDMAN

RYAN LOOKS in the crib and sees the child is still sleeping.

"Liza, why don't you stay here with the kid, I'm gonna go next door and try to initiate contact with this Birdie person. Amanda, you can come with me."

Amanda nods. They close the door softly behind them and walk to the next suite, which, other than the lack of a crib, looks like the room they just left—a bed against the wall, a window with the blinds closed, a round table with a couple of chairs, and a small desk in the corner. Ryan sits down at the circular table, and Amanda follows suit.

Opening the laptop and establishing the secure connection, Ryan mutters, "Here goes nothing." He assumes Brit and other unknown CIA agents are probably monitoring his activity, but he's not worried about it. His main issue is completing the mission by making the toddler trade and collecting the full amount of money promised him. Accomplishing what the feds couldn't— bringing Amanda's brother back—would also be a coup. He turns his attention to the screen in front of him and notices there's nothing on the computer except an email program, which Ryan opens, and he types up a quick message.

Birdie:

A different birdie told me you are the person I need to negotiate with. We have the president's grandson. We're not interested in money, just the return of Justin Michaels, and our safe departure thereafter with no retribution from your government. You've got 30 minutes to respond affirmatively. If you don't, dire things will happen.

Ryan pushes the computer around for Amanda to see. "What do you think?"

"It looks fine. What are the dire things you're talking about?"

"Don't worry, that's only if they don't cooperate."

Fifteen long minutes go by with no response. Ryan asks Amanda if she could watch the child so Liza can come see him for a few minutes. Amanda obliges, and she and Liza switch rooms.

"I'm assuming you haven't heard anything yet?"

Right at that moment, the laptop chimes.

"Your timing is impeccable, Liza," Ryan replies and smiles. He looks down and reads the email:

We know who you are. I cannot act for the Chinese Government. Please understand, the Chinese Government did not kidnap any one. You need to release Bin Lai within the next 60 minutes or you will face very serious retaliation. I am sorry I cannot provide more information to assist you.

- - Birdie

"This isn't going well," Ryan responds rhetorically before he taps in a response.

We don't care who took Justin Michaels. You either find him and make the arrangements, or little parts of the president's grandson are getting detached from his body. You have 15 minutes left. Don't test me.

Looking over Ryan's shoulder, Liza reads the message. "Are you intending to carry out that threat?"

"I don't make idle threats, you know that. Go join Amanda and the kid. I'm going to grab a few things and be over in a minute, then you and Amanda will come back here. I need to take care of phase two of this operation alone."

Liza returns his gaze with a concerned look, but complies. After closing the laptop and gathering some of his gear, Ryan also heads into the next room and tells Amanda, "Go to the other room with Liza, I need to be alone with the grandson to make my point clear."

Liza and Amanda warily walk out and Ryan closes and locks the door behind them.

The awaited response appears:

Friend:

I told you that Chinese Government did not play any part in Justin Michaels kidnapping. I believe it was a Chinese pharmaceutical company, LuLiXi. We do not control them. You must release the child or the government will locate you within the hour.

- - Birdie

Ryan stares at the message. He knows he can't be tracked because of the encryption on his messages. *Time to call their bluff.*

CHAPTER 107

URGENT MEETING

AMBASSADOR FONG HAS HELD his post at the Chinese Embassy for eleven years and is a familiar fixture in Washington. Striding across the room in his black custom-tailored suit, he shakes Brett Stein's hand.

"It's been a long time, Mr. Ambassador. I understand there is an emergency you need to discuss with us today."

"Yes. Let's sit down and we can begin," Fong replies.

The other representatives from the FBI and CIA join them on one side of the table across from the two assistants Ambassador Fong brought to the meeting. As a server rolls a small cart toward the table to begin the tea service Stein ordered, Ambassador Fong starts to explain the situation.

"Mr. Stein, I don't know what you learned through your own sources, but the grandson of our president was kidnapped by terrorists in Beijing. The timing of the kidnapping raises the concern that someone is attempting to disrupt the summit between the North Korean leader and our president. Our credible information is that the terrorists may be Americans."

Fong watches Stein's reaction carefully as he speaks the last sentence, then remains silent, hoping Stein will offer some intel.

"We haven't been able to confirm if Americans are involved, however, our Beijing office is aware of the situation. We can assure you our government was not involved."

Stein's words are hardly out of his mouth before the ambassador fires back. "If you have any idea who they are, you must turn their names and whereabouts over to the Chinese government immediately so we can take action and retrieve the president's grandson."

Stein glares across the table at the ambassador. "We only have unsubstantiated evidence about who may have done it. Again, our agencies are in no way involved in this outrageous plot, but we will do everything we can to determine the location of the kidnappers and we'll turn over any pertinent information we obtain to your government."

One of the ambassador's aides who has been looking at his phone during the discussion looks directly at Fong to get his attention.

"Excuse me, Mr. Stein," the ambassador says, leaning to his right to listen to the message from his aide. "I have an urgent message from our embassy staff. Is there a place where I can take the call privately?"

Stein asks one of his aides to show the ambassador into an adjacent room with a pocket door, and the two men, along with one of Fong's aides, walk out. Once inside the room, the aide hands the phone to the ambassador, gives him brief instructions on obtaining an outside line, and leaves the room, closing the door behind him.

Ambassador Fong places the call. "Who am I speaking to?"

"Sir, this is Jang-Chung, from the embassy. We opened direct communication with those identifying themselves as the kidnappers of Bin Lai. The communications are in English. It is not confirmed they are Americans, but we are fairly certain they are."

"How did you establish this communication?"

"One of our American sources said he could place me in contact. We were not able to track any of the email communications, but we think the kidnappers are still in Beijing."

"What is their purpose? Are they trying to disrupt the summit? Have they demanded money? Remember, we don't negotiate with terrorists."

"Sir, they're not asking for money and I have no proof they are trying to interrupt the summit. They want Justin Michaels, the kidnapped son of Ron Michaels, the American researcher. They say they will turn over Bin Lai in exchange for the boy."

"I don't remember being told about this kidnapping of Justin Michaels."

"We were informed right after it occurred, about a year ago. We assured the United States that the Chinese government did not kidnap him."

"How can we return Justin Michaels if we aren't holding him?"

"We have intelligence that associates of LuLiXi pharmaceuticals may be involved."

"We gave that company too much power. The president needs to rein them in," Fong fumes.

"We must advise the president. Mr. Ambassador, would you like to be the one to do that? He may give us instructions on how to handle this, including our interaction with LuLiXi."

The ambassador places his hand over the phone for a moment and whispers to his aide, "Go tell the Americans we made contact with the kidnappers and apologize for the delay, we are trying to determine the details."

The aide heads back to the main room to deliver the news, and Fong returns to the call. "I will discuss this with the president and also try to find out what the Americans know. Please find out anything else you can and call me back as soon as possible."

"Give me a few minutes Mr. Ambassador, and I will call you back," Jang-Chung promises.

CHAPTER 108
HOLDING PATTERN

WHILE BRETT STEIN waits for the Chinese ambassador to return, his cell phone vibrates on the table. He looks down and recognizes Steve Solarez' number. Striding off toward another adjacent room, he answers the call, pulling the door shut behind him.

"I hope this is good news, Solarez. I'm in a conference with Ambassador Fong, but something's up. He's in the other room taking a call, and I have a feeling he's learning something about the kidnappers."

"Interesting. Maybe you'll find out they have the Michaels kid. Or if they don't, maybe they can exercise control over whoever has him."

"Hopefully it's one or the other, because we need to get this thing resolved. But that's not why you called me, is it?"

"Have you thought any more about our conversation last night?"

"About detaining the ambassador and his aides?"

"Yes, for only 30 minutes to an hour. By the time they lodge all of their complaints and make their threats, you'll be able to let them go."

"That would violate every tenet of international diplomacy."

"I don't need to remind you how vital the Michaels family is, do I? We're also hoping to possibly find out where Ron Michaels is, assuming the Chinese are behind his disappearance too."

Stein sighs. "I didn't think to connect this with Ron Michaels. You're right, they could be holding both of them."

"Just don't let the ambassador or his aides leave until I give you the word."

"I can only imagine the fallout over this—"

"Worse things have happened, believe me."

CHAPTER 109

SINGLE DIGITS

RYAN REACHES into the duffel bag and pulls out some of the supplies. He opens a small tripod on the desk and screws on a video camera no bigger than a cellphone. A razor-sharp knife sits next to rolls of white gauze and medical tape.

They're not taking me seriously, Ryan thinks, looking at the baby, but that will end very soon.

When he finishes and the video is recorded, the baby's left hand is wrapped with white gauze and tape, through which blood has seeped. In the center of a bloodied white hand towel laying on the table is a tiny pinky finger. He uploads the recording to the laptop through a USB cable attached to the camera and reviews his work, making sure it doesn't reveal the location by showing any identifying information in the room. He then strips all metadata from the file and after saving it, carefully inspects the metadata a second time.

In the adjacent room, Liza and Amanda hear a loud thud, several unidentifiable noises, then crying. As the baby's cries become more incessant, Liza taps on the door and whispers through the door, "What's going on in there, why is he so upset?"

"He probably wants to eat, but I can't come out just yet. Give me a few minutes," Ryan replies in the middle of typing his message.

Birdie:
You obviously aren't taking us seriously. Whoever you need to

*contact inside your government or at the pharma company, you
better do it now. In 30 minutes the kid's going to lose another digit.*
He attaches the short video and hits the send button.

Birdie stares at the message, wondering what the hell is going
on. Then he clicks on the attachment. Horrified, he sees the tiny
finger laying on a white towel, surrounded in blood, and the
bandaged left hand of the baby, with tears under both eyes.

Jang-Chung, aka Birdie, a high-ranking diplomat in the
Chinese embassy in Washington, D.C., has been fastidious in
concealing his double-dealing up to this moment. He places the
fingers of each hand on his temples, thinking about how he
acquired the information and acted on it. After running through
many possible explanations he could give if he was ever
suspected, he decides he must notify Ambassador Fong, the
director of the MSS in Beijing, and the Chinese president. The
thought of doing so while the summit is still underway makes him
shudder, but he initiates the call.

"I need to speak with the president. It concerns his grandson.
We made contact with the kidnappers," he explains to MSS
director Fong.

"I'm outside the conference room. I will go in and ask the
president if he can speak with you. What is the nature of the
negotiations?"

"They're refusing to return Bin Lai unless their demands are
met. And they sent a video showing they severed one of his
fingers."

"What? The kidnappers are torturing him?"

"It appears that way. As I said, I need to talk to the president."

"Hold on, this may take a few minutes."

Birdie waits. Finally, he hears the president's familiar voice
join in on the conversation. "I understand you have information
about Bin Lai?"

"Yes sir, this is Jang-Chung from the Embassy in Washington.

We just received an email from the kidnappers with a short video-tape. They severed your grandson's pinky finger and are demanding the return of Justin Michaels, the baby of American biological researcher, Ron Michaels. Do you know about the telomere research involving—"

"The terrorists cut off one of his fingers?"

"Unfortunately, it appears so. We can provide you the videotape—"

"No, I could not bear to see it. Do we know where they are?"

"We are trying to locate them, Mr. President, but efforts to trace the emails have not been successful yet."

"Do we have any information on the location of this Justin Michaels boy?"

"The Chinese government was not involved in this kidnapping." Director Fong says.

"That is true, Mr. President," Jang-Chung interjects. "However, our intelligence agencies believe the pharmaceutical company, Lu Li Xi, continued its efforts to obtain telomere research information from the United States, which they promised to share with our citizens. Our sources indicate they may have seized this Justin Michaels boy right after he was born in Canada and are hiding him in China."

"We have a significant amount of control over this company. Contact the chairman of LuLiXi and order him to release this child if they have him. We extended them every government privilege and benefit, now it is time for them to do something for our government in return. Tell him the Chinese government will withdraw the company's certificate to transact all business unless they give up the boy at once. How long will it take to get an answer, Mr. Fong?"

"We can contact the company right now, Mr. President. How would you like us to communicate their response back to you?"

"There is nothing more important than getting my grandson back. I would postpone these talks now if I didn't think the media would make a major story out of my failure to be present. My position is simple: if these kidnappers have harmed Bin Lai as you say they have, they are not to leave China. I want them—dead or alive. Do you understand?"

"We understand, sir." Fong confirms.

"Thank you. Report back when my grandson is in your

possession, and the terrorists are captured or killed. That will be all." The president hangs up.

"I will send agents to see LuLiXi's chairman right away," Fong tells Jang-Chung.

"Excellent. if I obtain any new information, I will contact you immediately."

After the call, Birdie opens his laptop and replies to Ryan.

Friend:

I conferred with our president. We will demand the return of Justin Michaels from those who may be holding him. Do not harm the president's grandson any further. I will send another email as soon as the details are worked out.

-- *Birdie*

Ryan reads the incoming message and a smile crosses his face. *I knew they would see the light.*

Light but insistent knocking comes from the other side of the door, followed by Amanda's voice this time. "Open up! What the hell are you doing in there?"

Sighing, he gets up and walks to the door. "Stop worrying, I'm getting results."

"Results? Awesome, but I still want you to open this door."

"No can do, not yet."

Amanda knows how stubborn Ryan is, so she returns to the other room and sits down next to Liza. "He's still refusing to open the door, but I don't want to make a scene since there's probably a hidden camera in the hall. What the hell did he do to the kid?"

"He's playing hardball, I just don't know how. It happens in situations like this."

CHAPTER 110
HIGHER AUTHORITIES

IT TAKES Jang-Chung 10 minutes to obtain the cell phone number for the chairman of LuLiXi, Hong Xi. More importantly, during this time, Jang-Chung coordinated the dispatch of two MSS security officials to Xi's mansion in one of the country's most exclusive neighborhoods. Unaware of what is transpiring, Xi is enjoying his afternoon by the saltwater swimming pool, which continues under a glass wall into his 15,000 square-foot residence.

All real estate in China, including the chairman's mansion, is essentially controlled or leased in some fashion from the Chinese government. And that which is given can also be taken away.

Two oversized SUVs hightail it down the long driveway to the mansion, where they are met by a security guard and a gate closer to the home. The lead agent flashes his credentials to the security guard while explaining they are with MSS and were dispatched by the Chinese president to meet with the chairman. The security guard radios his counterpart inside the residence. The gate swings open and the SUVs proceed down the drive and park in front of the home. As two agents exit the vehicles, a single agent remains with each SUV. The two lead agents walk up the massive steps to the main entrance, another guard stands near the entry door, and waves them through. Once inside, an aide ushers them into a small library full of dark wood, books lining an entire wall, and a conference table with eight cushioned chairs. The chairman enters the room from the other side.

"This is most unusual. What is the nature of this visit?" the chairman inquires. The lead MSS agent answers.

"MSS is well aware of the major exportation by LuLiXi of black-market opioids, which flood into the United States, but since the Chinese economy derives substantial income from your illicit activity, and the damaging effects of the sales do not affect Chinese citizens, your side business is countenanced."

The Chairman seems shocked by the blunt truth. But the lead agent is only getting started.

"We are here on behalf of the president. He asked that we deliver a clear message to you. If your company does not produce Justin Michaels, the young American boy who was seized last year, he will withdraw your certificate of approval for all pharmaceutical business, including import and export. And the government may bring criminal charges as well."

The chairman's complexion loses all color. "But our certificate was just renewed two months ago for the next calendar year."

"And it can be withdrawn just as quickly. First of all, the President states, you must confirm this child is in your custody."

"Our company had nothing to do with any kidnapping—"

One of the agents smashes his fist down on the table, disrupting several pieces of fine china displayed in its center.

"Our instructions are to arrest you now, unless you assure us you will produce the child within two hours. Answer wisely, or you may never conduct business in this country again."

The chairman bows his head. "I can make a phone call."

"There is no time for any further lies. How long will it take you to produce Justin Michaels?"

The chairman keeps his head bowed and stares down at the table for several seconds.

"I need answers! Where is this child being held?"

"Just outside Beijing," the chairman finally responds.

"So, I can tell the president this boy will be available within the next 90 minutes?"

"Yes."

"Let's start making some phone calls. As further incentive," the MSS agent continues, "we know about the money you are leaving in foreign bank accounts. This could be a serious criminal violation, but we are not currently planning to pursue this matter."

The Chairman now looks more shocked than when he learned the government was aware of the kidnapping. "I will help. We are united, we are one."

"We appreciate those words. We believe you have contractors still in Beijing. We need to ensure they do not interfere with this operation."

"I will start calling now."

The operative offers his satellite phone to the chairman, who turns it down.

"Not necessary, my security guard's phone is secure." Hong Xi motions for his security guard standing by just outside the door.

CHAPTER 111

RESULTS

RYAN FLIPS through the current issue of a sports car enthusiast magazine Liza placed in his bag per his request. His plan is to buy something pictured in it with the proceeds from this mission. He stares longingly at the red Ferrari on one dog-eared page, then turns back a few pages to the black Maserati. *Ferrari? Maserati? Such a hard decision.* Then a chime sounds on the laptop.

Friend:

I made contact with the company holding Justin Michaels. They claim he is healthy and they are willing to turn him over in exchange for Bin Lai. We are prepared to do this in Beijing, in the rear parking lot of the Westin Beijing Chaoyang Hotel, Sanyuan Bridge Road. We would like this transfer to be in the next two hours.

- - Birdie

Ryan has no intention of allowing *them* to set the meeting place. He already cased his proposed location during his surveillance days before. And he holds an insurance policy he didn't mention to Amanda or Liza. He types on the keyboard:

Birdie:

I can't agree to that location. This is where we will meet: entrance to the Beijing Fenghuangling Nature Park, a few meters west of 6th W. Ring Road, near the red gate. No vehicles allowed, you must carry Justin Michaels or bring him in a stroller from the parking area. We will bring Bin Lai.

The meeting time is two hours from the send time of this email.

We will not show you the president's grandson until we see Justin Michaels. Then we will make the trade, and you will provide us safe passage out of China. Confirm.

- - Friend

Ryan looks around the room, relieved that Bin Lai stopped crying and is sleeping peacefully. He wraps the finger back up in the bloody towel, puts it into a zippered-top plastic bag, seals it, and drops the bag into a small cold pack that he places inside the oversized duffel with his other supplies.

The laptop chimes.

Friend:

Representatives will appear with Justin Michaels, look for men in green coats. You will not be followed from the area of the trade, however I provide no assurances on your safe exit from China.

- - Birdie

Good enough, Ryan decides. He walks over to the door, unlocks the bolt, and enters the room where Amanda and Liza are waiting.

"We're going to be making the trade in two hours."

"Unbelievable, you are a genius Ryan. How did you convince them to do it?" Amanda asks.

"I'm a persuasive kind of guy."

"What did you do?" Before he can answer, Amanda strides out into the hallway and opens the door to the next room. Her eyes are drawn to the white gauze oversized bandage covering the child's left hand with blood oozing from the area around the fingers. Ryan and Liza are not far behind her.

"What the hell did you do?" Amanda now gingerly holds the child's arm aloft to make her point, trying not to awaken him. "Tell me! What did you do?"

"I had to give them one small reason to cooperate with us." He points his single pinky finger upwards toward the ceiling.

"You chopped off one of that little kid's fingers?" Liza asks.

"That's torture! I can't believe you!" Amanda shrieks.

"This is not a situation where we send polite requests ladies, where we ask them to return Justin Michaels please, with a cherry on top. Pointing artillery at 'em was the only thing that got us results." Despite feeling he did the right thing, his response still comes out a little too loudly and sounds defensive.

Both women avoid direct eye contact with the man who disgusts them at the moment, but deep down they realize what he did appears to have worked.

"What's our next move?" Liza asks.

"We're going to wait about an hour and a half before heading to the meeting point I selected. I'll confirm there is a car here for our use, then it'll be show time."

He finds the burner phone to contact Britt, not only about the vehicle but also about any additional logistical support, and powers on the facial recognition mobile device to check its function. Britt explains they can survey the area via satellite, and they will text him if anything suspicious occurs. A jamming device will be mounted on a rooftop with a view of the meet point, which will interfere with any radio waves the Chinese might try to use to detonate an explosive device during the exchange. Ryan provides her the wave bandwidth for a device he may be forced to use at the scene, should something not go as planned. She confirms the band, but purposely doesn't mention several of the operatives from the embassy will be at the scene monitoring the activities.

Britt confirms where she and an agent will be parked, two blocks from the Singapore embassy, how they will watch Ryan pass, and assuming everything looks fine, she will radio the Singapore embassy staff to have the gate opened for their arrival.

CHAPTER 112
SIDE PROJECT

SOLAREZ CALLS BRITT HAYES.

"All right, the Chinese delegation is now at the old executive office building. Time for step two."

Two vehicles park a half block away from a small but ornate two-story row house in a residential district of Beijing. A team of six covert CIA operatives enter through the rear grounds. There are no guards, no protection. Once inside the home, the agents silently slip to the second floor, where the residents are sleeping. They roust a woman in the master bedroom, and the lead agent, who speaks Chinese, explains to her she is not to scream, and as long as she cooperates, she will live to see her husband, Jang-Chung.

He asks her to indicate how many children are in the house and she raises two fingers; he leads her into the hallway and asks her to point out which rooms the children sleep in, and she again complies. After the children are awakened and told to keep silent, all three are allowed to put on shoes and coats, but they are ordered not to take any belongings. The youngest of the children, a 10-year-old girl, doesn't understand and grabs a doll from her bed. The agents overlook it and lead their captives out the back door, through the backyard, and into the waiting SUVs.

One last SUV follows the others, the CIA agent purposely follows about a half block. He turns to Britt Hayes who seems pre-occupied with tapping something in to her mobile satellite phone and asks: "why are we holding the family at the embassy compound, anyway?"

"That's need to know information, and, uh, yeah." Britt replies.

Solarez answers the internal embassy phone.

"Sir, we have the family rounded up, and they are safe inside the residential apartments in the rear of the compound." Britt reports.

"Excellent work. Thank you." Just as Solarez ends the call, he notices one of the Embassy analysts approaching his desk.

"We have answers on the death of that biologist on Ron Michaels' research team, the one who supposedly jumped from the roof of the Constable Inn near Sherwood. It was no suicide. We scoured all the surveillance cameras from every approach road or highway to the hotel. We then did facial recognition on a subset of the male, lone drivers, in the 24 hours before Fletcher's death. We also did a similar review of all surveillance cams on the island of St. Martin, of every highway surveillance cam near every hotel within a couple miles of the harbor where Odette was murdered. Then we looked for any facial recognition match, and we got only one. We had nothing on the subject. Then, we checked with all our allied intelligence agencies in Europe. Bingo. We got a dossier from the Czech Republic's Committee for Intelligence Activities."

"That's unfortunate." Solarez says, looking at the picture of the subject, on the top page of the thin file that the analyst has placed on the desk.

"What?" She asks.

"He's just an everyman, I mean."

"He's a contract killer who may be non-descript. They don't have a real name either, or any bio. Just his moniker. Charon." She says.

"Care-ron." Solarez repeats, slowly, phonetically emphasizing each syllable the way she did.

"So, this seals it. He took out Odette and Fletcher." She says.

"Any intel on whether he's here in Beijing?"

"Nothing."

"Will the Chinese share their surveillance cam footage with us?" He asks.

"No. They never have."

"Can we hack in?"

"Maybe, but where do we start?" She asks.

"Dunno, but maybe we will get a lead. Get this picture out to all our agents in China," he says, staring at the photo of Charon inside the file. "Thanks, that's good stuff."

She walks away a step or two, then stops and twirls back.

"Pretty sicko handle if you ask me, sir."

"Huh, how so?" Solarez asks.

"I had a great prof in college who taught us all the Greek mythology. Charon would ferry the recently deceased souls across the River of Pain, the River Acheron. As long as they could pay the fare. If they couldn't pay Charon's fee, they would wander the river banks for 100 years."

"I didn't learn any Greek myths." Solarez says. "And what if you could pay Charon, you were already dead anyway, right?"

"Those who died with a coin in their mouth, Charon would carry them across the river to Hades' realm. They could then stand before the Judges of the Dead, who decided how they would spend eternity." She says.

"Now I understand what you mean by sicko."

"I need to return to our embassy so we can act on this information," Chinese Ambassador Fong says to Stein, who pauses a second before responding.

"No, we need to stay inside the compound until the summit in Beijing is over. Then we can work together."

The Chinese ambassador stands and begins to lead his entourage out of the room. "We will conduct this operation from the Chinese Embassy, not from your executive office building."

"I'm sorry, that's not going to be possible. We have directions to be your gracious hosts, and to give you comfortable accommodations, but no one is leaving the building at this time. We will provide you a secure phone line to the Chinese Embassy in the conference room next door, and we will allow you to use our facilities as you desire, but you need to remain here. It is important we work together," Stein lies, knowing, in fact, there will be additional chess pieces acquired to make this work.

The Chinese delegation storms into the open hallway, where Secret Service agents lining the hallway make clear no one is leaving the immediate area. One agent explains to the ambassador all mobile communication devices must be handed over, and they will be returned when the situation has been resolved. One by one, the Chinese grudgingly hand over their cell phones.

Seeing Stein standing at the end of the hall, the ambassador confronts him. "This is a violation of international law. The United States will pay dearly for this."

"We need to confirm our citizens in Beijing are safe and on their way. I'm sure it will only be a few minutes."

CHAPTER 113
RAMSHACKLE

CHARON and his henchman stroll into the industrial warehouse strewn with tools and car parts. In one bay are three late model compact cars, each fifteen to twenty years old. Approaching the cars, both men examine the rear-most car first, opening the driver's side door and carefully checking out the almost threadbare interior. They close the door and go to the next car, which is light blue except for the spots of body compound scattered over the exterior. Again, Charon is most interested in the driver's door, opening then closing it without sitting in the driver's seat. The third vehicle is so faded it can hardly be called red, but all of the necessary parts, including the driver's side door, seem to be intact. As Charon finishes looking over the last car, a man who looks to be in charge approaches and stands about ten steps away.

Charon slams the door shut and looks at Chong, his associate. "Ask him if these cars are gonna run, cuz they look like crap."

Chong translates Charon's question, minus the derogatory remark, and the mechanic walks over to the nearest car and points to the inspection sticker on the windshield. Then he moves back a step, and points to the front tire, shaking his head as he talks.

"He assures me they all run and have current inspection stickers. The tires are worn but he says you said there was no need to replace them."

"Yep, he's right. Tell him two guys are gonna stop by later today to do some work on them, and he's not to ask any questions."

Charon digs into his left pants pocket as Chong translates, and pulls out a wad of Chinese yuan. He counts out the equivalent of $5,000.00 USD and places it in the mechanic's hand.

"Thank him for his work and confirm we'll be moving the cars outta here tonight."

CHAPTER 114

NATURE PARK

RYAN PUTS the finishing touches on his handiwork under the loose-fitting shirt they are using to make Bin Lai look presentable for the trade. A suicide belt is secured under the boy's shirt, and appears to be rigged to detonate remotely, but it's a fake. They will arrive at the meeting point with Bin Lai under a blanket in a stroller with the canopy raised. Liza or Amanda will enter the park pushing the stroller, leaving Ryan to carry a diaper bag over his shoulder while hiding his Uzi under his jacket.

They stash the stroller in the back of the SUV and the four of them drive through the embassy gates and head west to the nature park. Ryan selected this park for two reasons: because of its large public square occupied by parents and kids, which doesn't make for a great bullet-ridden death zone, and because the parking lots are several hundred meters away from the red arch meeting point at the park entrance.

One hour before rendezvous, Britt Hayes and three other agents take up positions surrounding the entrance, one of whom launches a drone in a deserted area just outside the park. The other two agents study the satellite images on their laptops, which show remarkable details of the park and the surrounding buildings and topography. Inside a room on the top floor of the only tall building in the area, which houses the administrative offices for the park personnel, an electronics engineer controls the jamming equipment. Several thick antennae point toward the large closed window facing the park entrance. In one of the many images on her laptop, Britt watches Ryan and his entourage enter the park.

"We have a serious problem," one of the agents reports.

"What's that?" Britt asks.

The agent gestures toward the screen. Britt leans in closer and squints at the video feed from the drone. On the flat roof of the administrative building, a sniper lays prone behind a large rifle mounted on a short tripod. The barrel of the weapon projects through a drainage hole in the stub wall encompassing the roof. She locates the burner phone in her purse and calls Ryan.

As he enters the park, Ryan hears the still unfamiliar ringtone coming from the phone he's only answered twice since he's been in China. He slows down and pulls over, realizing there is no good reason why someone would be calling him now.

"Yes?"

"When you pull into the parking lot, don't exit your car, stay put until I get back to you. There's a sniper on top of the tallest building. I'm going to contact our facilitator."

Britt hangs up and dials Solarez on a different phone. As soon as she explains the problem, he types an email message to Birdie:

"*Someone's trying to sabotage this deal. If your president wants his grandson not to be in several pieces, you call your contacts and tell them to remove the sniper. They've got five minutes. If he's not withdrawn, he'll be taken out and the trade will be off. Don't respond to this message, we'll visually confirm he is gone and will proceed to the agreed exchange location.*"

The next few minutes seem like hours to Solarez.

Britt watches the drone footage as the sniper sits up from his prone position, then reaches for a narrow black bag. He detaches the rifle, folds up the tripod, and places it and his rifle in the black bag before disappearing from the roof area. She waits another few minutes to assure he walks from the building's ground level.

She texts Ryan: *All clear.*

Liza directs Ryan to the rear of the administrative building where he parks the SUV. Not seeing anything suspicious, they get out and quickly set up the stroller. They are a mere 10 minutes from the rendezvous point. As they slowly make their way down a sidewalk toward the main entrance, Amanda notices the inscription on the red arch and asks Liza what it says.

"Something like 'Enjoy the natural beauty of the world around you.'"

They keep their eyes peeled for someone bringing Justin. There are many people enjoying the sunny day, wheeling strollers, riding bikes, or walking in and out of the park. Finally, 50 yards from the entrance, they see four people including at least one woman, standing near the entrance, with a stroller. The child is concealed by a blanket and canopy, just like Bin Lai, but two of the adults are wearing forest green coats and they are hovering around the entry gate, so Ryan assumes they are the ones with Justin.

"I'll walk ahead, you both stay about 10 yards back. Amanda, once I get a visual of the child, I'm going to come back to get you. We need to verify it's Justin, it'll be your visual assessment plus the mobile device Britt gave us."

Amanda nods, but realizes the facial recognition software will be critical.

Ryan continues. "I'm also going to let them know Bin Lai is wired so they don't try anything after the trade."

Liza feels in her right pocket for the Glock Britt came up with at her request. They all move forward with Ryan running point.

"Which of you speaks English?"

The female replies, "I speak English. Do you have Bin Lai?"

"Yes, but I need to make sure the child you brought is Justin Michaels."

She motions to the man behind the stroller and he pulls the blanket down, revealing the boy's face. Other than knowing what Amanda looks like, Ryan has no idea how Justin should look since he was abducted at birth.

"Hold on, I need someone else to verify his identity." He motions to Amanda, who walks the short distance and looks down at the stroller as the man pulls back the blanket again. The little boy has distinctive Michaels features, she then holds up the mobile device Britt supplied and snaps a picture. She takes a step or two back, and waits for the response. Sure enough, the green checkmark fills the screen, so she nods affirmatively at Ryan.

Realizing they are satisfied the child is Justin, the woman in the green coat says, "Now we need to see Bin Lai."

Ryan and Amanda lead the woman back to their stroller. As they approach, Liza pulls back the blanket just enough to reveal Bin Lai's head.

"Please show me his arms."

Liza pulls the blanket back further to reveal the child's arms, including the one ending in the large bandage. The lady frowns, but confirms the child is Bin Lai. "Bring the stroller closer and we will make this trade."

Ryan takes the handles of the stroller from Liza and the three of them follow the Chinese woman. When they are all together again and Amanda holds the handles of Justin's stroller, Ryan pulls the blanket off of Bin Lai and raises his shirt, revealing the suicide belt.

"The remote synced with the explosives in this belt can detonate them within a one-mile range. If anyone tries anything when we leave, we'll hit the button and blow Bin Lai and the rest of you to pieces."

This revelation infuriates the female agent, who translates the information for her partners.

Ryan smirks. "It's been a pleasure doing business with you."

Amanda doesn't need any instructions, she immediately starts pushing the stroller toward their vehicle. Over their shoulders, they see the Chinese walking in the other direction to a different parking area with Bin Lai.

They put the stroller in the back of the SUV, get buckled up, and speed out of the park.

"We did it! You're brilliant, Ryan!" Amanda exclaims.

"It ain't over till the fat lady sings," Liza warns. "We know that, don't we, Ryan?"

"Truer words have never been spoken," he agrees, looking in his rearview mirror just in time to see two SUVs pull off a side road in pursuit. However, they don't get more than a couple blocks before two more vehicles appear from another side street and park across the main road, blocking their path. Britt Hayes' maneuver thwarts the would-be pursuers, who put their SUVs in reverse and speed off in the opposite direction.

Proceed with contingency plan.

Charon stares at the text. It's a go. No one else appreciates the weight of these words like he does. He takes a deep breath, then another. Still, his heart rate quickens. He scrolls through his phone for a suitable playlist and finds the one titled "Prophecy Conditions." Smiling at the title and its unfulfilled feel, he cranks up the first tune and drowns out all outside sound.

CHAPTER 115

EXFILTRATION

CHARON HOPS off the scooter and slides it into the metal rack within the row of dozens of motorbikes on the sidewalk. The surface of the rack and the concrete are flecked with dingy soot from the smokestacks of the industrial factories nearby. He and Chong grabbed some breakfast before he thanked him for his help and sent him on his way.

As he enters a Beijing café, patrons stare at their tablets, phones, and laptops, and an espresso machine grinds loudly over the music. The scene is the same as one would encounter at Starbucks, but this cafe has a Chinese name that means celebrity star cafe, or maybe movie star café—he doesn't remember exactly what Chong said it meant when they stopped in the day before. He flips open his laptop, joining the other device users, and brings six different video feeds up on his screen. Each feed features one of three intersections, with one view close up and one further away.

He looks at his watch. *Anytime within the next fifteen minutes*, he figures. He then retrieves from his backpack three mobile phones, each numbered one through three on a piece of tape on the bottom. Finally, he pulls a set of noise-cancelling earbuds out of his pocket, along with his own cell phone, and turns on his playlist, starting with "This Is What You Came For" by Calvin Harris and Rihanna. The music pulses into his ears.

His attention turns back to his laptop, watching every vehicle that approaches each intersection, until finally he sees a black

SUV. He looks at the close-up camera view and sure enough, a small red glow appears on the rear bumper, confirming it is the one he has been watching for.

"Oh my God, Justin, I'm so glad to have you back!" Amanda hugs her young brother, trying not to squeeze too hard. She doesn't have a car seat for him, so she cradles him tight in her arms in the backseat of the black SUV. Justin looks bewildered uttering single, unconnected words, some in English and many most likely in Chinese. Amanda doesn't care what he's saying, or who taught him Chinese words, she's so thankful to have him safely in her arms. The only piece of the plan left now is getting out of China and back home.

As Ty Ryan speeds down the road, he watches the rearview and the side-view mirrors, knowing this won't go down easily. He is surprised to see no one tailing them, which raises his adrenaline level.

"I didn't chop off the kid's pinky finger," Ryan blurts out, shifting a tad to see Amanda's face in the rearview mirror.

"What?" Amanda asks.

"Yeah, explain that." Liza says.

"I staged it. Got a kid's finger from the Beijing children's morgue. The big bandage, the seeping blood, all faked. It wasn't his pinky. Worked like a charm."

"I think I just decided to like you more," Liza says, a broad smile now on her face.

"Maybe so, but you should've told us from the start," Amanda adds.

"Nah, I wanted you both invested."

Amanda shakes her head and stares at Justin's face, barely able to contain her satisfaction and joy.

They finally approach signs of civilization—industrial factories bordered by paved sidewalks filled with bikes, scooters, and motorbikes.

"This is where I exit," Liza says.

Amanda leans a bit forward to be heard in the front seat. "Wait, I thought you were going to stay with us all the way out of China, you're our translator."

"Nope, I never said I was leaving China." Liza turns in her seat to face Amanda. "No one knows I have any role in this, so no one's searching for me, and I want to keep it that way. Ty, pull over right here, I'm gonna disappear into the masses."

Ryan looks at her questioningly, but doesn't argue. He checks the mirrors again, sees no pursuers, and pulls off to the right, near a packed row of parked cars.

"Liza, you're the best. How long till you're back in New York?" he asks, his voice showing no emotion.

"I don't know, I'm going back to our factory for now. I'll lay low for a few days, handle some legit business, then I'll fly back."

"I'll wire your funds as soon as I'm back in D.C." He adds. As Liza slides toward the open door, she pauses to look back at Ryan, and they fist bump. Then she smiles at Amanda and Justin.

"Can't thank you enough, Liza." Amanda says.

The door closes and Liza melds into the throngs of young Chinese workers already crowding the sidewalk.

Charon watches the SUV stop on the video. He leans closer, and sees someone get out. He can't see the woman's face, but he watches the gait and concludes it's definitely not Amanda Michaels, he knows her walk. *Who is that woman?* Seconds later she disappears in the crowd.

Pumped as a prize fighter bursting out of the dressing room and taking the short trip to the ring for his biggest fight, he cranks up the volume on his earbuds and lets the music take control. *It's show time.*

As the SUV approaches a faded red four-door, Charon picks up cell phone # 3 and presses the button. The close-up video feed on his laptop immediately goes black, but the distant video shows a massive explosion at the intersection. *Oops.*

He coils up the earbud cords and stashes them in his pocket, closes the laptop, slides it and the cell phones into his backpack, then walks out of the café. Jumping on his scooter, he makes an immediate left turn at the first corner, cutting off one of the micro-sized business trucks that seem to be everywhere. Once he reaches his destination, he sees scores of people shouting and gawking at the aftermath of the massive explosion.

Dropping the kickstand under his scooter, he maneuvers it against the curb. He elbows his way past several Chinese workers to get a better view of what's left of the black SUV. Near the rear, ribbons of fire still rise from what was presumably the gas tank and parts of the doors are blown off. Another car parked near the corner is nothing more than a bombed-out chassis. Some people start to run away, disturbed by the grisly scene, while others push their way toward it.

Charon examines the SUV from the passenger side. In the front seat, he sees Ty Ryan's burned and lifeless body slumped partially forward and toward the side; in the backseat, Amanda cradles a small child in her arms—both motionless and charred.

You don't kidnap the Chinese president's grandson and get away with it.

He nods to himself and walks back toward his scooter, where he taps in a message on his cell phone:

Confirmed.

Then, he scrolls back to his playlist and cranks up his earbuds again. As he speeds off, the crowd continues to expand and sirens grow louder.

A satellite image captures the explosion. The information is conveyed within seconds to the U.S. Embassy in Beijing. Moments later a black SUV screams out through the gates, it stops two blocks away, Britt Hayes jumps in the front seat, and the SUV accelerates towards the bomb scene.

An ambulance speeds by Charon, and then another, on their way to the remnants of the two vehicles. The black SUV arrives shortly after. Britt Hayes and a paramedic associate from the embassy, an Asian-American who speaks Chinese, leap out of the SUV and run to the wreckage. Britt flips open her badge and shows it to the rescue paramedics.

"Tell them we are prepared to take control of the bodies because they are Americans."

Her associate conveys the information to the rescue paramedic who wears a white face mask and small brown frame glasses. He peers into the car at the bodies, then feels Amanda's neck for a pulse. He turns with a frown and speaks to the man interpreting for Britt.

"What did he say?"

"He said they're all dead."

Britt tries to lean in to touch Amanda's body, but the paramedic with the face mask pushes her away gently, respectfully.

In Chinese, he says, "You are not authorized. Please move back."

"Tell him they are Americans, diplomats from the U.S. Embassy. We are entitled to take custody of them."

Her associate talks to the paramedic who still refuses Britt's request.

"He said because they are deceased, they have control of the bodies and will take them to the morgue. I told him I'm a paramedic too. He could care less."

"No! The girl can't be dead, tell him," Britt insists. "She can't be dead."

The masked paramedic turns and looks at Britt, shaking his head and responding once more in clipped Chinese.

Britt's associate looks at her. "He said you are crazy American. Nothing can be done for them."

Lifting Amanda's arm slightly, the paramedic assesses Justin's lifeless body still cradled in her lap.

He moves a few steps away from the car's interior and speaks into the radio on the right shoulder of his white uniform.

Britt seizes the opportunity and jumps into the backseat. She feels Amanda's wrist but detects no pulse. She begins CPR on her in feverish desperation. Blow in, chest compressions, blow in, more chest compressions. She also presses on Justin's tiny forearm but finds no pulse.

When the masked paramedic turns back toward the vehicle and sees Britt perched in the rear seat, he yells something at her and wraps his arms around her waist, trying to pull her out. Britt resists, and another paramedic rushes over and helps him pry her away from Amanda's body.

The crowd around the SUV has grown to 50 or 75 onlookers who are being held back on the sidewalk on either side of the street by police. The paramedics load the gurney carrying Ryan's body bag into one ambulance and Amanda and the child into another. Another rescue squad deals with two other young Chinese workers who were literally blown away by the blast.

"Quick, give me the medical bag." Britt tells her associate, grabbing it from his hand, before he speaks.

As the rescue squad tech swings the doors closed on the second vehicle, Britt flashes her badge, grabs one door before it shuts, and climbs into the rear of the ambulance, leaving the U.S. Embassy employee standing nearby, dumbfounded. He pulls out his cell phone to call the Embassy as both ambulances pull away, lights activated and sirens blaring.

"She's acting crazy. There's nothing I could do. She going to the morgue with the bodies."

Inside the ambulance, Britt's own words echo in her head.

No. She can't be dead, tell him.

Britt begins unzipping Amanda's body bag.

The female tech gestures at Britt to stop and unfastens her seatbelt to intervene. Britt reaches inside her jacket and pulls out her pistol, pointing the muzzle toward the tech, then toward the jump seat. No Chinese language skills required. The tech backs up to the jump seat and re-fastens her shoulder harness.

Britt unzips the bag, revealing Amanda's charred head and torso, and resumes mouth-to-mouth and CPR.

She can't be dead.